HOPE, HEARTS & FOREVER

A SMALL TOWN DUAL TIMELINE MYSTERY ROMANCE

HOPE & HEARTS FROM SWAN HARBOR
BOOK 6

SOPHIE BARTOW

CONTENTS

My street team;
The Wall-Giennie Wicks-Delaney,
Connector Inspector- Linda Hagerty
Reactor Inspector-Jami Fenton
Plot Catcher- Barbara Berry
Sign Crew- Kate Semenyuk

*The Clean-up crew: Debbie, Laura, Kim, Maggie, Sylvia, and Pam whose
feedback was valuable.*
And my family, who are still waiting for me to clean the house.

**Inspiration began,
when a lost girl fell for a lost boy**

Two Hearts Press
An imprint of LLIPSS, INC.
Copyright © 2021 by *Sophie Bartow*

Cover Design by Kate Semenyuk

SOME RESIDENTS OF SWAN HARBOR
PRESENT DAY

Killian Reade: Investigator for the Swan Harbor Sheriff's Department. Brother to **Liam Reade** and son of **Finley Reade**. Engaged to **Emma Foster**. Their story is told in **Kittens, Puppies & Love.**

Emma Foster: The Veterinarian and owner of Swan Harbor Veterinary Hospital. Daughter of **Ava King** and **Peter Foster.** Is engaged to **Killian Reade**.

Liam Reade: Chief Paramedic for the Swan Harbor Fire Department. Married to **Elsa Winters**. Their story is told in **Brothers, Hope & Hearts.**

Elsa Winters: She owns a pediatric practice in Swan Harbor and is best friends with **Emma Foster.** Married to **Liam Reade.**

Finley Reade: Owns a real estate business in New York City and is involved in a business venture in Swan Harbor. Father of **Liam** and **Killian**. He is married to Ava King. Their story is told in **Kisses Family & Hope.**

Ava King: Philanthropist and businesswoman. Mother of **Emma Foster**. Married to **Finley Reade**.

Aiden Jones: English professor at the Swan Harbor University. He is the cousin of **Killian** and **Liam Reade** and is **dating Harper Taylor.** Their story is told in **A Tree, Mistletoe & A Sunset.**

Cameron Hunter: The son of Mary and Clint and is an architect with

HCI. He is married to **Jessica Prince Hunter**. Their story is told in **From Darkness into Love.**

Dylan Prince: The Sheriff of Swan Harbor and married to **Molly Barnes Prince**. He is the brother of Jessie and the late James and son of the late Ruth and Robert. Their story is told in **The Innocence of Love**.

Terri Patterson: Matriarch of Swan Harbor. Widow of the Dean Patterson and mother to Danny, Beverly, Troy, Laura, and Rhonda. Grandmother to many. Her story is told in **Guided by Light.**

Captain Jack: Retired Naval officer and local legend of Swan Harbor who gives out sage advice to the locals of the town. Owner of Captain Jack's Fine Dining, located at the newly renovated pier in an old Spanish galleon. **The Journey to Love.**

SOME RESIDENTS OF SWAN HARBOR
1700S

Ian Jones: Captain of El corazón del Rubí. Ancestor of Killian and Liam Reade and Aiden Jones.

Geoffrey Prince: Sheriff of Swan Harbor. Husband of the late Christine Swan and father to Martin, Hope, Alan, and Luke. Ancestor of Dylan and Jessie Prince.

Hope Prince: Daughter of Geoffrey Prince.

Anne Michaels: Caretaker for Geoffrey's children.

Isabelle Williams: Daughter of Anne Michaels.

Henry Patterson: Friends of Ian Jones and brother to Faith Patterson.

Faith Patterson: Brother of Henry and best friends with Hope Prince.

Kitty Swan: Owns The Weavers with her husband, **Phillip**. Hope's aunt. Ancestor of Jack Swan, Ava King, and Emma Foster.

D.D. Timmons: First Mate of El corazón del Rubí. Father figure to Ian Jones.

Jenny Hunter: Friends of Hope and Ian. Married to **David Hunter** and mother to **Gilbert** and **John.** Ancestor to the Hunters.

Welcome to Swan Harbor

A Haven of Hope for Lost Hearts.

PROLOGUE

The Origins of Swan Harbor
By
M. Prince 1965

IN MARCH 1692, PRINCE GEOFFREY AND HIS BAND OF LIKE-MINDED travelers arrived at the port in what is now Boston, Massachusetts. They had been forced to leave their homes in England for refusing to sign an oath of allegiance, pledging their support to the Jacobites. The Colonies offered them an opportunity to start over.

Determined to provide a place for the new settlers to call home, their caravan began traveling north. Geoffrey was looking for a place where the land was fertile, the water was plentiful, and the opportunities were endless. After four weeks of traveling, on foot and by wagon, he'd begun to think he was searching for the impossible.

Then, almost as if they were being given a sign, they spotted a wedge of beautiful swans in the distance.

"We must follow them," he told the others.

There was much grumbling among the men of the group until Anne Michaels stepped forward. "We follow the swans," she proclaimed in a soft, albeit forceful, voice. "Look, they are even being guided by a black swan."

Everyone gasped and glared at her with identical frightened looks on their faces. "But one black swan in a bevy of white? Isn't that an omen?"

"Some say," Anne explained, "black swans are a reminder to reclaim your personal freedom. Isn't that what we're doing?"

The arguing continued until Geoffrey stepped forward and gently touched Anne on the shoulder.

"She's right," he cried. "We left England for a fresh start. Those swans will lead us to water." Within hours, they decided, and while several family units went in other directions, the majority remained. The swans led them farther north, past what is now Portland, and then they flew east and disappeared.

"What do we do now?" they asked Geoffrey.

"Why, we follow of course."

And they had, using whatever tools they had brought and could find, to cut through the heavy foliage that lined the path. It was lush and green, and once they broke through, they discovered they'd been right to follow the birds. The cliff overlooked the blue of the ocean, and wildflowers of every color surrounded them. Spring had arrived, giving them a new beginning with endless opportunities.

Far below from where they were standing, there were two harbors, and resting peacefully in one were the swans. On that day, it was decided that the area would be known as Swan Harbor. Then, in 1714, it became a town. For two-hundred years, the little town thrived. The grass grew as green as the brightest emeralds, and the sea sparkled like sapphires.

In the early 1900s, Louise Carmichael moved into the diner in the center of town, and Granny's became the diamond in Swan Harbor. Gossip, romances, and break-ups. If it involved the residents, you'd find it there.

Then the 1920s came, and with it the Great Depression. Swan Harbor teetered on a precipice, and there always seemed to be an urgency in the air. And while the swans still arrived each spring, there were fewer of them, and their eggs didn't always hatch.

By the end of World War II, businesses moved away, and factories closed. The question was no longer whether the town was going to thrive, but *whether* it was going to survive. Then, just as they worried would happen, the swans disappeared. Hope was in short supply.

. . .

In April 1969, Rose Dawson added a handwritten note to the book.

For the first time in years, a swan has appeared in Swan Harbor. He is pure white, and beautiful, and swims in the harbor with his head held high.

The pall that has hung in the air for years seems to have disappeared. The town is once again thriving, and the people are communicating. Our air smells sweeter, and the water is bluer and more fruitful. Jonesy, as Jack has named the swan, has become our sign that Swan Harbor will survive forever. He's brought us hope.

Except swans don't live forever, and the key to what has a hold on Swan Harbor still needs to be found. The answer supposedly lies within the charms of the bracelet that's been in the Swan family for centuries. We need to find the key to set us free. Until then, Swan Harbor is living on borrowed hope.

ONE

PRESENT DAY

QUICK NOTE: *If you enjoy* Hope, Hearts & Forever, *be sure to check out my offer for more Hope and Ian at the end. While reading, you can listen to the Hope Story's playlist -* **Hope, Hearts & Forever**
   With that, enjoy!

Emma & Killian's Home
February 12
6:00 a.m.

"Jonesy!" Doctor Emma Foster screamed, sitting straight up in bed. Her heart raced, and tears clogged her throat at the image in her dreams.

"What's wrong, Doc?" Killian murmured. "Nightmare?"

For a heartbeat, Emma considered snuggling a little closer and letting Killian, the man she loved and planned to marry, distract her for a few hours. But she'd tried that, and as much as she'd enjoyed those moments, *it* was still there. How was she supposed to save a swan *and* Swan Harbor's hope?

"I failed," she whispered. "I didn't believe Jack. And now ... Jonesy is dying."

"Jonesy was fine yesterday when we checked on him."

"Jack tried to tell me ..." Emma went on as if she hadn't heard him. "I should have listened.

"Talk to me."

Emma sighed, willing some of the weight around her shoulders to fade away. She finally linked their fingers and pressed her head against his shoulder.

"Can we really get married with this hanging over our heads?"

Their wedding day was in two days, Valentine's Day. A day they'd been looking forward to for eight long months. But every time they'd made plans, something always seemed to get in the way. It had her wondering if their happy beginning was in jeopardy because they hadn't located the 'key.'

"We've talked about this," Killian sighed. "Jack believes our marriage will give Swan Harbor another burst of hope."

"But can we find the key before Jonesy dies? If we don't, are we doomed?"

"We've made progress."

"I know, but it was my job—"

Killian kissed her quiet. "Doc, listen to me. Yes, you're a veterinarian. Yes, you've worked many miracles—but with dogs and cats—that's your superpower."

"I know," she sighed. "I just feel like ..."

He tilted her chin, and the love looking back took her breath. Slowly, he leaned down and kissed her. It was so tender, tears rushed to her eyes. A part of her wanted to say, '*I don't deserve to be treated that way.*' While the other side just wanted to bask in the attention.

"You feel you should have done more, right?"

"Yes."

"Tell me again, Doc. Tell me everything you've done."

Emma leaned back just enough to see his expression. It was one she'd seen before, and usually when in the center of an important case. Something inside seemed to settle, as it also reminded her she wasn't alone.

"What do you want me to say?"

"I'm a detective, right?"

"Well, yes, but how—"

"Just go with me here."

Emma's heart flipped, and she blew out a breath, trying to get her insides to calm down. Something told her that whatever Killian was asking would require her to think logically—and not emotionally.

"Okay. Sorry. Go on."

"Pretend that Jonesy is a case you're trying to solve."

"He is a case," she exclaimed. "But I don't know what's wrong—"

"Doc," Killian cut her off, except he never raised his voice. It remained the same soft, lilting tone she loved. "Hear me out?"

"Oh, okay."

She mimed zipping her lips and leaned back against the pillows. When she lifted an arm to cross it over her stomach, Killian wrapped his fingers around her wrist.

"Now, shush." He whispered a kiss across her mouth. "Listen."

"I will."

"Promise?"

Emma opened her mouth, but before any words came out, she turned her head slightly, her gaze colliding with Killian's. Just like always, his dark blue eyes, rimmed by long, thick black lashes, captured her whole being. Her heart pounded, and all she could think about right then was that she would do anything for him.

"I promise."

"When Jack first told you about Jonesy, what did you do?"

"Blew him off."

Killian side-eyed her, but said nothing.

"Oh, okay. I examined Jonesy ... or as best as I could. Except that didn't matter because he continued to get sicker."

"He did," Killian hummed. "Did you give up?"

She gave him a wry smile. "I wanted to."

"Go on."

"I called the organization that helps save wild birds, and we moved Jonesy to the zoo aviary."

"Was that it?"

"You know it wasn't."

"Emma." His voice was low, husky, and caused a flutter deep inside.

"I had a vet who specializes in wild birds do blood testing."

"And nothing showed up?"

"No, that's when Jack told me Jonesy needed to be free."

"Go on, Doc. I'm right here," Killian murmured.

"But it was winter, and I knew he would die if we set him free." She took a deep breath and continued the story. "It wasn't until Jack found the place by the cave that I agreed."

"You agreed it might be what Jonesy needed?"

"I did," Emma sighed. "The rocks would shelter Jonesy, and the water was warm enough for him to swim and feed. It's just ..."

"It's just what?" Killian asked quietly.

She blinked back the tears that threatened, not wanting to give in to the ache inside.

"Doc?"

"Hmm?"

Killian tugged her a little lower, and rolled over on top of her, pinning her to the mattress. He cupped her jaw, and while his thumbs brushed back and forth across her chin, he dropped kisses randomly around her face.

Her forehead. One cheek. A closed eye, then her mouth. The other cheek, her chin, before returning to her mouth. With each pass, Emma's limbs relaxed, and slowly, the tension in her back and neck subsided—mostly.

Killian propped his body up, and for some reason, his expression reminded her of the day Jack had shown her Jonesy's new retreat.

When she'd climbed in her van to drive back to the clinic, Jack had asked if she and Killian had read Ian and Hope's journals. Her answer had been no, and even before Jack said anything, she knew whatever he said would make her feel guilty.

'Read them,' Jack begged. 'I don't want to lose you too.'

That hadn't been the end of the guilty feelings, though. Especially when she'd told Killian what Jack had said. Her fiancé's message had hurt the most.

'I don't want to lose you either, Doc. I love you.'

LOOKING DOWN INTO HER BEAUTIFUL FACE, KILLIAN WISHED, NOT for the first time, he could wrap her in his arms and carry her away. Wished he could take on her burdens, because hearing the anguish in her voice tore him apart. Wished he could take away the clouds in her beautiful green eyes.

Except that wasn't his job. His job was to be by her side—working with her, and not against her.

Killian kissed her again, then rested his forehead against hers. "What do we need to do, Doc?"

Her eyes flared, and her lips curled into a gentle smile. "Find the key." She pushed on his chest until he rolled over. "Save the town."

And you.

"And save hope," he answered out loud.

Emma nodded. "And save hope." She crawled out of bed and disappeared into the closet. "Jack wasn't the only one who told me Jonesy was losing his hope, so did Elsa."

Killian was waiting for her when she came out of the closet, pulling on a sweater. "We both know how that sounded."

"Even on our first date at Captain Jack's Fine Dining," Emma went on. "You told me Jonesy seemed so alone."

"And you said he'd probably lost his mate," Killian reminded her. "His hope hadn't been part of the equation."

She was quiet, and for a second he thought she was listening. But then he saw her putting on her boots.

"It's bloody early, Doc! Where are you going?"

Emma stopped in front of the mirror, ran a brush through her long blonde hair, and pulled it back into a ponytail.

Their gazes met in the mirror. "What is one thing you've pushed since the beginning of our relationship?"

Killian took a deep breath as somehow, she'd outmaneuvered him.

"To share our burdens."

"That's right." Emma sidestepped him. "And I've been doing that. Telling you how I feel about Jonesy and Jack and this ridiculous notion that we can save the swan by finding a key. Right?"

"Aye," he stretched out his answer. "I'm happy I've been there for you. It's where I want to be."

"Then why," she backed him up, "have you refused to give me the same consideration?"

"I ..." He paused, what he'd planned to say fading. "Bloody hell."

"What was that?"

"You win." Killian dropped onto the bed and tugged her onto his lap. "Are you sure you want to hear this?"

"Killian, I love you." Emma leaned against him. "I know when you're hurting. And you've been hurting for at least two weeks, but haven't shared. That hurts me."

"I'm sorry, Doc. It's just difficult—"

"—To admit you need help?"

"To admit I'm scared of losing you," he clarified.

"I'm not going anywhere," she murmured. "Where did you get that idea?"

"Nightmare."

"What happened?"

"We were worried about finding the key," he began, "and Jonesy."

"Both true."

"When I woke up, you were gone and had left me a note saying you were going to the cove."

"I'm with you so far."

"I drove out to the cove to check on you and ..." He opened and closed his mouth several times, but the words refused to form.

"And what?" she asked. "When you got there, Jonesy was dead?"

"No, Doc," Killian whispered. "You were."

"I was? Not Jonesy?"

"You had slipped on the rocks." Killian shuddered, the image still crystal clear, even with his eyes closed.

"We can't stop living, Killian. This is my job."

He sighed, not sure what to say.

"I get scared when you're on a case," she murmured. "Yet I don't stop you from going to work, do I?"

"No," he grumbled. "I'm trained—"

"—And carry a gun," Emma hummed. "I get that. I'll be careful."

Their eyes clashed in the early morning light, and he wanted nothing more than to carry her back to bed. Except she was right. He needed to trust her, and they needed to find the bloody key.

"Alright."

"Thank you." She kissed him once more, and on her way out, handed him the charm bracelet that had belonged to her grandmother. "We know the answer is in these charms. You're the detective. Detect. Just hurry, Jonesy is running out of time, and if he dies …"

For generations, the women in the Swan and Prince families had not lived to see their forty-fifth birthday, until Ava. And Emma was a Swan.

Killian grabbed her hand before she could leave and tugged her into his arms. He'd always felt protective, but since his dream, it had been even more difficult letting her out of his sight.

"I love you, Doc."

"I love you, too."

He kissed her and, for the moment she was in his arms, he allowed himself to believe everything would be alright. That in the next few hours, they'd find the key, save Swan Harbor's hope, and in two days they'd finally be married.

"Hurry," Emma reiterated. Then, with another quick kiss, she ran down the stairs.

As soon as the outside door closed, Killian spread the charm bracelet on the table. Before he had time to study it, their three *Felis catus*, Millicent, Trudi, and Nina, demanded his attention.

"You guys first, huh?"

Once he'd taken care of the cats, Killian set up his evidence board and willed Ian Jones to speak to him.

Emma's charm bracelet was silver, made from pieces of eight that had been part of the Spanish Treasury Fleet in 1715. Its charms were melted on and included a key, the number 2, a heart, an eye, a swan, a ruby, a timepiece, and a cluster of stars.

If he looked at them individually, the only one that meant something was the key, which had been used to open two locks. But was that it? Or would they need it again?

Killian pushed the bracelet aside and reached for Ian's journal.

14 February 1720

Geoffrey was right, we need a miracle for all the pieces to come together at once. But I have faith that the higher power that guided me to Swan Harbor and Hope has a plan. Until then, the town will have to rely on the bursts of hope from the special occasions. And I will bide my time by lending my hope to the tiny town that holds my heart.

According to Captain Jack, the bursts of hope were no longer enough. While they'd been lucky with many pieces, they were still missing the most important one. Was this yet another task he needed to rely on others to complete?

A glance at the time had Killian grabbing his phone and hitting dial.

"Killian?" his father's calm voice came across the line. "Is everything alright?"

"Emma had a dream Jonesy died. She's having second thoughts about getting married until this is resolved."

"What do we need to do?"

The sick feeling that had been creeping up inside relaxed at his father's words.

"Emma went to the cave," Killian explained. "Can you have Ava check on her?"

"Of course," Finn assured him. "And you, Killian? What do you need?"

The rest of the tension he'd been holding dissipated quickly. "Can you meet me at Captain Jack's?"

"The ship?"

"Aye. I have a hunch."

"Alright, Killian. Shall I call your brother?"

"Would you?" Killian agreed. "Will you ask him to call Aiden as well? I'll send a message to Dylan."

"We'll see you at the pier."

"Thanks, dad."

"It's what families are for, Killian," Finn reminded him. "We'll see you there."

Killian hung up and sent a quick text to Dylan. Since the curse had begun with the Prince and Swan families, he knew Swan Harbor's sheriff would want to be involved. With the next step set, he went to shower.

Lover's Cove
February 12
7:00 a.m.

WHEN EMMA ARRIVED AT THE CAVE, HER HANDS WERE SHAKING, and she couldn't make herself get out of the van. She kept telling herself she shouldn't have listened to Jack. That Jonesy was safer in the zoo's aviary.

But if it's his hope?

That the hope of Swan Harbor being tied to swans dated back to 1692 still made no sense to her scientific mind.

And Killian's dream?

She understood why he'd not shared it with her, but they both were guilty of holding back when they shouldn't. Even though they had come a long way, they still had a lot to learn.

Which brought her back to a conversation with her new stepfather, Finn, who was her soon to be father-in-law. A situation that still felt a little like a soap opera.

They'd been dancing at Elsa and Liam's engagement party.

"Elsa said Swan Harbor has a way of reaching out and drawing people in."

"Swan Harbor is unique," she finally settled on.

Finn twirled her around a few times, his expression contemplative. "You two make it sound as if the town is a living, breathing entity."

Emma smiled. "There's just something about living here that gives you hope there is such a thing as a happy ending."

"Or is it a happy beginning?" Finn hummed.

"The first day to the rest of your life," she murmured, almost to herself. "I like that."

Was her happy beginning doomed if she was unsuccessful in saving Jonesy?

She refused to believe that. They had all the pieces except one, and it was close. It had to be.

Emma grabbed her medical kit and hitched it over her shoulder before she carefully made her way to the cave. She expected to find the swan foraging in the warm water. When he wasn't, her heart picked up speed. She climbed down into the cave, but again he wasn't in one of his usual places.

"Jonesy?" she whispered.

A sound alerted her to his whereabouts. He had moved farther away from the water than she'd expected and was slumped over. His eyes were closed, and the thought, *he looks hopeless,* floated through her head.

"Oh, Jonesy."

Her eyes welled, but she shoved the tears down and took out her stethoscope. As she approached him, he opened one eye, and she was afraid he would try to get away. Except he was too weak. Slowly, Emma knelt next to him and laid the drum on his chest.

"Let me listen."

A car door slammed, alerting her she was no longer alone, but her focus was on the swan. His heartbeat was faint, and so slow it was a surprise he was still alive.

"Oh, Jonesy," Emma sighed. "I'm so sorry. How did you get mixed up in Swan Harbor's hope, anyway? I wish ..." Her voice died as the time for wishes was over.

A stillness settled around them for a second, and then he looked at her again. When her eyes met his, she couldn't stop a few fanciful thoughts from floating through her mind.

Just listen, his eyes seemed to say.

TWO
IT WAS 1717 AND ...

Swan Harbor

May 1717

It was her youngest brother Luke's third birthday, and this year had been no different. Their caretaker, Anne Michaels, had planned a party, and they were all expected to attend. Except, just like the rest of her family, Hope Prince hadn't been in the mood to celebrate.

Her father, Geoffrey, had been the first to disappear, most likely drinking in his study. Then, after they cut the cake, her oldest brother, Martin, and his wife escaped. Hope had tried to pretend, but the pain was still too fresh. Her grief was still too close to the surface.

Half an hour later, she snuck out the back door, and started toward the woods behind her home. Unlike other times, though, instead of following the stream toward the cliff, she turned in the opposite direction. After a day of pretending everything was all right, she needed to hear that her feelings mattered. Needed someone to tell her that what she felt inside was normal.

Except, the closer she drew to the tavern owned by the Pattersons', her best friend's family, the more she second-guessed her decision. Was it fair to take her morbid self into their home? To subject them to her sour mood?

But you have every right to your feelings.

She did, and she knew they understood that. Faith's family had both drawn her closer and given her space for the last three years.

Hope had almost reached the tavern door when it opened, and the raucous laughter from inside caused her to reconsider. She skirted around the building and headed back into the woods.

With every step she took, the feeling of being watched grew stronger. So much so, she ducked behind a tree and looked back over her shoulder.

A group of men were standing right outside the tavern, and something about their laughter unsettled her. She knew they couldn't see her, but that didn't stop her from taking another step backward and pressing closer to the trunk of a tree. When she stepped on a twig, and it snapped beneath her foot, her breath caught, and fear of being noticed climbed inside. Especially when she remembered she had on a new gown, described as 'sunshine yellow,' that stuck out among the greens and browns of the foliage.

Hope gathered her petticoats tight to her legs and peered back around the trunk. The group had moved on, except for one man. Tall, dark, and ...

Dangerous, she couldn't help but think. He was a pirate after all, and dressed accordingly. Black boots and breeches topped by a billowing black shirt that exposed his broad chest. However, the longer she looked, another word appeared ... *intriguing*.

She stared, unable to look away, and then the strangest thing happened. He touched his chest, and his expression changed. The look had her fading further into the woods, as it caused feelings inside she wasn't sure how to describe.

"Don't go off alone, Hope."

"Those woods are not the place for a young lady."

"Be careful, Hope. You never know ..."

But she couldn't seem to stay away from the stream that meandered into the hills surrounding Swan Harbor. She'd spend hours studying the wildflowers, picking the berries and watching the small animals.

Yet, the feelings inside refused to allow her to enjoy what normally gave her pleasure. Instead, they pushed her forward, searching for peace, only settling when she was on the cliff overlooking the ocean. It was there, with the blue sea in front of her, the wind in her hair, and a field of wildflowers behind, her insides calmed. For it was there she felt closest to her mother.

Hope stepped near the edge, wrapped her arms around her waist, and held on. The pain, sorrow, and anguish she kept a tight lid on most of the time bubbled up and ... spilled over. It had been three years since her mother's untimely death. Yet the pain never completely dissipated. Christine Swan Prince had been the light in their family.

When she had died after giving birth to baby Luke, everything had changed inside their home. The servants became more subdued. Her father spent more time away from his family, and she, as the only girl, had been expected to take over. Until Anne, who had been her father's nanny, had stepped forward. Then, Hope had been left alone ... just as she wanted.

Do you really?

That was what she told herself anyway. If she wanted company, there were Faith and her family. Most days, they helped take some of the loneliness away.

During those times, Hope survived. Yet, it never stopped her from wishing for more. Wishing for someone or something to fill the hole her mother's death had left in her heart.

It was during those times she ended up on the cliff, staring out at the blue water, and the songs within spilled over. She sang from her heart, rarely paying attention to the words. As the haunting melody echoed around the town and out to sea, she was left open and vulnerable.

Hope knew people talked about her family. How could they not? However, since her father was the law, the talk was hushed and said behind their backs. And while it should have upset her, she was unable to make herself care. What mattered was searching to find the happiness her mother had promised was waiting.

Complete happiness had so far eluded her, but she could admit, with the return of the swans to the cove, she had felt a subtle shift inside. It was as if the force her mother believed they brought was being shared. That finally, what had been waiting had arrived.

Far below her, the swans that had been coming to their small town since her birth floated in the cove. The bank was dotted with females on nests, and just the glimpse had what suspiciously felt like hope blooming inside. Unintentionally, her melody changed, becoming lighter and brighter.

Hope was in the air.

El corazón del Rubí
May 1717

"Is the Siren singing again tonight, Cap'n?"

Ian tore his gaze away from the vision in yellow and relaxed his stance when his first mate, D.D., joined him on the bridge.

"She is." His eyes drifted back to the lass on the cliff. "There's something different, though."

"Her song has changed."

"You think so?"

"I do." D.D. hesitated several moments before offering, "Today, there is more hope than sorrow in her song."

"Perhaps."

"You think not?"

"I ..." His voice faded when he was unable to find the right words. Once again, he lifted the spyglass and studied her features. Tall, slim, with a fair complexion and long red-gold curls. "She crossed my path earlier," he surprised himself by admitting.

D.D. leaned against the railing, and Ian could feel his friend's attention on him, rather than on their siren. "Is there a story there?"

"Not much of one." Ian shrugged it off as if it were not important. "When I left the tavern, she was heading into the woods."

And the yellow of her dress had caught his eye, and in the vicinity of his heart a warmth had bloomed.

Except those were words he could not utter out loud.

"She's young," he settled on.

"Does she work at the tavern?"

"No," Ian responded, then quickly amended his answer, "at least I do not believe so."

"You sound besotted," D.D. exclaimed, surprise in his voice.

Ian wanted to scoff at the possibility. However, the warmth in the center of his chest when looking at her had been new ... different.

"She's young," he repeated.

D.D. smirked. "So was my wife when I first met her, and look how ..." His expression sobered, and Ian knew where his thoughts had traveled.

Instead of responding, he turned his attention back to the cliff. Without his spyglass, he couldn't make out the Siren's features, but there was something about her that took his breath. Her long yellow gown rippled in the wind, and the way her arms were wrapped around her waist told him she was in pain. What was it that could have brought such pain to one so young?

"Look at her," he murmured. "What is her story?"

"With your penchant for stories," D.D. teased. "I'm surprised you did not ask."

"I wanted to." Ian winced. "However, before I had a chance, she was gone. And then I ..."

"You were afraid?"

"No," Ian denied. "It was she who was afraid."

"You are scary," D.D. laughed. "Next time, try smiling."

"Perhaps," Ian replied before turning his back on the Siren, and to the reason they had gone into town. "Did you find any news?"

For a moment, D.D. looked like he was going to say something else, but with a shrug followed Ian's lead. "That your friend Henry was seen with the First Mate earlier."

"Henry?" Ian frowned. "Why? Where?"

"He is *your* friend," D.D. pointed out. "Perhaps you should ask."

"Perhaps I should."

Ian had taken several steps toward the ladder when D.D.'s voice drifted through the air, "Perhaps you can also ask about the Siren."

"Perhaps."

"Ian," D.D.'s voice was closer, "are you sure ...?"

"Stop!" Ian snapped. "The decision was made. We are here and must continue on the path to see where it leads."

"But what if the path is not of our choosing?"

Ian blew out a breath, and once again glanced toward the cliffs. "Do any of us get to choose our paths, D.D.? Or are they chosen for us?"

"You know what I mean."

"I do," Ian acknowledged. "Sometimes, though, the decision is not ours to make. Are you coming?"

He was surprised when D.D. followed him quietly off the ship and toward the tavern. It was not like him to keep his thoughts to himself. Was there more going through D.D.'s head than he was sharing?

They slipped into the tavern and took a table in the corner. The noise seemed louder than usual, making him wish he'd stayed on the El corazón.

"Relax." D.D. set two glasses and a bottle of rum on the table. "You might scare away the ladies."

Ian poured a healthy amount of rum, tossed it back and poured again. "We are not here for the ladies." However, if the vision in yellow walked by ... he would look. Anything else, he would see.

"Here comes Henry," D.D. murmured. "Maybe he knows who the Siren is."

"Let's stay bloody focused, shall we?" Ian grumbled.

"Stop being surly," D.D. tossed back.

"Professor. D.D.," Henry greeted them, "I thought you had business elsewhere."

"Who told you that?"

"I heard," Henry frowned and pulled out a chair. "What am I missing?"

Ian set his glass down and leaned forward. "Why were you talking to Sly Bill today?"

"Sly Bill?" Henry echoed.

"Black hair, and has a scar that runs from one eye to his chin," Ian described the man.

"Oh, Billy," Henry exclaimed.

"Billy?" Ian exchanged looks with D.D. and the thought, *Were we wrong?* flew between them.

"Yes, Billy Smith," Henry went on. "Showed up at the beginning of the year. Doc Williams patched him up, and since then , he's been helping at the mill. Why?"

"Are you sure?"

"Yes. I found him." Henry looked from one to the other. "He'd washed up not far from the new lighthouse."

"I trust you," Ian responded. "But do not trust him."

Henry laughed. "I'm not a greenhorn, Professor. Why do you believe Billy is not trustworthy?"

"Your Billy," D.D. explained, "is not as innocent as he appears. He's a pirate."

"And?" Henry's brows arched. "As are you."

Ian winced, his comments to D.D. earlier coming back around. "Some choose their journey, such as your Billy," he offered cryptically. "And for others, the journey is chosen."

"Which means?" Henry grumbled.

"It means," D.D. offered. "You need to be vigilant around him and his kind ..."

A flash of yellow pulled Ian's attention away from the conversation to the corner of the room.

"The Siren," he murmured.

"The Siren?" Henry repeated, looking over his shoulder. "Are you talking about Hope?"

"Hope." The name rolled off Ian's tongue as if it had been created just for him. "Her name is Hope?"

As quickly as she had appeared, she disappeared through a door that was nearly hidden from sight. "Does she work here?"

"Hope? Hardly." Henry shook his head. "She's my sister Faith's friend. Why?"

There was much he could have said, but opted for the simple, "I heard her singing. She has a beautiful voice but seems so ... sad."

"From the cliff?"

"Yes."

Henry shrugged. "Since her mother passed, Hope has struggled. My mother says give her time and allow the swans to rebuild her hope that tomorrow will be better than today."

"The swans?"

"Of course," Henry exclaimed. "You know the story of how Swan Harbor was discovered, right?"

Something inside Ian stirred, and the thought, *A story*, flashed through his head. "I'm listening," he responded, leaning a little closer, as there was nothing he enjoyed more than a great tale.

"It started in 1692," Henry began. "When my family and many others left England. The story goes they had just about given up when a group of swans were spotted, led by a lone black one."

"And the swans led them to this piece of land?"

"Yes," Henry nodded. "They gave the settlers hope that something better was waiting for them. And Swan Harbor has flourished."

Ian grunted, as he had not heard that before, but rather than asking more questions, he filed it away to research later. And while he wished for more information about the lass, Hope, he moved on.

"How's the construction of the lighthouse?" he asked, knowing the device to guide ships around a dangerous area was something his friend was excited about.

Henry's face lit up. "It is almost complete. I just need to ..."

The Patterson's Home
May 1717

Hope ducked into Faith's room and slid onto the floor with her knees bent, her gown billowing around her. It took several seconds before her pulse steadied. Once it did, her thoughts went back to what had happened as she'd passed through the tavern.

She'd been going in and out of the same set of doors her entire life, and never had she experienced the same sensation. It had been as if she could hear another heart beating. Feel it racing alongside hers. Where had that come from?

Her head dropped onto her crossed arms resting on her knees, and her emotions rolled over her. While they were still heavy, they felt lighter for some reason. It was as if she ...

When the door opened, her thoughts scattered. Hope shrunk back against the wall, not wanting to see anyone except her best friend, Faith.

"Hope!"

"I'm so happy to see you," Faith gushed.

Hope frowned at her friend's apparent excitement, as surely, she remembered what day it was.

"Here I am," Hope muttered. "Did you need me for something?"

Faith giggled and twirled around, and the first thought that flew through Hope's mind was her friend's happiness involved a boy.

"He's here," Faith sighed, falling back on her bed. "Did you see him?"

"Who's here?" Hope questioned.

"Him," Faith repeated. "Henry's friend."

"Henry's friend?" Hope echoed.

"The Professor," Faith reminded her. "I told you about him."

Hope thought back on their last few conversations. And while she had a vague recollection of Faith being excited about something, she realized she must have missed much of what had been said.

"I'm sorry," she admitted. "Tell me again."

"The Professor," Faith repeated, "is a friend of Henry's. He is also a pirate."

That last bit had come out in a whisper, and Hope found she had to rush to catch all the pieces and connect them.

"Henry has a friend, who is a pirate," Hope murmured. "But he's called The Professor?"

"Yes!" Faith nodded her head exuberantly. "He's really, really smart."

"If he were smart, he would not be a pirate," Hope pointed out.

"Oh, Hope," Faith sighed, completely ignoring the comment. "You should see him. Tall, dark wavy hair that touches his shoulders. Brooding dark eyes and a mouth that—"

"Faith!" Hope interrupted her friend.

Faith giggled. "I was wondering if you were paying attention."

"Of course, I was," Hope assured her. "Why were you looking at this man? I thought your parents wanted you to marry Benedict."

"Pah!" Faith wrinkled her nose. "He's just a bore."

"True," Hope agreed. "But I thought it had been decided."

Faith shrugged. "I understand my parents' marriage was arranged, and it seems to have worked out. But come on, Hope! This is 1717. I want to choose the man I'm to spend my life with. Do you not wish for the same?"

The feeling inside when she'd seen the man outside the tavern flashed through her mind. It reminded her of the stories her mother had told about fighting for her father, Geoffrey.

"I think so," Hope admitted quietly. And because she wanted to listen and not think, she encouraged, "Tell me about your professor."

"My professor," Faith giggled. "I wish."

"What do you know about him?"

"He's the captain of the ship El corazón del Rubí. His all-black clothing makes him look ..."

Hope's attention spiked at the mention of all black, and she remembered the man whom she'd seen outside the tavern.

"Dangerous?" she supplied, even though that word was not the one she would have chosen.

"Yes." Faith buried her face in her hands, and when she looked back up, her dark eyes were sparkling, and her cheeks were pink. "He makes me feel—"

"—Like you are being pulled toward something you have no control over," Hope murmured, finally able to label the feeling she'd experienced when her eyes had met those of Faith's professor.

"You do know!" Faith exclaimed.

"I do," Hope acknowledged, but refused to say it was in reference to the same person.

"I just have to get him to notice me," Faith murmured. "Maybe the next time he comes into the tavern, I can ..."

With every new suggestion, the pain in the center of Hope's chest grew. She had known Faith her entire life, and there had been nothing but support between them. Why was it that suddenly she felt they were on opposite sides of something?

THREE

Timber Creek, Maine
July 1717
6:00 a.m.

Ian kicked at the burned-out remains and studied the carnage around him. "There's something different about this village. It's almost too perfect."

D.D.'s brows shot up. "How so?"

"I cannot say … yet." Ian placed his hands on his hips and turned completely around, his gaze drifted from one pile of debris to another. "There is … too much consistency," he finally offered.

"Meaning?"

"Remember the last village, Pine Bay?" Ian pointed to the building they were standing next to and then to the closest pile of debris. "Everything was burned. But here, what do you see?"

He waited while D.D. studied the area around them but had no doubt the older man would come to the same conclusion.

"Piecemeal," D.D. finally proclaimed. "Most of the buildings appear as if they just toppled over."

"And every few piles were set on fire," Ian nodded. "But why?"

"Hiding something—"

"—Or someone," Ian murmured, as an idea began to crystallize in his head.

"Someone?" D.D. looked at him as if he had grown an extra head. "What are you thinking?"

Ian glanced at the pile of wood and rocks next to where they were standing. "Help me!"

After several minutes of moving debris and not making much progress, Ian called for some of the crew to help them.

"Listen."

What he was hearing sounded more animal than human, but after another layer was uncovered, they realized an underground chamber had been found.

"A dog?" D.D. murmured.

There was something about the pitiful sound that sent a chill up Ian's spine. They pushed aside the last layer, and the sight huddled in one corner had his stomach twisting.

"Children."

"And their dog," D.D. whispered, his eyes meeting Ian's. "But where are their parents?"

It was several more moments before they were able to lift the children and their dog from the depths of the pit. Except they were so frightened, if Ian's reflexes had not kicked in, they would have run.

"You have children, D.D." Ian nodded to the boys. "Now what?"

D.D. squatted in front of the oldest child. "Here now. Do not be frightened. You are safe." His voice was low and soothing. "What are you called, son?"

A second passed, then another, and the young body trembled under his hand. Then, gradually, Ian felt his muscles relax.

"John, sir," the child responded. "My name is John. This is my brother Gilbert and our dog Mutt."

The scraggly dog whimpered and pressed tighter to the smaller boy, and once again Ian had to fight off the memories.

"Where's your—?"

"Cap'n," Freddy called from several feet away, "there's more."

Which he had somehow expected, he realized, not surprised by the news.

"What did you—?" Ian was cut off mid-question when, all around him, there were more shouts.

"Here's another!"

"And two more!"

Then the younger lad, Gilbert, stiffened. "Mama?"

"Gilbert! John!" Ian heard before he was roughly pushed away. "Get your filthy hands off my boys!"

Her cloud of red-gold hair took him aback for a split second as she tore the boys from him and wrapped herself around them. It had been over two months, yet each time he saw hair resembling that of the Siren's, the warmth in his chest bloomed.

"We mean them no harm, Mistress," Ian tried to assure the mother. "We were just—"

"Hunter," she snapped. "Mistress Jenny Hunter, Pirate. And I know exactly who you are."

Ian exchanged glances with D.D. "Tell me, who am I?"

Her brown eyes flashed hatred, and slowly, Ian began putting together the pieces.

"Listen up," he demanded, his usually quiet voice louder, more forceful, earning him the attention he desired. "Gather the survivors and take them to the ship."

"The ship?" the woman screeched. "We'll not go with you."

"And what will you do?" Ian questioned. "Stay and wait until the pirates return?"

She blanched, and there was a part of him that regretted his harsh words. "Where are the men?"

Jenny dropped her eyes, refusing to look at him.

"This was staged," he tossed out, satisfied when she glanced back in his direction. "But please tell me they are not out searching for El corazón de la Rosa."

Their eyes clashed in the early morning light, and then, he saw a crack in her armor. She whispered something to John, and after he'd taken his brother's hand and the boys were far enough away, took a step closer.

"Yes," Jenny hissed. "Many of us have survived an attack by the pirates sailing on El corazón de la Rosa. When they began to prey on our new village, we decided to take the law into our own hands and go after them—"

"—Before they could come after you?"

"Yes."

"How long have you been hiding in these underground dwellings?"

She shrugged. "Just a couple of days."

"How did you know it would work?" Ian asked. "That the black-hearted bloke who captains the Rosa would not set fire to everything?"

What little color was left drained from her face, and he saw D.D. step closer to catch her lest she fall.

"We prayed," Jenny admitted. "Then we got word that the ship had bypassed us and was on the way north."

Ian's blood chilled at her comment. "North? What do you know?"

"Our men," she pointed into the lush foliage that surrounded the area, "they went through there, toward the town where the Rosa was heading."

"By foot?" Ian frowned.

"No, by horse," Jenny clarified. "There is a small town about a day's ride ... called Swan—"

"—Harbor," Ian finished.

"Yes," she nodded. "The men hoped to gather more citizens in Swan Harbor to fight the pirates. They hoped there would be strength in numbers."

"Sometimes hope is not enough," Ian murmured, not realizing how cynical he sounded.

"Sometimes hope is all you have," Jenny retorted.

"She's right," D.D. agreed.

Ian nodded in acknowledgment and gave orders for everyone to board. There was no time to lose.

"How did the Rosa slip past us, D.D.?" he asked his first mate. "And will we be able to catch them before they do to Swan Harbor—"

"Stop!" D.D. demanded. "We will catch them."

"How can you be so sure?" Ian questioned, the older man's hope still strong after so many months.

"Hope," D.D. whispered. "Because without it, my life would be worth nothing."

"Hope," Ian repeated.

While he gave the orders to set sail toward Swan Harbor, Henry's story about the swans bringing hope filtered through his head. Behind those thoughts were ones of the Siren. Was she still making her trips to the cliff to sing? If so, there was a part of him that hoped today she would stay home. Especially if, as was thought, El corazón de la Rosa was on its way there. He hated to think what would happen to her, and her town, if the men were set free.

Swan Harbor
July 1717
8:00 a.m.

When Hope heard Geoffrey's boots outside her door, she jumped from the bed and peered out her window. It wasn't long before his loose-legged walk carried him to the barn. After a few minutes, he led his stallion outside and climbed on. Then, once he'd ridden out of view, she rushed to get dressed.

Hope tossed her sleep shift one direction and pulled another from the drawer she had altered to wear beneath her 'riding' clothes. The shortened shift slipped over her head, stopping mid-hip, and she covered it with one of her older brother's shirts. She had a pair of his breeches halfway on when her door was suddenly pushed open.

"Hope!" Anne whispered. "Please tell me you are not planning to ride."

"I cannot," Hope hedged, even knowing it would not get her far.

"But Hope," Anne pleaded. "You heard your father last night. There are pirates ..."

Except every time the word pirate was uttered, Hope kept seeing the tall, dark man Faith called Professor. If, as she'd expected, he was the man outside the tavern, his return did not instill fear inside of her ... but intrigue.

"I will be fine."

Anne shook her head. "How can you guarantee no harm will come to you?"

Hope studied the older woman and, while on one hand, she understood where the worry came from ... on the other ...

"If I show you," she began. "Can I trust you to keep my secret?"

A pinched look crossed Anne's face, as if she couldn't believe what she was about to say. "Fine."

Hope fastened her breeches and opened her wardrobe, taking out the sword she'd been learning how to use.

"Hope!" Anne practically screeched. "What? Where?"

"Uncle Phillip," Hope admitted.

"Does your father know your uncle is encouraging this behavior?"

"What do you think?" Hope dropped the sword and tied a piece of rope around her waist. "Of course, he does not know. But are you surprised?"

"No," Anne shook her head, "especially not after what happened to your aunt."

Hope grimaced and stepped in front of the window, using it to see her reflection while she twisted her hair on top of her head. She covered it with a cap and turned back around.

"Even father admits no one knows who attacked Aunt Kitty," Hope admitted. "But Uncle Phillip just wants me to be safe."

"Is he teaching your cousin too?"

"Ellie? Yes."

"There is nothing I can say to stop you?"

"Not today, Anne." Hope slipped the scabbard over her head, the sword draped across her back. "I will be fine," Hope promised the older woman. "Just fine," she reiterated on her way out of her room.

"Eat something," Anne's voice followed her down the hall.

Except Hope was too excited to take much time and instead filled the breeches' pockets with nuts on her way out to the barn. If she got hungry, there were wild berries in the woods.

Her horse was waiting for her and nickered softly as soon as she entered the barn. Big Red had been her gift from her parents for her thirteenth birthday. Easily standing fifteen hands, he was a magnificent beast.

However, since her father's prized stallion and her mother's beautiful mare had sired him, it had been expected. He was temperamental and allowed no one else to ride him. Hope knew the minute she climbed on his back, he would feel her mood; for they were connected.

"Hello, Big Guy," she murmured as she fastened his saddle and led him into the yard. "Are you ready to run?"

He nickered and bobbed his head as if he understood, but otherwise waited patiently for her to finish her tasks. Hope climbed on, and his muscles quivered in anticipation.

"Ready?" she whispered, tightening her knees against his big body.

Big Red tossed his head in the air, gave a spirited whinny, and took off.

The freedom Hope felt spilled over as his walk moved into a trot. When his speed increased to a canter, she couldn't keep her laughter inside. By the time he had reached full gallop, she was bent over his neck, pushing him forward with her soft-spoken words.

The wind whipped her cap off, but rather than stop, she glanced over her shoulder and wished it farewell. Her long red-gold hair flew around her head. With the smell of wildflowers in the air, and the warmth of the sun on her skin, she didn't care.

She lost track of how long they rode but, as if Big Red knew what she needed, he led her toward the cliff. Just as she had for the past two months, she immediately checked the dock. His ship wasn't there, but somehow, she knew he would soon return to Swan Harbor. It was how she knew that made no sense.

Her attention drifted to the swans below, where the nests were empty, and the white birds dotted the cove. She was too far away to see clearly. Yet, she knew the swan that had appeared the year after her mother's death was there. Majestic, graceful, leading her young around, just not the four that had hatched, as only two remained. Was there a meaning there she was missing?

The sound of Big Red's whinny was her first indication she was no longer alone. Slowly, Hope turned to see three men step around a group of boulders, the menacing look on their faces sending a chill through her.

"What 'ave we 'ere, mates?" the tallest of the three questioned.

Hope measured the distance between where she was standing and her horse. *Could she make it? Should she try?*

As if anticipating what she was thinking, one man cut away from the others, heading for her horse.

"Are you sure you want to do that?" Hope asked, more bravado in her voice than she was actually feeling.

"'E's a 'orse, Missy. I know 'orses."

"Not this one," Hope pointed out, edging away from the cliff, farther into the field of wildflowers.

"'E's a 'orse," the man repeated, reaching for the reins.

Hope opened her mouth to warn him, just as Big Red blew out air and reared up on his hind legs.

"Bloody 'ell!"

He jumped back, and thinking she had an opening, Hope took several more steps, except she had forgotten the other two men.

"Going somewhere?" the tallest asked, the threatening note in his voice sending another shard of fear through her.

She wasn't sure what, but something reminded her of the scabbard hanging on her back. Suddenly, Hope pulled her sword and moved into the stance, just as her uncle had shown her.

"Stay away," she growled, jabbing the sword toward the closest man.

"Oh, lookee 'ere," he chortled to his friends. "The missy wants to play. I'm game." His sword was brandished, and he struck first.

The clang of metal on metal kicked Hope's adrenaline into high gear. He was stronger, which meant she had to be smarter. But while she could back him up a step with one move, his next would bring him closer.

She lost track of the time, the sweat rolled down her face, and her muscles began to wear. The thought that she should have listened to Anne had just flown through her mind when a dark head appeared over the cliff.

"Looking for a fight, fellas?" the man she'd seen outside the tavern asked conversationally as soon as he was standing on the cliff.

"Leave us be," one man yelled. "We found her first."

The man Hope had been fighting jabbed his sword toward hers, and because her focus was broken, he knocked it from her hand. She sent panicked eyes first to her horse, then to the newcomer.

"Go!" he screamed, running in her direction. "Go!"

Hope heard a cry and looked around to see more men running from a copse of trees in the distance. *Were they friend or foe?* flew through her head.

"Go!" the man cried again.

Big Red reared, pushing the man closest to her back, giving her space to make a quick decision. Hope grabbed her sword, threw herself onto the horse's back and before she was even seated, they were running.

Just before the trees swallowed her, Hope looked over her shoulder. The scene gave her a sick feeling in the pit of her stomach, clenching. Was that it? Had the Professor just sacrificed himself for her? If so, how was she going to explain what happened to her father ... and to Faith?

El corazón del Rubí
July 1717
9:00 p.m.

Ian groaned, unable to pinpoint which part of his body hurt most.

"Shhh," a quiet voice whispered, seconds before a cool cloth brushed across his forehead.

He struggled to organize his jumbled thoughts, but the more he tried, the worse his head pounded.

"Just rest," the voice murmured.

Except without more knowledge of where he was, and what had happened, Ian fought the need to give in to the darkness. What ...

... standing on the deck ...

... Siren ... but not ...

... frightened sound from a horse ...

... Go! ...

As bits and pieces of information floated around inside his brain, another groan escaped.

... follow them ...

But ...

... Go ... go ...

"No worries," the quiet voice murmured, soothing the cloth on his hot face.

... come on ...

... walk with me ...

... Trust ...

More fragments filtered in and out as Ian remembered leaning on his friend, Henry. He dug into the last remaining bits of his energy and forced himself to focus.

The gentle sway told him he was on his ship. However, the hands touching his brow were unfamiliar. He forced his eyes open, but even with the moonlight filtering in through the portholes, his vision was hazy. "Henry?"

"If you believe that," a melodic voice laughed. "I might need to call Doc Williams again."

The warmth in the center of his chest bloomed and spread out, as the woman who had been invading his dreams for months was standing in his cabin. "My siren."

"Your siren?" she questioned.

Of their own accord, his lips curved. The skin pulled taut, and the pain had a hiss escaping instead of clever words.

"Now, look what you've done," the Siren scolded. "You're bleeding again."

The cool cloth returned. This time, though, to dab at his mouth, and the metallic taste of blood touched his tongue.

"Rum," he croaked, thinking it would not only take the taste away, but the pain.

"It will sting."

"Rum," Ian repeated, ignoring the stubborn tone in his voice.

"Well, if you insist."

He tracked her movements across his cabin, and it wasn't long before she returned and handed him his flask.

"Do you need help?"

"No," he grunted, rolling over on his side to take a drink. The minute the spout touched his sore mouth, he hissed and yanked it back.

"Tsk, tsk," she clucked. "You're as contrary as my brother Luke. And he's three."

Ian growled and tried again, this time pouring the liquid into his mouth without touching his lips. It burned going down, but no more than usual. Then, after several sips, the pain had dulled enough for him to focus on his caretaker.

She was standing next to his bed holding a basin, which explained where the water had come from. The moonlight was hitting the side of her face in such a way, it highlighted her ivory skin and made her hair look more gold than red. But she wasn't close enough for him to read her expression.

"Why are you here?"

"Why do you think?"

That she might care what had happened to him was his first thought, but instantly discarded. He hadn't had anyone care about his well-being in many years.

"Tell me."

"Do you not remember what happened?" she asked, taking the basin across the room, and placing it on a sideboard.

"I remember enough. However, that does not answer my question, Hope."

"You know my name?"

I know more about you than you think, he wanted to say, but only offered, "Of course. Now answer the question."

"I came to check on you," Hope admitted quietly.

"And your father allowed this?"

"My father does not know where I am."

"If you are found with me," Ian tried to push up, needing to get her off his ship before his men returned. "It is not a situation you wish to happen."

"So, they talk," Hope shrugged as if it were no big deal. "That would be nothing new."

There was a tone in her voice that had him wishing he were not in pain. Had him wishing he could ask her what she was thinking. But he did not have that luxury, not at this moment anyway.

"As you can see, I am fine," he replied. "Your services are no longer needed." Then something had him amending his response. "I thank you for checking on me. You really need to leave, though."

Their eyes clashed in the dark room, and while he could not tell their color, there was something about the intensity that took him aback. He had stared down more than his fair share of adversaries, and none had affected him as she did.

"Thank you," Hope mumbled, "for you know. I'm just sorry ..."

"You're most welcome," he offered softly. "I'm happy everything turned out well."

She took a deep breath, nodded her head once and stepped toward the door. With her hand resting on the latch, her soft voice floated across the space between them. "Thank you again ... Ian."

Hearing her say his name temporarily rendered him speechless, but before he could say anything, she was gone. Ian pushed out of the bed and used the edge to lean on while he watched her scurry across the dock. She had just vanished from sight when he saw D.D. and several other men coming from the opposite direction. *Too close,* he couldn't help but think.

The echo of footsteps below him reminded him to move, and he'd just lowered back onto his bunk when D.D. entered his cabin.

"Why are you here?" D.D. was carrying a lantern and set it next to his head.

"Where else would I be?"

D.D. sent him a concerned look. "You promised. It's the only reason we went ..."

Ian waved his concerns aside. "Forget it. Did you catch them?"

"No, Ian," D.D. grumbled. "However, I did figure out how we keep missing the ship."

"How?" Ian's heart raced, as knowing how they were losing sight of the El corazón de la Rosa put them one more step closer to catching her.

"The lighthouse."

"Henry's lighthouse?" Ian repeated.

"Yes." D.D. nodded and pulled a chair close to the bunk. "Henry's lighthouse is giving the El corazón safe passage into a small but well-hidden cove. It's a wonder Swan Harbor has survived this long without an attack."

"Bloody hell," Ian muttered. "Help me up. I need to talk to Henry."

"Forget it," D.D. told him, using what Ian considered his fatherly voice.

"Forget it?"

"Yes," D.D. repeated. "I spoke to Jenny's husband. He and his men will meet with the Sheriff."

"We'll go after the ship," Ian stated, thinking once they'd completed their task, then perhaps ...

"I'll take care of it," D.D. promised. "You look like hell."

He felt like it too, Ian couldn't help but think, laying back in his bunk once more. And because he now had memories of how Hope's touch felt, he closed his eyes and allowed the dreams to take over.

FOUR

Swan Harbor
October 1717
11:00 a.m.

THE FIRST SATURDAY IN OCTOBER, AND THE ARRIVAL OF THE merchant ships, meant it was market day in Swan Harbor. Since her mother's passing, Hope had always attended with Ellie, Faith, and their mothers. This year was no different, as they were looking for material for a specific occasion; her eighteenth birthday ball.

As soon as they had stopped at the docks and she saw *his* ship, something inside her shifted. It had been over two months since the day he had rescued her on the cliff. Over two months since she had snuck onto his ship to make sure he was well. Two months since she had brushed his hair off his forehead and wiped it with a cool cloth. When she closed her eyes, her fingers still tingled from the feel of the silky strands. Thoughts of him appeared more often than she was completely comfortable with, and more often than not at the most inopportune times.

None of those were more unfortunate than when she was supposed to be focusing on something else.

"Not that table, Hope." Aunt Kitty forcibly turned her around. "This one."

Hope stared down at the table, not only full of colorful rolls of material, buttons, and threads but also plates, vases, and other pieces of crockery. Except, once again, she found her attention drawn to other, more pressing matters.

"Have you chosen your material yet, Hope?" her Aunt Kitty asked again.

"Not yet," Hope replied, barely holding in the sigh that threatened. Except the truth was, she was only paying half attention to the material. Her primary focus was on the ship, and hoping for some sign he was all right.

"It's him," Faith looped her arm through Hope's, turning them toward the El corazón, "the Professor. Look!"

Hope clamped down on her emotions and schooled her face into a nonchalant expression. "What did you say?"

"The Professor," Faith repeated. "He's just ..."

"Dangerous?" Hope offered.

"No, silly. Dishy," Faith giggled, holding aloft a porcelain bowl decorated with intertwined flowers.

"What was that?" Kitty asked, suddenly appearing between them. "You like that dish?"

Hope's eyes met Faith's, both fighting their grins that wanted to break free.

"What do you think of this dish, mother?"

"That's just too fussy," Kitty decreed.

"Really," Faith murmured for Hope's ears only, "I think he's quite ... handsome."

Against her better judgment, Hope glanced toward the ship to see the man in question standing on the deck talking to an older man. Ian, as she privately thought of him, was bareheaded, and as his hair blew in his face, he constantly pushed it back.

"Soft," she murmured, remembering the feel beneath her fingers.

"Soft?" Faith questioned. "What?"

Hope felt her face heat, and she quickly grabbed the nearest cloth. "This material," she held it up, "it's soft."

Faith fingered it and wrinkled her brow. "Doesn't feel very soft to me."

Deep down, Hope had to agree but couldn't say anything without giving away she'd been distracted. "Maybe this would be better?" She held up a gold material, the cloth velvety soft beneath her fingers.

"I like that." Her Aunt Kitty took it and draped it over Hope's shoulder. "It looks beautiful with your fair skin and red hair. Now, we just need to decide how much to buy."

"He's coming," Faith hissed as soon as Kitty had moved.

Hope glanced over her shoulder just as Ian was leaving the ship. The way he looked walking down the gangplank had her biting her lip to keep from swooning. He was wearing fawn-colored breeches and a creamy white shirt covered by a long, dark brown duster that billowed behind him. Definitely 'dishy,' she had to agree with Faith's description.

When he turned in the opposite direction from where she was standing, Hope felt equal parts relief and frustration.

"He looks recovered," Faith murmured, causing Hope's thoughts to scatter in search of a safe follow-up question.

"Recovered?"

"Oh, yes," Faith replied in a hushed voice, not wanting the others to hear. "I overheard Henry talking to Doctor Williams."

"Henry was talking to the Doc about I—," she quickly amended it to, "your Professor? Why?"

"Henry found him bleeding in his cabin," Faith explained. "Took him to the doctor, but once he was patched up, insisted he had to be back on his ship."

"Is it bad luck for pirates to be away from their ships?"

"I'm not sure," Faith shrugged. "He seems to have made a full recovery, though."

"Did Henry say how he was hurt?" Hope still hated she was keeping secrets, but sometimes it was necessary. Especially if you didn't want to disappoint others.

"Apparently, the professor was taking a walk and rescued someone."

Hope's pulse spiked as she remembered that moment when his dark head had popped over the cliff.

"But no idea who? Or why?"

"No." Faith studied her for several minutes. "Does it matter?"

Don't let on, she scolded herself.

"Matter?" Hope squeaked, cursing her weakness. "No. Just with Aunt Kitty's attack and all."

"Right." Faith started to say something else. Before she could, though, they were hurried to the buggy for the return trip home.

The older women climbed in first, and just before it was her turn, Hope glanced in the direction Ian had gone. He was climbing onto the back of a stallion, all black except for a patch of white between his eyes. Then something was said that caused him to throw back his head and laugh. She sucked in her breath and hurried into the buggy, yet couldn't stop staring in the direction he'd ridden.

"I wonder where he's going," Faith whispered, the very question Hope herself wanted to know.

"Maybe to see the person he rescued," Hope murmured, almost to herself.

Faith inhaled sharply, and a pained look crossed her face. "Do you think so?"

"I cannot say," Hope opted for instead of the truth, which caused pain in the center of her chest. While she couldn't explain what she was feeling, she did know that even though Faith had seen him first, her friend knew him as the Professor and not Ian. There had to be a difference, right?

As the buggy left the docks, Hope's aunt kept tossing out ideas for her dress. And while she tried to listen, she found her thoughts wandering. Where had he been going? Did he have someone he fancied? But no one knew.

"Do you want to come over and talk about your dress?" Faith asked after her aunt and cousin had been dropped off.

"Maybe tomorrow."

Faith studied her for several moments, and Hope fought not to squirm. "Is everything all right?"

"I'm fine, why?" Hope hurried to respond, then instead of keeping her mouth shut added another lie, "Just a little headache."

"If you say so."

"I'll come tomorrow," Hope promised, wishing to appease.

"Well, all right," Faith agreed. "If you are sure nothing is wrong."

Hope forced a smile she was not feeling and waved the Pattersons off.

Once inside though, she found her thoughts were running riot. Taking an apple, some nuts, and her book, she snuck back out. Fallen leaves softened her step as she wove her way deeper into the forest. With the trees changing colors and the weather becoming cooler, the woods were quieter. Unconsciously, she turned away from the cliff, angling toward one of her favorite places.

The 'thinking' stone was a large, flat boulder perched above one of the hot springs that dotted the hills around Swan Harbor. Protected by ivy hanging from the trees, many had named it 'The Bride's Veil'. You could lie on the rock, study the clouds, and contemplate life. It made you feel as if you were the only person in the world. It was truly solitude at its finest.

Hope pushed aside the ivy and stepped inside the natural arbor, expecting to be alone. What she saw both brought her up short and sent her pulse into overdrive.

The black stallion she'd seen Ian ride away from the docks on bobbed his head a couple of times in greeting. Hope gentled him with a calming pat, her thoughts on what she should do.

Was he alone?

She had to admit the possibility that he wasn't alone gave her a sick feeling. Should she turn back and not say anything?

Then she heard whistling. The tune was haunting and familiar, and before she realized her feet were moving, she pushed the brush aside. The view had her slamming her eyes shut and forgetting to breathe. Several impure thoughts worked their way through her brain, and slowly, she opened her eyes for another peek.

Skin!

He tossed his breeches onto a rock with the rest of his clothes and dipped his toe in the hot springs. Her gaze trailed down his broad back, taut backside, and long legs. When he angled slightly, it was enough for her to get a peek of his lightly furred chest and the line of dark hair that led ...

Once again, Hope slammed her eyes shut, the sight overwhelming, spiking her pulse and causing her face to flush.

"You can open your eyes, Siren," Ian teased. "I'm covered."

Something inside said she should be exasperated, but somehow, she couldn't work up that emotion.

"It matters not to me." Hope shrugged nonchalantly as if she walked in on bare men daily. "But why are you here?"

"I'm bathing. Why are you here?"

"Bathing?"

"Yes, bathing. You know the process of dipping oneself in water and—"

"I know what bathing is," Hope interrupted. "But ... you bathe?"

When Ian threw his head back and laughed, the sound stirred something inside. Why was she staying and not running? What was that feeling coming to life inside? Was it as she had read in her mother's journal—the waking of one heart because of another?

⚜

Ian watched the many expressions cross Hope's face, and the more she questioned, the more she fascinated him.

"Of course, I bathe," he replied. "Would you care to join me?"

Her mouth dropped open, her eyes flew wide, and he finally found the answer to a question he'd been wondering. Blue, her eyes were as blue as the sky on a cloudless day.

"No, thank you," Hope answered primly.

But again, she surprised him by tossing out another question.

"What were you whistling just now?"

"Whistling?" Ian repeated, as he'd been unaware he had been.

"Yes," she pushed and attempted to imitate.

"Oh," his gaze locked with hers, "you mean this?" He whistled the tune he'd heard her singing on the cliffs. One that had haunted him since May.

"That's my song."

"It is," Ian acknowledged.

"But, but why?" Hope tilted her head, and the sun seeping through the branches set her hair on fire. "Why would you even remember my song?"

What did he say? He wondered. Did he want her to stay, or did he want to scare her away?

"Does it matter?" Ian opted for while he tried to figure out what it was about her that caused the warmth in the center of his chest.

"It," and then she hesitated, and it was as if he could hear her thoughts, as they ran along a similar vein as his. Except, she surprised him yet again when she responded. "It matters."

"I cannot forget—"

"I'm sorry," Hope interrupted, not allowing him to finish.

"And what are you sorry for?"

"That my voice—"

"Is beautiful," Ian cut her off before she could disparage her voice any further. "Do you not know that?"

Hope shrugged, but instead of answering the question directly, she threw another one at him. "How did you know I needed—?"

"—Rescuing?"

"Help," she went on as if he hadn't interrupted.

Again, another dilemma as to how much to say. "I saw you."

She inhaled quickly, and her eyes grew wide. "You saw me?"

Ian splashed water on his face and brushed his hair back, trying to push the memory of how he'd felt when he'd spied her on that cliff that day.

"When we docked, I saw those men step away from the rocks," he admitted. "I cannot even think about the possibility of what would have happened had I not."

Her face blanched, and he cursed his mouth, but she needed to understand the danger.

"In fact, why are you even out alone?" His voice had sharpened, fear for her causing him to snap.

"That was months ago," Hope shrugged it off. "Nothing has happened since that day."

"Yet," he spit out. "You need to be careful."

"While I might not have my sword today," Hope offered. "I'm not completely defenseless."

She reached into her pocket, pulling out an apple.

"You're going to throw an apple?" Ian laughed. "Come now, lass. You know that won't deter."

"No," Hope smiled, very nearly taking his breath that she was so beautiful. "But perhaps they'll think twice when they see this." She brandished a knife he hadn't expected.

"Do you know how to use it?"

"I'm not daft," she retorted.

"Did I say you were?"

"You did not have to," Hope murmured. Except, instead of giving him an opportunity to respond, she threw out another question. "Why do you call me siren? What is a siren?"

"Every sailor knows the legend of the siren," Ian's voice grew teasing. "Am I to assume you have never been on a ship?"

"I have too been on a ship," she tossed back. "Your ship."

He laughed, "Right. How could I forget? You took a chance coming to my ship, you know?"

Hope tossed her head, and the way the sun caused it to sparkle, once again took his breath.

"I had to." Her voice was so soft, he almost didn't hear all the words. "I needed to know you weren't dead."

"But why?"

Their eyes locked across the distance, and the warmth in his chest expanded, flowing outward. What was she doing to him?

"I was worried," Hope admitted, but he could tell she hadn't wanted to make the admission. "My friend Faith has her eyes on you—"

"Come now, Siren," Ian cut her off. "It's just the two of us here. What's the real story?"

It was quiet for so long; he had just about given up she was going to answer.

"I know not what it is," Hope confessed. "But I could not rest until I had made sure you had not died saving me."

The connection isn't in my head, flew through his mind. He wanted to dig into what was going on, but before he could say any more, she sat on a rock and looked at him expectantly.

"What?"

"You never told me the siren story," she reminded him.

"You're right, I did not." Ian wanted to shake his head to see if it would clear the picture surrounding him. She'd seen his naked arse, yet she hadn't given him the 'come hither' eyes. Nor had she run screaming. Instead, she was sitting on a rock waiting for him to tell her a story. He'd never met anyone like her.

"If it's story time, perhaps I should ..." He began to stand.

"No!" Hope held her hand up to halt his movements. "You're just fine over there."

"Afraid?"

"No," Hope scoffed. "I have brothers. I've seen the," she waved her hand toward him, "parts before."

Ian chuckled, and his voice deepened. "But not my parts."

"Just tell me about the siren, Professor."

Ian grinned. "Now, I'm back to being the Professor?

"Why are you called the Professor, anyway?"

"Which should I answer first?" he couldn't help but tease. "Just moments ago, you insisted I tell you about the siren story, and now ..."

Hope groaned. "Just stop. Tell me the siren story."

"You don't want to know why they call me Professor?"

"You can tell me that some other time."

"There's going to be some other time?"

An expression he hadn't expected crossed her face; one he could only describe as hopeful.

"So?" Hope pushed. "Get on with it."

"You'd make a good captain." Ian chuckled at the look of outrage that crossed her face and hurried to add, "That's meant as a compliment."

Hope successfully fought the smile threatening to break free, but she couldn't stop her eyes from sparkling.

"Beautiful," he murmured.

Hope's quick intake of air was his first clue she'd heard him.

"You don't agree?" Ian surprised himself by asking.

"That I'm beautiful?" she snorted. "Hardly."

Ian wanted to touch her, but since in his current state that was impossible, settled for allowing his gaze to linger on her face. He wasn't sure how or when, but he vowed that somehow, he would convince her she was indeed beautiful.

"Sirens," he began in his best professorial voice, "are dangerous creatures who lure ships to their island, where they crash."

"Do you think I'm dangerous?" Hope asked him quietly.

"To my ship?" Ian raised a brow. "No."

"But?"

"The word 'but' was not uttered," he tried to back away from what he'd not wanted to say.

"You were thinking it, though," she pointed out.

The connection, he couldn't help but think. They'd worked their way back around to it.

"How do you know what I'm thinking?"

Hope was quiet for so long that he wondered if he'd finally found the question she wasn't going to answer. Then her eyes met his. "Your heart is racing."

He glanced down at his bare chest, and while he could feel how fast his heart was beating, they weren't touching.

"How do you know?"

"I can *feel* it," she whispered. "But that makes no sense."

Was it the same as his ability to know when she was near?

"It doesn't," Ian agreed.

"You believe me?" The look on her face when she asked took him aback.

"Should I not?"

She dropped her head, and suddenly he needed to be closer. The need to ask her why she had asked. And why she seemed to doubt he would believe her.

"You might want to turn around," Ian warned.

Hope lifted her head just as he stood. "You should have warned me!" She whirled around.

"I did," he pointed out conversationally, using the rag he'd brought to dry off. "What's wrong? I thought you said my parts were nothing impressive."

She whipped around toward him, and the look on her face was equal parts embarrassed and shocked.

"I did not say that!"

"Are you always this easy to rile?" Ian asked curiously.

"You think I'm easy to rile?" Hope suddenly stood and moved closer to him.

Her hair glowed, her eyes sparkled, and his breath lodged. "I think you're beautiful."

"You're," Hope huffed, "making my head spin. Good day!"

"Hope?" Ian cried, unsure how he'd lost the upper hand. He was torn between going after her and letting her be, but he had been serious when he'd warned her about the danger. The El corazón de la Rosa was still out there, its men plundering and looting. If anything happened to his Siren, he'd ... well, that was not something he wanted to consider, he thought, rushing to dress.

FIVE

Swan Harbor
2, October 1717
3:00 p.m.

Hope looked up and, not for the first time, cursed her impulsiveness. If he had not flustered her, she would not have run away.

You knew he was there.

Except he was whistling my song, she tried to tell herself, that was the only reason she had stepped through the brush.

That did not explain why she had stayed, though.

Because he draws you.

However, that made no sense either. Would rereading her mother's journal help her understand what she was feeling? But that would have to wait, she thought disgustedly, staring at the rock prison she'd fallen into.

"Help!" Hope called, not for the first time.

Where was he? Was he just lazing around?

"Help!"

The ground around her vibrated, and her heart rate ticked up a few beats.

"Help!"

"Hope?" Ian called, and she practically wept with relief.

"I'm here," she cried.

"Keep talking," he instructed. "Lead me to you."

"Keep talking, he says," she muttered but then realized he couldn't hear her and raised her voice. "Why are you called professor? Why are you a pirate? How long have you been a pirate? What's taking so long?"

"You are full of questions." Ian's voice was closer.

"It's your own fault," she accused. "You said talk."

"And so, I did," Ian called from directly above her. "Are you all right?"

Hope sent him an exasperated look. "Does it look like I'm all right? I fell in this hole, tore my dress, hurt my ankle, and my hands are dirty."

"You also have dirt on your face, and your braid came loose," he teased. "Can you climb out?"

She groaned. "What do you think? I did not do this on purpose."

"I did not say you did," Ian replied. "But now that *you* say that ..."

"Oh, stop, and get me out of here," then, remembering her manners and muttered, "please."

"Since you ask so nicely," he smirked. "Just a minute."

His face disappeared, and Hope sank back against the rock wall of the prison she had fallen into.

"Here, Hope." A rope dropped next to her. "Tie this around your waist, and I'll pull you up."

"I fail to see how this will help," Hope grumbled, doing as he asked.

"Trust me?"

The gentle tone of his voice had that part of her inside that responded to him warming. Her eyes met his, and what she saw made her heart race. And somehow, she knew their thoughts were in sync.

"I do."

Ian smiled, and that funny feeling inside grew stronger.

"Now what?"

"Are you ready?"

"No, wait ... let me think," Hope huffed. "Of course, I'm ready."

He disappeared again, and when he returned, leaned down inside the crevice where she had fallen. "As I pull, I want you to hold on to the rope and try to walk up the side of the rock."

"But ..."

"Trust me," he repeated. "When you are close enough, I'll take your hand."

Hope met his gaze head-on, and all she saw was care and concern. "I'm ready."

The rope tightened around her waist as he tugged on it, and once it pulled taut, Hope wrapped her hands around it and put her foot against the rock.

"Are you sure there's no other way?"

He chuckled, "If you would stop complaining ..."

As she began climbing, the pain in her ankle caused tears to spring to her eyes. But little by little, she drew closer to him.

"Just another step," Ian encouraged. "Then I want you to reach for my hand."

Hope gritted her teeth, moved her right foot, then left and reached for his hand. As soon as his fingers closed around hers, a line of heat zipped up her arm. Her eyes flared, meeting his, and the look on his face said he'd felt it too.

Ian lifted her and pulled her over the side next to him. Their hearts were beating as one, and they were so close, she could count his eyelashes and see each individual whisker on his face.

"Are you all right?" Ian asked quietly, and the husky tenor sent a chill up her spine.

Hope wanted to say something witty, something memorable, but words didn't seem to be enough. The thought that maybe he was short-circuiting her ability to speak had her scrambling up and moving back several steps.

"I'm fine." She winced when she put her full weight on her ankle.

He pushed up and gave her a look that said he did not believe her. "Let me see."

The memory of the heat from when they'd touched had her clapping her hands together and holding them aloft. "See, just a little dirt."

But he kept coming, and because she did not want to fall back into the crevice, she sat and lifted her skirt. Her ankle was swollen over the top of her shoe, and not for the first time she wished she'd ridden Big Red.

"There, are you happy?"

"Oh, Hope."

Her name was but a sigh, and goosebumps appeared on her arms. He knelt in front of her, and when their eyes met, she forgot to breathe.

HOPE WAS STRONG AND FIERCE, AND EVERY TIME HE SAW HER SHE pulled him a little deeper under her spell. He'd even caught himself looking for her a time or two, and when her bright hair had drawn his attention at the docks earlier, he'd wanted to be near her. But while he'd purposefully tried not to seek her out, he had to wonder if his subconscious had known she would cross his path. Had a part of him been waiting for her to appear?

"May I?" Ian held out his hand and waited for her to place her foot ... and her trust in him.

"Are you a doctor?"

"Would it matter?" he countered.

"Then you would know what to do," Hope pointed out. But she placed her foot in his hand, which felt momentous.

"You asked why I'm called the Professor," Ian stated, slipping off her shoe and gently pressing on her ankle. "It's because of my penchant to read everything and then teach others."

"That hurts," she murmured, pulling back slightly.

"I'm going to wrap your ankle," he told her, ripping the bottom off his shirt. "It will give you a little stability."

"And this is something you have read?"

Ian grinned up at her. "No, I just wanted an excuse to hold your ankle."

Her mouth dropped open, and her leg tensed, and he wondered if she was going to pull it back even more. However, she must have seen something on his face because she relaxed and leaned back.

"Thank you," he whispered, positioning the cloth around her foot.

"Does your crew listen?" Hope asked, circling the conversation back.

"My crew," Ian repeated, surprising himself at what he was about to say. "They listen really well."

Hope frowned. "That does not fit. I thought pirates were just a sorry lot of misfits."

"You're not far off," he chuckled. "Each has a story revolving around their village or family."

"I still do not understand."

Instead of answering her, Ian fastened the makeshift bandage and leaned back. "There. How does that feel?"

She studied him for several seconds before pushing to stand. Her balance was off, and before he'd asked, Ian took her elbow to steady her. The current he'd felt earlier vibrated just under the surface, and the warmth in his chest continued expanding.

"I need my shoe." Hope bent to reach for it, and if he hadn't been holding on to her, she would have fallen.

"Stop being so stubborn," Ian scolded. "There is no way you can walk with that ankle as it is."

"But I need—"

"To be quiet," Ian told her, picking her up. "I think Realta would be happy to give you a ride."

Hope turned her head in his direction, and he was once again graced with the potent power of her blue eyes. "And how will you get down the mountain?"

"How do you think?" Ian whispered.

"Are you sure this is a good idea?"

Ian said nothing while he helped her up onto the saddle and climbed behind her, tucking her against his chest. They sat there for several heartbeats, surrounded by nothing but trees, and he was overwhelmed with the amount of trust she had instilled in him.

"Do I think it's a good idea?"

She tilted her chin slightly, and the silkiness of her hair brushed the underside of his chin. "Yes, Ian. Do you think this is a good idea?"

He made the mistake of looking into her upturned face, and her lips were just inches from his. She was dangerous to his sanity, but it was as if he needed her to feel alive.

"Remember what I told you about Sirens?" Ian asked a question without answering hers.

"Of course," Hope nodded. "They lure ships and cause them to crash. But you said I was not dangerous to your ship. Did you lie?"

"I do not lie," he replied, more sharply than he'd intended. "While you are not dangerous to my ship, you are to me."

"To you?"

A little wrinkle developed between her brows, and he had the strangest desire to smooth it away. Which made just as much sense as anything else when it came to her.

"You said you could feel my heart beating," Ian reminded her. "Can you feel it now?"

Hope closed her eyes, and it was as if she were taking inventory of what was around her.

"I can," she murmured. "It's racing. Can you feel mine?"

"Your heart?" Ian shook his head and moved the horse into a gentle walk. "No, but I can *feel* you. Whenever you are near, there's something inside of me that warms. And the more you're near, whatever *it* is, expands."

"And this has not happened to you before?"

"Never," he murmured, enjoying the feel of her in his arms as the horse carried them down the mountain. "It makes no sense."

"I know."

"Have you heard of this before?"

"Maybe."

One word was all she gave him, which confused him even more. Because it was her that brought the warmth to the center of his chest. More so her presence, but sometimes just the thought.

Except she was so young. How could that be?

"Maybe?" Ian pushed a little more, hoping she would explain what she was thinking.

Hope took a deep breath and sighed, making him wonder if she was going to give him words he would not like.

"I think," she hesitated a heartbeat and then another, "I think my mother wrote about it in her journal."

"What did she say?"

"Something about hearts speaking."

Laughter escaped before he could call it back. "I'm sorry, Siren. But did you say it had to do with hearts speaking?"

She straightened against him. "What if I did?"

"Why, that's," he searched for an appropriate word, finally settling on, "ludicrous."

"Wh-Wh-Why would you say that?"

"You said it yourself," Ian reminded her. "I am a pirate. You are not."

"You are a man, and I am a woman," she countered.

"You are a child," he tossed back, needing to create some distance between them.

"I will be eighteen next February," Hope shot back. "And my mother always said the heart wants what the heart wants, and when it speaks, you need to listen."

Was there merit in what she was saying? Which was a question he could not answer.

"That is where the danger comes into play, Siren," Ian murmured patiently. "I can just imagine what your father would say if you brought me home."

"Well, you are a pirate."

Ian was, but he was so much more, and there was a part of him that wanted to show her.

Hope suddenly stiffened in his arms. "Let me down now."

"What is it?"

"My father," Hope hissed. "Hurry."

Something inside him twisted, but Ian pulled up the horse and helped her off. "Will you be all right?"

She had taken several steps away from him, when suddenly she turned back. "Thank you for rescuing me ... again."

There was more he wanted to say. However, the look on her face said the time was not right. "My pleasure. Be well, Siren."

With a little wave, Hope stepped behind a tree and disappeared from his sight.

Ian sat there for a few more moments, waiting for the warmth in his chest to fade. Except it didn't as it had before. The heat burned brighter, and an anticipatory feeling surrounded him.

When the answers eluded him, he turned his horse toward the pub. Perhaps he'd learn news of the Rosa, and they could take up the chase again. For only when his reason for becoming a pirate ... this time, had been eliminated, would he be able to go back to being Ian Jones, the Professor.

Hope's Home
2, October 1717
7:00 p.m.

HOPE SAT IN THE KITCHEN, HER FOOT SOAKING IN A BASIN OF water and some smelly concoction Anne had created. She'd tried to hide the fact her ankle hurt, but once they'd finished eating, there had been no choice.

"How much longer do I have to keep my foot in this water?" she asked, hating the whine she heard in her voice.

Anne, who was sitting across from her mending one of Geoffrey's shirts, glanced up over the top of her glasses. "Ten more minutes."

"Ten more minutes, right?" Hope murmured, trying to focus on the rip in her gown.

Except after a half-dozen stitches, she gave up and set the gown aside. Her concentration was gone and had been since she'd arrived home.

"Do you want to talk about it?" Anne surprised her by asking.

Hope's startled eyes met the older woman's. "Talk about what?"

"What has you out of sorts?"

"I'm not out of sorts," Hope quickly denied.

Anne raised a brow but said nothing until she'd tied off what she was sewing and set it aside.

"Hope, you may have your secrets, after all you will be eighteen soon. But promise me you will be careful."

"I'm always careful," Hope replied.

"Well, all right then." Anne held a towel and, as soon as Hope set her foot in it, took the bowl of water to empty. "Will you promise me something though?"

Hope dried her foot, slipped her stocking back on and stared at her ankle. While Anne's potion had helped with the swelling, she was worried when she stood, Ian's bandage would still be needed. Except how was she to explain its use?

"What would you like me to promise, Anne?"

The other woman dried her hands and set the bowl aside before turning back toward her. "I kept your secret regarding your new knowledge, did I not?"

"Yes." Even when she'd returned that day after Ian had rescued her, Anne had looked at her differently. But so far had said nothing.

"Then promise me, if you need me, you will talk to me."

Hope studied her, and while she knew Anne could never take the place of her mother, there was something about her she trusted. "I promise."

"Thank you," Anne smiled. "That is all I can ask." With a last look, she picked up her sewing and went upstairs, leaving Hope alone for the first time since she'd returned from her escapades.

It was then the events of the day began playing in Hope's mind, as if they were a moving picture. Ian on his ship, walking down the gangplank, riding away from the docks, and finally walking into the hot springs. Her face flamed, her heart raced, and there was a part of her that was ashamed of just how brazenly she'd behaved.

I'm a pirate, and you're not.

You're a man, and I'm a woman.

You're a child.

Words she assumed meant to create another barrier between them. However, if what her mother believed was true, there was a reason she could feel Ian's heart beating. And if it was true, their hearts were speaking, then that was not something to be taken lightly. Was it?

Hope needed answers, but she was unwilling to share her burdens with anyone besides Ian. Since he was just as lost as she was, her only option was to rely on her mother. Or at least, in Christine's journals.

She found what she was looking for in the one her mother had been writing her seventeenth year. More specifically, almost five months before her mother turned eighteen.

August 1695

The most amazing thing happened to me today, and even after my mother explained what it was, I am still floating. Will this lead to something more? I can only hope ...

This morning while at my father's store, I was weaving, and the door opened, signaling the arrival of a customer. When I looked up, my eyes met those of Geoffrey Prince, and as clearly as if he had said it out loud, I heard, "You're beautiful."

I blinked several times, assuming I'd been daydreaming as usual, but then it happened again.

"You are so beautiful."

My breath lodged in my throat as I stared at him, and even with the distance between us, it was as if I could feel him. As if I could hear his heart beating, and our hearts were beating as one.

His eyes were blue, like the sea, and as they spoke to me, there was nothing I wanted more than to ask him, if he'd felt it too. But the moment was lost when my father began discussing the shirts he was making for Geoffrey.

Except I needed to know what was happening to me. Was I going crazy?

The answer is simple, my mother told me with a smile. Your heart has located its mate, and they are communicating.

My heart is communicating? What does that mean?

Love, dear daughter, she said. Your father and I were not meant to be together, but when we saw each other, our hearts connected. And we had to fight to be together. It appears your heart has chosen.

Geoffrey, I murmured several times. It felt right and somehow; I knew I had met the man who was meant to be my forever. The question was, did he agree?

Her mother had written those words when she had seen her father. Which had been close to five months shy of her eighteenth year.

Just like me. Hope set the book aside and hobbled to the window. What would Ian think if she showed him the passage? Would he laugh as he had earlier? Or would he consider the possibility? Was that what she wanted? If so, how did she tell her family ... and Faith?

SIX

El corazón del Rubí
15, December 1717
7:00 a.m.

IAN TURNED THE HELM OVER TO FREDDY AND MADE HIS WAY toward the forecastle to watch Swan Harbor come into view. It had been over two months since he'd seen Hope, and she still lingered in his thoughts. Except, in those sixty-odd days, he'd not come up with answers as to how hearts could communicate. Yet it hadn't stopped him from searching.

Their last chase of the Rosa had led them to Boston, where he'd purchased *The Anatomical Exercises of Doctor William Harvey.* He'd not read it yet, but there was a part of him that worried once he had, he'd again be disappointed. But as they were on the last leg of their journey, he escaped to his cabin, holding a little 'hope' in his heart.

As he read, and learned nothing new, his hope began to wan, and frustration once again set in. When the motion of the ship changed and they had docked, he was unable to stop the rush of disappointment that flew through his system. The professor wasn't used to failure.

"Cap'n," D.D. stuck his head in the door. "If it's all right, I'm going to set the crew free."

"Fine," Ian waved him away.

When D.D. made no response, Ian thought about ignoring him but, knowing his first mate, he glanced back up. "Is there something else?"

D.D. stared out the porthole for several seconds, which told Ian he was working around to something.

"Spit it out, D.D.," Ian finally barked. "I don't have all day."

"While I might have an idea, what caused you to behave in such a contrary manner," D.D. told him. "The crew does not."

"It's no business of theirs."

"Do you really believe that?"

"I ..." since he was unable to respond in the negative, he let it drop.

"Do you want to talk about it?"

"Not really," Ian grumbled, pushing the book across his desk and stalking to the porthole. Then, as if the words had a mind of their own, they fell from his mouth. "Something happened the last time we were in Swan Harbor that I do not understand."

"What did the Siren do?"

"Why do you ask that?"

D.D. raised a brow, but saying nothing, he pointed to the book. "How many of those have you read since we were last in Swan Harbor?"

"Three," Ian hesitated a beat and then admitted, "five."

"Did you find what you were searching for?"

Ian blew out a breath before reciting, "The heart has four chambers, two ventricles, and two auricles. Located between the fourth and fifth ribs, its main purpose is the transmission of blood throughout the body. But not one bloody word about the heart's ability to communicate with other hearts."

D.D. looked at him as if he had suddenly grown a second head. "You're saying," he snickered. "You're looking to find if hearts engage in verbal communication?"

His chuckle grew into full-blown laughter, leaving Ian looking at his first mate as if he were the one who had grown a second head.

"I fail to see what is so comical."

"You." D.D. wiped his eyes, and sent him one of his fatherly looks. "Care to share what the Siren said? Maybe I can help."

Ian turned back toward the porthole, and while a part of him wanted to say no, he found himself sharing. At least he shared about some things, anyway. Except the more he tried to explain the warmth he felt when Hope was near, the less sense it made.

"When I try to put what happens into words," Ian murmured. "It feels too trite."

"As if the words cannot fully encapsulate the feelings inside," D.D. offered.

"Yes," Ian sighed. "The warmth in my chest expands, my heart races, and my breath—"

"—Lodges in your throat," D.D. said what he could not. "And what to say is not readily on the tip of your tongue."

"You've felt this way?"

"Oh, yes," D.D. replied. "The answer is simple, really."

"Simple?" Ian scoffed. "I'm feeling as if I have an affliction of some sort, and you say the answer is simple."

"It is," D.D. confirmed. "It's called love."

"Love?"

"Yes, love."

"But ... love is not something I've experience with."

"Nor did I until I saw my wife," D.D. explained. "And held my first child."

"I do not know if my mum loved my father." Ian thought back to when both of his parents were living under the same roof. Except there were no memories to give him answers. "You love your wife?"

"I do," D.D. smiled. "And, while you are used to marriages arranged for the benefit of the families, I will say that love is worth fighting for."

"Love ..." Ian shook his head, confusion still running riot inside. "How can I love someone I do not know?"

"Perhaps your heart is a step ahead of you," D.D. suggested.

"But ... she is so young," Ian brought back the handy excuse.

"Love knows no age."

"What should I do?" Ian found himself asking. "I highly doubt her father would be accepting of a pirate courting his daughter."

"You could always explain what we are doing."

"And to what end?" Ian responded. "I would still be a pirate."

"Are we really?" D.D. posed. "Or are we masquerading as pirates because it serves our purpose?"

"Does it matter?" Ian shot back. "Until we have—"

"Ian," D.D. cut him off. "This does not have to be your fight."

Ian turned back to D.D., and while there was a part of him that understood what he was saying, he could not completely agree.

"I promised," he repeated what he'd said time and again. "Until we've saved your son, as you saved my brother, I will help."

D.D. studied him for another moment before nodding slightly. "Fine. But that does not stop you from getting to know the Siren, now does it? After all, where there's a will ..."

Should he take advantage of the time they were in Swan Harbor to get to know Hope? Or, more importantly, to allow her to get to know him?

Swan Harbor
15, December 1717
11:00 a.m.

HOPE SAT IN THE BACK ROOM OF HER UNCLE'S SHOP, HER FINGERS twisting thread and material to create a design for her new dress. Instead of giving all her attention to Kitty, her concentration was split. Half of it was focused on her aunt, as she gave a rundown of what remained to be done with regard to the birthday ball. The rest felt as if it were waiting for something. Or more specifically, waiting for someone. Waiting for a certain man.

A man she should not be spending energy thinking about. For not only was he a pirate—and her father would not approve—but he was also someone her friend had her eye on. Plus, keeping secrets from Faith was getting more and more difficult.

Her attention was redirected when something her aunt said had her tuning back in to hear;

"... wearing masks until midnight."

"Wait," Hope frowned. "What did you just say?"

Aunt Kitty gave her an indulgent smile, one that set her teeth on edge. "Your Ball is a masquerade party, dear. You knew that, right?"

"But why?"

"It's a special occasion, Hope," her aunt persisted. "Then at midnight, the masks will be removed, and your father can introduce you, and ..."

The flow of her speech was halted when a customer arrived in the front of the shop.

"Excuse me," Kitty murmured.

Hope's fingers stilled as the air around her seemed to shift, and she didn't even need to look to know … it was him. He had returned … at last.

Ian.

She quickly set aside her sewing and ran to peer through the door to see she had been correct. Ian was standing next to an older man, who was involved in a discussion with her aunt. And while *he* looked the same, there was something different about him. But what?

Slowly, as if he were a puppet, his head lifted, and their eyes met. The intensity burned, scorching a path, heading directly to her soul. It stole her breath and had her fighting to remain still.

She needed to talk to him. And now she knew he was back, there would be no focusing until she had.

With that thought in mind, Hope packed her sewing away and, when her aunt returned, pleaded a headache.

"But, Hope," Kitty reminded her. "We have more to discuss."

"Tomorrow," Hope promised, just before rushing out the door.

Instead of immediately fading into the woods, she couldn't keep from hurrying to the front of the building. She inched around the side, hoping for another peek, but the walkway was empty. And while she really wanted to go looking for him, she was not in the mood for questions as to why she was without her chaperone. Which gave her only one option.

Hope hurried to the forest and tracked back to her home. Once there, she raced up the stairs, changed into warm riding clothes and, on her way out, packed a lunch.

Big Red was waiting, and as soon as he was saddled, Hope climbed on, and they were off. The wind was cool and damp on her face, and there was a second when she wished she would have taken an even warmer cape. Except there was no turning back.

Her horse knew what she needed and, without being directed, he took her to the cliff. When she dismounted, the thunder in the distance had him pawing the ground and side-stepping farther away from the edge. The fact she hadn't noticed the weather was further proof of her tumultuous thoughts and feelings. Except when she glanced in the direction of the docks and saw his ship, she knew she was where she was meant to be. Otherwise, she might have ... well, at the moment, she wished not to consider that.

The storm moved closer, with lightning strikes and thunderclaps. Each one coming quicker than the one before. It sped across the ocean, bringing forth winds, and when a drop of water hit, she knew it was time to seek shelter.

Hope slipped between two large boulders, and leaving Big Red under an overhang, pushed aside the vines guarding her hideout. The cave was warm, dry, uninhabited, and perfect. Thunder crashed, lightning popped, and the heavens opened, but where was he?

Then she heard, "Hope, it's Ian," just outside the mouth of the cave. "Can I come in?"

Instead of wondering how she'd known he was nearby, she was curious how he'd gotten so close without Big Red announcing his presence. A fleeting thought of how she looked zipped through her head.

When she peered out, she found Ian standing next to her horse, water dripping off his leather duster and streaming down his face.

"You're wet."

"I've been wetter," he smirked.

"You can hang your duster there." Hope pointed to a broken rock. "Then you may enter."

She hadn't realized how uppity she'd sounded until he grinned. Then, worried she'd make it worse, Hope scooted back into the cave and waited.

But do you know what you want to say?

When Ian climbed inside, the space seemed to shrink. He was so close, she could smell the outdoors that surrounded him, and if she stretched out her hand, she could touch him.

His body created longer shadows, making it harder to see his face. Harder to read his expressions.

"Do you know how to build a fire?" Hope asked, reaching for some sticks.

Ian's gaze met hers, and the way he was looking at her caused that part inside that always woke when he was near to feel funny. Almost as if there was a large flower in the center of her chest, and one by one each petal was unfurling.

"A fire?" he whispered. "Do you think that's a good idea?"

"I think ..." The way he was looking at her had the words dying and made her wish for something to drink.

"Are you cold, Siren?" he asked. "Is that why you want a fire?"

Hope worked her tongue around until she was able to initiate a swallow, and her gaze drifted around their surroundings. The intimacy had her scooting back a little and quickly moving the meal she had brought between them.

She could feel how fast his heart was racing. Feel his heat reaching toward her and hear him breathing. Why, then, was she not frightened? Why did she have the strangest desire to touch him?

"I'm not cold," Hope whispered. "Are you?" But then a little shiver worked its way through her system.

"Are you sure you're not cold?" Ian asked again. "Did you get wet?"

The wind whistled, and another clap of thunder sounded, this one so loud it felt as if the ground vibrated around them.

"Oh." Her cherry-red lips formed a perfect O, and once again his eyes were drawn to them.

In the dim light, he tracked her features from memory. Coppery hair, bright blue eyes, an angelic face, and a voice that shimmered along his skin. If he'd thought anything had changed in the time he'd been away, he'd just been given his answer. No! What he'd felt when in her presence in October was but a fraction of what he was currently feeling.

"Oh, all right," Hope gave in. "Maybe I am just a little cold."

Ian refused to allow the thought that perhaps he could offer to warm her form and busied himself gathering sticks for a fire. It took several minutes, but finally, he was able to start a small one. Except once he sat back, it was as he'd wondered. The firelight highlighted the copper in her hair and made him want to touch.

It's called love.

There were things he wanted to say, and one look at her, he had no doubt she was thinking the same. Except how was it to be brought up? Did he just blurt out, *D.D. thinks I may love you?*

No! That would make him sound like a loon.

What about her? Did he wait and allow her to say something first?

"I ...," Ian began, but then changed his mind and tossed out an innocuous topic. "I noticed the swans are gone."

A sad smile flitted across her face. "Yes. My swan and her mate left in October."

"And that made you sad."

"Melancholy," she admitted.

"You said 'your' swan," Ian pointed out. "How is a swan yours?"

Hope's smile grew, and she tossed him an apple before taking one for herself and leaning back against the rock wall.

"You know the story of how Swan Harbor was founded, right?"

"That a wedge of swans led the settlers to this plot of land," Ian repeated what Henry had told him.

"That's right," Hope smiled. "My father was the one who led the group here. And my mother said each summer, when the swans returned, it was as if the town was renewed. Then, even though the birds came to Swan Harbor for several years in a row, their young were never born."

"The eggs didn't hatch?"

"No," Hope frowned. "It went on for two or three years, and the townspeople began to worry."

"Because they looked at it as if fewer swans meant the town's hope was diminishing?"

"Yes." A smile crossed Hope's mouth he was unable to interpret. There were both sadness and hope in it, which he was having a hard time combining. "Then I was born in February 1700, and a few weeks later, the swans returned."

"But they had never stopped coming, right?"

"Right," she agreed and adjusted her answer. "That summer, though, the eggs hatched."

"Hence, you brought the town 'hope,'" Ian grinned, still unsure how much he bought into the whole concept of hope being tied to a bird.

"It's what my mother told me," she repeated primly. "And one swan she named Hope."

"Your mother named a swan, Hope?" He laughed lightly before he realized she was not teasing. "But why? And can you even tell your swan from another?"

"I asked her the same thing," Hope shared. "When I was four."

Her laughter caused her face to light up, and the sound took Ian's breath. He ducked his head, unsure if he was ready for her to see how much she affected him.

"And what did your mother say?" he asked huskily.

"She pointed to the swan, Hope, and then to another swan and told me to look at their necks."

"Their necks?"

"Yes, their necks." Hope gave him a look that dared him to disagree. "*Hope*, the swan has a different color of neck. It's more copper than white."

"Which mimics your coppery strands?" Ian unconsciously reached out and fingered a long curl.

Her breath hitched, and Hope's eyes flew wide. Only then did he realize what he had done. Ian quickly dropped the strand of hair, as if it had burned him, and looked away, afraid to meet her eyes.

"I'm sorry," he murmured.

"It's ... it's all right."

There was something in her voice that had him once again lifting his head to meet her gaze. The curl he'd held was falling over her shoulder, and he had the strangest desire to touch it again. It was as if he needed to assure himself it really was as soft as he'd thought.

It's called love.

"Your heart is racing," Hope murmured.

Which told him she could still feel his heart beating, he thought, concentrating on what her body was telling him.

"As is yours."

"You can feel it?" she asked breathlessly.

Ian couldn't take his eyes off her, and rather than focusing on his surroundings, he concentrated on Hope. Her heartbeat, her thoughts, her breaths. And the more he stared, the more that warmth inside spread.

Their breaths synced, their hearts aligned, and he could feel her insides running riot, until eventually, they became one.

"It's there," he whispered, hesitant to break whatever spell was weaving around them. "Can you feel it?"

Hope was quiet for several long moments, and while he couldn't *hear* her thoughts, he knew they were running just as wild as his.

"Yes," she murmured. "What does this mean?"

Dare he tell her what D.D. thought? Or did he toss it back to her? After all, were females not better at emotional issues than men?

"You tell me, Siren," Ian replied, never taking his eyes off her. "What does it mean?"

He thought she would have jumped right in, but then she surprised him.

"You mean you don't know?"

"That something is happening between us that cannot be explained with words," Ian finally offered.

"Maybe."

The look in her eyes said she knew more than she was saying.

"Are you sure you're ready to hear?" she asked quietly.

"Were you?"

Hope shrugged a slim shoulder as if it were no big deal. "Our hearts have recognized their mate."

"Which scientifically cannot be explained."

"You researched it?"

There was a tone in her voice that had him ducking his head. Needing to step away to regroup, he turned his attention to the fire and tried to reorganize his thoughts. He already felt foolish enough. If she thought the same, he wasn't sure how he'd respond.

SEVEN

The Cave
15, December 1717
3:00 p.m.

Hope mentally shook her head at how she'd just blurted out what she'd learned in her mother's journal. She'd meant to ease into it gently, but he'd pushed.

"Did you?" she pulled on that thread a little harder. "Research it?"

Ian cleared his throat and sent her a sheepish smile. "I told you I have a penchant for reading everything."

"And you went searching to see if hearts what?" Hope mused out loud, "If you could find something that said hearts spoke to each other?"

Ian glanced up under his brows, and the look on his face caused that funny feeling inside to spin, making her dizzy.

He's adorable, she couldn't help but think.

"What did you find out?"

"In the books?"

Hope nodded but saw no need to fill the empty space.

"The heart has four chambers, two ventricles and two auricles. It is located between the fourth and fifth ribs. And its main purpose is the transmission of blood throughout the body," he rattled off so quickly she almost missed part of what he'd said.

"There was nothing there about hearts speaking?" she asked innocently.

"You know bloody well there wasn't," he grumbled. "But my first mate seemed to understand what I was trying to find."

"The older man you were with today?"

"Yes. His name is D.D.," Ian told her. "He gave me a label. But I ..."

"Do not believe him."

Ian shrugged. "It's more that I have no experience with it."

"I see."

"Do you?" His eyes met hers. "You said before you thought your mother had written about it. Is that correct?"

"Yes."

"Did you find it?"

"I did." Hope grinned when Ian grunted and pushed her to give him more. "She'd experienced it with my father. It was almost five months before her eighteenth birthday."

His breath caught. "The same as you?"

"Yes."

"And then what happened?"

"My mother asked her mother what it meant," Hope explained. "Grandmother Swan said, 'love, my dear daughter. It appears your heart has met its mate.' It was then, my mother realized my father was the person who was to be her forever."

"Love," Ian repeated. "That's the label D.D. gave me."

"You act as if love is a foreign word." Hope hesitated before continuing. "Your parents' marriage was not one of love?"

Ian sighed. "I'm not sure."

"You're not sure?" Hope frowned. "How can you not know?"

"Are there signs?" he surprised her by asking. "Something they might have done that alerted me there was love?"

Hope thought back on moments when her mother had been alive. Moments when they were a family.

"Did they ever touch? Hold hands, laugh or smile at each other?" she asked. "Were there times they talked or looked at each other, and you knew they were reading each other's minds? Or did you ever hear them talking quietly, cooking dinner together or helping each other?"

"I do not remember."

Hope studied Ian and thought back to what she knew about him. Dark hair, dark eyes, and he made her feel things she'd not experienced. He was known as Professor, liked to read, and sailed the El corazón del Rubí. And he was a pirate.

Yet, she was never frightened he would hurt her when in his presence.

"Tell me your story," she surprised herself by asking.

"My story?"

"Yes." Hope pushed the remnants of their lunch aside and, folding her knees up under her skirts, rested her arms on them. "Who is Ian Jones?"

He looked taken aback for a minute. "What do you want to know?"

What did she want to know? She wondered, but the only answer she could come up with was … everything.

"For example," Hope began. "My father and the early settlers came to the Colonies from England in 1692. In 1695, my father courted my mother, and they were married in February 1696. I have three brothers—Martin, Alan, and Luke. Since my mother died after my youngest brother was born, Anne takes care of our home. Now it's your turn."

"You really want my story?"

"I do." Hope assured him and prompted, "You're from England?"

"Yes." A faraway look appeared in Ian's eyes. "I was born in May 1690 and have an older brother, Simon. My father went to debtor's prison when I was three or four. After he returned home, he was never there for long. My earliest memories are of my mother pushing us into a hiding place under the kitchen floor. Somehow, we survived."

"You had to hide?" Hope asked. "But why?"

"Soldiers," Ian shrugged. "People looking for my father. I know not. But my mum did the best she could, and time passed. When I was sixteen, I joined the Royal Navy and set sail on the Windsor."

"But why?" Hope frowned.

He tilted his head in thought, and the way the firelight glittered off his skin, had her turning away. There was something about him that tugged at her, and the more she looked, the stronger the pull. That he could have such power over her was what frightened her.

"Stability," Ian finally replied.

"Stability?" she exclaimed. "On a warship?"

"Regular meals, a place to sleep," he shrugged, "and mates."

"You made friends?"

"I met Edward Teach," Ian grinned. "Eddie had all sorts of exciting ideas. And in 1715, after hearing how several ships from the Spanish Treasury Fleet had gone down in a hurricane, I joined him in the search for gold."

"Is that when you became a pirate?"

"The first time."

As he went on to explain how they'd ended up capturing a ship that had survived the hurricane, Hope saw more signs of Ian, the man. He was thoughtful, articulate, and smart.

"After we captured that first ship," Ian admitted. "There were several failures, and Eddie decided it was the ship's fault."

Hope snorted. "Why?"

"Because the ship's name had been changed."

"And that's bad luck?"

"If you're superstitious."

"You aren't?"

"Not really," Ian added. "Besides, I beat Eddie in a game of chance and won the ship. She's been more than kind to me."

"How so?"

"She brought me here." Somehow, Hope heard what had not been said. That the ship had brought him to her.

"Then what happened?"

"I'd decided I was going back to England to attend the university. I found I did not enjoy a pirate's life any longer. Plus, I really was not ready to die."

"Were you called Professor, even then?"

"Yes," Ian laughed. "I was much more interested in the books than I was in the gold."

"But here you are," Hope replied quietly. "A pirate yet again. Why?"

WHILE HE'D BEEN TELLING HIS STORY, IAN HADN'T BEEN ABLE TO look at Hope. He'd been afraid of what he might see in her eyes, but when she asked why, he'd chanced a glance. Her blue eyes were just as potent in the light from the fire, but he saw no judgment ... only curiosity. Was he really going to share the rest of his story?

"Do you really wish to know?"

"I do."

"My brother had gotten into some trouble, and ...," he hesitated, unsure how much of D.D.'s story to tell.

"You cannot stop now," Hope prodded when he did not immediately continue.

"Let's just say that D.D. happened to be in the right place at the right time," Ian settled on, "and saved my brother."

"But since you are here and not teaching at some university, you must be repaying the debt."

She already knew him; he couldn't help but think.

"I am."

"Why?"

"His son."

"D.D. has a son who needed rescuing?"

Ian took a breath and went on with the story. "His son is special ... slow and innocent. Captain Pence of the Rosa preys on people weaker than he by promising them what cannot be given. Many of the men on Rosa's ship were coerced and ..."

"Your crew is aware of this?"

Dare he tell her the rest? It was the look on her face that had him spilling the biggest secret.

"My crew," Ian admitted. "They are not real pirates."

"Excuse me?" she sent him a look of disbelief. "You're telling me your crew are not real pirates?"

"That's what I'm saying. Do you remember how I described them?"

"You said they each have a story."

"And they do," he confirmed. "One man's a brother, another's a son, a nephew ..."

"And your plan is ..."

"To rescue the men who wish to be rescued," Ian explained. "With any luck, Pence can be taken to the authorities in Boston. There is quite a fee awaiting his capture."

"Is it possible?"

"If we can catch them. But," he hesitated a second before continuing, "they always seem to be a step or two ahead of us."

"I ...," Hope shook her head, confusion written on her beautiful face. "I do not understand why you're pretending."

"Information," he shrugged as if it were not a problem. "Pence is slippery, but with winter coming, I'm beginning to think he's gone south."

"You're leaving?" Hope whispered. "But you just arrived."

There was something in her voice that had Ian studying her. Was it possible she honestly believed there could be something between them?

"I must."

"But ...," Her mouth dropped open, and several expressions he was unable to decipher crossed her face. "For how long?"

"I cannot say," Ian admitted. "If we could catch Pence, then it would be over."

Then maybe he could consider what was between them.

Hope dropped her head, and Ian was torn, unsure how to handle what was going on inside. He had no wish to hurt her, but ...

It was then that he realized he could not stay in her company any longer. The more he was with her, the more he wished for things he could not control. The more he wished there were something to what D.D. had claimed, and that love was in the cards for him and his siren.

"You, you just arrived," Hope repeated.

"So, I did."

The look on her face had him backpedaling. "What did you think, Siren? That once we spoke, everything would change?"

"I ...," She surprised him by taking the conversation in another direction. "What has become of Simon?"

"Simon?"

"Yes," Hope nodded. "You said D.D. helped him out of his difficulty, and yet it is you who is searching for D.D.'s son."

"That is because Simon is married to D.D.'s daughter," he explained.

"So, shouldn't he be repaying his father-in-law?"

"His wife was with child," Ian told her.

"And you stepped into his place," Hope completed what he'd been about to say.

"I volunteered."

"Why?" Hope pushed. "You no longer wished to go to the university? You felt his life was worth more than yours?"

"I ...," Ian stared into her large eyes, at a loss for words. And not for the first time, he was struck with how much she confused him.

The absence of sound had him turning his attention to the weather. Ian stepped out of the cave, and when the north wind hit, he quickly slipped into his longcoat.

"How did you know I was up here?" Hope asked, coming up behind him.

"I followed you."

"You followed me?" she repeated. "Why?"

Ian frowned, trying to figure out how he'd lost control of the conversation.

"Why do you think?" he tossed out, following her as she led her horse out into the open. "I wanted to talk to you about ..."

"About?" Hope tilted her chin, and her red-gold brows arched. There was something about her that had his breath catching in his throat. So much so that he had to walk away.

"About?" she pushed.

"You know what!" Ian whirled in her direction. "About this connection between us."

Hope shook her head. "So you do admit there is a connection between us, but you're still leaving."

"What would you have me do, Hope?" Ian brushed his hair back and blew out a frustrated breath. "Yes, there's a connection between us. Except what can we do about it? I'm still a pirate, and you're still not."

⁂

Every time he said that, Hope knew he was trying to put distance between them. This time, though, she knew the truth. He was pretending to be a pirate. And this time when he'd uttered the words, there had been pain in his voice that hadn't been there before.

"But you're still a man, and I'm still a woman," she repeated the words she'd said to him before.

Ian cupped her face. "Do you really believe that would matter to your father? That he would be all right with a man such as I knocking on your door."

"If you told my father—"

Ian placed his thumb across her mouth, startling her into silence. "Nothing can change ... now."

That part inside of her that was affected by him twisted, causing her to retreat into herself. She closed her hand around his wrist and stepped back. "I understand. But I need to go."

Ian took a step back, and Hope walked stiffly to where Big Red was standing. "Have a safe trip," she told him through gritted teeth.

When she climbed on her horse, Hope tried not to look at Ian, afraid that if she did, she would lose control. Big Red had only taken a few steps, when she chanced a glance over her shoulder. The look on his face had her wishing she had not turned back.

Ian stalked toward her, stopping next to her horse. "May I ride down with you?"

Could she do that? Ride next to him, feel the heat of his body so close, and not respond?

"Do you think that's a good idea?" Hope threw the same words at him as the last time they were on a horse together.

"You are still dangerous to my sanity," Ian told her, not directly answering the question but climbing on behind her. "And so far, I have not been able to stay away."

Hope flicked the reins, and as Big Red began the journey back down the mountain, she tried to hold herself stiff. But with every rolling step, she ended up bumping against Ian.

"Come here," he whispered, wrapping his arms around her, and taking over. "Is that better?"

His warmth surrounded her, and she was unable to stop her body from sinking into his. "It's all right."

Ian chuckled, and the sound vibrated against her back. "It's more than all right, Siren."

As they walked farther away from the cave, cracks in her tightly held emotions began to appear. She wanted him to stay. Wanted him to need to see what was happening between them. So much so, she lost track of how far they'd walked until Ian pulled Red to a stop.

"I'd better get off here," he responded to her unanswered question. "And this path is the quickest way to the docks."

Hope nodded but couldn't get any words out around the lump in her throat. His eyes locked with hers, and she had to fight not to jump off the horse and into Ian's arms.

"Remember me, Hope," Ian whispered. "I'll be back."

There was a part of her that wanted to say she didn't care. A part of her that wanted to say she wouldn't be waiting. Except she knew enough to realize words said in haste often had unhappy consequences.

"Until next time." Hope caught Red's reins in one hand and guided him back onto the path. This time, though, she refused to look back as she rode away. With every step her horse took, the tears just below the surface threatened.

She'd thought she'd succeeded in controlling her emotions until she reached the incline that looked down toward the docks. The sight of the El corazón against the fading sun had one tear slipping free, followed by another, and then another.

Hope wearily climbed off Red and led him into the barn, thinking she'd hide out for just a little while. She'd just begun to brush him when she heard her name being called.

"Hope," Faith stuck her head inside the barn. "Where have you been? You'll never believe what I just heard."

Do not bring up Ian, she pleaded silently.

"That you have to go to my Ball with Benedict?"

Faith rolled her eyes. "No! This is about you!"

Hope had to fight to stay calm and sighed. "Come on, Faith. You know people talk about me all the time."

"But this was your father," Faith whispered. "And he was talking to mine."

Hope's heart rate spiked, and before saying anything more, she put away Red's brush and led Faith from the barn. "Do I want to hear this?"

"Probably not," Faith winced. "But if I were in your shoes, I would want to know."

"It's something I'm not going to like, isn't it?"

"You're most definitely not going to like it," Faith informed her. "Especially not with your parents' history."

"My parents' history?" Hope frowned. "What do you mean?"

"Oh, you know. How it was expected that your father would eventually marry Isabelle Michaels but didn't."

Isabelle was Anne's oldest daughter, and while Hope had heard the story, she'd never given much credence to it. Especially when she saw how Geoffrey had looked at Christine. One look at the pair, and it had been obvious there had never been anyone else for either.

"That was because my father saw my mother," Hope pointed out. "Once their hearts connected, there was no doubt they would marry."

"True," Faith agreed. "Which is why I found what your father was saying so surprising."

The sick feeling in the pit of Hope's stomach was churning. This one said something was going to happen over which she had no control. But more importantly, it said she wasn't going to like it.

"What did you hear?"

Faith squeezed her fingers in support. "Geoffrey has invited three men to court you."

"What?!" Hope practically screeched, her stomach churning. "Who?"

The look on Faith's face said she hated being the one to share the news.

"Oliver Maddok."

Hope grimaced. "He has a weak chin."

Faith nodded her head in agreement. "But better than Nigel Randolph."

A shudder worked its way through Hope. "Boorish."

"That's being kind," Faith said. "I would have said mean. Hugh Griffin was the last name mentioned."

A feeling of distaste rose inside, at how she felt whenever she saw Hugh Griffin. "Old."

"But rich," Faith murmured.

Just not who her heart wanted.

"I need to talk to my father," Hope responded, her thoughts running in circles. Betrayal was the main emotion she was feeling. "He'll listen to me."

"Good luck with that. You've said yourself he's changed."

"But to pick the men he wants to court me?"

"Oh, it's more than that," Faith gave her the final piece of the puzzle. "He wants to announce your engagement at your Ball in February, and have you married by April."

"April?!"

"That's what he said."

"I will not listen." Hope tightened both her hands into fists with determination. "Martin was able to choose the woman he wanted to marry. I expect to be given the same consideration."

"Good luck, Hope." Faith sighed.

Hope sent her friend a thank-you smile and stormed into the house. She had a few hours until her father came home, and then they would talk. There was no way she was going to marry someone she did not love.

EIGHT

El corazón del Rubí
28, February 1718
4:00 p.m.

Ian practically stomped up the gangplank, not caring if the entire ship ... bloody hell, the entire town could hear him. He'd spent hours up in the mountains waiting for her, and she'd never shown. Had she not felt him near as she had the other times? Had she not thought of him as he'd thought of her?

It had been almost three months since they'd been in Swan Harbor, and he'd thought he'd be missed. Had thought their connection would have grown stronger as it had every other time. But yet, she'd not been there to greet him. And, bloody hell, he wanted answers.

He'd had time while away to think of his siren, and while the concept of love still felt new, there were several things he could admit. Hope had never been far from his mind. Plus, he couldn't wait to see how the gift he bought for her looked against her copper hair. And since she hadn't come looking for him, he needed ...

A shaggy dark head exiting the apothecary gave him an idea and put a skip in his step. "Henry," he called, running back down the gangplank. "How goes it?"

"Professor!" Henry smiled. "It's nice to see you again."

"Have time for a pint with an old friend?" Ian asked, hoping to garner some information.

The look on Henry's face gave Ian his answer before the words were uttered, "Sorry, Professor, you know normally I'd jump at the chance. But I've no time today. Have to get ready for the Ball."

"The Ball?" Ian questioned. "In February, in Swan Harbor? It must be a big occasion."

There was something rolling around in Ian's head that filled in a few blanks, even before Henry responded.

"It is," Henry laughed. "It's Hope's birthday. *And,*" he emphasized, "I have a wager on which suitor captured her attention."

"Which suitor?" Ian repeated, his stomach beginning to churn.

"Yes," Henry went on as if he hadn't noticed Ian's discomfort. "Geoffrey, her father, chose her suitors in December."

December?! He should have stayed!

"I was not aware the process of choosing suitors for one's daughter was carried out in Swan Harbor," Ian retorted. "And the Siren is all right with this?"

"I'm not sure 'all right' is quite the way I'd describe her," Henry smirked. "In fact, she was spitting mad for a few weeks, and the entire town heard about it. Lately, though ..."

The more Henry talked, the more the warmth in the center of Ian's chest seemed to fade. His heart felt as if it were being squeezed, leaving him adrift.

"Lately?" Ian prodded. "Something changed?"

"It's ... as if she's resigned," Henry finally offered. "Hope has become passive. Which isn't like her."

Passive? His Hope?

"Anyway," Henry went on, "I have a wager with Martin, her brother, on which man will be her choice."

"You're wagering on the lass' choice?" Ian repeated, attempting to make light. "And what gent did you place your money on?"

When Henry looked around, as if he were making sure no one was listening, Ian became even more curious.

"I do not believe Hope will choose any of them," he finally admitted.

"No?" Ian had to fight the need to toss the questions at Henry faster, asking more and more in-depth ones.

"No." Henry shrugged. "She has been friends with my sister, Faith, for many years. If I had my guess, I would say someone else has captured her attention."

Ian's heart lightened, and once again the warmth inside his chest grew.

"And what if she chooses none?" Ian posed. "Will her father accept her decision?"

Henry mulled over the answer for so long that Ian found both hands folding into fists.

"I cannot say, Professor," Henry finally answered quietly. "Since his wife's death, he's a changed man. It's as if he blames himself not only for her death but is haunted by something else."

What could be haunting him, Ian had to wonder. And was Hope aware of this in December when they'd last met? If so, why had she said nothing? He needed to talk to her, but how?

"I see." Ian searched for a way to find out more information, but when he could think of no solution offered, "It sounds like a very entertaining evening."

"It could prove to be so," Henry agreed. "Perhaps a pint tomorrow?"

"Tomorrow?" Ian nodded absently. "That should be fine. You can fill me in on Sly Bill."

"Sly Bill?" Henry frowned, but then the connection was made, and he grunted, "Billy Smith. Right. He's locked up."

"In the brig?" Which explained why there had been no sightings of him when they'd happened upon some of the Rosa's destruction while down south. "What happened?"

"He drank a little too much and bragged about trying to catch himself a woman," Henry shared.

"And the woman did not wish to be caught," Ian hazarded a guess.

"The woman is the sheriff's sister-in-law," Henry clarified.

"Hope's aunt?"

"Yes, Kitty Swan," Henry confirmed. "Happened last summer, I gather." He hesitated a moment and then nodded once. "You were right about him. Billy has a nasty temper when he drinks."

Which did not surprise Ian, especially if Billy were of the same ilk as those he'd fought in July.

"It's good everything turned out all right."

"It is." Henry held up the apothecary bag. "I should be on my way. My mum will be accusing me of getting lost."

"Right." Ian waved his friend off. "Good luck with your wager."

"Thank you," Henry laughed. "I'll see you tomorrow."

Ian smiled but didn't comment, his concentration on how he could speak to Hope. There was no bloody way he was going to allow her to marry some other bloke. He just had to figure out how to tell her.

Hope's Home
28, February 1718
5:00 p.m.

Hope dropped the curtain and rubbed her hand over her queasy stomach. It wasn't as if she could see his ship from her window, but she knew he was back in town. And every time she'd tried to escape, something had prevented it.

Anne.

Faith.

Her father.

However, as much as she'd wanted to see him, a part of her was scared too. She was afraid it would make what she needed to do that much more difficult. Which was hard enough without having to answer Ian's questions.

Ian.

It still hurt to think about him, but she'd run out of options, or at least she thought so.

"Hope."

The calling of her name had her grabbing her dressing gown and slipping it over her shift before answering the door.

"Yes, Father."

His jaw tightened, telling her he was annoyed she was no longer calling him papa.

"Do you have a moment?"

Hope walked away from the door, leaving it open for her father to enter. Except she wasn't going to make anything easy for him.

"I suppose."

For a split-second, as he stared at her, his blue eyes softened, and a part of her hoped …

"How do you plan to wear your hair tonight?"

"What does it matter?"

"This was your mother's." He handed her a pearl and diamond hair ornament, Hope remembered reading about in Christine's journal. "I think she would have liked to see you wearing it."

"I'm not getting married," Hope snapped, moving farther away from Geoffrey. "That's when mother wore it, isn't it, father?"

Geoffrey winced. "Yes, but I thought—"

"You thought what, *Father?*" Hope interrupted. "To appease me by giving me something of mother's? Something you knew I would love?"

"Well, yes." He sighed, and his blue eyes met hers. "I realize you are not happy with this situation—"

"You think?"

"But I am doing this for your own good," he said the same words he'd said multiple times. "For the good of our family."

"Right," Hope cried. "And yet, you refuse to explain what you mean by that."

"I cannot," he admitted. "You must trust me."

"I'm sorry, father," Hope tossed right back. "You did not trust me when you offered me up as if I were some great prize. You did not trust me when you insisted I choose one of the men you allowed to *court* me. Therefore, I cannot trust your word."

"Hope," he continued to plead as he had done many times during the past three months.

"Now, if you'll excuse me." Hope grabbed her door, willing her emotions back under control. "I must get dressed."

Geoffrey bowed his head, and she watched as a myriad of expressions crossed his face. She couldn't help but wish he would trust her with whatever was going through his mind.

"We leave in an hour," he finally murmured.

His eyes locked with hers once more, and she thought, maybe. But without saying anything further, her door was shut, and she was alone.

Her eyes drifted to her new gold dress hanging in her wardrobe before landing on the hair ornament. Could she wear it and make it through the night? Or would it make it worse? Would it make her feel more cheated than she already did?

Hope didn't have long until Anne would be in to help her dress. And before she could change her mind, she took out her mother's journals and quickly found the date of her parents' wedding. \

<u>14, February 1696</u>

I'm getting married today! When I woke this morning, I had to take a second and then a third look at the calendar. In some ways, it seems as if I have loved Geoffrey forever. And in other ways, it all feels brand new. But when the night ends, we will finally be considered one under the law. Something we have felt in our hearts for months.

As I'm writing this, I'm having difficulty keeping my eyes off the gift my mother left for me. She says it has been in her family for generations, as it belonged to her mother and her grandmother before.

The gift is a hair comb decorated with pearls and diamonds. Reportedly, it will bring me a long life, fertility, and enrich the commitment between myself and Geoffrey. And while I believe with everything inside that he is my forever, it never hurts to have a little extra help.

It hadn't given her a long life, Hope couldn't help but think. Except, that wasn't what Christine would say. Her mother had always looked on the bright side of a bad situation. Had always assumed that because Swan Harbor was founded on 'hope for a better tomorrow' that was how everyone thought.

"You would have said two out of three is not bad, would you not?"

Hope murmured, closing the book, and picking up the hair comb. When holding it caused tears to rush to her eyes, she knew she couldn't wear it. The luck had played out. "I'm sorry, mama," she whispered, tucking it into a drawer.

❧

El corazón del Rubí
28, February 1718
6:30 p.m.

IAN PACED FROM ONE END OF HIS CABIN TO THE OTHER, HIS MIND filtering through options for how to get to Hope. So far, though, every idea he'd come up with, he'd discarded. He'd just about given up when he glanced through the porthole to see D.D. strolling toward the ship, as if he had nary a care in the world.

"D.D.!" Ian bellowed through the open porthole. "Get your arse up here now!"

D.D. sauntered into the cabin whistling the same tune he'd been stuck on the past month and dropped a package on the bunk. "You rang?"

"Stop being cheeky," Ian grumbled. "I have a situation."

"And would this be a situation involving the siren?"

"How do you bloody know that?"

D.D. laughed, "You've not been too good at hiding your thoughts lately."

"I've not?"

"No," D.D. scoffed. "Most of the trip, you were a might grouchy. Even the crew noticed and assumed it was because of a woman."

"Do they—?"

"—Know you have your eye on the lovely Hope?"

"Yes."

"They know not who it is," D.D. assured him. "Have you declared your feelings to her and explained the situation to her father?"

Ian frowned. "Why would you ask that?"

"You rushed off the ship almost before she was settled," D.D. shrugged. "I just assumed ..."

"You assumed wrong." Ian paced back and forth a few times trying to decide what to say. "It seems tonight is Hope's birthday Ball, and if I want to talk to her ..."

"You need to go to the Ball?"

"Yes." Ian slipped into his long, black leather duster. "Once you help me come up with a way to attend the Ball, I'll be on my way."

"You want to crash the Ball?" D.D. exclaimed. "Like that?"

Ian glanced down at his clothing. "These are my finest. My coat even has buttons with the Jones family crest. What do you find so offensive about them?"

The way D.D. examined him made Ian feel as if he were a piece of meat, but he stood stoically.

"As a pirate, you'll do," D.D. began. "As a father, though, there are many things that would make me question your intentions."

"Wha—?"

D.D. cut him off before he'd even completed the question. "Your breeches are too tight, your shirt needs to be buttoned, and your hair is too wild."

Ian sighed and dropped into his desk chair. "I see."

"I see," D.D. echoed. "Is that it?"

"What would you have me do?" Ian grumbled. "I spent hours waiting to speak to Hope. Then I find out she's had suitors for the past three months. Yet, by my clothing, I am still not what she needs."

"Ian, Ian, Ian." D.D. opened the package he'd tossed on the bed earlier. "Do you love the lass?"

Did he? Was he willing to give the connection he felt to Hope the label love?

"Is this what love feels like?" Ian shrugged out of his duster and looked at the gift he'd purchased for Hope while he was away. "Like I'm standing on a cliff one minute and then free-falling the next? As if I cannot wait to see her, but worried when I do, she will not return my feelings? In the time we've been away, I've—"

"—Not felt complete," D.D. added.

"But with her father choosing her suitors," Ian cried. "Who am I to say he is wrong?"

"You're the man who loves her," D.D. told him solemnly. "I've learned love is not always simple, nor is it always easy. If it is something you want, you must fight. If *she* is the one you want, you must fight."

"How, though?" Ian jabbed his finger toward the porthole that looked out over Swan Harbor. "I know not where this Ball is being held. Plus, even if I did, how would I get in?"

"Those are not the words of a man ready to fight," D.D. scolded. "It's a good thing I happened to be in the right place at the right time today."

"What did you do?"

"Oh, nothing ... much," D.D. chuckled. "I just helped myself to someone's invitation and found you more appropriate attire."

D.D. took a pair of black wool breeches, a bright blue waistcoat, a cravat, and a black tricorn and laid them on the bunk.

"What are those?"

"Exactly what they look like," D.D. grunted, "your evening wear."

"You mean me to look like a dandy?" Ian posed.

"If you want to be with Hope tonight," D.D. pointed out. "You'll wear them, and this." He tossed a black mask next to the waistcoat. Then handed him a card. "And you'll present yourself as Reginald Goodfellow."

Ian choked back a laugh. "Do I want to know what happened to the real Reginald?"

"Oh, he's sleeping off too much port laced with a bit of laudanum," D.D. waved away his concerns. "Now hurry. The lovely Hope will be waiting."

Ian's gaze drifted from the frocks he was supposed to wear, to the gift he'd purchased, then to the town beyond. Was she what he wanted?

"And you think this will work?"

D.D. shrugged. "It will get you in the door. After that, it's up to you. What you need to decide is whether she's worth the fight."

Ian didn't have to mull the question long before he had begun the process of removing the pirate to become a dandy.

The Ball
28, February 1718
8:00 p.m.

As soon as the music came to an end, Hope barely kept the wince off her face when Oliver Maddok bowed over her hand.

"Thank you for the dance." Oliver sent her a smile that made her insides crawl. "Shall we?" He waved to a corner where the refreshments were set up.

"I think not," Hope brushed her suitor aside. "If you'll excuse me."

"But ..." He tried to get her attention.

Except Hope's gaze was fixed on the opposite corner of the room, where Faith was talking to their new friend, Jenny Hunter.

"Jenny," Hope exclaimed. "I'm so happy you made it. Were John and Gilbert too disappointed they were unable to come?"

Hope had met Jenny and her boys one day a few weeks back when she'd stopped by the tavern with her brothers. As Alan and Luke were similar in age, the boys had become fast friends. It had given her someone to talk to, and started a kernel of an idea rolling around in her head.

Jenny laughed, "Only for five minutes. But once they saw David tying his cravat, they ran the other way."

Hope smoothed her skirts and tried to take a deep breath, but with her stays tightened, had to agree with the boys. The freedom of breeches and an oversized shirt sounded like heaven.

"Your dress is gorgeous," Jenny complimented her. "Kitty was right about the coloring against your red hair."

"As she was correct about that shade of brown with your red hair," Faith admired the other woman's dress.

The conversation continued to swirl around her, but Hope found her thoughts floating. As angry as she was at her father, he had gone out of his way to give her the birthday ball she'd dreamed of for years. And even though just about the entire town was in attendance, the people were not there for her. They were there for her father and to see and be seen.

She'd only had a small say in the attendees, Faith and Jenny being the only two non-family guests. While it was nice to have friends, the one person she really wanted to hear say happy birthday to her wouldn't have the chance.

"Hope," Jenny stepped closer and lowered her voice. "How are you feeling?"

Betrayed. Lost. Desolate.

"Determined," Hope murmured. "Thank you in advance."

Jenny's smile was sympathetic. "I told you we had much in common. There was no one to help me, so whatever you need."

Hope blinked her eyes several times behind her mask, willing the tears not to fall. It wasn't just Jenny's cloud of red hair and brown eyes that reminded her of her mother. Her demeanor was also much like Christine's. Plus, with someone else sharing their hope, somehow, she did not feel quite so alone.

"Thank you," Hope whispered.

"You're very welcome," Jenny replied, just as a ripple of excitement ran through the room.

"Who is that?" Faith exclaimed, her eyes trained on the door.

Hope opened her mouth to say she couldn't care less when suddenly, her heart was whole. It was him. Somehow, he had come for her.

NINE

The Ball
28, February 1718
8:30 p.m.

Ian fought the need to loosen the cravat, as he handed his cape and tricorn to the valet.

"Your invitation, sir," someone asked.

He looked up to respond, but his gaze happened to land on the woman's who'd never been far from his mind, and he couldn't make himself turn away.

"Your invitation, sir," Ian heard again.

He tore his eyes away from the vision in gold and handed over the card D.D. had pilfered.

"Reginald Goodfellow, of Boston," was intoned. Yet, Ian had eyes for only one person.

"Reginald," someone grabbed his arm, halting his progress as he crossed the room. "I'm so happy you were able to make the party. We have much to discuss."

Ian's thoughts swirled, and his heart raced at the possibility that someone knew the real Reginald. He turned toward the person who had stopped him, and even behind his mask, he knew the man. The look of curiosity and not outrage on the other man's face told him his identity was safe.

"You must be Geoffrey." Ian shook Hope's father's hand, wishing he knew what business Goodfellow had come to town to discuss. "Lovely party."

"I just hope my daughter agrees," Geoffrey murmured. "Did you bring those pieces to show me?"

Pieces?

"I ah left them back at the hotel," Ian hastily tossed out. "Perhaps tomorrow or the next day? A party is not the time to discuss business, now is it?"

Geoffrey looked at him as if he thought he was daft, but eventually nodded. "That would be fine."

"Good, good." Ian slowly let out the breath he was holding. "Now, if you would be so kind as to introduce me to your daughter, I would like to extend my best wishes."

There was something about the way Geoffrey was looking at him that had Ian wondering if the request was to be declined. Then, as if he'd just decided, he relented and led the way to where Hope was standing with several other women.

"Ladies," Geoffrey addressed the group. "May I present Reginald Goodfellow? He's the blacksmith from Boston I'm trying to lure to Swan Harbor."

"You're a blacksmith?" Hope's blue eyes sparkled behind her mask. "How did you meet my father?"

Ian raised a brow at being put on the spot, but knew it couldn't be seen behind his elaborate mask. Except how did he get out of this? He sent her a look, its message, *You'll pay for this,* loud and clear.

"I've not met your father before," Ian offered, fairly sure he had that part of the story correct.

"No?" Hope turned her direct gaze on Geoffrey. "How did you hear of Mr. Goodfellow's work, Father?"

When Geoffrey took up the story of how he'd met Reginald's brother, a silversmith, Ian allowed his attention to wander. It drifted over Hope's elaborate hairstyle, to her slim throat above the bodice of her new dress. She looked like a princess, and very nearly took his breath away.

"And this is Mistress Jenny Hunter," Geoffrey brought Ian's attention back to the group. "Pirates burned her family out of their home."

Ian stilled himself and bowed over her hand, hoping she did not recognize him. "It's a pleasure."

Jenny looked at him, and there was something in her smile that set him on edge.

"Your brother, Elias, crafted my wedding ring. He does lovely work."

Ian fought not to let go of the breath he was holding at once. "I'll tell him you said that."

"See that you do," she nodded.

He had to get away from the group, Ian couldn't help but think. There was more going on than he understood.

"And now, if you ladies will excuse me." Ian turned his dark eyes back onto Hope. "Would you care to dance?"

Her eyes flared, and he had the strongest desire to spirit her away. To just carry her onto his ship and sail off, just the two of them.

"I'd be honored." Hope placed her hand in his, and he had to fight the need not to pull her close.

"No, it is I who am honored," Ian replied, leading her away from the group.

She tightened her fingers around his and, as they lined up for the Minuet, his heart climbed into his throat.

Could he give her what she deserved? He wasn't sure, but with her hand in his, he knew he was bloody well going to try.

"Do you know how to dance?" Hope whispered, a lilt in her voice.

"I guess we'll see, will we not?" Ian winked as the music started.

She should have been surprised when he executed the first few steps perfectly, but then again, he was a reader. Had that been how he'd learned to dance? Or had someone taught him?

As they circled around each other, the dance made her think of a courtship. They spiraled together, and when she put her right hand in his, and he squeezed her fingers, she could feel his heart racing. It was with reluctance that they released the others' hand and retreated.

"Your hands are not sweaty."

"I should hope not," Ian replied, taken aback. "Did you expect them to be?"

"Just an observation," Hope replied when she was close enough not to shout and—she could admit—because she needed to keep talking. Or, she was afraid she'd get lost in his eyes.

"What else do you observe?" he asked conversationally.

Hope studied his appearance and had to bite her tongue to keep from making a comment about missing his unbuttoned shirts. As well as his tight breeches.

"That's quite the mask."

His lips curled into a smile, and his teeth shone brightly against his tanned face. "Like that?"

The mask was black and covered the top half of his face, which she did not mind. It was the elaborate design of shiny stones and feathers that set it apart.

"It's you."

"I thought so."

Nothing else was said as the music came to a close. Except unwilling to walk away from him, she searched for a way for them to continue to talk. When their eyes met, she read the same feelings.

"I'm sorry."

"About what, Siren?"

"That I was unable to meet you at our place."

"Why is that?" Ian asked, a tone in his voice she had not expected.

"I tried," Hope admitted. "But Anne, then Faith, and then my father kept me from sneaking away."

"Your father," Ian murmured. "Why did you not tell me about the suitors?"

He's hurt, she realized. Except he wasn't the one having men paraded in front of her as if she were a prize.

"Would it have mattered?" was out of her mouth before she could stop it.

"Bloody hell, it ..."

"Mistress Prince, I believe this is our dance." Hugh Griffin stepped in front of Hope, waylaying their journey across the room.

"Sorry, old chap. She's promised this dance to me," Ian retorted before she could figure out how to respond.

Hope found herself relaxing slightly, but then Hugh stepped in front of them.

"I know not who you are, sir. But this is my intended. Now if you will excuse us."

Hope felt Ian's heart rate pick up speed and saw his jaw tighten.

"Is he correct, Mistress Prince?" Ian asked, his voice dangerously soft. "Is this your intended?"

What now?

Hope wanted to be with Ian, but she also needed to keep the ruse going for a few more hours.

"I'm sorry, Mister Griffin," her voice dripped saccharin. "This is Reginald Goodfellow, the blacksmith my father really would like to lure to Swan Harbor. He asked that I make him feel welcome."

"Geoffrey did?" Hugh looked from her to Ian before glancing across the room to where her father was in a discussion with several other men. "If you say so."

"I do." With a little bow, she led Ian toward the refreshments.

"And is he, Hope?" Ian asked when they were out of Hugh's hearing range. "Your intended?"

She stopped and looked over at him, but she couldn't tell him everything just yet. Would he, unlike her father, trust her?

"We need to talk."

"We do."

"But not here."

"You tell me where."

Hope's mind was awhirl with how to get everything to work out as it was meant. But to grab a few minutes to gather her thoughts, she turned back toward the bar.

"Hope?"

"Have you had champagne, Reginald?" Hope handed him a glass. "I love how the bubbles tickle your nose when you drink it."

Ian sipped the drink, his dark eyes boring into hers over the rim of his glass.

"Isn't it lovely?" she asked, leading him away from where a group had congregated.

"Lovely," he murmured, but the way he was looking at her gave her the feeling he wasn't talking about the drink. And that thought caused her head to swim more than the champagne she was drinking.

Hope took another sip, her mind searching for the perfect place for them to talk.

"Well, Hope," Ian hissed. "Where should we talk?"

"Do you trust me?"

He studied her for several seconds before nodding slightly. "I do."

Her shoulders relaxed, and she had a fleeting thought she wished her father did, before throwing out, "Meet me in the woods behind our barn at 11:45 p.m."

"11:45 p.m.?" he frowned. "Do you not ...?"

Hope gave a quick shake of her head and whispered, "11:45 p.m., in the woods behind the barn." Then, seeing she was being beckoned to the front of the room, added a little louder, "If you will excuse me, Mister Goodfellow, I'm needed to cut the birthday cake."

"11:45 p.m.," Ian whispered as she walked away.

Every step became more difficult than the one before. However, she was playing a game; and it was important for all the pieces to fall into place.

Swan Harbor Woods
28, February 1718
11:55 p.m.

Ian stomped to the edge of the woods and pulled out his timepiece. Hope was late.

"Bloody hell," he murmured, kicking a stone in frustration.

He paced some more and strained his ears for her arrival. When she'd suggested the meeting place, he'd wanted to argue. Then she'd tilted that stubborn chin of hers, and the way she'd asked about his trust had him feeling he was being tested. Once more, he checked the time—11:59 p.m.

Where was she? He'd not even told her ...

"Ian."

"Happy Birthday, Siren," Ian offered before he quizzed her. "I wanted to ... you know ... tell you before your birthday had passed."

Her smile could have lit up the darkest space, and caused that warm spot in the center of his chest to glow hot and spread outward.

"Thank you. I was hoping ..."

"I would remember?"

"That ... and," Hope took several steps closer to where he was standing, "you would say the words."

"I would have said them earlier, but ..." except he couldn't bring back the wasted time.

"Ian," Hope broke in. "I did not know my father was going to allow suitors when I last saw you."

"No?"

"No!" She visibly shivered, pushing Ian to remove his cape and wrap it around her. "Thank you. I forgot mine."

"Were you not meant to choose which suitor you fancied at midnight?"

"I had no intention of choosing one of those men ... *Reginald*," Hope told him, with a little giggle in her voice. "But perhaps I should set my sights on Mister Goodfellow."

"No!" Ian exclaimed, a little too harshly. "You cannot."

"How did you end up with Reginald's invitation, anyway?"

"D.D.," Ian gave her a sheepish smile. "Apparently, I've been a grumpy sort since we left."

"Oh?"

Internally, he'd been scolding himself since she'd arrived. Trying to put certain thoughts out of his head. But with the moonlight highlighting the copper in her hair and creating shadows on her face, there was no way he could resist.

"Bloody hell, Hope!" Ian wrapped his hands in the front of the cape and tugged her against his chest. "I'm sorry."

"What are you sorry for?"

"This ..." Ian barely got out before his mouth was on hers.

Hope gasped, and he took advantage, sweeping his tongue inside. It was their first kiss, and he wanted to go slow, not to push her too fast. Except it felt too good, and she tasted too sweet, leaving him no other option but to sink in with plans to stay.

Their lips met and meshed, and the innocent way she responded told him everything he needed to know. Her father might have chosen the suitors, but they'd never stood a chance. Her heart belonged to him. And as much as he'd tried to fight it, his belonged to her.

One of them groaned, and Ian lifted his lips. "Shall I apologize again?" he asked, backing her against the trunk of a tree.

Hope hummed. "That depends."

Her breath blew across his mouth, and a little shiver worked its way down his spine.

"On?"

"If you apologize," Hope slid her hands up his chest and around his neck, "are you going to stop doing what you're doing?"

Ian lifted his chin, allowing the cool air to blow across his face. "I should."

"You do not wish to kiss me?"

"That is not it at all," Ian countered. "I wish to kiss you more than anything. But ..." He was unable to resist dropping another kiss on her upturned mouth.

"But we need to talk." Her fingers tightened on his neck temporarily before she brushed her hand down his cheek and stepped away.

"What now?" Ian asked her softly. "You might have walked away tonight. However, what about tomorrow, next week, or next month? And how *did* you get away tonight?"

Plus, how did Henry know she would not choose one of those suitors? Was that something that needed to concern them?

"Jenny."

"Mistress Hunter?"

"Yes." Her eyes met his across the shadowy ground. "She knows who you are."

Ian inhaled sharply. "What did you say?"

"You heard me," Hope murmured. "Jenny knows who you are."

"My name?" Ian shot back. "If she knows who I am, why did she not tell everyone? Are we safe? Or should I go?"

While he was waiting for her to answer, it felt as if the warmth in the center of his chest was suspended. Waiting for what, he knew not. But the sense of anticipation was great.

"Jenny knows you as the Captain of the El corazón," Hope explained. "She has also figured out there was a connection between us. Except, I did not get the entire story from her before we left."

"Before you left?" Ian repeated. "Mistress Hunter left with you? What am I missing?"

THE WIND KICKED BACK THE EDGE OF THE CAPE, AND ANOTHER shiver worked its way through Hope's system. She tightened her hold on the garment and tried to find the words to explain to Ian what she was planning. But wearing his clothing, with his smell surrounding her, had her thinking about one thing ... his lips.

"Hope," Ian cupped her jaw and brushed his thumb across her cheekbone, "I'm right here."

She knew that, as she could feel his heart. That was what made it so difficult.

"When Faith told me she'd overheard my father speaking to hers regarding the suitors," Hope began. "I did not believe her."

"Your father had never said anything?"

"No," she hesitated, the look on her father's face every time she fought him tearing her apart. "My mother used to talk about '*when I fell in love*.' But now, he just shuts me out."

"I saw Henry on the docks today," Ian admitted. "He told me you were choosing tonight, and he had a wager."

"What did you think?"

"That there was no way you were marrying some other bloke."

"What?"

"You heard me," Ian smirked. "I couldn't allow you to marry anyone else."

"Why?"

Hope felt his heart rate speed up, and when he stepped closer and pulled her against his chest, hers was racing just as fast.

"You know why," Ian whispered.

"I do?"

"You do. And I brought you a gift to prove my devotion.

Devotion?

"A gift?"

He fished in his pocket and took something out and opened his hand. "Happy Birthday, Hope. This is my promise to you."

Hope took the hair comb that in many ways reminded her of the one her mother had worn. But this one was a pearl-encrusted semicircle.

"It's beautiful."

"Just like you. May I?"

She handed him the comb, and he gently slipped it into one side of her hair.

"This is a promise of my devotion to you. As our connection continues to grow, there will come a time when I ask you to be mine. On that day, I will give you the other end, and the combs will form a perfect circle.

"No beginning and no end," Hope whispered, a little in awe at how far he'd come in just three short months.

"Until I can offer you everything you deserve, I will hold on to that other half. Can you wait for me?"

Hope's stomach clenched as she wanted to scream, *Yes*. She would wait forever. What of her father, though? Would he continue to push the suitors? And why had Jenny been so helpful?

"Hope?" Ian asked hesitantly.

"There was a reason I had no plans to choose one of those suitors, Ian," Hope tried to explain. "You are the only man I can imagine giving my heart to. After all, we are connected."

"We are." Ian wrapped her in his arms and rested his chin against the side of her head. She supposed it should have felt suffocating, and yet, she felt safe. "And what of Jenny?"

"I know not the entire story," Hope admitted. "But I gather Jenny and David ran away to be together. She reminds me of my mother."

"Does she commune with swans?" he teased.

"I'll ask."

Ian chuckled. "Jenny helped you because she had to run away to be with her husband. And how did you get away?"

"I'm sick." Hope stepped from the warmth of his arms. "Jenny told her husband she was bringing me home. Then David told my father. Which means I should go in."

"I do not wish to let you go quite yet."

"No?"

"No," Ian murmured against her mouth. "I could get used to the feel of you in my arms."

His words were causing Hope's head to spin and her heart to flip. Kissing Ian, she decided, was her new favorite pastime.

"So could I."

"One more?"

He swung her around and dipped her before bringing her close to cover her mouth. Their hearts connected, and she couldn't help but think it had been her best birthday ever floated by.

TEN

Swan Harbor
5, March 1718
10:30 a.m.

Ian rowed the small craft into the cove beneath the lighthouse and tugged it up onto the beach. With his connection to Hope growing stronger every day, he was reaching the point where he periodically regretted his lot in life. Then, he would remember that had he not offered to help D.D., he wouldn't have met Hope. And the thought of not having her in his life was quickly becoming unbearable.

However, to give her the life he wanted, the El corazón de la Rosa needed to be found, caught, and passed on. Which meant he needed to be proactive.

He lifted his hand to knock on Henry's door, hoping he wasn't asking too much.

"Cap'n," Henry answered the door, then glanced around as if he was expecting someone else. "Everything all right?"

"It's fine, Henry," Ian assured the other man. "But I need your help."

"My help?" Henry repeated, surprise clear in his voice. "Sure, Cap'n, anything."

Ian waved toward the wooden lighthouse that sat on a narrow strip of land jutting out into the sea. It was bordered by two of Swan Harbor's smaller coves. The one that housed Hope's swans, and one that had been harboring the Rosa.

"Can you show me how that works?"

Henry stepped the rest of the way outside and looked in the direction Ian had pointed. "You want to know how the lighthouse works?"

"Yes."

"Can I ask why?"

Ian searched for the words, not wanting to say too much. Yet, not wanting to say too little.

"You know I've been looking for the Rosa, right?"

Henry nodded. "I assumed it was because they had taken something from you."

"You did?"

"Well, isn't that what pirates do?" Henry shrugged. "Take things that aren't theirs."

"Some pirates," Ian agreed. "This time, though, it's not things I'm looking to save ... but people."

"People?" Henry frowned. "Are you saying the captain of the Rosa has kidnapped someone?"

"Someones," Ian winced. "When the ship comes north, we think they're hiding in the cove."

"That's what Geoffrey, and another fellow tried to tell me." Henry's tortured eyes met Ian's. "Except I did not believe them."

Ian knew D.D. had spoken to Jenny's husband the previous summer, but why had Henry not believed them? Plus, why had the sheriff not pushed harder to find if it were true or not?

With no immediate answers, he turned his focus to the cove in question. It was guarded by numerous boulders shooting up through the water on either side, creating a narrow channel. Then once you'd passed those guardians, it was a straight shot.

Inside the cove, there were several paths. One led directly along the waterline toward the docks, the other into town, and if he wasn't mistaken, the third was a straight path to the cave.

"Perfect," he murmured, thinking it would make it easier to sneak away to see his siren.

"You must be seeing something different from me, Professor," mused Henry. "That channel looks a might tricky."

"It's just geometry," Ian shrugged. "If that bloke Pence can sail through with nary a problem, so can I."

"Geometry?"

"Math concerned with shapes," Ian offered a simplified view.

"If you say so."

Ian glanced back at Henry, feeling as if he were still missing something. "What's on your mind?"

"Are you sure a large ship such as yours could slip into that small cove?"

"You do not believe it's been done before?"

Henry shrugged, "I just ... do not wish to be responsible for allowing the ones you are after to hide."

"I understand your concerns," Ian acknowledged. "But what of the men you have chosen to keep watch at night? Are they trustworthy?

"I think so." Henry led the way into the wooden structure. "From now on, I will keep a closer eye on them."

"I appreciate that, Henry," Ian replied. "I do not wish to cause any dissension between you and your friends and family."

"Thank you." Henry waved toward the ladder that led up to the top of the lighthouse. "Shall we? And I'll do my best to explain."

"I'm sure you will, Henry," Ian nodded.

Henry smiled, and there were a few moments when Ian thought he was going to say something else, but then he turned away.

"The person on watch stands there," Henry pointed to a platform. "His job is to keep an eye out for ships sailing in this direction. When it gets dark, he lights the lantern, hoping they will steer clear of the rocks."

"That's it?" Ian climbed out onto the platform and took in the view. "Is it manned all night?"

"It is," Henry confirmed. "Is there anything else you need?"

"No," Ian sent Henry what D.D. called his wicked smile. "Here's what we're going to do."

❧

Hope's Home

5, March 1718
1:00 p.m.

It had been close to a week since her birthday ball, and Hope could honestly say it had been the best time of her life. The more she was with Ian, the more she wanted to be with him. And the more times he kissed her goodnight, the more she was convinced he was her forever.

However, with all the uncertainty surrounding them, she was forcing herself to be patient. Which was not her. She wanted to jump in with both feet and everything else be damned.

Since the Ball, there had been more times than she could count when she had wanted to share her happiness. Except every time the words threatened to escape, she pulled them back. She couldn't chance something happening unless it was of her choosing.

"Alan, Luke," Hope called up the stairs. "Are you ready to go?"

Their running feet echoed through the house before they clamored down the stairs. Anne was following behind, albeit her pace much more sedate, carrying their caps, shoes, and balls.

"Where is it you're taking the boys again?" Anne asked, directing them to chairs to put their shoes on.

"The Lighthouse Park," Hope reminded her. "We're going with Jenny and her boys, and a few others."

"That sounds like fun." Anne studied her for a minute, and Hope fought not to squirm. "Are you feeling all right?"

"Fine, why?" Hope frowned. "Do I look like I'm feeling ill?"

"No." A small smile played on Anne's face, making Hope wonder what she was seeing. "Your cheeks are a touch flushed, and your eyes are shining."

"I'm fine," Hope assured her, hurrying the boys along and trying to come up with a convenient excuse. "Just happy the weather is cooperating."

And you're hoping you'll see Ian.

"How are you getting to the park?" Anne asked yet another question. "Are you riding?"

"Riding?" Hope repeated. "Not with the boys. Why?"

"No reason," Anne replied nonchalantly. "You've just been riding a lot lately."

But before she could come up with a handy excuse, Alan jumped in, "John and Gilbert's mama is taking us. They got a new wagon."

"They did?"

"They did!" Alan exclaimed, his voice getting louder the more excited he grew. "Listen!"

Anne sent Hope a conspiratorial smile. "I hear bells."

"That's them!" Alan squealed before bouncing out the door, Luke hard on his heels.

"Bells on horses?" Anne asked.

"The boys like them," Hope explained.

"I see. Well, enjoy your day."

By the time Hope made it to the buggy, the four boys were making so much noise, she didn't have to worry about what to say as they got under way.

The Lighthouse Park was located not far from where the new lighthouse had been built. Open fields for the children to play, trees that provided shade for the adults, and a walking path, if desired.

They spread an old blanket under a large tree, handed the boys their toys and sat down. Yet, even then, Hope couldn't figure out how to approach the situation about Ian.

"You're trying to decide what to say regarding the Professor, aren't you?" Jenny asked before she'd come up with the right words.

"Maybe," Hope hedged, but then one look at Jenny's face and she amended her answer, "okay, yes. How did you know? Why did you not say something? I mean, I thank you for not saying anything, but still. Why—?"

"Hold up," Jenny laughed. "Let's take them one at a time, shall we?"

Hope gave a quick head bob, but held her tongue, worried too much would fall from her mouth again.

"How did I know?" Jenny chuckled. "When you've had a good look at the captain's strong jaw, it's hard to forget."

"What?" Hope's mouth dropped open, surprised by the answer she'd just been given. Although she had to agree. Ian was the most handsome man she'd ever seen.

"You heard me," Jenny grinned. "Your Captain cuts quite the dashing figure."

"But ... you're married."

"And happily," Jenny agreed. "But I'm not dead."

"Does David know you were looking at the Captain?" Hope asked. "Plus, when were you looking at him?"

"David knows all," Jenny laughed. "And on the ship, when he found us."

Hope knew the story of how the women and children had been brought to Swan Harbor after being found hiding by Ian and his crew.

"As to why I did not say anything," Jenny sighed and adjusted on the blanket. "That's a bit more complicated."

"I'm listening."

"Because of what happened with the men from the Rosa, I was predisposed to hate all pirates," Jenny began. "Especially when the Professor insisted we all board his ship without asking us what we wanted."

"Did you feel safe in your village alone?"

"No," Jenny's voice softened. "But I refused to let him see that."

"That I can understand." Hope hesitated, then asked, "What changed your mind?"

"On the way here," Jenny shared. "Your captain was always surrounded by the young boys. He was so patient with them, I decided there had to be more to him."

"There is," Hope sighed. "A lot more."

"But that's his story," Jenny guessed.

"It is. Except how did you know about–?"

"You and the Captain?"

"Yes."

"When you told me what your father had arranged," Jenny shared, "there was a wistful tone in your voice. It reminded me of when I was about your age and my father did the same thing."

"Tried to choose the men to court you?"

"Tried to choose the man I was to marry," Jenny clarified. "But I had my eye on David."

"And your father wouldn't listen?"

"No." Jenny gave her a melancholy smile. "My father arranged everything, and on the way to the wedding, David hijacked the buggy and kidnapped me."

"Are you serious?" Hope glanced at Jenny; sure she wasn't telling the truth.

"Very!" Jenny exclaimed. "We're from south of here. It's a place called

Virginia. After David pulled me from the buggy, we began working our way north. We were married in Boston."

"Do you miss your family?"

"Sometimes," Jenny admitted. "However, I wouldn't trade David, John, and Gilbert for anything."

Hope couldn't help but wonder what if the same thing happened to her? Would she give up her family and her home for Ian? She hoped she would never have to find out.

"But how did you put me with the Captain?" Hope pushed.

"When he walked in and you saw each other," Jenny's smile turned dreamy. "It was as if you were the only two people in the room."

Hope's breath lodged. "Do you think anyone else noticed?"

"No one said anything," Jenny assured her. "It seems your secret is still safe."

"Good," Hope murmured, her eyes drawn to the sails of the El corazón, anchored farther away from the dock than usual. "I wish I could introduce the man I know to my family. And explain everything to Faith. But at least I have you."

"Yes, you do. Anytime you want to talk, I'm here."

The Lighthouse Park
5, March 1718
3:00 p.m.

It had taken longer than he'd anticipated to anchor the El corazón in the cove. Once it was, Ian left D.D. in charge of the crew and went looking for Hope. He knew she was bringing her brothers to the park and wished to see her. While he didn't anticipate anything beyond a glimpse. However, if something were to happen that put her in front of him, he wouldn't complain.

Ian took the path through the entrance to the park and saw her across the way. She was sitting under a tree with two other women; her head thrown back with laughter. That he imagined he could hear the sound clear across the grounds showed how far gone he was. It also propelled him farther along the path; out of the line of sight, lest he do something he shouldn't. Except he couldn't make himself go back to the ship.

He wanted to walk along the path with her arm tucked through his. Wanted to press her against a tree to steal a kiss.

"Ian."

Was that his wishful thinking, hearing her call his name in her soft voice?

"Ian."

The second time his name was accompanied by the crinkle of leaves, pushing him behind a tree.

He peered around the trunk just as Hope stepped off the path between two large pine trees and stopped to look around.

"Ian," she whispered again.

"Mistress Prince," Ian stepped back onto the path, "is there something you need?"

"Oh, I'm quite sure you know what I need."

Ian indicated they should continue walking, looking for what he did not know.

"I did not think you saw me."

"I didn't." Hope slanted him a quick look. "But I did feel you."

"Just as I felt you," he murmured, stopping to take her hand. "It's getting stronger, is it not?"

"The connection between us? Yes."

Her blue eyes were piercing, causing his heart to race. It took strength he wasn't aware he had, but he tore his gaze away before he took liberties best not taken.

"Did you speak with your friend Jenny as to how she knew about me?"

Hope blushed, making him wish he'd been privy to the talk. "I did."

"And?" Ian brushed a finger down her soft cheek. "Based on your high color, it must have been some conversation."

"She recognized you," Hope shrugged.

"That's it?" Ian slanted a side-eyed look at her. "There seems to be quite a bit you are not saying."

"Perhaps." A corner of her mouth lifted, and the twinkle in her eyes grew. "Perhaps not."

Ian took a step closer, the tips of his boots touching hers. "What will it cost me?"

"What are you willing to pay?"

His eyes dropped to her mouth before bouncing back up. "What do you want?" he countered.

"I want," Hope pushed him back a step, then another, and another, "this."

Her hands were wrapped in his coat, and her lips on his before he'd figured out what she was going to do. But with her in his arms, who was he to argue?

Ian tightened his hands around her slim waist and allowed her to control the kiss. She'd learned much in the week since her birthday, and before he was ready, his body was waking and longing for a bit of attention.

"Hope," Ian attempted to set her back a step, "maybe we should ..."

But before he could finish the sentence, the sound of others approaching had him pushing her away.

"It's best you not be seen with me."

He'd barely ducked behind a group of trees when he heard Hope calling his name. Had he been mistaken, and it had been an animal? Ian stepped back around to encounter Henry and his sister.

"Come out here, Ian." Hope took his arm and tugged him close, her eyes boring into his. "We need help."

"Help? I do not understand."

"Are you not tired of hiding behind this?" She fingered his linen shirt, unbuttoned to the bottom of his chest. "Do you not wish to spend time with me beyond when we are on the mountain?"

"You know my thoughts on both of those."

"Then trust me."

She was back to the trust again; he couldn't help but notice.

"Always."

"Good."

Her smile caused that place inside to grow warmer, making him yearn for all those things he'd never thought possible.

"Faith, come with me." Hope squeezed Ian's fingers, then pointed to Henry. "We'll meet you at your home in a bit. It's quieter."

Then she looped her arm through Faith's and disappeared down the path.

"What just happened?" Ian asked when the women were out of sight.

"I just found out I was right on several counts," Henry smirked. "And that Hope is a miracle worker."

"Why do you say that?" Ian questioned.

"Did you see how quiet my sister was?" Henry laughed. "That never happens."

"I see."

"You do not have sisters," Henry told him while they strolled toward his home, "or you would understand. But now, tell me about you and Hope."

"Hope," Ian murmured with a grin on his face, "is wonderful."

"This is not something I expected," Henry admitted.

"And you think I did?"

"You did not seek her out?"

"Seek out Hope?" Ian looked around to make sure they were still alone. "Hope just happened. And now, more than ever, Pence and the Rosa need to be found."

"Why now more than ever?"

"Hope," Ian shrugged. "I wish to give her the world. But until Pence is no longer in the picture, I'm stuck in this." He fingered his shirt, which was quickly becoming his albatross.

"You do not wish to be a pirate?"

"Certainly not, Henry," Ian exclaimed. "I wish to be a professor."

"A Professor? Why?"

"Why, to teach you about geometry, of course."

Ian laughed at the other man's look of outrage as he followed him inside his home. He just hoped Hope knew what she was doing.

ELEVEN

The Thinking Stone
21, March 1718
4:00 p.m.

HOPE WRAPPED THE REMAINS OF THEIR DINNER IN AN OLD CLOTH and shoved it aside. The last few weeks had only deepened her feelings for Ian, but ever since he'd arrived, she'd been waiting for something. Exactly what, she wasn't sure.

"Come here." Ian took her hand and settled her next to him, his arm snug around her waist. "Talk to me."

Hope frowned. "We talked throughout our meal."

"You told me about the party Anne was planning for Alan. And that you were going to be sad when Jenny and the other residents of Timber Creek went back home."

"And that is not the kind of talking you want?"

"It's alright," he assured her. "If there are not other things we need to speak of. Things that put a little wrinkle here." Ian tapped the frown between her brows. "What has you so vexed?"

"I know not."

"You know not?" Ian's brows shot up. "I think you can do better than that."

Hope hadn't wanted to worry him, especially since she had nothing definite to rely on.

"Remember what my father did?"

Ian blew out a harsh laugh. "Are you referring to the fact he set you up with suitors?"

"And expected me to choose one the night of my birthday. Yes."

"How could I forget?" Ian grumbled. "What about it? Has he said anything?"

"No."

"But is that not a good thing?"

"I'm afraid he's," she shrugged, "setting up something."

"Why do you say that?"

"Last week," Hope went on. "When I came home, I saw one of the men he'd allowed to court me leaving our house."

"And your father said nothing?"

"No."

"But if he were," Ian asked. "Would you not know?"

Hope shivered and was happy when Ian tucked her a little closer against his side. She certainly did not want to think what she was thinking. Except her father had shaken her trust.

"I keep remembering Jenny's story," Hope admitted. "If her father can plan her wedding without telling her, do you not believe mine could do the same?"

"Marry you off to some bloke," Ian exclaimed, "without your knowledge?"

"Yes."

"Do you really believe that?"

"I do not want to!" Hope cried. "But I do not trust him."

Ian tugged her onto his lap and cupped her face. "You're not marrying one of those other blokes."

"I'm not?"

"No."

He kissed her, and just like every other time, the funny feeling inside swooped and swirled. Hope tangled her hand in his hair and held on, following his lead. His kisses set her on fire, making her want things she did not quite understand. One thing was clear, though. Whatever the feeling was in her chest, she never wanted it to end.

"Give me a minute, love," Ian pressed her against his chest, his breaths coming fast.

There was a part of her that wished to ask why he had stopped, but the other part of her understood. After all, she knew about *that*.

"Is there ..." Then she had second thoughts. In the end, though, she plunged forward. "Is there anything I can do?"

He chuckled. "Hope, love, your kisses are why I'm needing a break. They wreck me."

"They wreck you?"

"Yes, love." He kissed her again, but this time kept it quick. "You wreck me."

"I'm sorry, Ian," Hope caressed his face, "I do not mean to wreck you."

He studied her for several moments before a corner of his mouth kicked up. "Hope. Your being able to wreck me is a good thing."

"It is?"

"Yes!" He moved her aside, so he could stand and tug her up. "And please continue, as I would despair if you stopped."

His comment swirled in her mind, and that female part that thrilled with his words allowed her gaze to travel up his body.

There was the ever-present unbuttoned shirt and, in deference to the heat, he'd tossed his coat aside. While she enjoyed burying her nose in the soft fuzz on his chest, she didn't believe that was the problem. It was once her eyes dropped below the waistband that she got an eyeful.

"Oh!"

Ian squinted, and a teasing smile crossed his face. "Keep staring, and I cannot be responsible for what might happen."

"Really?" Hope could feel her eyes growing wide.

"Really." Ian slipped on his jacket and once more tugged her against his side, before leading them away from their picnic spot.

"Would I enjoy what you're thinking of?" she teased.

But instead of teasing back, his body language changed.

"Don't tease a man, Hope," he murmured before she could say more.

"Ian?"

Hope turned toward him, and the sun bounced off her hair comb. He wished with everything inside, he could give her the other half. No longer was he terrified of the word love. He'd learned it was something you could not really explain, but it created powerful emotions that vacillated from highs to lows. It made you feel on top of the world when you were with that person. Then plunged you to the bottom of the sea when apart. His heart no longer belonged to him, but to the Siren with glorious red hair and sky-blue eyes that pierced his soul.

Ian Jones loved Hope Prince.

Tell her!

"Talk to me," Hope threw his words back before he could declare his feelings.

"I wish I could," he told her. "But I ..."

"Ian." Hope fisted his shirt, and the touch of her skin against his sent a bolt of lightning zipping through him. "Why can you not?"

Instead of responding, he kissed her and led them to where Big Red was waiting.

"Soon." He climbed on the horse, and then situated her in front of him. "Soon."

Hope snuggled against his chest, and he tried to think of something to say to take his mind off how good she felt in his arms. But with every step Big Red took, she undulated against him, and his body grew hotter than the midday sun.

By the time they arrived at the fork in the path, he'd begun thinking about his geometry angles. Anything to get his thoughts of the warm woman in his arms out of his head. But as he helped Hope off the horse, she was firmly planted there, pushing him to put some space between them.

"Will I see you later?" she asked, shielding her eyes from the sun.

"I thought you were going to Jenny's?"

"I am, but ..." Hope stepped into his arms, the space once again disappearing, "she knows of us."

His Siren was right. Jenny did know about them. Except, would that not be tempting fate?

"I will try," he settled on.

Her blue eyes met his and once again, the desire to toss her over his shoulder was strong. To allow it to be just Ian and Hope and everyone else be damned. Except he couldn't take her from her family. From her younger brothers, who had lost their mother. And, heaven help him, even from her father, who was trying to marry her off.

"Do not pout, Siren," Ian teased, dropping kisses randomly on her face. "Just keep singing that pretty song of yours."

"Is it my song that lures you then?" The twinkle once again in her eyes.

Her question brought a feeling unlike any he could remember washing over his body.

"Oh, Hope. It's your song, your eyes, nose, and these lips." With every declaration, he placed a light kiss on each spot he named. "Your hands, body … you. There is no part of you that does not lure me."

"Ian," she sighed, and a single tear slid down her cheek.

"I love you, Hope."

Hope smiled and everything inside of him wanted to sing.

"I love you too," she whispered, her tears falling fast and free.

Her words had him wanting to step to the edge of the mountain and shout, 'Hope Prince loves me,' just to hear it bounce back to him. Instead, he settled for giving her a few long, and hard kisses, trying to imprint the feel of his mouth on her, just as she was on him.

Jenny's Home
21, March 1718
7:00 p.m.

HOPE HELPED JENNY CLEAN THE SUPPER DISHES OFF THE TABLE and waited. There was something the older woman had been working her way around to saying, but as of yet … nothing.

"You have news you wish to share, do you not?" Hope asked when she could stand the silence no longer.

Jenny looked up from wiping off the table, "And what makes you think a thing like that?"

"Could it be you've washed the same spot three times?"

"One can never clean too much with young boys in the house," Jenny retorted. "Especially, in a small house, such as this."

"True." Hope glanced around at the small three-room home that had been built for the Hunter family after they arrived in Swan Harbor. "Little boys can be messy."

"See," Jenny scurried across the room to wipe the countertop ... again.

"Did I ever tell you how you remind me of my mother?" Hope tried another tactic.

"We both have red hair," Jenny offered. "About your parents. But that is all."

"Like you, my mother always saw the positives," Hope smiled. "And she always saw the good in people. She never believed someone would purposefully hurt her ... or her family. You are much like that."

"Your mother sounds as if she was a special woman," Jenny replied. "I do not see myself as you describe, though."

"No?"

"No," Jenny sighed. "I am just a woman who loves her family. And ..." Once again, she picked up the rag to wipe off another counter.

"My mother also cleaned when she was trying to hide from bad news."

It was quiet for several moments, and Hope had just about given up. But then Jenny tossed the rag aside and pointed to a chair.

"You're right," Jenny told her. "I do have news."

"Is this about Ian?"

Jenny reached out and covered Hope's hands that were sitting on the table, "No, nothing about Ian. But ..."

"But?" Hope pushed, her insides becoming more anxious by the second.

"We're leaving Swan Harbor," Jenny spit out in a rush.

Hope tilted her head and tried to read the other woman's expression, "I knew that. *We* knew you were not staying in Swan Harbor forever."

"I know," Jenny shrugged. "The day always seemed so far off."

"And it's not?"

"No." Jenny dropped her head and somehow, Hope knew she wasn't going to like the answer. "We are leaving March 30th. David wants to get home, so we have all summer to rebuild."

"March 30th?" Hope sat back in the chair, the sadness welling up inside. "So soon?"

"I know." Jenny's lower lip trembled. "After everything my father did to keep David and I apart, I wanted to be here for you. The stranger to run interference. Especially since David and Geoffrey get on so well."

"Is David not the Sheriff of Timber Creek?"

"He is," Jenny acknowledged. "Which gives them common ground."

"I keep hoping my father has given up this crazy notion of his. But I fear something is brewing."

"Why would you think that?"

"Because I caught Hugh Griffin leaving our home one day," Hope explained, and even the thought caused her stomach to churn.

"Would he have business with your father ... besides you, that is?"

"Maybe," Hope shrugged. "However, if he were in need of a sheriff, I believe he would discuss it at the office."

"Do you really believe he's going to try to marry you off, as my father tried?"

"I cannot say," Hope admitted. "If my feelings mattered, why not ask me? Why not ask me whom I would like to marry? Or why not choose the son of one of his friends?

"Like Henry?"

"Yes!" Hope exclaimed. "It's as if he wants me to marry the most vile person. But to what means?"

"I cannot tell you," Jenny answered. "Have you thought what you'll do if he tries? Is your Ian ready to claim you as his?"

Hope smiled, Ian's words of *I love you* still echoing in her head.

"He told me I wreck him today," Hope shared. "And said it was a good thing."

Jenny laughed for the first time all evening, "Oh, I would say that is a very good thing. It means he wants you."

"Yes," Hope nodded. "That is what I thought. Especially after I saw the evidence in his breeches."

Jenny started coughing, and Hope rushed to get her something to drink. "Are you all right? Did I say something wrong?"

"No," Jenny forced out once her cough was under control. "I just was not expecting what you said."

Hope frowned, searching her memory for what she'd said, "Especially after I saw the evidence in his breeches." The second time the words escaped her mouth, she realized how they sounded. "No, no, no," she quickly backpedaled. "I did not mean. It's just his breeches are tight and ..." Then she gave up and buried her face in her hands.

"It's quite all right," Jenny was suddenly there, kneeling next to her chair. "I know what you meant ... now. I'm just glad it was me you were saying those words to."

"Me too, Jenny," Hope smiled. "Ian loves me, and I love him."

"Then somehow, you will be together," Jenny promised her. "And I will always be there for you."

Hope's Home
21, March 1718
11:00 p.m.

Ian rushed toward Hope's home, making sure to stay in the shadows. He'd wanted to give her time with Jenny, as he knew from D.D. the news of their departure. And now that information had been given, he had some news of his own. How she would receive that, he knew not.

He was pleased when he arrived at her home to see the lights had been extinguished. It decreased the chances Geoffrey would come after him, his weapon drawn. But it also increased the odds Hope would not hear his call.

Her windows were on the side of the home, her view facing the mountains. Ian had brought several small stones and pulled them from his pocket. He aimed, his goal to rouse his siren and not the entire house. When the rock pinged off the windowpane, and she didn't appear, he worried. Was that not her room?

It took him several more moments to work up the courage to try again. He tried a larger rock, and when it hit, the ping was a little louder.

The sound of a door opening had him ducking behind a bush and holding his breath. A heartbeat, then another, and another, until the rhythm was pounding in his ears. Until his breaths were coming hard and fast.

"Ian, is that you?"

His heart steadied, and he blew out a slow stream of air and stood. She was on her balcony, looking down on him, and he very nearly died on the spot.

"Beautiful," he murmured, even knowing she could not hear him.

Hope was leaning against the balcony railing, wearing a light-colored dressing gown. Her red hair was hanging loose, its long curls blowing around her shoulders. And the way the moonlight brought out the coppery tones had his fingers itching to touch.

"I'm here." He stepped in front of the tree and glanced up, "Did I wake you?"

"No," she admitted. "I was lying in bed thinking of you."

Ian's heart kicked up a notch and brought his body along with it. And, heaven help him, he should say his piece from where he was standing, but he could not. "Can I come up?"

"Up here?"

There was laughter and something else in her voice. Perhaps their thoughts were of one accord.

"Unless you want to come down here."

He heard her breath catch. When she looked back over her shoulder, he had to wonder what she was seeing. *I'll catch you*, he wanted to say; but that was impossible.

Ian dropped the last of the stones he'd brought and studied the wall next to the balcony. There was a vine that climbed up the side of the home, and as he felt around, he discovered a lattice-like structure. Would it hold him?

"Here I come," he promised, placing his foot on the first rung.

"It won't hold you."

"How do you know?" Ian flashed her a quick smile. "Have you tried?"

"No, but ..."

"Trust me, Siren."

Ian had to focus on where he placed his foot, but shortly, he was even with the balcony.

"Be careful," Hope cautioned.

He took two more steps and then wrapped his hands around the bars to pull himself up.

"Ian!"

There was enough room between the bars for him to wedge his foot in, which gave him leverage. He pushed up enough, so he was standing on the outside of the railing. It was either lift his leg over or return the way he'd come.

"Are you stuck?" Hope took a handful of steps closer to where he was wedged.

"No," Ian tossed out nonchalantly.

"Then what are you waiting for?"

"An invitation."

"An invitation?" she grinned, placing her hands close to his on the railing. "Let me see."

"Bloody hell, Hope," Ian grumbled. "Just say the words."

Hope leaned closer and kissed him, "Would you like to come up, Ian?"

He lifted his leg over the railing and dropped onto the balcony. As soon as his feet were on solid ground, he reached for her, and she was in his arms.

Her lips were soft and, as he'd hoped, she melted into him. He allowed the kiss to continue until he reached a point where all he could think of, was carrying her through the doors.

"I can never get enough of those."

"My kisses?"

"Of course, your kisses."

"Good." She giggled lightly, then stepped out of his arms, "What is it?"

Ian dropped his head and took a breath before taking her hands and pulling her close once again.

"As soon as I get back to the ship, we're setting sail," he broke the bad news. "Henry believes he spotted the Rosa, but for some reason, she turned around."

"You're going after it?"

"Yes." He hesitated for a moment, but then realized he couldn't wait any longer. "Do you remember what I said to you on your birthday?"

"You said much to me that day." She looked up and her eyes sparkled in the moonlight. "Are you referring to your *devotion*?

He winced, wondering what he'd been thinking, labeling what he was feeling anything but love.

"Yes," Ian murmured. "I love you, Hope."

"And I love you too, Ian."

"Then ... will you be mine?" His heart was beating out of his chest at his next words. "Will you wait for me–?"

"Why is your heart racing, Ian?"

"If you would allow me to finish."

"By all means."

"As I was saying," he began again. "Will you be mine forever?"

Hope tilted her head, her eyes never leaving his. "What are you saying?"

"Will you marry me?" Ian finally shared the words that were in his heart.

"You ... you want to marry me? Really?"

The thought that maybe he'd read her wrong crossed his mind.

"Yes, really." Ian frowned. "Why would you ask?"

"You aren't just asking because you do not wish me to marry some other bloke?"

"Remember what I said? I love every part of you ... and no, I do not want you to marry someone else. That is because I want you to marry me."

"Yes," Hope whispered. "Yes, I will marry you."

He took the other half of the comb and laid it on her palm. "A perfect circle, that has no beginning and no end. Just like my love for you."

"Oh, Ian."

"Give me that mouth," Ian growled, sealing their lips, and wishing with everything inside that their trip would be successful. Then, he could return to Swan Harbor, explain everything to Geoffrey, and claim Hope as his.

TWELVE

Swan Harbor
29, March 1718
3:00 p.m.

Hope stood with her arms held stiff while her Aunt Kitty pinned the back and bottom of her dress. There was much she wanted to say, but it wasn't her aunt's fault her father was being such an overbearing clod.

"Are you about done?"

Kitty looked up, her dark eyes kind. "Almost. But Hope …"

"Do not tell me to accept this quietly, Kitty," Hope snapped. "You would not do this to Ellie. It was not done to you. Nor was it done to my parents. Why am I so different?"

Kitty didn't say anything immediately, but momentarily sat back on her heels. "Your father has changed since your mother's death."

"And that's my fault?"

"No," Kitty shook her head. "It just is."

"Then why am I made to pay for *his* change?" Hope tossed out.

Kitty straightened the bottom of the skirt and then gathered her supplies and scurried around putting them away.

"Aunt Kitty?" Hope tried again. "I do not want to marry someone older than my father."

"I know."

"What shall I do?"

Kitty stared at her for so long, Hope wondered what was going through her mind.

"Mister Griffin is a man of great means," Kitty finally offered. "He will make sure you have what you need."

Except love.

Except her heart.

Where was Ian?

"Are we finished?" Hope asked through gritted teeth. "You've done what you must. Now it's my turn."

"Don't do anything rash, Hope," Kitty warned.

"Oh, you mean, such as marrying off your only daughter to an old man?" Hope snapped, disappearing behind a dressing screen.

"Hope."

Hope tore off her 'wedding' dress and pulled on her old gown. She slipped on her shoes and stepped back around the screen.

"Here," she threw the offending garment toward her aunt. "I need to go."

"Hope!" her aunt's voice followed her out the door.

The time had come for her to confront her father. And even though just the idea made her stomach twist into knots, it was quickly becoming a situation of now or never. Because if she could not get him to see things her way, the time for her to control her own fate was running out.

However, the fear of what she was about to do almost had her taking a detour to see Jenny. Except, the older woman couldn't make the problem go away. This was something she was going to have to deal with all on her own.

Hope ran up the stairs to her front door, and words she'd heard her mother say many times floated through her head.

The heart wants what the heart wants. When you are lucky enough to meet someone who loves you and you love them. Then grab hold with both hands and fight with everything inside. For true love is rare and special and worth every ounce of energy it takes to make that person yours.

Well, mama, Hope thought, slamming the front door behind her. *I'm on my way to fight for what I want. Will papa listen to me, as he always seemed to listen to you?*

"Hope?" Anne met her at the bottom of the stairs. "Is everything all right?"

"What do you think?" Hope spit. "Were you the one who suggested Hugh Griffin?"

Anne frowned. "What are you saying?"

"Just stop pretending you care," Hope cried.

"Hope, honey," Anne began.

Except Hope needed to deal with Geoffrey and brushed her aside until later.

"Father, we need to talk." Hope slammed her palm against her father's den door. And the resounding thwack, as it bounced against the wall, added to the feeling of satisfaction coursing through her system. As did the resigned look on her father's face when he glanced up from the papers he was reading.

"Hope," Geoffrey stood and moved to the front of his desk. "What can I help you with?"

She blew out a breath and powered forward. "What do you think you can help me with? How dare you expect me to marry a man twice your age!"

"He's not—"

"How could you even think I'd marry anyone of your choosing?" she cut him off. "Where did this idea come from?"

"I'm your father."

"And that gives you the right to have a say about whom I marry?"

Geoffrey took a deep breath, and the look on his face had her thinking maybe she'd gotten through to him.

"I'm doing what has to be done." He cleared his throat and added, "It's for your own good."

"*How?*" she pleaded, wishing he would tell her the entire story. "How can marrying someone I do not love be for my own good?"

"You have to trust me."

"Come on, Father." Hope waved at the painting of her mother that hung over the fireplace. "I've read mother's journals. I know about your hearts being connected. She told me many times how much she loved you. How can you take that experience away from me? I know you loved her."

His eyes pleaded with her, but for what, she had no idea. "Of course, I loved your mother."

Hope brushed away the errant tear, unwilling to show him how much he was hurting her. "Then how can you deny me the same opportunity? To find a man who loves me, just as you loved mother. To have a family someday."

His face crumpled, and again she thought, maybe.

"What did love do for me?" Geoffrey surprised her by asking.

"What did love do for you?" Hope took another breath and forced the words out around the lump in her throat. "How can you even ask that? You had almost twenty years with a woman who loved you. Every day she was the first thing you saw in the morning, and the last thing you saw at night. We were a happy family. She gave you Martin, me, Alan, and she gave her life to give you Luke. Yet this is how you remember her? By throwing me to the highest bidder? What do you think mother would say if she were here?"

Geoffrey stared at her but said nothing.

"I'll tell you what she would say," Hope sniffed. "Mother would say, 'Geoffrey, is it not better to have loved and lost than to never to have loved at all?'"

"You don't understand," he cried. "It's all my—"

"Just forget it," Hope cut him off, not willing to hear any more excuses. "You should have trusted me."

Then without waiting for him to say anything more, Hope ran out the door, down the hall and away from the house. She wasn't quite sure how everything was going to work. However, she was going to control her own destiny.

El corazón del Rubí
29, March 1718
6:00 p.m.

With Freddy at the helm, Ian went looking for D.D. He was agitated by everything that was going on around him. The weather, the crew, but mainly because he'd not accomplished everything on this trip he'd hoped to. The only positive thing had been running into his old friend, Eddie Teach, who had told them where Pence was heading.

Except after making the detour to the islands of Bermuda, what did they have to show for it? They had a scared child who hadn't said anything, and not much else.

Ian located his first mate in the galley, hovering over the child. Bernie was sitting with a biscuit and milk in front of him, but rather than eating, he was staring at something only he could see.

"Has he said anything?" Ian asked as soon as D.D. stepped across the room.

"Not much," D.D. admitted. "He's scared because a pirate is a pirate."

"That's a bloody lie," Ian snapped. "We rescued him. Pence kidnapped him."

"I know that, and you know that," D.D. sighed. "To a five- or six-year-old scared kid, though, it's not as easy to understand."

"But ..." Ian turned away, his entire being vibrating with frustration. Being so out of control was not a feeling he experienced often.

"I know you wanted to be back in Swan Harbor before tomorrow," D.D. consoled him. "But the stop in Bermuda—"

"—Saved the boy," Ian brushed away anything else. "For that, I am happy. It's just that ..."

"You want to be with Hope."

"Am I that transparent?" laughed Ian.

"To me," D.D. gave him a *What do you think,* look. "But that's only because I've known you since you were a boy. I'm happy for you."

"I'm happy for me too." Ian flashed him a grin. "Until my job is done, though, I'm where I need to be."

D.D. looked at him as if he were going to argue, but then the boy's soft voice captured their attention.

"I safe?"

"Yes, Bernie, you are safe." D.D. squatted next to where the boy was sitting. "Can you tell us anything about the Rosa?"

"Rosa?" Bernie frowned. "What's Rosa?"

"Captain Pence's ship."

A look of distaste flew across Bernie's face so quickly that if he hadn't been looking closely, Ian would have missed it.

"Bad man," Bernie grunted.

"I agree," D.D. replied softly. "He took my son."

"Son?"

"Yes," D.D. nodded. "His name is Richard. Do you know him?"

"Richard is nice," Bernie grinned. "He's okay."

"He's okay?" D.D. repeated. "Really?"

"Really." A huge smile suddenly blossomed on Bernie's face. "Can I go home now?"

D.D. laughed and lightly ruffled the boy's hair. "Yes. Tell us where home is, and we'll take you."

"Home?" But then Bernie's face crumpled, and he murmured, "I forgot."

"Bloody hell." Ian's eyes met D.D's. "What now?"

D.D. shrugged. "I guess he goes back to Swan Harbor with us. Perhaps on the way, he'll remember."

"Perhaps," Ian murmured, but not holding out much hope for it to be true.

The sudden change in the rolling motion beneath his feet had Ian rushing back up to the bridge. Bloody hell, he'd forgotten the weather.

"Cap'n! Storm!"

Ian looked in the direction Freddy was pointing, and his stomach clinched. The sky was black, and the clouds were churning. Great bolts of light shot straight toward the water, and loud claps of sound reverberated around them. Did they sail through or go around?

The wind kicked up, the sails billowing. Every wave was bigger than the one before.

"Which way?" Freddy yelled over the noise.

Ian studied the clouds, watching them. He was trying to see if he could figure out which way they were moving.

The waves were breaking, and the sea was climbing higher with each minute. However, as the storm moved toward land, the sky lightened. With that information, he decided they were going around it.

"Reef the mainsail," Ian cried and pointed starboard. "Take us out."

"Won't that take us off course?" D.D. asked, coming up behind him.

"Yes," Ian agreed, keeping sight of the starboard side as Freddy headed out to sea. "But better than going through that."

The end of his sentence was drowned out by another snap of light from the clouds. Which was followed by a boom, louder than three cannons combined.

"Hold on." Ian grabbed a line from the jib that flew past. "It's going to be a wild ride."

D.D. gave him a look as if he thought he was crazy, but Ian was too busy keeping an eye on the boom sail.

"You're actually enjoying this, aren't you?"

Before he could respond, there was a snap, another boom, and the clouds opened up. Ian was instantly soaked and laughed when the kerchief D.D. had tied around his head blew off.

"Keeps me busy," he cried.

Which was what he needed. At least then he didn't think about all the possibilities. The ones that involved Geoffrey Prince going ahead and making plans to marry Hope to some other bloke. If so, he'd do no less than David Hunter had done in rescuing Jenny. As he'd told her, his siren was marrying no one but him. Of that, he was positive.

Hope's Home
29, March 1718
11:00 p.m.

Hope paced in her room, from her bed, to the window, to the door, to the wardrobe, and back to the bed. She lost track of how many steps she took, but everyone brought her closer to the time.

There were so many questions when it came to what she was about to do. But after talking to Jenny, she didn't feel she had many options.

The gold comb Ian had given her glinted in the candlelight. She'd worn it several times, and every time she'd done so, it had made her feel closer to him. Except she'd thought he'd be back. After all, he'd known what was happening on March 30th. Did he not know she needed him?

Of course, those thoughts were quickly followed by ones of how she was behaving like a child. That somehow he knew, and when he could, he would return.

However, with the decisions she'd made, she wouldn't be waiting for him.

Would he know where she'd gone? Would he come to her? Would he understand?

She stopped pacing when the footsteps she'd been waiting for were heard on the stairs. Before they came any closer, she blew out the candle and climbed into bed.

There was a moment of hesitation when the door did not open as she'd expected. Then the steps backtracked, and slowly it was pushed open.

Hope held her breath, praying nothing was said. Hoping he would not come any closer. She squeezed her eyes shut, let the breath she was holding out slowly, and listened.

"I'm so sorry," her father's soft voice carried across the room. "I did not know what she would do. When I saw Christine, I knew she was the woman meant to be mine. How could we have known that our love was going to unleash such hate in another person? But as you've said to me many times. Your mother always saw the best in everyone. She never believed that words uttered in a moment of anger would have such a monumental effect on our families. We hoped our love would snuff out the danger. That by keeping the secret, no one would be harmed. But she died, and until I can figure out the next step, this is what must be done. Forgive me, Hope."

When his voice broke on her name, tears sprang to her eyes, and she wanted to ask him to explain. While she didn't understand the overall message behind what he'd said, there was one thing that still rang true. If she stayed, he expected her to marry Hugh Griffin. And as much as she loved her family, that was never going to happen.

As soon as the footsteps had faded, Hope climbed from her bed and relit the candle. Her dressing gown was tossed aside and within minutes, she was wearing her outfit of breeches, a man's shirt, and boots. All she needed to do was write a letter to her father. The question was, what should she say?

29, March 1718

11:45 p.m.

Dear Father,

As I write this, I have to wonder if you will be surprised when reading it. You and mother raised me to fight for what I wanted. You taught me that just because I am a female, that it did not mean I didn't matter. That I had a brain and to use it. And when mother was alive, you treasured that part of me.

Then mother died, and you behaved differently. I know most say you blame yourself for her death. That if she hadn't been pregnant, she wouldn't have died. However, you and I both know she wouldn't have thought that. She believed that everything happened as it was meant to.

I do not understand why you have decided it is necessary for me to marry someone such as Hugh Griffin. While I wish I could trust that you have a reason, I cannot allow it to come at my expense.

My future is just that—_my_ future. Until you get this notion, I cannot be married off as if I have no say. I must do what is best for me and leave. Just as you and mother chose to love each other, I am fighting to have the right to love a man of my choosing.

Perhaps someday, you will decide to trust me with your reasons for why you have done what you've done. Maybe then we can be a family again. Trust that my decisions have not been made in haste. Just to be clear, they are _my_ decisions.

Hope

With the letter written, the last thing she needed to do was complete. Once it was done, something inside of her settled, telling her she was making the right choice. She was choosing love above all else.

Hope left the note on her desk and slipped the scabbard over her head. Since she'd already hidden a small pack of clothing in the barn, all she needed to take care of was her hair.

She swept the long red strands up onto her head in a simple style and fastened them securely. Then she took the combs Ian had given her and slid them into her hair, forming a circle.

A perfect circle, just like my love for you.

Hope crammed a cap on her head and took a last look around. There were things she'd wanted to take with her, but those were just things. *Perhaps someday,* she told herself, stepping out onto the balcony.

Then, just as Ian had done two weeks previously, she climbed over the railing and took hold of the trellis. And with every step down, she was that much closer to freedom.

THIRTEEN
PRESENT DAY

The entire time I climbed down the trellis, I kept waiting for something to go wrong. The rungs to break, or I would slip and fall, or my father would be waiting at the bottom. But none of those happened, and once my feet touched the ground, I sighed with relief.

Big Red was waiting for me when I walked into the barn. That he didn't greet me with his usual sounds didn't escape my attention. Somehow, he knew this was not our usual type of ride.

He stood stoically while I saddled him and tied my packs across his back. Instead of jumping on him right then, I led him away from the barn, out of the yard, and into the woods. Only then did I feel comfortable climbing onto his back and giving him the freedom he desired.

As we traveled toward the path where I was told to wait, it was pitch black, and I realized anything could happen. But as I had written in my father's note, I was fighting for love. Because my heart did want what it wanted. It wanted Ian Jones, and as Jenny had stated, I too believed someday we'd be together.

Big Red carried me up into the mountains and onto the path that would take me to my new life. I did not wish to leave Swan Harbor. However, I realized it wasn't the place that made the home, but the people. While I would miss many, it was Faith and Henry who were on my mind. They had been good friends, even providing cover for Ian and me in the month since my birthday. Both knew where I was going, though, and I couldn't help but think we'd one day meet again.

It was true that I was leaving one set of friends, but I was also being helped by another. David had rescued Jenny from being forced to marry someone else. With Ian away at sea, they were saving me. In my head, that made us family. My hope was that someday I could return and introduce Ian as my husband.

When I reached the spot where I was to wait, I tied Big Red close and settled between several large rocks. My cape provided warmth, and as I drifted to sleep, I couldn't help but wish Ian were with me. For only then would I be truly home."

A shiver ran through Emma as she finished reading Hope's words. She'd known there was more than just thinking about the death of her ancestors that made her hesitant to read the journal. Finally, though, after reading what Ian and Hope had gone through to be together, she was beginning to understand why the task had been so overwhelming.

"What is it, Doc?" Killian asked softly.

Emma frowned. "I'm finally understanding my hesitancy with regard to reading Hope's journal."

"You told me it had to do with so many women dying young," he reminded her. "Is that not it?"

"It's more complicated than that." She set the journal aside and angled toward him on the bed. "Do you remember what Captain Jack said when we were at Sally's earlier?"

"Jack said a lot of things, Doc," Killian laughed. "What specifically are you referring to?"

"I was referring to why he thought you and I should read the journals."

"The same things he's been saying." Killian shrugged. "He believes it's because you are Hope's descendant, and I am Ian's."

"That," Emma nodded, and went on to add, "he also said it had to do with our wedding date being the same as was on the rings we found with Hope's journal. Jack believes it brings everything full circle."

"Which is why you finally picked up Hope's journal when we got home," Killian guessed. "Am I right?"

"Well, yes," Emma agreed. "Except I've begun to think it's bigger than just you and me."

"That's never been questioned," Killian reminded her. "It's why the others were at Sally's today."

Emma shook her head, frustrated she wasn't able to put her thoughts into words. It just kept feeling as if the story was bigger somehow, especially when it seemed as if the hope of Swan Harbor was riding on the 'key' being found, and soon.

"I think it's more than that," she added, her thoughts continuing to coalesce. "If the words were meant for just anyone, then don't you think Jack and Aiden would have read them when they had the opportunity?"

"Aye," Killian admitted. "But both said it felt as if they were reading words meant for others."

Emma thought back to what they had learned so far. It had taken months to gather the small pieces of information about the couple. And when it came down to everything they had discovered, they were *all* involved. Ava had received a letter. Aiden had brought the journal page. Terri had solved the riddle. Killian had unlocked the compartment. Then Jack had put the book back together.

Except that was just for Ian's journal. For Hope's journal, it had been Ava who had located the trunk. Emma who had the key. And both who had taken the journal back to Jack.

"Killian," Emma said quietly. "We are *all* involved."

He studied her for several seconds and nodded. "So what are you saying, Doc?"

"While Hope and Ian are the main characters of their story," she murmured. "They aren't the only ones. From their journals, we've learned there are multiple minor players who helped."

"Aye," Killian nodded, the look on his face telling her he was beginning to understand. "D.D. was instrumental in helping Ian get into the Ball."

"Even if he didn't know it," Emma replied. "Henry shared information about Hope with Ian. He then provided them cover for a month after her birthday."

"Let's not forget Jenny and Faith," added Killian.

"Which brings us back to everyone who was at Sally's today." Emma circled around to where her thoughts had been after finishing the last entry in the journal.

"Jack, Ava, and you," Killian began are connected to Hope. "Liam, Aiden, and I are connected to Ian."

"Harper is connected to Henry," Emma continued, "Dylan and Jessie to Geoffrey. Cameron and Gray to Jenny."

"The last being Catherine Gold, who is connected to Anne and Isabelle Michaels."

"Right," Emma winced. "Which is interesting since she at one time was connected to Dylan."

Killian sent her a look that had another chill running up her spine. "The connection between all of our families started in 1717, didn't it?"

"It did," Emma agreed. "Which means the town of Swan Harbor has once again doled out information in her own sweet time."

"Typical female," Killian quipped.

"Watch it," laughed Emma. "But as much as I hate to admit it, Jack's right. You and I do connect the families in the way Hope and Ian would have done."

"Bloody hell." Killian grumbled. "Do you want to call your mom and have her call Jack, or shall I call dad?

"Why?"

"Because, Doc," Killian climbed out of bed and grabbed his phone. "We shouldn't be reading the journals alone. We should be reading them aloud."

"With everyone else?"

"Aye."

And somehow, with that decision made, it felt right.

"I'll call mom," Emma offered, "and she can start the phone chain. You can call Dylan."

"Good idea," he grinned. "Then we can get to other, more enjoyable activities."

She laughed. "You know, we still have to listen to the C.D. Tyler sent over and choose our wedding music, right?"

"That has to be done tonight?"

"It was supposed to be done a few days ago, but ..."

He gave a long-suffering sigh. "And we can't just choose songs A, B, and C?"

"What do you think?"

"I think a man's work is never done." Killian tugged her up and into his arms. "Perhaps we can do a little of this while listening to the music," he dropped a kiss on her mouth, "and a little of that."

Emma slid her arms up and around his neck. "Perhaps."

He kissed her again and just like every other time, she expected to get lost in the feel of his lips against hers. Except she found a piece of herself unable to let go.

"What is it, Doc?" Killian brushed his hand across her cheek. "You usually respond to my kisses in a more vigorous manner."

Emma sighed and instead of responding, leaned her head against his chest. The steady thump of his heart soothed her, and somehow that made her even more sad.

"I'm sorry," she murmured. "It's just, I've known what happens with

Hope and Ian for months. But after reading a little about their relationship, somehow it just makes it that much more sad. You know?"

"Because they never got their happy ending?"

"Or their happy beginning," Emma added. "I'm almost scared to read the rest of it."

Killian cupped her face and when her eyes met his, she knew he somehow understood. "But isn't the hope that as we read, we find the key? And then not only do Hope and Ian get their happy ending, but the town of Swan Harbor as well."

"Do you really believe that?"

His lips touched hers briefly. "I have to, Doc." He kissed her again. "I have to."

Emma and Killian's Apt.
January 29
10:30 p.m.

"That's it, right?" Killian asked hopefully.

"What's wrong?" teased Emma. "Are you tired of dancing with me?"

"Never that, Doc." He tugged her back into his arms. "But the songs were all ..."

"Sounding the same," she guessed.

"Aye."

"I'll just send a quick message to Tyler and then we can go to bed."

Killian wiggled his eyebrows. "For those more enjoyable—"

But before he could finish his comment, his cell buzzed. He almost ignored it until he saw who it was.

"Who is it, Killian?"

"It's my dad." He grabbed his phone. "I'll meet you in the bed."

Emma acted as if she wanted to say more, but he threw her a smile, that meant 'go on.'

"Dad," Killian answered just before it went to voicemail. "Is everything alright?"

"I called to ask you that, Killian," Finn replied.

A part of Killian had expected that. After all, his father was married to Emma's mother, and understood how it felt to love a Swan woman.

"I'm fine," he gave the same answer he always did.

"Did you learn anything new in their journals?" asked Finn. "Regarding the reason why so many Swan and Prince women die before their forty-fifth birthday?"

"Not yet," Killian sighed, not wanting to say much, just in case Emma was close.

"But knowing what you know," Finn guessed, "and what the outcome will be, is weighing heavy on your mind."

"Something is," Killian agreed. "But I do believe that reading the journals as the one big, connected family we are, is the right thing to do."

"Alright, son," Finn acknowledged. "We'll see you in a few days. Get some sleep."

"Thanks, dad. Night."

Once he'd hung up, he didn't go directly to bed. He walked through the building, assuring himself once more the doors were locked. Then he poured a couple of fingers of rum and tossed them back. There was an unsettled feeling inside that he couldn't quite name.

When he turned the lights off, he found Emma in bed asleep. Their cat Millicent was curled up on one side, and the kittens, Nina and Trudi, on the other.

"Come on, little loves," he crooned to the cats as he climbed into bed. "Give me some room here."

Millicent blinked her green eyes at him, but otherwise didn't move.

"Killian," Emma murmured. "Everything okay?"

"With dad and Ava, yes. But our bed is too full."

She laughed. "I guess we need a bigger bed."

"I guess we do," he agreed.

When he laid his head on the pillow, he couldn't make himself close his eyes. They were focused on the woman in the bed with him. Focused on thinking of how much his life had changed in the two years since he'd moved to Swan Harbor. Except he wouldn't trade it for anything in the world. He just wished ...

"Killian?"

"Hush, Doc." He physically moved Nina and Trudi and pulled Emma into his arms. "There. Sleep now."

It wasn't until Emma's breathing evened out he allowed his eyes to close. But every time they closed, he struggled a little more to get them back open. It was almost as if his subconscious was trying to tell him something.

However, a point was reached where he could no longer drag them open. He was drifting along, with his body relaxing into sleep, except his mind kept reaching. Searching for answers and trying to connect all the pieces.

"The Swan women don't live beyond their forty-fifth birthday."

Killian fought the feelings of helplessness. Fought to try to open his eyes. Somehow, he knew, this was where he needed to be. There was also something that said, beware.

Find the key …

"My grandmother died when my mom was just a few months old," Emma explained. "And my mom's grandmother was in her early forties."

Killian's breath lodged in his throat, and his heart raced. No! He couldn't think about not having fifty years with Emma.

"My mother died when she was forty-four," Jack explained. "Then I went to live with Rose. I've been looking for the key for fifty years."

The Swan women don't live beyond their forty-fifth birthday.

No! He refused to accept that. They would find a way to give all of them their happy ending.

"It's not just the Swan women," Dylan added. "The Prince women have been affected too. My great-grandmother, grandmother, mother …"

"Why is this happening to our families?"

Jack shrugged. "I believe that somehow the destinies of the Swan and Prince women have been interconnected. Their futures cut short way too soon. Was it because of a curse, the power of suggestion, or just fate?"

But that didn't tell them why?

"My mom is the only Swan woman to live beyond the age of forty-five in centuries."

"I don't want to lose you," Killian said after she'd returned from finding a place to let Jonesy be free.

"Killian," Emma wrapped her arms around him, "you aren't going to lose me."

Why was this happening?

"I found Anne Michaels's diary," Aiden said. *"And happened upon a passage that seems to answer one of our questions."*
"Which question, Aiden?"
"Why."
"Anne wrote,"

December 1695,

Today Geoffrey made known what I have suspected for some time. He is in love with Christine Swan and not, as I had hoped, my daughter, Isabelle. But since the heart wants what the heart wants, I am happy for them and will wish them well.

Unfortunately, I am not able to say the same about poor Isabelle. She is a willful child and made some rash comments. When I returned home, I found my book titled Magical Charms, missing from my shelf. And while my use of the book has been the sections on lessening pain, that is not all it holds. The book contains several other cures and curses, some which are said to be very powerful. I fear Isabelle's anger will lead her to do something she will one day regret. Something we all might regret.

"So, I was right," Jack murmured, his dark eyes meeting Emma's, *"it is a curse. And only the key can set us ... and Swan Harbor, free."*
"The key?"
"Yes, Killian, the key." Jack replied. *"Jonesy is running out of hope. We need to find the key."*
"And then what?"
"Set him free."
"But didn't you set him free?"
Emma nodded. *"But he doesn't look good. I'm worried he isn't going to make it."*

"And if Jonesy dies?" Killian asked, even though he didn't really want to know the answer.

"Jack says, 'all hope will be lost.'"

"Meaning?"

"I don't know," Emma sighed. "But I don't think I want to know."

"We need the key."

"Where's the key?"

Killian knew he was asleep, but as much as he tried, he couldn't open his eyes.

Wake up!

Emma! Help!

But she wasn't lying next to him. Instead, she'd left a note on the table.

> Killian,
>
> I have a bad feeling about Jonesy. If something happens to that swan, Jack is going to be upset. I've gone to the cove. Keep searching for the key. We need to find the key.
>
> Love,
>
> Emma

The key! How were they supposed to find the bloody key when they had no bloody idea where to look?

Were the answers in the journals?

Then suddenly, he was in the car and on the way to the cove and Emma. Killian parked and as soon as he stepped out, a shiver ran through his body. Something wasn't right.

Jonesy!

Emma!

The ground was slippery as he tried to step over the rocks leading to the cove.

"Emma!" he screamed. "Where are you?"

His voice echoed around him, but there was no answer from the woman he loved.

"Emma!" he cried again, running toward the cove where they had freed Jonesy. "Emma!"

Killian climbed up over the rocks and then down into the cove. He saw Jonesy first, but it wasn't until the swan moved that Emma could be seen.

She was lying at an odd angle, as if she had slipped on the rocks when checking on Jonesy.

"Emma!" he cried, running toward her. "Emma!"

Killian dropped down onto his knees and reached to brush away the blonde hair covering her face, "Doc! Look at me!"

As soon as her face was uncovered, he understood why she wasn't answering. Her eyes were open, staring up at him ... sightless.

"Emma!"

FOURTEEN
IN 1718 …

Swan Harbor, Maine
1, April 1718
4:00 a.m.

Ian cut a glance at Bernie, who had become his shadow since they had picked him up in Bermuda. The child didn't say much, but periodically something interesting fell from his mouth. Especially since Pence had kept him close.

They had learned Bernie had been Pence's cabin boy. His responsibilities had included bringing the Captain his meals and picking up after him. What Ian still wanted to know was why he'd been left in Bermuda. Had he run away? Or had someone left him? If it was the latter, why?

However, those were questions for another day. He lifted his spyglass once again. Just like every other time he'd looked in the past four hours, there was no movement.

"How long do you plan to stay here?" D.D. asked, dropping beside him. "It's been hours."

"I'm aware of that," Ian grumbled. "But I have a hunch—"

"And you need to see it through?"

"Something like that," Ian agreed.

They'd arrived in the waters near Swan Harbor the evening before. Instead of docking or sailing into the smaller cove, Ian had anchored them offshore, near a small island.

He hoped that if the Rosa had been following them, they would see them first and could chase. The idea that someone from Swan Harbor helping Pence was still there. Whether that was on purpose or inadvertently was yet to be seen.

"Explain it to me again," D.D. requested after they'd sat there a few minutes, and it was quiet.

"My hunch?"

"Of course, your hunch," D.D. groused. "I need something to keep me awake."

"You're not needed," Ian reminded him. "Bernie and I are just fine."

D.D. sighed. "Just tell me."

"He's afraid we're going to talk about him," Ian muttered to Bernie. "He's a nosy old man."

"D.D. nice man," Bernie exclaimed.

"Thank you, my boy," D.D. grinned.

"You told him to say that, didn't you?" Ian accused the older man.

"What if I did?" D.D. shrugged. "Right on cue, too. Now about that hunch."

"It's just the only thing that makes sense," Ian told him. "We've been after the Rosa for a year, and she's always one step ahead of us."

"Pence is—"

"Don't say smarter," Ian barked. "We both know that's not true. Lucky maybe, but not smarter."

"You're quite touchy, Professor," D.D. murmured. "All right, who's helping him?"

Ian pulled out his spyglass and scanned the area again. In the distance, he could see another ship traveling in their direction.

"That, I don't know … yet," Ian admitted. "But I think it's one of the men who take care of the lighthouse overnight."

"Did you ask Henry who they were?"

"No. I just asked him if they were trustworthy," Ian confessed. "And while Henry didn't offer any further information, he didn't appear to be hiding anything either.

"But if the men who work in the lighthouse overnight are helping," D.D. frowned. "How? What are they doing?"

"That's why we're sitting here," Ian pointed out. "I'm hoping to find a pattern."

"A pattern?"

"It's the only thing I can come up with," Ian sighed. "There has to be a way someone on land is warning the ship. How else but through the lighthouse?"

"Makes sense," D.D. agreed.

"I thought so," Ian acknowledged, watching the ship coming closer. "But here comes a frigate now."

"Friend or foe?"

"Black Dandy," Ian muttered.

"In these waters?" D.D. asked.

"My thoughts too. Here she comes."

He watched the lighthouse flash, so the ship missed the treacherous rocks. Then it sailed around the land where the wooden structure was located before pulling into the docks. But as Ian watched several individuals run toward the ship, he became aware the child was muttering softly.

"Long, long, long, can't go wrong," Bernie murmured. "Long, long, long, can't go wrong."

Ian exchanged looks with D.D., and something inside of him sparked.

"Bernie, lad," Ian asked softly, not wanting to startle. "What did you just say?"

Bernie looked at him for several seconds, his fingers holding tight to an old piece of cloth. Then he pointed at the lighthouse and smiled. "Long, long, long, can't go wrong."

Ian laughed. "That's what I thought you said. Who told you that?"

Bernie shrugged. "Bad Man liked it."

"Pence liked it?"

"Yes," Bernie shook his head excitedly. "Did not like short."

"Short?" asked Ian.

"Short, short, short, abort, abort," recited Bernie.

"Bloody hell," Ian exclaimed. "I was right."

"Yes, and Bernie, my lad. You were brilliant." D.D. praised the boy. "Now what?"

"Now, we sleep," Ian replied. "Then later this morning, we will sail into the cove, and I'll talk to Henry."

"And get that spot on the bow fixed that your joyriding caused," D.D. reminded him.

"My joyriding?" Ian grumbled. "It was the storm."

"And you just had to tackle that last wave," D.D. kept complaining.

"You're just jealous it wasn't your idea."

D.D. grumbled under his breath the rest of the way down, but Ian let him carry on. His thoughts had already moved off his ship and onto his siren. While he wouldn't be able to spirit her away and marry her quite yet, he did have a few plans for when he got her alone. Plans that involved just the two of them, he thought, wondering what he was going to do with Bernie. They definitely needed to find the boy's family.

Timber Creek, Maine
1, April 1718
9:00 a.m.

Hope's life had changed since arriving in Timber Creek. Gone was the privacy afforded by having her own room. And gone was the freedom to do what she wanted, when she wanted.

Instead, she spent her days doing what needed to be done for them to survive. They were also spent thinking of Ian, for he was never far from her mind.

"Are those deep enough?" Hope asked Marie, the woman she was staying with.

"I guess." Marie dropped a seed in each of the holes and stood back, waiting for the next set.

Hope sighed and moved forward to dig some more. She felt sad for Marie, who'd lost her family before settling in Timber Creek. Except how did you help someone when you weren't sure what they were going through?

"How many more?"

Marie showed her the pile of seeds she had in her pocket and then stood waiting for her turn to plant.

Hope went to work on the next set of holes and made a mental note to talk to Jenny. She'd been the one to introduce Marie, and said she'd hoped having a young person to care for would bring the other woman back to life. Yet, Hope felt at a loss.

"What is it we're planting again?"

"Vegetables," Marie offered.

"Vegetables?" echoed Hope. "Such as ...?"

"Beans, squash," Marie tossed out. "Vegetables."

They finished planting the seeds, and Hope brushed off her hands. The dirt stuck, though, especially under her fingernails.

"Come," Marie suddenly instructed. "Come."

"What is it?"

"There's clean water." Marie waved her hand toward the woods surrounding them. "I'll show you."

"Really?" Hope asked, surprised the woman had initiated conversation.

"Yes, come." Marie didn't wait to see if she was coming, but picked up a wooden pail and took off.

Hope followed her around the garden and into the trees surrounding their camp. As soon as she stepped into the forest, she could hear the water bubbling. It immediately reminded her of the stream that ran in the woods behind her home. The thought of missing her family zipped through her, taking her breath, it was so painful.

"See." Marie led her to a shallow pool. "It's clean. Tastes good."

Hope smiled at the older woman and dipped her hands in the water. It was cold, but refreshing, and before she'd thought it through, she'd taken off her stockings and dipped her feet in it.

"Hope!"

"What?" Hope asked innocently. "It feels good. Try it."

"But your ..." Marie pointed to Hope's bare legs, her face turning red with embarrassment.

"It's just us," Hope assured her. But the image of Ian holding her foot in his hand had her pulse kicking up a notch.

For the next few moments, it was quiet, with only the sounds of the forest surrounding them. She gave her thoughts permission to drift and took Ian's combs from her hair. Somehow, holding them made her feel closer to him.

"Those are pretty." Marie sat next to her, dipped her toes in the water and then suddenly began to giggle, surprising Hope. "It tickles."

Hope nodded, "I agree. The bubbles do tickle."

"You were right," Marie murmured. "The water is refreshing."

"Very."

They sat there for another minute, and Hope thought of and discarded several topics. She didn't want to make the other woman uncomfortable, which made it difficult to know what to say.

"I saw you."

Marie's declaration had Hope's stomach tightening with worry. But why, she wasn't sure, since they were no longer in Swan Harbor.

"You saw me?" Hope frowned. "When?"

"At the dance."

"My birthday Ball?"

"Yes," Marie added. "I was helping serve."

Which cleared up how she'd gotten into the Ball. Except why was she acting as if she had a secret?

"I saw you with that man."

Ian? Had she too recognized him just as Jenny?

"Which man?" Hope asked.

"You were dancing with him." Marie shivered, and a look of distaste crossed her face. "He had light hair, but darkness always surrounded him."

Maddok!

"There was a darkness around him?" Hope questioned. "What do you mean?"

Marie glanced around, and there was a part of Hope that wanted to remind her they were alone. Instead, she held her tongue.

"I see colors around people," Marie admitted quietly. "His colors were very dark. Evil."

"Evil? Oliver Maddok?" Hope remembered how he made her feel when he'd held her hand. "I don't care for him. It's one reason I left Swan Harbor."

"You could not marry someone you did not love."

"Which is what my father wanted."

"But the other man," Marie explained. "His colors varied."

"Which man was this?"

"The Captain," Marie whispered.

"The Captain's colors changed?" Hope exclaimed, not even pretending she did not know to whom Marie was referring.

"Yes," Marie confirmed. "Blue, red, purple. He loves you."

Her first inclination had been to deny, but since she was in a new town, Hope smiled and held up the combs. "He gave me these. But I'm not sure where he is. I thought he would be back by now."

"I think he's a good man," Marie said. "He'll come for you as soon as he can."

"I hope so."

"You miss your family."

"What makes you say that?"

"I've seen you watching John and Gilbert," Marie admitted. "And every now and then a sad look crosses your face."

"John and Gilbert are friends of my brothers," Hope told her. "I know Alan and Luke probably miss Jenny's boys too."

"Just like I miss mine," Marie whispered.

Hope held her breath, wondering if Marie would say anything more, and searched for what to say.

"I'm sorry," she finally settled on, even knowing it wasn't much. "Jenny told me what happened to your family. How long has it been?"

"Three years," Marie sighed. "Yet, it still hurts."

"What happened?"

"Pirates," Marie murmured, sending goosebumps up Hope's spine. "They swarmed the town; killing, pillaging, plundering ... kidnapping."

"Yet you still trusted Ian, and believe he's a good man," Hope said, a little awe in her voice at what the other woman had gone through.

"His colors were always bright," Marie explained. "Even when he was yelling for us to board his ship, his colors were always good. Hope surrounded him. The Captain of the Rosa, though? Dark colors. He's a bad man."

The same ship Ian was after. Perhaps when he had captured the man who had D.D.'s son, maybe that would help Marie too. Then happiness would prevail, for all of them. They just needed to have hope.

⁂

Swan Harbor, Maine

1, April 1718
11:00 a.m.

"What you're saying is," Ian grumbled. "George wasn't feeling well, and someone else worked his shift in the lighthouse?"

"That's what he said," Henry retorted, meticulously working on the crack in the bow of the El corazón.

"And George can't remember who that was?"

Henry stopped what he was doing and glanced up. "There's obviously something you're trying to say. What is it?"

Ian had tried to work his way around to the light flashes accusing no one, but that didn't seem to work.

"Bernie," he called the young boy over. "Tell Henry about the lights."

Bernie smiled, seemingly happy to be the center of attention. "Long, long, long, can't go wrong. Long, long, long, can't go wrong."

Henry repeated the words and frowned. "You believe there's someone who's signaling the ships using my lighthouse?"

"Yes," Ian nodded, excited it had taken little to get the point across. "Tell Henry about the short lights," he instructed Bernie.

"Short, short, short, abort, abort."

"Abort, abort," snickered Henry. "Do you really think …?"

"You do not believe me?" Ian barked, his ire rising at many things, primarily at his current lot in life.

"I cannot say that," Henry admitted. "But I cannot say I believe you either. It's just …"

"I know!" Ian relented. "I too have a difficult time believing there could be meaning behind light flashes. Then give me another way Pence, or any other ship, would know when it's safe … or not safe to dock."

Henry said nothing right away and went back to work on the bow. However, from the way he was focusing, something told Ian his mind was working.

"Maybe I can look at the dock ledger," Henry offered. "And compare it to the lighthouse one."

"Meaning?" Ian probed.

"Meaning," Henry winced. "Maybe I was a bit hasty in laughing at your suggestion."

"Because?"

Henry glanced back up. "Just a few conversation pieces I've heard at the tavern. Plus, George has a weakness for the liquor."

Ian let go of the breath he'd been holding and smiled at Bernie. "That's the sign of a good man, my boy. He admitted he might be wrong."

Bernie nodded, his eyes huge in his small face. "Yes, Professor."

"Bernie," D.D. hopped off the ship, "come with me. Let's see if we can find you some clean clothes."

Bernie cut a look at Ian and then quickly back at D.D. "Clean clothes?"

"Yes, come."

It took D.D. several more minutes of coaxing before the child followed him down the dock toward the Weavers. Ian watched them go, and a part of him wondered if his siren was visiting her uncle's place of business.

"I'm ready for the pitch," Henry pointed to a pail on the other side of him.

Ian grabbed the bucket, the smell so strong it caused his eyes to water. "Stuff bloody stinks."

"It gets the job done," Henry reminded him. "How did this happen again?"

"Storm," Ian grunted.

Henry gave him a look that said he'd been talking to D.D. and went back to the job at hand.

"You know you can't leave until—"

"I bloody know that," Ian cut him off. "Just hurry, though. I'm eager to see Hope."

Henry's hand stilled, sending Ian's heart into overdrive. "What?" he barked when nothing was said right away.

"You don't know?" Henry murmured, and then he shook his head and went on as if talking to himself, "Of course, you don't know. You had already left."

"I'm standing right here," Ian hissed. "Stop mumbling and tell me!"

Henry didn't respond until he'd finished what he was doing. The entire time he was waiting, Ian fought to stay calm, the news he was expecting to hear growing worse by the second.

"Hope's gone."

"Gone?" Ian repeated. "What do you mean, gone?"

"You're saying you really didn't know," Henry's eyes met his. "That she was planning to leave."

"No, I bloody didn't," Ian snapped. "We made a promise to each other before I left. She was going to wait for me."

"Hope didn't have a choice," Henry admitted.

"How?"

"Geoffrey went behind her back," Henry shared. "He scheduled her to be married without telling her."

"To bloody whom?"

"That's where it gets strange," Henry winced. "No one knows."

"No one knows?" Ian questioned. "How can that be? What of the three suitors?"

"Nigel Randolph disappeared," Henry explained. "Everyone thought he was the favorite. And Hugh Griffin died."

"Died?" Ian exclaimed. "Natural?"

"Fire."

"And the third?" Ian questioned. "Was he involved?"

"I'm not sure," Henry confessed. "There's some speculation, so maybe."

"So, Hope went with Jenny and David?"

"Yes," Henry nodded. "How did you know that, though?"

Ian shrugged. "I'm not sure. Maybe it was said by one or both of them the last time we were all together."

"I'm assuming you'll go to her?"

"I'd leave now if I could—" Ian was cut off by rushing feet. "What the ...?"

A group of men ran past him toward the Black Dandy, and just as Ian was prepared to go after them, Henry hissed.

"What?"

"Fire!" Henry dropped what he was doing and took off running.

Ian's thoughts pinged all over the place. "Henry," he chased after the other man. "We need buckets."

"Buckets?"

"Anything to get water to the fire," Ian explained, drawing from something he'd read a while back.

Henry stopped and then took off toward a small warehouse at the end of the dock. Along the way, he shouted for help until, once they arrived, they were being followed by a large group. "There are empty barrels in here waiting to be traded for full ones."

"That will work." Ian grabbed several men and pointed between the fire and the water. "We form a chain and pass the full ones up, and empty ones back."

As soon as he'd barked out orders, Ian grabbed a full barrel and took off toward the smoke. There was something about the direction from which it was coming that had him pushing to go faster.

"Geoffrey!" someone screamed. "Geoffrey is in there!"

Ian glanced at the woman and then back at the building. "The Sheriff is in there?"

"Yes!" she cried.

He wasn't sure exactly what to do, but he knew he couldn't allow Hope's father to die.

"You." Ian pointed to a dandy who had come out of a shop to stand next to the woman. "Give me your cravat."

"What?" the man sputtered.

"Hurry!" Ian wiggled his fingers impatiently. When the man still didn't comply, he barked, "Or do you want the sheriff to die?"

"Edmund, do it," the woman cried.

"But, Isabelle," he whined. "It's my favorite."

"Just do it!" she snapped.

It took several precious moments before the cravat was placed in Ian's hand. Acting purely on instinct, he tied the cloth around his head, covering his nose and mouth.

"Professor," Henry grabbed him by the elbow. "What are you doing?"

"Saving Hope's father," Ian murmured, pouring the water from his bucket over his head. "Just keep the chain going."

"I hope you know what you're doing!"

"So do I, my friend. Perhaps you should get the doctor, just in case."

Ian took another full barrel and waded into the smoky building. It was eerily quiet inside, just the pops from the flames, and the hiss when the contents of the barrels hit. As he made his way through the debris, he used the water to tamp down the hot spots.

He found Geoffrey midway between the front and back rooms. The older man's leg was bent at an odd angle, and there was blood on his temple. When he couldn't be roused, Ian used the rest of the water to open a path. Then, with the Sheriff over his shoulder, he ran outside.

"Over here." Henry rushed forward to help, which was good as otherwise Ian wouldn't have been able to see him.

"Here, Professor," Doctor Williams helped him lower Hope's father to the ground.

Ian ripped off the cravat, and the black covering it gave him an idea of what the rest of him looked like.

Geoffrey began coughing, and Doctor Williams tried to get him to be still, but he fought.

"Where's," Geoffrey coughed several times and tried again, "where's Bill?"

The doctor looked at Ian for an answer. "I didn't see anyone else. But there were flames everywhere."

"Was Sly Bill still locked up in there?" He moved farther away to ask Henry.

"As far as I know," Henry admitted.

And almost as if it were a moving picture, the pieces began clicking into place.

Geoffrey Prince had gotten lucky this time, Ian couldn't help but think. Would he be able to say the same about the victims of the next fire?

FIFTEEN

Timber Creek, Maine
3, April 1718
7:00 a.m.

Hope fought not to open her eyes. Because in her dreams, there was still information she needed. Information that filled in the blanks and protected her from shadows. Those were what threatened everything she held dear.

"Hope."

She buried her head deeper into the mat, attempting to ignore the voice. However, it was too late, as the answers were fading.

"Hope."

Reluctantly, Hope peeled her eyes open to see Marie standing next to her, a look of concern on her face.

"I'm awake," she mumbled. "What did I miss?"

"Miss?" Marie frowned. "Nothing yet. But you were crying out in your sleep. Are you all right?"

Hope pushed into a sitting position and rubbed her hands across her face. She was surprised when they came away wet.

"I was dreaming," she looked up at Marie. "I just don't remember what about."

"Your colors kept shifting," Marie told her.

"My colors?" Hope thought back, trying to bring some of her dream to the forefront of her mind. "My mother was in it. She was telling me something."

Marie hummed and stepped away, giving her space. "As long as you're fine."

"I am," Hope assured the other woman. And she was ... fine. She was also confused. Especially since it seemed as if Marie wanted to tell her something.

"The mercantile ship will be here soon," Marie advised. "Would you like to go?"

The mention of the ship reminded Hope of going shopping with her aunt, cousin, and Faith. What were they doing? Had her dream been about them?

Except that didn't feel right. It felt as if her mother was trying to warn her about someone closer to her. But what? Or who?

"Just let me get dressed."

"Take your time."

But when Marie left her alone, her thoughts immediately went back to her dream. What had her mother been trying to say?

The question stayed with her while she dressed, brushed her hair, and ate some fruit. When she stepped outside the one-room shelter, Marie was waiting, an expectant look on her face.

"You were dreaming of your mother?"

"Yes," Hope acknowledged as they started walking toward the beach where the mercantile ship would dock. "It felt as if she was trying to warn me about something."

Marie glanced in her direction and smiled. "Your colors are bright today. No worries."

"That is good," Hope stretched out the response, not quite understanding Marie's color comments. "But if there was a message from her, what could it be about?"

"Perhaps it was about the man you danced with at your Ball."

"Perhaps," Hope agreed. "Since I am not in Swan Harbor, I guess I do not have to worry."

"But your family is," Marie tossed over her shoulder on her way to join a group of women who were waiting for the ship to dock.

Hope hung back from the others, her thoughts on her family. Were they in danger? Except if they were, what could she do about it?

"Hope?" Jenny gave her a puzzled look. "You appear to have a lot on your mind."

Hope shrugged, "Just a dream. How are you?"

"I miss Swan Harbor."

"What did you say?" Hope looked carefully at her friend. "Did you just say you miss Swan Harbor?"

Jenny sighed. "Silly, isn't it? Missing a place. Especially since we were there for just a few months. But there was something about it that gave me so much hope for the future."

"The swans," Hope replied. "They have a way about them. When they were in town, everything just felt right. Which makes no sense, except it just is."

"Swans," Jenny laughed. "That, I wouldn't have guessed. I would have said the people."

"The people are important," Hope agreed. "My mother used to say it was the presence of the swans. She said they encouraged everyone to put their best foot forward. And you know, there was something to that."

"Why do you say that?"

Hope shrugged and turned to watch the mercantile ship dock. "When the swans left, there was always something missing. Except when ..." Her voice faded, as she wasn't even sure if what was rolling around in her head made sense.

"What?" Jenny encouraged.

"I was just thinking that when the swans were gone, there was always a sense of anticipation in the air." Again, Hope hesitated, surprised she was going to say what was on her mind. "Except when there was an engagement, wedding, or someone was expecting a new baby. During those times, hope was alive."

"That sounds wonderful," Jenny murmured. "Much like Serenity Cove was at one time."

"Serenity Cove?"

A flash of something flew across Jenny's face, and Hope wasn't sure she was going to respond.

"Our home," Jenny explained, "before Timber Creek."

"The pirate attack," Hope suddenly understood. "Is that where Marie's family ...?"

Jenny nodded. "Serenity Cove was much the size of Swan Harbor. It's south of Boston, and where David and I moved after we were married. Then one evening we woke to screams, and ..."

The knot in Hope's stomach grew as she recalled what she'd felt when those men had attacked her on the mountain. What would she have done had Ian not shown? A little shiver ran through her system that she worked to push away.

"How did you escape?"

Jenny's dark eyes were haunted. "It's all a blur. David grabbed my hand, and John. I had Gilbert, and we ran. However, there were so many families that weren't so lucky."

"Like Marie's."

"Yes." Jenny winced and went on to add, "Marie's husband was killed, she was left for dead, and when she came to, her sons had disappeared."

"Disappeared?" Hope repeated. "I thought they'd been killed."

"Oh, we were sure they were dead," Jenny proclaimed. "Especially since everything had been burned. In many ways, it would have been better for Marie had she seen it happen. Because without bodies ..."

"There was no closure."

"Right." Jenny glanced around to make sure they were still alone. "How are you two getting along?"

"We're doing all right," Hope admitted. "Marie told me Maddok, one of my suitors, had evil surrounding him."

"She read his colors."

"You knew about that?"

Jenny laughed. "Everyone knows about that. And that doesn't surprise me about Maddok."

"Me neither," Hope admitted. "Marie knows about Ian's feelings for me."

"Anyone with half a head knows," Jenny grinned.

"Really?"

"Well, if you're willing to look beyond the pirate to the man," Jenny acknowledged. "I think that gives him the ability to slip in and out without people paying close attention."

"Because they fear the pirate?"

"Because they fear pirates," Jenny clarified. "It's like when that man, Billy, was arrested. People knew he'd been a pirate ..."

"But because he showed up injured and worked an honest job," Hope added. "They thought he was harmless."

"Yes, it's a good thing your aunt hit him with her sewing bag," Jenny replied, "or the ending could have been different."

Hope agreed, but the whole situation gave her an unsettled feeling—even knowing Billy had been caught.

"Shall we?" Jenny waved toward the wares. "We've had enough serious talk for one day."

They wandered around, looking at the items the ship had brought. And while Hope saw several things she liked, nothing she felt she needed. It was as if her life was in limbo, and she was waiting for something.

"Pirates!" someone shouted, and a ripple of nervousness ran through the group.

Then someone else shouted, "Friend!" And everyone relaxed.

Hope shielded her eyes, and while the ship was still pretty far away, she knew it was Ian. She could feel him.

"It's your man, isn't it?" Marie asked, coming to stand close. "Will he take you away?"

"On his ship with him?" Hope exclaimed. "Somehow, I doubt that. But I wish."

What would they do, though? When she'd run from Swan Harbor, she hadn't worried about anything but herself. She hadn't wanted to marry someone of her father's choosing. Except now that she was free, what was next? Was Timber Creek to be her home? Or would Ian have other plans? Would he still want her?

"Look!" Marie pointed to where the El corazón had anchored, and a small boat was being lowered. "Seems your Captain is a might eager to see you."

"How do I look?" Hope asked, suddenly unsure of herself.

Marie studied her carefully for several seconds. Then she tilted her head in one direction, then in the other.

"Marie!" Hope gave an exasperated cry. "How do I look?"

Marie chuckled, "You're colorful. He'll approve."

"Colorful? Is that a good thing?"

"The best," Marie agreed. "Happiness is coming off of you in waves."

Hope tossed a quick "Thanks" over her shoulder before her feet started to move. Except did she walk slowly, quickly, or run?

Ian waited for D.D. and Bernie to settle in the small boat before picking up the oars.

"Ready?" he asked, not for the first time.

"Just about," D.D. replied, moving around in the small space, causing the boat to rock.

"Just hurry," Ian grumbled.

"Bernie, my boy," D.D. laughed. "That's called impatience."

"Impatience," Bernie repeated slowly, trying out the new word. "Professor Impatience."

"Professor Impatient," D.D. corrected. "Perfect."

Ian huffed, "If you two are through disparaging my name, I would like to get on with it."

"Carry on," D.D. muttered, the boat finally settling.

"Hold on." Ian pushed away from the El corazón and set his sights on shore.

The water was smooth, and with each stroke of the oars, he was a little closer to Hope. There was much he needed to tell her. Much he wanted to say. However, those things would wait. Because above all, he just wanted to hold her. Was it possible for them to have an entire evening with friends ... as a couple?

"Why was it you and Bernie needed to come again?" He tossed over his shoulder.

"Why, to help, of course," D.D. proclaimed.

"Help with what?"

"Rowing."

The boat shifted slightly as D.D. stuck his oar in the water. "It might help if you used both of them," Ian mumbled.

"Perhaps," D.D. agreed. "But that would require work."

"And Bernie," Ian glanced around at the boy, who was staring wide-eyed at the mercantile ship they were passing. "Why did you come?"

"I help too."

Ian didn't respond as he realized he needed to change the angle they were coming into shore. That became his focus for the next few minutes.

The water grew shallow, and he was just getting ready to jump from the boat to pull it in when he glanced up.

"Hope." Her name spilled from his lips almost reverently. And while his mind was screaming run to her, his body was paralyzed.

The boat rocked as D.D. and Bernie jumped out, and before he'd realized it, the boat was tied.

"Well," D.D. gave him a nudge. "Are you going to just sit there all day?"

"What?" Ian glanced around him and finally climbed from the boat. "I guess we're here."

"He's a bit daft," D.D. mock whispered.

"Daft," Bernie laughed. "Professor Impatient daft."

"Stop being cheeky, you two," Ian groused.

He took a step, and then another, in Hope's direction and heard Bernie mutter, "What is cheeky?"

D.D.'s response was lost when Ian took off running across the sand.

She's here, she's here!

Ian jumped over the rocks and ran around a display of wares, and then he noticed she had stopped.

"Hope." His voice was low and rough, and he couldn't help but wonder what she was thinking.

She dropped her head, and when she glanced back up, his nervousness evaporated.

"I missed you," Ian whispered, even though they were separated by a distance greater than he was tall.

"You did?"

"I did." He couldn't stand being separated any longer and deliberately took a step toward her.

"I missed you too."

"You have a funny way of showing it."

Her eyes flared. Hope glanced left, then right, then they both ran toward each other, and she was in his arms.

"You're here." Her fingers clutched his shoulders, then his neck, before settling in his hair. "I'm sorry I wasn't in Swan Harbor."

"I'm sorry I wasn't back quicker," Ian began. "But we …"

A screech cut him off, and then he heard, "Bernie! Is that you?"

Ian slipped his arm around Hope's waist and plastered her against his side as he turned toward the crying woman.

"Do you know her?" he whispered.

"Her name is Marie Martin." Hope stepped away from him and went to the crying woman. "Marie, what is it?"

The other woman pointed to where D.D. was standing with Bernie. And the look on the child's face was equal parts hope and fear.

"D.D., bring the lad closer," Ian instructed.

"What is it, Ian?" D.D. asked when he was close enough.

Ian held his hand out for Bernie to come to him and squatted to eye-level. "You trust me, right?"

The little boy nodded, his green eyes round. "Trust you, Professor."

"Thank you, Bernie."

"Ian," Hope moved close enough to place her hand on his shoulder. "Is Marie right, and this little boy's name is Bernie?"

He squeezed the little boy's fingers, trying to instill a little comfort in him. Between their hands was the piece of cloth Bernie was never without.

"Bernie, meet Hope," Ian introduced them. "The lad joined our crew in Bermuda."

Her eyes met his, and in them, he saw questions for which he had no answers. However, something was telling him he might have just found the child's family.

"D.D., will you stay with Bernie while Hope and I speak to Marie?"

As soon as they had walked away, Ian glanced toward Marie. She had sunk to the ground and was staring at Bernie, almost as if she were afraid he would disappear.

"I'm assuming that somehow Marie's child was taken."

"Children," Hope clarified.

"Children?"

"Yes." Hope's chin quivered. He wanted to take her in his arms. Instead, he settled for holding her close while she told him the story. "About three years ago, in a town called Serenity Cove."

"Charles was twelve and Bernie was two?" he asked when she finished.

"Yes."

Ian's thoughts went back to what had transpired in Bermuda. The Rosa had been anchored on the opposite side of the island from the El corazón. Instead of taking the time to sail around, Ian and several of his men had gone after it by land.

Somehow Pence's crew knew they were coming, and a chase had commenced. They had gone down a dark alley and turned the corner, expecting a fight. But instead, Bernie was waiting. Ian had tried to follow, but a flash of a young face was all he had before the last of the crew vanished. Could that have been the brother?

"Which could explain why Bernie has no memory of his home."

"None?" Hope asked hesitantly.

"Not that he has shared." Ian gazed down into her blue eyes, and the hopeful look on her face made him want to give her the world. "Do you think she'll speak to me?"

"I think so," Hope smiled. "She says you have bright colors and are a good man."

"She what?"

"Never mind." Hope slipped her hand into his and nodded toward where Marie was sitting. "Come on. Let me introduce you."

Ian went with her, and they sat next to the older woman on the hard-packed sand. He took a deep breath and prayed for the ability to say the right thing.

"Marie," Hope whispered. "You remember Ian, don't you?"

Marie's eyes met his, and the anguish in hers almost brought him physical pain.

"How are you, Professor?" Her voice was so soft he had to strain to hear over the waves rolling in.

"Better now," Ian grinned at Hope. "I heard about your encounter with Captain Pence and his crew. That was three years ago?"

"Yes," Marie murmured. "It was three years ago this month."

"And your boys?"

Marie swallowed and brushed her hand across her face. "Charles was twelve. We had just celebrated Bernie's second birthday. The pirates killed my husband and knocked me out. When I woke, my children were gone."

Ian knew what he was going to say was going to cause the woman pain, but he wasn't sure what else to do.

"Pence's men left Bernie behind," he explained. "I did, however, get a look at one of the men. He had light hair, shockingly light hair."

"That sounds like my Charles," she smiled. "He always protected his little brother."

"They were close?"

Marie nodded, and a faraway look appeared in her eyes. "Bernie was all he had left. His sisters had died the previous fall."

"Bernie doesn't remember his home," Ian gave her the news he'd been dreading.

This time when Marie's eyes met his, there was a spark in them he hadn't seen before. "I'm his mother. I birthed him and sat up with him when he was sick with fever. Let me talk to him. We are connected."

Ian glanced in the direction where D.D. was talking to Jenny and David, and Bernie was playing with John and Gilbert. Who was he to deny this woman the chance to see if she could reach her son?

"All right. Let me go talk to him."

He left Hope with Marie and approached D.D. and the Hunters.

"What do you think?" Ian asked them. "Is Bernie her son?"

Jenny's dark eyes flashed. "Who are you to keep her from seeing for herself?"

"Jenny, Honey," David calmed his wife. "That's not what he's trying to do."

"It's her son," Jenny proclaimed. "Look at them side by side. Same green eyes, same shape of face, and same color hair."

Ian did as she'd asked, and he had to admit, the similarities were there.

"Bernie," he called the child over. "You told us you couldn't remember your home, right?"

The child said nothing, just nodded, his eyes large and taking in everything.

"Was Charles with you when we found you?"

"Charlie," Bernie nodded. "Say goodbye."

"Charles told you goodbye?" Ian asked. "Why?"

"Bad man mean." Bernie's chin trembled, but still he stood stoically.

Had Charles somehow made a point of making sure his little brother was safe? Unless they found the older son, that question might remain unanswered.

"Come with me." Ian held out his hand and, as soon as Bernie slipped his inside, held on. "I have someone I think you will enjoy meeting."

Bernie's steps were slow, measured as they walked across the sand to where Marie and Hope were still sitting.

"This is Marie." Ian guided Bernie closer to the other woman. "She believes she is your mum."

Bernie scrunched his face in concentration and looked up at Ian. "Really?"

"Yes, really. Why?"

Bernie held up the cloth he was never without. "Charlie say, 'give mama.'"

Marie whimpered, reached into her pocket, and pulled out what looked like more cloth of the same color.

"I think this bear will look better if we sew back on his ear," Marie whispered to Bernie. "Don't you?"

As soon as Bernie took Marie's hand, Ian let go of the breath he was holding and looked away from the reunion.

"Are you all right?" Hope asked, stepping close.

"Why do you ask?"

"You just looked sad there for a minute." She slipped her hand into his. "Memories?"

Ian squeezed her fingers and brought her against his side. "How did you guess?"

"I don't know," Hope shrugged. "Perhaps you can tell me about it someday."

He looked down into her upturned face, and his thoughts quickly moved away from the past. "Perhaps. I have more important things to take care of right now, though."

"Oh?" Her eyes dropped, and she went to step away from him.

"I don't know what you're thinking, Siren," Ian turned them toward the woods where he hoped to find a bit of privacy. "But there's nothing more important than you."

"Oh!" When she looked up this time, her eyes sparkled. "Where are we going?"

"To take care of the most important thing." He backed her against a tree and brushed his knuckles down her cheek. "This." When their lips touched, he showed her how much he'd missed her.

SIXTEEN

Timber Creek, Maine
5, April 1718
9:00 a.m.

Hope wound her hair up on her head and slipped Ian's combs around her bun. With her morning dressing done, she was left with nothing to do but think about how much had changed in Swan Harbor since she'd left.

Nigel gone, and Hugh dead. Men she'd had no desire to marry, but she hadn't wished for them to die. And to think that whatever happened to them may have been caused by her other suitor, Oliver Maddok. The man Marie had proclaimed evil surrounded. How had she known what so many had missed?

What of her father, though? Had he known about everything? Was Oliver the one who set the fire to the sheriff's building? What would have happened had Ian not been there? Would anyone else have gone into the burning building? She thought not.

"Hope," the minister's wife stuck her head into the room where Hope had slept. "Your young man is waiting for you."

When she was gone, Hope double-checked the room and went looking for Ian. She found him waiting outside, pacing frantically back and forth.

"Ian?"

His eyes met hers, and she couldn't help but notice the look on his face. One she couldn't decipher.

"Are you unwell?"

"Am I not well?" Ian repeated. But then with a shake of his head, he went on, "No, yes, I'm fine."

"But?"

"Your guard dogs," he glanced over her shoulder where she assumed the minister, his wife, or both had stepped outside. "They will not allow you to accompany me back to Swan Harbor."

"What?" she exclaimed. "Why? Do they not know I need to get home and check on my father?"

"Well, yes, but—" Ian tried again.

"You said we could go on your ship," she reminded him.

"And you refused because I would not allow Big Red on the El corazón."

"Then you said fine," Hope sighed. "We go by horse, and you would have D.D. captain the ship. I do not see what the problem is."

"The problem is—"

"—You are not married," the minister interjected. "I would be remiss in my duties to the church if I allowed you to go with this man."

"But," Hope's gaze flew to Ian's. "We have made promises to be married."

"You have?" The minister perked up. "Have you asked her father for permission? Has it been announced at your home church?"

"Well," Hope winced, trying to figure out exactly what and how much to say. "Not just yet."

Ian slipped his arm around her waist. "I wanted to be able to ask for Hope's hand after I finished my search for D.D.'s son," he admitted. "But please know, I want to marry Hope more than anything."

The minister stared at them for several minutes before nodding once. "Fine. Prepare for a wedding in a few hours," he told his wife on the way back into their home.

Hope frowned. "What just happened?"

"I think we're getting married."

"Married?" Hope squeaked.

"Come along, Hope," the minister's wife took her hand. "We have much to do."

"Ian?" Hope glanced in his direction, fear racing through her veins.

"May I?" He took Hope's hand and led her away from the other woman. "Tell me what you're thinking."

"I'm thinking this is crazy," she admitted. "But there is nothing I want more."

"Then I'll see you at the altar." Ian winked, then kissed the back of her hand, taking her breath.

"All right."

"Come now, Hope."

Instead of leading her back into the home where she'd slept, Hope was taken to Jenny and David's.

"There you are!" Jenny exclaimed, dragging her inside. "We've been waiting."

Hope glanced around the small room and was surprised to see Marie and several others. "What am I missing?"

"You're getting married."

"And?"

Jenny stopped fussing around her and took her hand. "Remember when I said you and Ian would be together?"

"You would be there for me," Hope remembered. "Yes."

"This is me keeping my word." Jenny pointed toward the wardrobe in the corner. "We've recovered much of what we had hidden from Pence. Which means ..."

"We have a dress." Marie squeezed Hope's hand. "And we're helping you get ready to be married. It's the least I can do after what your Ian has done for me."

Hope smiled through the tears. "How's Bernie?"

"Quiet," Marie admitted. "But he's home, and I couldn't ask for anything more."

Then Hope lost track of time as the women scurried around her. They removed her old dress and replaced it with a new one. When all was done, a wreath of flowers was placed on her head and one in her hands.

"It's time." Jenny told her. "Are you ready?"

"To marry the man I love?" Hope smiled. "I'm more than ready."

"We'll see you at the minister's." Jenny took charge and pushed everyone out of her home. "Before we go, is there anything you wish to know?"

"About?" But the way Jenny's face turned red filled in the blanks for Hope. "Oh, you're talking about *that*."

"Yes," Jenny nodded, probably relieved she didn't have to spell it out.

Hope thought back to the time Ian had told her she wrecked him. Somehow, she knew that everything she needed to know about *that*, he would show her. She didn't plan on asking how he'd learned.

"It's, it's sweet of you to ask," Hope assured her friend. "But no, no, it's unnecessary."

"I'm glad." Jenny's smile relaxed. "And I'm really going to miss you when you leave."

"Me too." Hope bit her lip, trying not to cry. "Will you promise to come see me?"

"I promise." Jenny wiped her hand across her cheek. "David has been warned. If Timber Creek has not become home by next summer, we're moving back to Swan Harbor."

"I'll hold you to that."

Jenny took her hand, and when they stepped inside the minister's home, in a way everything felt surreal. There was music, and Ian was standing in front of the minister, waiting for her.

"Good luck," Jenny whispered, stopping next to David.

The heat in Ian's eyes warmed her heart and made her feel so many things. There was a part of her that wished everything had been different. That Faith, Henry, and her family were here. But as her mother would say, things happen for a reason, and she was where she was meant to be.

Hope glanced down at their entwined hands, and with her heart in her eyes, tuned into the minister. She was ready to pledge herself to Ian.

"We are gathered here today to join this man and this woman," the minister began.

Timber Creek, Maine
5, April 1718
12:00 p.m.

Ian knew he should be listening to the words. Except, standing next to Hope, his senses were overwhelmed. The candlelight bounced off her creamy skin. Her hands were soft in his. And the sweet smell of the flowers from the bouquet in her hair surrounded them.

"You are beautiful," he mouthed.

She smiled, and he felt ten feet tall. The minister had warned him that their marriage would be legal under God's eyes, but not according to the state. They would have to marry again. But as he listened to what the minister was saying, the enormity of the situation washed over him. There was no doubt in his mind that, if need be, he would proudly marry her over and over again.

The vows continued, and her eyes flared when she was asked to obey. His siren had a mind of her own, and those words would give her pause. If she were one to go willingly along with others, she would have been wed to another. That was something he could never stand.

Then he heard,

"... as long as you both shall live ..."

He knew their love would last forever. An eternity to show her what she meant to him.

"You may kiss your bride." The minister nodded to indicate Hope was his.

Ian pulled her into his arms, and when his lips touched hers, the kiss felt different. There was a freer feel to it, and only the minister's quiet 'humph' had their lips parting.

"Let me introduce Professor and Mistress Ian Samuel Jones."

"Professor?" Hope murmured, her sparkling eyes meeting his.

"That is the man I wish to be," he squeezed her fingers, "for you."

She smiled, and he couldn't help but think their thoughts were aligned. It was time to return to Swan Harbor.

"We want—"

Before he could complete his sentence, the door was opened, and a bell rang.

"It's time," Jenny shouted. "We know you are ready to leave, but you must stay for one last meal."

"But, we thought ..." Then he got a look at Hope's expression, and there was no way he could deny her.

"Well, wife," Ian teased. "Shall we?"

"Wife?" she giggled. "I'm your wife."

"And you're already being impudent."

"I am?"

"You did not answer the question," he pointed out.

"Oh!" Hope tossed her head, and once again he was besieged by the aroma from her head wreath. "You have seen nothing yet."

"That has me worried."

"You're not, are you?"

Ian winked and led her outside into the festive atmosphere. Music, assorted dishes, and even a small cake.

"I hope you like it," Jenny told them worriedly. "We were missing much, but …"

"Jenny," Hope exclaimed. "It's so much more than we expected."

"I hope you like it," Jenny repeated.

"We love it," Hope's gaze met Ian's, "do we not?"

"We do," he smiled.

For the next few hours, he tried to shut out the world. Tried to focus on his new bride. Yet there was something holding him back. Timber Creek had little to protect it from another attack. He and D.D. had tried to warn David and a few others. But they thought they were safe. How did he tell them they were not? That with one cove, they were very vulnerable?

"What is troubling you?" Hope surprised him by asking when they had a moment alone.

"Why do you say that?"

"Have you forgotten?" Hope questioned. "I can feel your heart." Then she hesitated and leaned closer. "I can feel you. And I feel your tension."

"I …" But neither did he wish to lie nor to worry her.

"Why, for instance?" she called him on what he'd hoped she'd missed. "Did you not move the El corazón to the dock once the mercantile ship left?"

"Noticed that, did you?"

"Ian."

He sighed, "I was worried about being boxed in."

"By Pence?"

"Or others."

She did not reply immediately, but just arched one of her coppery brows. "And?"

"The cove leaves you at a disadvantage," Ian finally admitted. "With the El corazón anchored as she is, we can see them before they see us."

"You have men watching?"

"Always."

It was still difficult for him to relax. So much so that once Hope was involved in an animated discussion with Jenny, he stepped away.

"You're worried, are you not?" D.D. asked before he'd said anything.

"How do you bloody know that?"

D.D. shrugged, "I feel it too."

"I was afraid you were going to say that." Ian trusted D.D. as no other but still hated putting burdens on him. "Are you sure?"

"Ian, son," D.D. began in his fatherly voice, "you have a new responsibility now. That is to Hope. Get your siren home to Swan Harbor. I will meet you there."

"If you are sure."

"I am." D.D. nodded toward where Hope was standing with Jenny. "Now get your bride, pack that big horse of hers, and go."

Ian grinned, his first relieved smile since they'd stepped outside, and went to collect his wife.

"Are you ready, love?" Ian whispered against the side of her head.

Hope leaned back against his chest. "I'm ready. Everything is packed and waiting."

"Let's go."

Ian took her hand, but before they could say their goodbyes, a shot rang out from the El corazón. Then five counts later, another.

"Pence," he spit. "D.D., I'll—"

"Take care of Hope!" D.D. shouted, already running toward the beach. "We'll see you in Swan Harbor."

With the men of Timber Creek taking charge of their residents, Ian looked around for Hope.

"I've got it," she came running, her packs in her arms. "Big Red just needs to be saddled."

Ian wanted to say so much, but there was no time. He had to trust and believe in others. D.D. would take care of the El corazón, and its men. And David would take care of his people. Hope needed him.

He climbed onto Big Red's back and adjusted to make room for Hope.

"Come on, love. Let's go home."

Halfway Home

5, April 1718
10:00 p.m.

THEY HAD STOPPED NOT FAR FROM TIMBER CREEK, AND HOPE HAD changed into her breeches. It was much easier to ride astride Big Red, and she felt secure in Ian's arms.

The position also allowed her to feel the tension Ian was holding onto. Hours had passed before he'd completely let go of it. As he'd relaxed, they'd both realized what was happening. They were married, alone for the first time, and with each step Big Red took, her backside rubbed against his front.

Ian had said nothing, but she knew he was affected. The question was, what was next?

They finally stopped for the night, and instead of allowing her to help, he sat her on a boulder. "I'll just be a moment."

She wanted to go to him, but something held her back. Once the fire was started, and she could see his face, she left him alone. He was nervous. Which somehow calmed her.

"Ian," Hope slid off the rock and slowly approached him as he spread a blanket on the grass. "That is not required."

His eyes met hers in the firelight, something mysterious hidden in their dark depths.

"Tonight ..." He shook his head as if the words mattered not. "You are so beautiful standing there. With the stars in your eyes, and the moonlight in your hair. Tonight is the night I will make you mine. And together we will be for the rest of time."

Her breath caught, and she wasn't sure who moved first, but she was in his arms. He cupped her face, and as he lowered his mouth to hers, she dug her fingers into his sides.

"Sweet." Ian's lips whispered across hers.

She could feel his heart race, and the longer, more drugging his kisses, the faster her heart beat. He dropped a kiss on her nose, and her stomach clenched. One on her cheek, and she wanted to grab hold, keeping him still.

Ian chuckled, the husky tone tightening the spell weaving around them. "I love you." He loosened the combs in her hair and carded his fingers through the long strands. "Your hair is just like fire."

Hope was reaching the point where it was no longer when was he going to touch her, but why wasn't he? Liquid heat settled in the pit of her stomach and slid down between her legs. Her knees weakened, and it was only the strong bands of his arms that held her upright.

The world tilted as Ian lifted her and bore her down to the blanket. "I wish I were lying with you on the finest silk," he murmured, burying his lips in her neck, and popping the first button on her shirt.

His lips never stayed in one place, and finally, she could stand it no longer. She grabbed fistfuls of his shirt and pushed him over, crawling on top.

"Now what?"

"What do you want?"

His question sent a shiver through her that had nothing to do with the night air. It was the way he made her feel. It was them.

"You, Ian," Hope told him, peeling her shirt off and tossing it aside.

"You're going to have to be more specific than that."

She studied him in the firelight, and something had her nipping his bottom lip.

"How was that?"

"Is that the best you can do?"

Hope slid backwards, over the fullness in his breeches, and his quick intake of air had her repeating the motion.

"Better?"

"Yes!" Ian whistled. "That feels much better."

But there was a tone in his voice that hadn't been there before. It was darker, hotter, sending thrills to that spot that needed his touch.

Her moves were unpracticed, and when she took off her shift and threw it aside, she wasn't sure what he would do. He hissed, his eyes trained on her bare breasts, their tips tight.

Ian licked his lips, and when they glistened, she wanted nothing more than to have them on her. She just wasn't quite ready for that yet, as she preferred to remain in control. Touching, teasing, and continuing to be in awe that such a man as Ian Jones had fallen for her.

"How did I get so lucky?"

It didn't take much to unbutton his shirt, freeing his entire chest for her perusal. The light fur on it was soft beneath her fingers, and she was helpless to stay away.

Hope placed a kiss in the center of his chest, and when he groaned, she felt it in *that* place. She could no longer resist and stretched out on top of him. Their sounds of pleasure mixed with the sounds of the night to create a world with only them.

Her movements were slow and unhurried, allowing her to feel her way. Allowing her to learn what he liked. Allowing her to learn what made him growl deep in his throat with pleasure. His body was hers to do with what she wished.

Then she realized his movements were becoming more frenetic. His hips lifting and lowering against hers. His hands touching and exploring in ways she'd never experienced.

"Am I wrecking you?" she asked, wondering how much more, and what she should do next.

His laughter should have warned her, but it wasn't until he'd reversed their position that she realized her power. He'd allowed her to touch, taste, and tease as long as she'd desired. With him gazing down at her, she could see what it had cost him.

"Now what?"

He rolled next to her and as her breeches disappeared, and the cool air brushed across their skin, her breath stopped.

"We become one." Ian's lips teased, mesmerized, and caused her to squirm against him. The ensuing friction between them generated a spark. She kept waiting for the inevitable pain, but the pressure from his fingers had her pushing to get closer.

"What's happening?" she asked breathlessly, feelings bubbling inside. "I cannot ..."

"That's natural."

He continued his assault on her senses until she could feel the tremors in his body.

"Ian!"

"Fight it not, love."

"But ..." Except before she could say anything, the feelings inside climbed and, before she was ready, slammed into her. She trembled, and tiny pinpoints of pleasure spread from the tips of her fingers to the soles of her feet.

"Hold on to me."

She wanted to say she was not going anywhere. Then he rolled her onto her back and settled between her legs. Ian covered her lips and gradually connected their bodies. The fit was tight and full, and Hope dug her hands into his waist as he moved.

"I'm sorry," he murmured, his speed picking up.

Hope kept thinking, *I need to do something*, but the feelings were too overwhelming. It was too much.

"Ahh, Hope," Ian grunted, and his big body shuddered, collapsing on top of her.

She wasn't sure how long he lay there before he propped himself up on his elbows. "I'm sorry, love."

"Is that not supposed to happen?"

"Oh, it's supposed to happen," he assured her. "But I wanted you to experience pleasure as well."

"I felt pleasure—"

"You did. With my fingers," Ian clarified. "I wanted you to feel pleasure with my body."

"Well, it was pleasant."

"Pleasant?" he repeated. "That's it?"

"You wished for more?"

"Yes, I bloody wished for more," Ian retorted.

"My mother always said, 'If you want to be good at something, you must practice.'"

He barked out a laugh. "Oh, she did? Then I guess we'll just have to practice."

Hope hissed when Ian moved too fast, and she was surprised when he just tucked her against him.

"We'll practice," he promised. "After all, we have all the time in the world."

SEVENTEEN

Halfway Home
6, April 1718
6:00 a.m.

Ian stared down at his bride and brushed a coppery curl off her face. She sighed softly and pressed her cheek against his hand. They'd just started their life together, and yet their bodies naturally reached for the other. How was he going to leave her behind to continue his mission?

"Wake up, Siren."

He kissed her lips and watched her eyes flutter open, her blue orbs locking on him.

"You're real," Hope murmured. "I thought I'd dreamed you."

Ian slid his hand up her bare torso and cupped one pert breast. "Does that feel like a dream?"

Her smile was shy, and a ruddy hue dotted her cheeks. He wanted to keep on touching but knew this was all new to her. Instead, he settled for a lengthy kiss.

"Why did you stop?"

"You're sore." He kissed her again because he couldn't resist. "Perhaps a soak in the hot springs would feel nice."

"That sounds lovely," Hope groaned. "Shall we go?"

Ian kissed once more, but rather than lingering, it was hard and quick. "To tide me over."

She laughed as he'd hoped and moved away from him to take care of her morning dressing. There was something that had him fighting not to pull her back. He'd never felt territorial about a female in his life, but with Hope, it was always there. A physical ache to have her nearby. What was it about her that made it so?

He forced himself to push it aside and readied Big Red for the trip. The horse was skittish, sidestepping away from the path, but Ian saw nothing. And then the wind picked up, blowing from the north, and he smelled it. Fire!

"Hope," he tried to hurry her without worrying her. "We should go."

When she stepped from behind a rock, she was busy winding her hair up onto her head. The image of them on a bed with silk sheets was so real, it almost brought him to his knees.

"Ian?"

He opened his eyes slowly, willing the dream not to fade. "I'm all right," he assured her. "But we should go. Do you smell that?"

"Smoke?" Her eyes grew large, wary. "In Swan Harbor?"

"It is coming from the north."

"But you know nothing for sure?"

"No, love."

They climbed onto Big Red and began their journey. It was quicker than the day before, and by mid-morning, they'd reached familiar terrain. As soon as they cleared the path and Swan Harbor lay before them, Ian knew something was wrong.

There was a thin layer of smoke hanging in the air. The smell lingered, settling over the cove, and decreasing visibility.

"I'm afraid that soak is going to have to wait."

"I know." Her tone said she felt something was off as well.

"Do you want me to take you straight home?"

"Or?"

"I thought I would stop by Henry's."

"Take me with you."

Ian reined in Big Red and turned Hope toward him. "What is it, love?"

"I cannot say," Hope admitted. "There is just something in the air I've not felt before. And it does not feel happy."

He had to agree, but rather than admitting that out loud, Ian held her a little tighter and directed the horse toward Henry's.

"Where shall we leave Red?"

"We can't tie him at Henry's?"

"What if he's seen?"

"That would require answering too many questions," Hope groaned. "Can we tie him in the cove or in the park?"

"We can try."

In the end, Ian led Red down a narrow trail toward the small cove where the El corazón had anchored. They tied him to a post and then took another trail to Henry's home.

"Do we tell him we were married?" Hope asked softly.

"I would like to shout it to the world," Ian assured her. "But your town, your rules."

Her smile was quick, and she grabbed his coat and kissed him. "We'll see. All right?"

Ian squeezed her fingers and knocked, hoping his friend was home, and alone.

It took several moments before the door was opened, and Henry stood on the other side. He was slightly more disheveled than usual. His hair was standing on end, as if he'd run his hands through it repeatedly. And his clothing was dirty, covered with something black. By the smell, Ian assumed soot.

"Ian, Hope!" Henry's body sagged with relief. "I ..."

"Henry?" Ian tightened his hold on Hope's hand. "What happened?"

Henry looked at him, distress clear not only in his voice, but in his body language. He said nothing, but turned and indicated they should follow him inside.

"My father?" Hope pushed when Henry didn't immediately offer any news.

"Your father has a stiff bandage on his leg, but he's alive," Henry assured her. "However, his head's not been right since the fire."

"I sense you are not sharing the entire story," Ian prodded. "What is it?"

Henry winced and buried his face in his hands. When he looked up, it was as if he'd aged. His eyes cut to Hope, and a sick feeling crawled into Ian's stomach.

"It's Martin, his wife," Henry hesitated a beat, swallowed, then continued, "and my sister, Marion, and her husband. They're gone."

Ian felt Hope sway from where she was sitting next to him, and he pulled her closer. "Gone? What happened?"

"I have to go home," Hope started to rise.

"Hold on, love," Ian whispered. "Just a little more."

Henry's eyes met his. "There was another fire."

Somehow, Ian had known that. He'd smelled it, felt Big Red's uneasiness, and noticed the telltale evidence left behind.

"They lived together?"

"In a way," Hope explained. "There was a large home that Widow Mars owned. At some point, it was divided."

"They were in their homes?" Ian asked Henry. "What about the others?"

"Eleven people perished in the fire."

"I have to go," Hope said again. This time, though, she didn't give him a chance to say anything before rushing to the door.

"Hope." Ian caught her just outside the house, her distress written on her face. "Let me go with you."

She leaned her head against his chest and, for just a second, he thought she would grant his wishes. But when she glanced up, and their eyes met, his hopes were lost.

"Ian, I want you with me," she told him. "But I cannot introduce you as my new husband in the middle of this grief. Especially since I have no idea how you will be received. Please tell me you understand."

"I understand," Ian sighed. "But I do not like it."

"Nor do I."

Her chin quivered, and Ian tugged her into his arms. "I would take your pain if I could."

"I know." Her arms tightened around his waist. "And I love you for it. There are just some things I must handle alone."

"May I see you later?"

"Will you be here?"

"I've nowhere else to go," Ian admitted, "until the El corazón returns."

"I'll find you," Hope promised.

Ian kissed her goodbye, pouring everything he was feeling into it, and slowly let her go. She waved and disappeared back down the path toward where they'd left Big Red.

"Hope's gone," he told Henry as soon as he'd stepped back into the house. "Tell me the rest."

Henry frowned. "How did you know?"

"That there was more?"

"Yes."

Ian shrugged. "The look on your face. What are you leaving out?"

"Where do I start?" Henry brushed his hands through his hair and moved to the window. "I compared the two ledgers."

"The dock ledger and the one for the lighthouse?"

"Yes." Henry sighed, his agitation on full display. "You were right ... about George, that is."

"How?"

"There were three times the Black Dandy docked," Henry explained. "And George was supposed to work."

"From the look on your face," Ian surmised, "George was not where he was meant to be."

"Right."

"Did you talk to him?"

"Yesterday."

"Spit it out, Henry," Ian cried. "What happened?"

Henry blew out a frustrated breath. "I went to George yesterday and asked him why. At first, he denied everything."

"Eventually, though, he admitted someone had paid him to 'be sick', right?"

"Yes," Henry nodded. "As I said before, George is fond of liquor and the cards."

"Who was it?" Ian barked, wanting to ask a few questions himself.

"Oliver Maddok," Henry admitted.

"Hope's suitor?"

"Yes."

The pieces swirled around in Ian's head, and after several trips across Henry's great room, a picture was forming.

"So, Maddok paid George to work the lighthouse," Ian began. "He 'signaled' to the ship whether it was safe to dock. What was in it for him?"

"Money," shrugged Henry.

"Did you confront Maddok?"

"No. I was going to do that today."

"Let's go." Then, Ian got another look at Henry's expression. "What have you not told me?"

Henry dropped his head, and a look of anguish crossed his face. "George and his wife lived in the same house as Martin and Marion."

"George is dead as well?" Ian frowned. "Do you believe Maddok took care of the other two suitors, set the fire at the sheriff's, and George's?"

"Yes," Henry nodded. "I also believe that after I left George, he spoke to Maddok."

"They lived close?"

"They lived in the same house," Henry sighed. "I think Maddok got nervous and set the fire, hoping everyone would assume he died too."

"But you're telling me that's not the case?"

"I am," Henry agreed. "Especially now that you're here."

"Meaning?"

Henry took a bag from the table and tossed it toward Ian. "Those were found in the debris."

Ian upended the bag, and five buttons dropped onto his hand. "Bloody hell."

"My thoughts too," Henry grunted. "But who had a duster with the same buttons as yours?"

"These are my buttons," Ian confided. "They have the Joneses crest on them. The question is, how did they get my duster? And who was it?"

"I know not," Henry replied. "Those buttons were found under a metal trunk, along with another body and some metal strips. Doctor Williams said the other person was a female."

"Why would he say female as opposed to it being Maddok?"

"He believes the metal straps were from a woman's stays."

"So, where's Maddok?"

"That's where we have a problem," Henry confided. "There was a merchant ship that left late last night. It's bound for Boston. I believe Maddok set the fire and jumped on the ship."

"Is that not good?" Ian asked. "That he is gone?"

"While there are many reasons, it is good," Henry explained. "There are just as many that are not, the most prominent one being, Swan Harbor's heart is missing."

"Swan Harbor's heart?" Ian echoed, his pulse suddenly racing.

"It's a ruby that's as red as blood," Henry explained. "It's believed to bring the town life, just as the swans bring us hope."

"Without this ruby, Swan Harbor will die?"

"As long as we have hope, Swan Harbor can live without its heart." Henry shrugged. "But if we lose hope—"

"Is Hope's father looking for the heart?" Ian interrupted.

"That's where the real problem comes in," Henry sighed. "Geoffrey believes the heart was stolen ... by pirates."

"Pirates?" Ian exclaimed. "Who?"

"You."

"Bloody hell!" Ian frowned. "Why me?"

"I know not," Henry admitted. "However, you were in Timber Creek, with Hope. Why then are you worried?"

Ian cut a glance in his friend's direction. The look on Henry's face was one of curiosity and not accusatory.

"Why would you ask?"

"Your expression, the tone of your voice," Henry shrugged.

Ian searched for the right words. "Can you draw me a picture of this ruby?"

"Why?"

"Humor me," Ian tossed back.

He held his breath for several moments before Henry nodded and went to get something to draw on.

"I'm no artist."

Ian watched as Henry drew exactly what he'd anticipated. One-half of a heart with shaded lines to show the many facets.

"The ruby varies from light red to dark," Henry went on in a hushed voice. "With the uneven edges of the stone, when the light shines on it just right—"

"—It appears to be breathing," Ian murmured.

"Yes!" Henry frowned. "Except how do you know about it?"

"I read about it," Ian admitted. But the look on Henry's face had him offering, "While I was at the University."

"Interesting," Henry hummed. "I was not aware there was a story behind it. All I've heard is it belonged to Hope's grandparents."

Ian wanted to say more, but that could wait. He had some research to do ... as soon as his ship returned.

※

Hope's Home
6, April 1718
1:00 p.m.

HOPE WIPED HER HANDS ON HER PETTICOAT AND TOOK THE LAST few steps to her father's den. Just as she lifted her hand to knock, the murmur of voices made her hesitate.

"What do you have to say for yourself, Geoffrey?" a woman asked. "All of this is your fault."

"My fault?" her father questioned, his voice sounding weary. "I followed my heart."

"When you should have listened to me."

Hope peered through the doorway and could see the side of her father. He was sitting next to the desk, one leg straight in front of him, as Henry had mentioned.

Isabelle Williams was pacing in front of the fireplace, her movements agitated and erratic.

Why was Isabelle blaming her father for something? And what was he being blamed for?

"I should have listened to you," Geoffrey went on, "about what?"

"The life we were meant to have," Isabelle cried.

Geoffrey sighed. "Isabelle, I've told you many times, Christine was my life. She was the woman I was meant to spend my days with. You just could not ... would not understand."

"Because you did not know your own mind," Isabelle tossed out angrily. "The things we said to each other before we left England—"

"Were the ramblings of two young people thinking they knew everything."

"But I loved you."

"When you love someone, do you not wish them well?" Geoffrey questioned.

"I wished you to be happy," Isabelle hesitated a beat, "with me."

"I loved Christine," Geoffrey repeated. "I never believed ..."

"What?" Isabelle wanted to know. "That she could make you as miserable as she did?"

"Do you really believe that?" He was quiet for so long, Hope wondered if he was going to tell Isabelle to leave. Then, he went on, almost conversationally. "I did not expect you to be happy for me. But I did expect you to accept my decision. When you muttered those crazy words on the night Christine and I announced we were betrothed, I brushed them aside."

Hope pressed her hand against her mouth to keep from crying out. Words? What words?

"You should have known better than that," Isabelle told him. "I rarely say things I do not mean."

"It was Christine who convinced me you were just speaking out of turn," Geoffrey replied tiredly. "She was the kindest, most caring, and most loving woman I have ever known. In her eyes, you were hurt and angry, and would eventually find a man of your own."

"Oh, yes," Isabelle spit, "good old Christine could do no wrong."

"No one is perfect," Geoffrey continued. "But she was just about as perfect as a person could be. When Swan Harbor took a turn, and it appeared our hope was dying, I reminded her of your words. I wanted to find a way to undo the hatred. You know what she said, though?"

"I'm sure you're going to tell me," Isabelle retorted.

"Christine said, 'Geoffrey, hearts connected by love is what will save Swan Harbor. And the more love in our town, the more hope and happiness there will be'. I wanted to believe she was right," Geoffrey sighed. "To believe that our love was the key to saving our family."

Hope dashed away the tears running down her face and tried to sort through everything she was hearing. While it reiterated her thoughts about her father keeping something from her. It did not tell her what.

"We could have that," Isabelle pushed. "Our love could save your family."

"You seem to have forgotten two very important facts, my dear," Geoffrey taunted. "You are married to Edmund. And I do not love you."

"But you could learn."

"Isabelle," Geoffrey's voice was low, each word enunciated clearly. "I'm never going to love you. If I had thought killing you would have saved my family; I would have done it long ago."

"You're not man enough," Isabelle taunted.

"I would do anything to save the future of my family, Isabelle. You should know that."

"Oh, that's right," Isabelle hummed. "Even marry little Hope off to someone she'd never bed. Stop the line, save the family."

Marry her off…

Hope's thoughts tumbled over, sorting through pieces of conversation regarding the men who'd courted her. Men her father knew were not good men. Had his hope been to keep her from having children and a happy home? But why?

"Leave Hope out of this," Geoffrey uttered. "You've won, Isabelle. I've lost everything. Christine was the light in our family and in my life. While I did not know what Maddok was ultimately capable of, my association with him has cost me my heart and my hope. And not just the feeling inside that everything will work out. It had cost me my daughter, and my son Martin and his wife. What are you waiting for? You want my beating heart too? Take it. I do not care what happens to me."

"It's not over," Isabelle hissed.

"You're mad," Geoffrey scoffed. "Take your husband and your two children and go live your life. Just know this. I will never stop searching for the key to set my family and my town free of your hateful words. They might have been muttered to make your heart heal. But they were vengeful, hateful words. Everyone who suffers, their pain, will come back to you. Hope will live on in Swan Harbor. The swans led us here for a reason. If even one is left, our hope will not die."

"And what about your heart, Geoffrey?"

"You know how it is, Isabelle," Geoffrey responded. "For years, you've held onto hope in that delusional mind of yours that we would be together. You have no heart. You're just an empty, soulless body. Which means that as long as there is hope in Swan Harbor, it can live without its heart. Now get out of my home before I throw you out."

Isabelle laughed, the sound sending a chill up Hope's spine. "You're all talk, Geoffrey. Just as always."

It was quiet for several seconds, and Hope waited. But then she heard her father take a quick breath, and the chair creaked as if he were moving.

"Isabelle, what are you doing?"

"What does it look like?"

A shot rang out, the sound echoing around the house.

"No!"

Hope pushed open the door, meeting Isabelle on her way out.

"I hope he dies," Isabelle snarled, shoving Hope against a wall where her head bounced, and everything went black.

EIGHTEEN

El corazón del Rubí
6, April 1718
5:00 p.m.

Ian pushed past D.D. and stalked across the deck to his cabin. How could he have forgotten the answers he had sought?

"Where's Hope?" D.D. called. "Ian? Talk to me!"

"What shall I say?" Ian snapped. "We arrived back in Swan Harbor, married and happy. Only to discover death and grief that seem to just keep getting worse."

"Keep going."

"Keep going, he says," Ian grumbled and quickly explained about the fire. "Hope refused to allow me to go with her. It's been hours, and I've had no word."

"There's more," D.D. pushed. "You've kept your love for Hope secret for months. What else happened?"

"When you saved Simon from a sure hanging, I thanked you," Ian began.

"You did," D.D. agreed. "And volunteered to help me rescue Richard."

"It was the least I could do." Ian hesitated and watched D.D.'s face closely as he uttered the next words, "However, the night before we left, I overheard a conversation that filled in a few holes."

There was a slight tightening in D.D.'s jaw, and Ian had to wonder if, at some point, his first mate had expected the conversation.

"What do you think you heard?"

Ian let out a dry laugh. "I think you know what I heard. While there are many answers I still seek, it explained all those times Mum hid Simon and me beneath the cupboard."

"To hide you from the magistrate," D.D. replied. "The ones looking for your father."

"Was it the magistrate?" Ian questioned. "Or were they treasure hunters ... land pirates, if you will?"

"Looking for?"

Ian opened the secret compartment and removed the contents.

"This." He opened his palm, and in it lay the ruby Henry had drawn. The matching half of Swan Harbor's heart.

"Bloody hell," D.D.'s mouth dropped open. "It's real."

"Did you doubt?"

"I did," D.D. frowned. "Especially after ..."

"After what?" Ian studied the other man and wondered if he'd jumped too far ahead.

D.D. ran his hands through his salt and pepper hair and moved to the porthole. When he began speaking, his voice was soft, and Ian had to concentrate to make out all the words.

"I first met your father in debtor's prison, not long after you were born. He carried on about a gemstone that held magical properties. Said the one holding it would have his greatest desire granted."

"Did he tell you he had this stone?"

"No," D.D. frowned. "It was just assumed."

"And so, when you were released from prison," Ian guessed. "You made sure my father was as well."

"I did." D.D. wandered around the cabin for several moments before continuing, "Years went by, and I thought nothing of the stone until Simon began courting my daughter, Clarissa."

"Then somehow the conversation came back around?"

"It did," D.D. confirmed. "Except I no longer wanted the stone for myself. I wanted it for my son, Richard."

"Was this before Pence took him?"

"Pence had been seen around the village recruiting," D.D. replied. "Richard was easily led, and I thought if I had the stone, it would give my son the knowledge he needed to move on to other things."

"Did you research the stone?" asked Ian. "Did Simon?"

D.D. shrugged, which gave Ian his answer.

"Then what happened?"

"Simon claimed your father had sold the stone to the Pickering's and well …"

"Old man Pickering did not take too kindly to Simon's insinuations?" Ian offered, although he knew the situation had been much more dire.

"But how do you have the stone?" D.D. questioned. "And why did Simon believe it to have been sold?"

Ian glanced down at the stone in his hand. With the light touching it, just as he'd told Henry, it appeared to be breathing.

"My father stole the stone, but I know not from whom," Ian began his tale. "When I returned to England to go to the university, my mum gave it to me. She wanted me to sell it, but I wanted to learn about it."

"And did you?" D.D. asked. "Learn about it?"

Ian laid the stone on the desk and opened his journal. "You know the myth of Vega and Altair, do you not?"

"She was a Goddess, Altair a man, and her father placed them in the heavens."

"Yes," Ian confirmed. "They are separated in the sky, and only together for one night every seven years."

"Why did you ask?"

Ian ran his finger over the gemstone, which felt warm to the touch instead of cold.

"There's more to the myth, a little-known fact," he explained. "The story is, Vega was so distraught, she took out her heart, ripped it in half, and flung the parts far and wide. But the next time her star was with Altair's, it was no longer the same, because their hearts were no longer beating as one."

"Let me guess," D.D. laughed. "The pieces must be reunited."

"So says the story," Ian acknowledged. "To locate the other half, you must listen to your heart. And to do that, you must have hope."

"Which brings you back to your heart research."

"How could this be?" Ian practically shouted. "Until today, I'd forgotten I'd placed this stone in that compartment for safekeeping."

"You've had other things on your mind," D.D. tried to console him. "What reminded you?"

"It seems," Ian confessed. "I was not brought to Swan Harbor randomly but led here by that piece of rock."

"Why do you say that?"

"Because I just learned," Ian sighed. "Hope's family has the other half. It's referred to as The Heart of Swan Harbor."

"The tone of your voice tells me there's more to that story."

"Swan Harbor's heart was stolen," Ian grumbled. "And Geoffrey believes I took it."

"That is a problem," D.D. agreed. "I'm assuming this means not only are we searching for Pence, but for the stone as well."

"It would seem so." Ian checked the time, deciding he'd given Hope long enough. He was going after her. "Perhaps my wife can share more information with me regarding their half of the stone, and its origins."

"Does that matter?" D.D. questioned. "If you and Hope marry, and reunite the stones, it seems everyone is happy."

"It depends," Ian confided. "On if that is the end of the story ... or just the beginning."

"Meaning?"

Ian sighed. "Meaning there might be more. Is it enough to have hope and locate both halves of the heart, or must the ruby also be reunited with something greater?"

"What are you saying?"

"I found mention of a ruby heart, the size of a man's hand, being part of a set called Las Joyas del Mar."

"The jewels of the sea?"

"Yes," Ian nodded. "So, which is it? Do I reunite the heart and leave it in Swan Harbor? Or do I reunite the heart and keep searching for the rest of the jewels?"

"What happens if the jewels are reunited?"

"Eternal life."

"Is that what you wish for?" D.D. questioned him. "To live forever, but alone?"

"Of course not," Ian shot back. "I wish to live forever … with Hope. Without her, life would not be worth living."

"There's your answer," D.D. pointed out. "So, now what?"

Ian slipped the stone into his pocket and put his journal away. "I'm going to see Hope. Her response will give me our next step."

D.D. nodded and left the cabin. But as Ian jumped into the small craft and rowed to shore, he couldn't help but think the story could have many endings. Not all of them to his liking.

On his way to see Hope, Ian took the trail through town. He wanted to know if there had been more information leaked regarding the fire … or the jewel. He saw no one, heard nothing, except for a coach followed by a wagon piled high.

Ian stepped out of its path, his eyes meeting those of a young boy, about twelve. The child appeared distraught and was staring out the window as if he were seeing the town for the last time.

A fire, Maddok leaving town, the missing heart, and someone moving when the rest of the citizens were in mourning. The child was pulled away from the window, and just before the coach turned, Ian's gaze met those of the woman he'd seen outside the sheriff's building the day of the fire. Her eyes flared with recognition—and something else. And he couldn't help but think she held the pieces to a puzzle—he just wasn't sure which one.

As he neared Hope's, he saw the home was dark, save for a lone candle. He almost returned to the ship, leaving her family to grieve alone. But the closer he drew, the more his heart ached. Except they weren't his feelings, they were hers.

Ian didn't think twice and climbed the trellis, landing quietly on her balcony. He tugged the door open, took one step inside, and before he caught his breath, she was in his arms.

"Ian," Hope sobbed. "You came. You came."

"Hope, what …?"

"Just hold me," she cried. "Please, just hold me."

His heart twisted, and while he knew she was upset regarding Martin, there was more to her pain. He could feel it.

"I'm here, love," Ian whispered, carrying her to the bed and sitting with her on his lap. "Talk to me."

Hope's Home
6, April 1718
11:00 p.m.

Hope lost track of how long Ian held her, and she cried in his arms. Eventually, the tears slowed enough for her to explain what had happened.

"Who found you?" Ian snapped. "Where's your father? Is he all right?"

"No one found us," Hope sighed. "When I woke up, I stumbled to my father's side. There was so much blood." The thought sent a shiver running through her body. But Ian tightened his arms and after several moments, she felt strong enough to continue. "I tore one of my petticoats and wrapped the rags around my father's hand and head."

"Was Geoffrey awake?"

"No." Hope closed her eyes, and the memory of seeing her father lying on the floor washed over her. "He was so still, and the only way I knew he was alive was by listening to his heartbeat. Except the blood wouldn't stop. It just kept soaking the bandages." She hesitated and wiped her hand across her nose before continuing. "I finally decided if help did not arrive, he would die."

"So, you ran to get Doctor Williams?"

"Yes, Anne was here when I returned." Hope sat up, her eyes meeting Ian's in the candlelight. "I did not tell her what I'd overheard."

"Do you not believe she could have filled in some of the holes?" Ian questioned. "She might even tell us the words Isabelle spoke."

"I know this ... in my head," Hope explained. "Except, how could I tell her that not only did her daughter possibly *curse* my family ... but Isabelle had shot my father?"

"Wait a moment." Ian's voice was tense, as if he'd just learned something displeasing. "Did you just say Anne's daughter's name is Isabelle?"

"Yes, why?"

"Their coach passed by me on my way here," he explained. "There was a boy, around twelve, with his face pressed to the window."

"She's running," Hope realized. "Just as my father told her to do ... before she shot him."

"Are you going to tell Anne and the Constable?"

"I have to say something," Hope admitted. "I just don't know what."

Then she remembered Isabelle's question about the heart and her father's response. There had to be more.

"At least my father did not wish me to marry those men." Hope pressed closer to Ian. "I just do not understand why he could not trust me."

"And what is meant by finding the key?" Ian murmured.

His hand rubbing circles on her lower back was meant to be soothing. But there was something about being alone in a dark room with her husband that sent her thoughts on a wayward trajectory. One more pass and Hope jumped from his lap and crossed to her bureau, her hands busy with her hair.

"Hope," Ian's husky voice whispered across her skin. "Look at me."

"I cannot."

"Hope."

She closed her eyes and finished removing her combs before turning around. "Yes, Ian."

"Did I do something wrong?"

"No!" Hope quickly assured him. "But ..."

"We're alone for the first time," Ian took a step in her direction, "since our wedding night."

"Yes."

He tugged her into his arms. "And you're wondering what it would be like to make love in a bed."

Hope pushed away and stormed across the room. "How evil must I be?"

"To what?" Ian questioned. "To want to spend time in your husband's arms in a big soft bed instead of on the hard ground?"

"Yes!"

"I want nothing more ... than to spend the rest of the night wrapped around you," he went on. "However, after you left, Henry shared more, and it just ..."

Hope's head popped up, but the look on his face didn't quite match his words.

His heart was racing. She could feel it. Except there were other emotions going on inside of him she wasn't familiar with.

"What is it, Ian?"

"It seems your father believes I've taken Swan Harbor's heart," Ian surprised her by saying. "In the conversation you overheard, were there any hints given about the heart?"

"Why would my father think you had taken Swan Harbor's heart?"

"I know not," Ian admitted. "But ..."

He stuck his hand into his pocket, and when he held it out, the heart lay on his palm.

A chill ran through her body. Perhaps the heart was the only thing he'd been looking for in Swan Harbor. But that made no sense.

"You found the heart?"

"No." Ian closed his fist around the stone, and the intense look on his face had her wondering what he was thinking. "Do you trust me?"

"Yes!" Hope slid her hands up his chest and around his neck. "Tell me."

The candlelight flickered in his dark eyes, and she couldn't help but wish things were different.

"Tell me," she urged him again.

Ian bowed his head, and his curls curtained his face, hiding his expression from her.

"Will you tell me about Swan Harbor's heart first?"

"Why?"

"Let's just say," a corner of Ian's mouth curved, "there are some details about this stone that are murky. Perhaps hearing about yours will fill in some blanks."

"All right."

Hope sat on the side of the bed and patted the space beside her. Once he was seated, she dug into her memory banks.

"The heart-shaped stone has belonged to my father's family for generations. It rested on a pedestal in the family home, and as long as it was there, the ground was fertile, and the people prospered. Then, the village was overrun by a group of miscreants, and as they were leaving, one of them dropped the stone, and it split in half."

"Two halves of a whole," Ian murmured. "When was that?"

"Long before my father and the others came to the Colonies."

"When was that?"

"1692." Hope studied him for a few seconds. "Why?"

"Did anything change when there was only half of the stone?"

"In the village?"

"Yes."

"I cannot say." She thought back to the conversations she'd had with her mother when she was younger. "Why?"

Ian shrugged and changed the subject so quickly, she had to rush to catch up. "You need a wedding ring."

"I do." Hope couldn't help but wonder what he was running from. "But we need to tell my father about us first. For now, though, finish the story."

Ian took a deep breath, and she could tell the story made him uncomfortable. "D.D. and my father met in debtor's prison a few years after I was born. My father told grandiose stories about a stone with magical abilities."

"Your father stole the stone from my family?"

"Not then," Ian shook his head. "However, I believe my father knew who did. Then somehow, he later ended up with it."

"Did he give it to you?"

"No, that was my mum, long after my father was gone," he admitted. "She told me to sell it."

"It's worth quite a large amount of money." Hope hesitated and studied the expression on his face for a second. "That mattered not to you, did it? What did you learn?"

A pink tint crawled across his cheekbones. "How did you know?"

"Ian ..." Hope arched a red-gold brow and waited for him to continue.

"Oh, all right."

He caught her off-guard when he cupped her face and kissed her. His lips teased, making her head swim. Hope dug her fingers into the bedding as the kiss went on, pulling her under.

When he finally released her lips, her heart was racing along with his. She wanted to crawl into his lap and spend hours in his arms. If only ...

"What I learned," Ian began, his voice husky, sending shivers up her spine, "is it could be Vega's heart."

"What?"

"Vega and Altair," Ian repeated, before explaining the myth. "Or ..."

"Or?"

"The heart could be a part of something bigger."

"What shall we do?"

"You need to find out why your father believes I took the bloody heart," Ian retorted. "I'll try to track down Maddok in Boston. Perhaps when I return, we can speak with your father."

Her heart flipped. "I want that." Then something floated through her head.

"What is it, love?"

"Jenny said something to me that has me wondering about the possibility."

Ian grinned, but instead of saying something, he kissed her cheek, then her mouth.

"I'm waiting." His lips whispered across her ear.

"Shesheshe," Hope cleared her throat and tried again. "She said people do not see the man you are because of your clothing. What if …?"

"I dress differently?" Ian pulled his shirt away from his chest, and his dark eyes clashed with her blue ones. "If I dressed more respectably, would your father allow me to court you?"

Hope's hands closed into fists. "Until we find out the words that Isabelle spoke, I cannot see my father wishing me to marry anyone. He believes he's protecting the future of our family."

Ian cupped his hands under her arms and scooted her up onto the bed. "Then we must find the bloody key. But now …"

His mouth covered hers, and as her heart raced to catch his, all thoughts of the key were shoved aside. Her focus was centered on uncovering all her husband's secrets.

NINETEEN

Henry's Home
15, September 1718
9:00 a.m.

As soon as the El corazón was docked, he left D.D. in charge and ran up the trail toward Henry's. The spring and summer had been among the most difficult times of his life.

Ian had been left doing what he could instead of what he'd wanted. However, in the past month, life had been looking up for them all. Which made him most eager to see how his plans were faring.

Since the incident in April, Hope had been left to care for her father. The lead ball from the pistol had gone through Geoffrey's right hand and then grazed his temple. With the loss of both his right arm and the vision in his right eye, he'd become uncommunicative.

Just how close he came to losing his life, Hope would not discuss. Except it had been too close for her to take the chance and tell her father about them. Especially since Geoffrey had still believed the pirate who had rescued him from the fire had taken the heart of Swan Harbor. They'd made the best of it, though. And Ian had to admit, he was getting rather adept at climbing the trellis.

He knocked on Henry's door and, while waiting for it to be answered, glanced toward the cove. There were three adult swans and one brownish cygnet left, with the rest already gone in anticipation of winter.

"Ian," Henry called, coming from the direction of the lighthouse. "How goes it?"

"Why are the swans still here?" Ian asked instead of answering Henry's question.

"The cygnet cannot fly yet," Henry explained. "Should be any day though."

Ian nodded, but when the thought, *they stayed to give Geoffrey hope with his healing,* flew through his head, he realized he'd become one of them.

"And everything else?" Ian asked, praying his plan had worked.

Henry's eyes twinkled as he led them inside. "I knew you'd expect me to have everything ready when you arrived."

"Sorry," Ian replied sheepishly. "It's just been weeks—"

"—Since you've seen Hope," Henry laughed. "I know."

"Speaking of females," teased Ian. "How is the lovely Felicity?"

"She's fine," Henry murmured, his face turning red. "Just fine."

"Just fine?"

"You know what I mean," Henry sputtered, spreading several pieces of parchment on the table. "There." He effectively changed the subject. "That should get your attention."

Ian looked over Henry's notes, impressed by how meticulous they were. "These are very thorough."

"I wanted to help," Henry mumbled.

"Plus, while Geoffrey was indisposed, it did not hurt you were working with the Constable," Ian pointed out, "who just happens to be Felicity's father."

"You are right. It did not hurt," Henry agreed. "I do not wish to be like you, married and forced to visit under the dark of night."

Ian winced. "I cannot say I blame you."

"I'm sorry."

"No, tis I who am sorry," Ian assured him, turning his attention to what Henry had uncovered.

The mysteries surrounding the fire were being revealed a little at a time. However, there were still two bodies without identities.

"So, the body found close to my buttons was not Sly Bill?" Ian asked, his mind going in multiple directions.

"No." Henry pointed to his notes. "My mother reported she left lunch for the Sheriff and Sly Bill at 12:00 p.m. and was back in the tavern before 12:30 p.m. However, Mercy, who works with her husband in the apothecary, reports seeing two men running from behind the sheriff's building around 2:00 p.m."

"Which was about when we saw those men running back toward the Dandy," Ian surmised.

"I believe so," Henry nodded. "Plus, one of the men on the bucket line says he thinks he saw Bill on the deck of the Dandy as it left the harbor."

"Bloody hell, Henry," grumbled Ian. "It's been almost six months. Why did he say something just now?"

"Said he was waiting to be asked."

"Do you buy that?"

"No reason not to."

"Which is what you said about George," Ian reminded him.

Henry winced, and for a moment, Ian felt remorse for giving his friend grief.

"Was one of the men behind the sheriff's building Maddok?"

"That's what Mercy said," Henry acknowledged. He pointed to the timeline he'd created. "The men from the Dandy went in through the front, tussled with Geoffrey and left with Sly Bill. Maddok set the fire, and he and one other left out the back."

"Which means the man with Maddok was another prisoner, or from the Dandy?" Ian groused. "How was it he was not stopped?"

"People see what they want to see," Henry replied. "It's why, dressed as you are, you can come and go as you please."

Which had been Hope's plan when she'd said the same thing, he thought, glancing at his new clothing. Fawn-colored breeches, a linen shirt, a striped waistcoat, and a velvet longcoat. "I appear quite the dandy, do I not?"

"Especially with that cravat tied as it should be," Henry smirked. "And with those spectacles and your hair cut short as it is, you are not recognized."

"They see not the pirate," Ian murmured. "But Professor Samuel Jones, who is much more respectable."

"I still do not understand why you will not step out with Hope, as the Professor."

"And neither does Hope," Ian confessed. "All I can say is I want to be able to step out with her ... as me."

"I pray that happens soon, Professor." Henry turned back to the last two things on the table. "And if this is what you were hoping ..."

Ian looked at The Boston Newsletter, dated 01 September 1718.

Geoffrey Prince of Swan Harbor attended the Governor's Ball last week. He was in Boston recovering the ruby that had been stolen from him earlier in the year.

"And?" Ian glanced at Henry. "Did it have the desired effect?"

"Well," Henry grinned. "I guess that all depends on what your goal was. If it was to get Geoffrey out of bed and on his way to Boston, it worked."

Ian couldn't keep from smiling. "That's excellent news, Henry. Now with a little luck, Geoffrey will locate Maddok, retrieve the ruby, and my name will be cleared."

"You're not hoping for much," Henry laughed. "Are you?"

"No, not much." Ian glanced around the room before finishing his request.

"If you're looking for the basket," Henry thumbed out the window. "It's waiting for you in the cave."

"Excellent!"

Ian quickly stacked the papers, and after thanking Henry, ran back down the trail to the ship. He left the paperwork for D.D. to study and took the back way to the cave.

He was eager to see his bride. The past few months had taken their toll on her, and her usual sparkle had been missing of late. With Geoffrey gone, he was hoping ...

Big Red's greeting had him leaving the cave behind to see Hope sliding gracefully to the ground. She glanced in his direction, and when their eyes met across the meadow, he had to grab hold of the rock to keep from racing to her side.

"It took you long enough."

Hope pushed the hood of her cape back, and when the sun glinted off her coppery curls, it took his breath.

"You did not say what time," she tossed out. "I believe the fault lies with you."

"Oh, you do?" Ian's steps toward her were slow, deliberate. "How can I ever make it up?"

She laughed, and there was an undercurrent he hadn't heard before. "I'm sure I can think of something."

"I'm sure you can." Ian tilted his head and studied her for a second. "But what's wrong?"

"How do you know something's wrong?" Hope blew out her breath.

"Because," he closed the distance between them and tugged her into his arms. Except with all her petticoats and cape, he was having a difficult time feeling the woman beneath. "You did not run into my arms as you are wont to do."

"And now it seems as if I must make it up to you."

Ian kissed her, not giving her a chance to say anything more. He'd missed her. His mouth captured her plump bottom lip, and he tugged her as close as possible. She sighed, and he willingly took the kiss deeper, thinking he would never tire of her taste. Nor of the feel of her in his arms.

Hope hummed with pleasure, and the image of them making love, surrounded by flowers, raced through his mind.

"That was nice," she murmured when he'd released her mouth.

"Nice," Ian scoffed. "It appears I need to work on my technique."

"Feel free." She puckered her lips at him.

"I'll show you practice." Ian swung her around and dipped her over one arm. Then he dropped a kiss on her mouth that he felt to the soles of his feet. "How was that?"

Hope said nothing right away. Instead, she laid her hands over her mouth, almost as if she were making sure her lips felt the same.

"That was ..." Hope's gaze met his and suddenly her eyes pooled.

"Hope," Ian tugged her back into his arms, "talk to me."

She buried her face against his chest, and he could feel her body shaking. Great sobs wracked her, and he tightened his arms around her. Wanting, needing to take her pain.

"I'm sorry," Hope murmured. "May we sit?"

"Yes, yes." Ian looked around for a place. "Hold on." He ran back to the cave to get the blanket he'd asked Henry to pack.

As soon as Ian was out of sight, Hope let go of the breath she was holding. There was much she wanted to say, but where should she start?

"We can sit on this," Ian returned, bringing with him a blanket. "Where shall I lay it?"

"There." She showed him a flat place that overlooked the cove, and the swans swimming below. "All right?"

He spread the blanket, but when they sat, she kept a slight distance between them.

"Hope?"

She glanced in his direction, and what she saw wasn't him. Slowly, Hope removed his spectacles and slipped them into his pocket. His cravat was tucked away. Then she couldn't keep from running her hands through his dark hair. "I miss your curls."

Ian chuckled. "Short is bloody better on a windy day at sea."

"I wouldn't know," she pouted. "My husband is a brute and will not take me sailing."

"He's going to have to remedy that."

"I'd like that."

Ian smiled at her, and just as always, that funny feeling in the pit of her stomach grew. But she couldn't say what needed to be said if they did *that*. She linked their fingers and scooted closer. "Is this all right?"

"Fine." His lips whispered across her cheek. "For now."

"My father is on his way to Boston."

"Henry told me."

"Will he find Maddok?"

"I hope," Ian admitted. "Did you find out why he believed it was I who took the ruby?"

"Maddok."

"Maddok?" Ian echoed.

Hope sighed, mentally and emotionally exhausted after six months of caring for her father. Months of not knowing whether he would live or die. If he could use his right hand or arm, see out of his wounded eye, or communicate in any meaningful way.

However, in the past few weeks, he'd begun to talk to her. His sentences were short, and sometimes he forgot what he wanted to say. Finally, though, he had trusted her with several important facts.

"I guess a day after the fire at the sheriff's office, Maddok came to the house. He wanted to know where I was. My father lied and said I was visiting friends. Then Maddok said, 'Good. I wouldn't want to think she was with that pirate. You know he's the one who took Swan Harbor's heart, right'?"

"What?" Ian stopped her. "Maddok knew about us?"

"That's what it sounded like." Hope thought back to that conversation. Something about it was off, though. "When my father asked how Maddok knew that, he was told a man wearing a long black coat had been seen sneaking away from the building. The same coat as the man who'd carried him from the fire."

"Part of that story is true," Ian grumbled. "Maddok and someone wearing my coat were seen behind the building. But did your father believe it was me?"

Hope thought back to her father's expression, and the look in his one good eye. "I think he knew the person in the coat, and the person who carried him from the building were not the same."

"What else did he say?"

"My father says he does not remember the words," she confided, knowing Ian wanted to know more about the curse. "Just the meaning behind them."

"I do not want to hear this, do I?" Ian wrapped his arm around her waist and tightened his hold on her.

"Probably not," Hope acknowledged. "But after his explanation, everything makes more sense."

"Tell me."

Hope took a deep breath, as she still had not spoken to Anne. Hurting the woman who'd taken over the care of her brothers was the last thing she wanted to do.

"He still believes we need to be set free with a key."

"Bloody hell," Ian retorted. "I need more to go on than that. How do I find a bloody key when I have no idea what I'm to search for?"

Hope tightened her hold on Ian's hand. She knew he was frustrated, but so was she. Especially since ...

"Remember what my mother said? She felt hearts connected by love would save Swan Harbor. And there is something to the idea that when there's an engagement, or wedding, or new baby coming, there's more hope in the air."

"I'm going to track down Isabelle," Ian confided.

"You will not hurt her?

"I could," he snapped, "and easily. But no, I will not hurt her."

"Do you think she cares how powerful her words were?"

"Someone who would say those words only cares about herself. But Hope," Ian tilted her chin, forcing her eyes to meet his, "if Isabelle had a broken heart, then your mother was right."

"About what?"

"That connected hearts can heal."

"The ruby pieces?"

"No, love," Ian whispered. "Connected hearts so full of love, they communicate in a way only they understand. Our love is powerful."

Hope blinked rapidly, trying to stem the flow of tears. "For a man who had never known much about love, your knowledge is great."

"I had an excellent teacher." He kissed her, and she fought not to get lost in the moment. "Hope."

"Oh, I ..." It took her a moment to realize he wasn't just referring to her. "You mean the swans."

"Not entirely," Ian confessed. "Because you have taught me much. However, there is something to having hope in your life. It gives you that extra feeling to conquer your dreams. Do you not believe the swans had something to do with your father's recovery?"

"Perhaps." Hope looked down at the cove where one swan seemed to watch over the others. "After my mother's death, that swan showed up," Hope murmured. "Except she does not come every year. Only in those years when I need her."

"Is it you she's watching?" Ian asked. "Or is it Geoffrey?"

"It feels as if she's watching us both."

"Perhaps," he agreed. "But why would you require her this year, when you have me?"

Hope cut a side-eyed look toward him, wondering if he was getting at something specific.

"I had a letter from Jenny," she offered a safer topic.

"Things are well with them, I trust."

"You can stop pretending you do not know." Hope nudged him with her shoulder. "She told me you stop to see Bernie and check on them every time you are in that area."

Ian gave her a sheepish smile. "I still feel Timber Creek is located in a very vulnerable place."

"Jenny also mentioned the El corazón had stopped at Serenity Cove. Is there a possibility they will move back?"

"I cannot say," he admitted cryptically. "We'll just have to wait and see."

Hope studied him, and something told her he knew more than he was saying, but she let it go.

"Did you also fail to tell me Jenny was with child?"

"I'm sorry." Ian dropped a kiss on her nose. "She wanted to tell you herself."

"It is good news."

"The best," he agreed. "Are you hungry?"

"I'm always hungry," Hope laughed. "However, I see no food."

"Wait here."

Hope watched him for several moments before turning back to observe the swans. There had been fewer of them this summer, and yet her mother's swan had appeared. How had she known Geoffrey was in trouble? Was there something to the connected hearts comment?

"What are you thinking, Siren?" Ian set a basket between them and began taking out several types of food.

"About the swans," she admitted. "There were fewer this year. Why? Is that because of those words?"

Her eyes met Ian's, and in them, she could tell he wanted to give her the world.

"I know not, Siren." Ian tilted his forehead against hers, and the gentle puff of his breath sent little shivers running up her spine. "I believe we shall take one problem at a time."

"Oh?" For the first time in a while, her heart felt lighter, as if some of her burden had been transferred. "What is first?"

Ian hummed. "First, I spread out this lovely supper Mrs. Patterson packed for us." He kissed her, making her head swim.

"And then?"

"We lie back on the blanket, and I show you Vega and Altair's stars." Ian kissed her again, this one longer and deeper than the first.

"I'm with you so far."

"Good, because the next item on the list is the most important."

Hope's heart raced in sync with his, and somehow, she could feel his emotions.

"You already know."

He chuckled and tugged her fully into his arms. "That you are carrying our child? Yes, I know."

"But how?"

"We might not have been able to spend every night together," Ian whispered. "But I know your body. I want to shout to the whole world that you are mine."

"Oh, Ian," Hope buried her face in his neck, "I want that too. But ..."

"I've been patient, Hope," Ian told her. "But with the babe coming, my patience is gone. When will the babe arrive?"

"January or early February."

"Here's my offer," he responded. "By December, I will turn the search over to D.D. and Freddy, and we will tell your father. Then by February 14, we will be married under the law. Is that acceptable?"

"You would give up your ship, your search, your life in England, for me?"

"Hope, love," Ian murmured against her lips. "You are my life. You and this babe ... if you'll have me."

"Forever, Ian." Hope needed to be closer and pushed until he leaned back, taking her with him. "I love you."

"I love you too." His kiss was drugging, causing her to forget what she was going to say as she reached for the buttons on his shirt. "What number is this on the agenda?"

"Whatever number you want it to be."

"First," her lips trailed across his chest. "Any arguments?"

He rolled them over, and as his lips descended, she could think of nothing but him.

TWENTY

Boston Harbor
30, November 1718
7:00 a.m.

Ian guided El corazón toward the dock in Boston Harbor, happy to be back on land.

"Here comes the Rosa, Cap'n," D.D. called. "Would you like the honor?"

Ian glanced to where his First Mate was standing shoulder to shoulder with his son, Richard. At long last, their journey was about over.

"It's all yours," Ian yelled back, "if you want it."

D.D. looked toward the Rosa, then turned back and slung his arm around his son. "I found my treasure. That one is all yours."

Ian bowed slightly in their direction, happy everything seemed to be working out as it should. There had been moments over the last few years when he'd begun to doubt. His marriage to Hope had given him more hope that the journey was soon to be over. Especially since he'd set an ending date.

The El corazón had sailed from Swan Harbor at the end of October, after Geoffrey had returned from Boston. Unfortunately, he'd not retrieved the ruby heart, but he no longer believed the pirate who'd saved him had stolen the gem. He seemed to understand that there were several forces involved. However, he'd made a decision that had created an obstacle.

It seemed the sheriff was interested in meeting the pirate. At the time, he'd not been ready to bring his pirate and professor personas together. With Pence caught, and Richard returned to D.D., once Ian was back in Swan Harbor, things would be different.

They had to be as, with his child growing in Hope's belly, there was no option. The curse had to be broken and their family saved. And with the capture of the Rosa, he had every hope it would continue to be so.

Ian left D.D. in charge and went searching for his contact, Jonathan Belcher. He'd first met Jon in England before embarking on his current journey. Then he'd seen the man in a Boston tavern, and learned his old friend was a member of the Governor's Council. That had been a most advantageous encounter for both.

"Professor, over here."

"Jon," Ian shook the other man's hand. "I appreciate your meeting me."

A corner of Jon's mouth kicked up. "It's the least I could do. You've brought me quite the big fish."

Ian glanced toward the Rosa, where Pence and several others were being led onto the docks.

"I trust you'll know what to do with those fish."

"You know I will," Jon assured him. "How did you finally happen upon Pence and the Rosa?"

"Sheer luck," Ian laughed. "A late-season hurricane pushed us off course, and there set El corazón de la Rosa with a broken mast."

"Which meant no running."

"Right," agreed Ian. "We boarded. And while not all of my crew could reunite with the individuals they sought, many were."

"Now what, my friend? What does the future hold for you?"

Ian smiled. "Happiness and a family. Is that not all a man should wish for?"

"Do you have someone in mind?"

"Hope." But he couldn't keep the secret any longer. "Hope and I are married, and she is with child."

Jon's smile grew. "That is wonderful news. I'm most happy to hear it."

The wind blew, and a chill raced up Ian's spine, the memory of what was at stake never far from his mind.

"Thank you," Ian sighed. "I'm eager to get home. The babe has not been kind to her."

"I'm sorry to hear that. Once you are back with her, that may help." Jon directed them away from the docks, into a small building where there were two other men waiting. "Let's dispatch this business. I know you have other things you wish to accomplish while in Boston."

"Did you find him?" Ian asked regarding Maddok.

"I did," Jon confirmed. "He's meeting us in a few hours."

"Meet us?" Ian questioned. "You believe he's willingly going to meet me ... and bring what I seek?"

"I said nothing about being willing," Jon laughed. "Now did I?"

"No," Ian studied the other man. "No, you did not."

"Then we're in accord." Jon spread several pieces of parchment on a table. "You need to sign a few forms, and the reward will be yours."

His and his crew's, Ian thought, quickly signing the forms.

"While I'm here," Ian posed. "Do you know someone who works with silver?"

"Silver?" Jon hesitated a beat. "Goodfellow, Elias, I believe his name is."

Bloody hell, thought Ian.

Swan Harbor
30, November 1718
11:00 a.m.

HOPE REPLACED HER QUILL AND REREAD THE JOURNAL ENTRY she'd just completed. Ian had been gone for thirty-three days, and just as she'd promised, each day she'd written a few lines of how she was feeling. She placed her hands over her growing belly. Lately, all she'd felt was tired.

"You know not the difference between night and day," she murmured to her unborn child. "Do you?"

"Hope?" Her father knocked on her door, and a shard of fear raced through her. Had he heard?

"Yes, Papa," Hope called lightly, but remained seated at her desk.

"How are you feeling?"

"I'm feeling tired. The ba ..." When she realized what she'd almost said, she quickly corrected. "My brothers kept me awake last night. How are you feeling?"

"I'll survive," he mumbled. "And Alan and Luke seemed to be sleeping peacefully."

In the month since Ian's departure, a mysterious illness had swept through the town. They would suddenly be overcome with a high fever, an inability to keep food in their stomachs, and extreme lethargy. Many had not survived.

"Did you need something?"

Geoffrey adjusted the black patch covering his right eye and took a letter from his pocket.

"I came to tell you I have to go to Boston again."

"Boston?" Hope frowned. "Why?"

He showed her the letter. "I received this from the Boston Sheriff. They have heard of a ruby that fits the description of our heart."

"Our heart?" Hope's pulse picked up. "Really? In Boston?"

"So, it seems," he murmured. "I have to go."

"It's all right, Papa," Hope told him. "I understand."

He studied her, and Hope fought the need to squirm. What was he thinking?

"Is there anything else?"

"I, I was wondering if you would walk me down."

The babe in her belly gave her a swift kick, reminding her she did not have her stomach covered.

"I need to finish this entry," Hope offered a simple excuse. "Then I'll be right down."

"All right."

Geoffrey gave her a small smile and shut the door behind him. Once he was gone, Hope put her journal away and, on her way downstairs, grabbed her cape. When she wrapped it around her shoulders, a sharp twinge in her back nearly took her breath.

"Hope?" Geoffrey met her at the bottom of the stairs. "Are you all right? You're pale."

"I'm fine," Hope hurried to assure him. "I just got a little dizzy."

"If you're sure," he murmured, still studying her carefully.

"I'm sure."

She was afraid he would insist they contact the doctor, but then he relaxed.

"Have you somewhere to be?" Geoffrey asked, waving toward her winter cape.

Since her pregnancy had become noticeable, Hope had been spending more time away from home. Initially, it had only been Faith and Henry who had been taken into their confidence. When the child growing inside her had not treated her too kindly, Ian had brought in Doctor Williams. That she could not share her condition with her father was something she wished she could change daily.

"I promised Faith I would sit with her mother," Hope quickly tossed out.

"Elizabeth is ill?" Geoffrey questioned.

"She is. But Doctor Williams feels she is improving."

"That's good." Geoffrey picked up his bag, but before he left, he grabbed her hand. "Thank you for being by my side."

Her breath caught, and tears immediately sprang to her eyes. "Where else would I be?"

He gave her a gentle smile, and for a second, she was reminded of her father before her mother's death.

"I'm sorry about those men," Geoffrey whispered, his throat thick with emotion. "I should have trusted you."

"You should have," she agreed. "But now I know. We will find the key."

"I pray you're correct." He squeezed her fingers. "I wish for you to have what your mother and I had."

Hope had to work not to spill the news. It was only the desire to tell her father with Ian by her side that kept her silent.

"I will, Papa," she promised him.

He kissed her cheek. "I love you, Hope. Look for me before Christmas."

"I love you too, Papa," Hope whispered, her tears spilling over. "Christmas will be special this year, you'll see."

Once he was gone, she was left with too much time with only her thoughts. Hope gathered her things and left by the back door, thinking to take the shortcut to the tavern. Halfway there, another pain in her back had her stopping to lean against a tree.

Was it the baby? It was too soon. Plus, she remembered her mother saying it felt like her stomach was being squeezed. It took several minutes before she could shake off the worry and walk the rest of the way to the tavern.

She found Faith in the kitchen stirring a large pot of soup. And the room smelled of newly baked bread.

"Hope!" Faith exclaimed. "I need help."

"All right," Hope replied hesitantly. "I thought you wanted me to sit with your mother."

"Oh, that," Faith waved away any concern. "I just told you that so you'd have a handy excuse. My mother isn't even here."

"Where is she?" Hope asked, glancing around the kitchen to see what needed to be done. A variety of vegetables were spread across the table, a sharp knife next to them. "Shall I slice those?"

"Please," Faith blew out a breath. "We have to make three more pots of soup and two more loaves of bread. Then after separating everything, we're to deliver the meals."

"To the families who've been sick?"

Faith indicated a piece of paper on the counter next to her. "My mother made that list. I'm just following it."

"All right."

The smell of the just-baked bread called to her, and before she'd even asked, Hope cut a piece. She had it halfway to her mouth when she realized how quiet it was. "What?"

"How are you feeling?" Faith asked, her brown-eyed stare all-knowing.

"Tired," Hope admitted. "Lonely."

"Have you heard from Ian?"

"No," Hope confessed. "I'd hoped to hear something, but I can only surmise they are still out at sea."

"And the baby?"

A feeling of love so strong washed over Hope, it brought tears to her eyes.

"Busy." She smiled, thinking of the continuous kicks and punches. "I think I'm having a boy."

Faith laughed. "Why would you say that?"

"Because my mother used to complain about how active Alan was when she was carrying him," Hope recalled. "After he began walking, she would look at me and say, 'see, boys keep you on your toes from before they're even born.

You have to watch them.' And this one," she rubbed her hands over her belly, "has certainly kept me on my toes."

"A boy," Faith repeated. "Ian will like that."

"He will," Hope agreed. "Do you want me to slice the vegetables or start the bread?"

Faith waved toward the table. "Sit and slice the vegetables. I'm sure you'd like to rest your back as much as possible."

If only you knew, Hope thought, sliding onto the bench. But as she reached for the knife, the remnants of the pain remained, and she vowed she'd say something ... if it became worse.

Hours later, she was helping Faith pack the food in boxes, and the pain had settled into a dull ache. It wasn't worse, she assured herself. Besides, she'd spent much time bending over the table and kneading bread.

"Ready?" Faith asked, giving her a concerned look.

"I'm ready." Inside though, Hope had to admit, there was a little worry. The problem was, what should she do about it?

"Henry said he would help," Faith whispered when they left the tavern to find her brother waiting with a coach.

"Is it because he's hoping to see Felicity while we're out?"

"Of course," Faith laughed.

Hope settled inside the coach, and after the first few stops; they developed a routine. She would hand the dish to Faith and check off the name on the list. Then they would move on. With every stop, her worry grew stronger.

Boston
30, November 1718
5:00 p.m.

"What did you say?" Ian stuck his finger in his ear as if he were clearing it out. "I'm not sure I heard you correctly."

Maddok sent him a quick side-eyed glance, worry written all over his face.

Good, thought Ian, *maybe I can get some answers.*

"I said," Maddok replied in a soft voice, "that I cannot give you the heart."

"That is what I thought you said." Ian took several steps closer to where Maddok was sitting and leaned on the table. "Where is it?"

"I gave it to Isabelle."

"Isabelle?" Ian frowned, as he hadn't expected that response. "Isabelle Williams?"

"Yes."

Ian exchanged looks with Jon before turning his attention back to Maddok.

"Why?"

Maddok seemed to shrink into himself, almost as if he were trying to decide whom he feared most.

"It was her idea for me to take it," he whined. "I just did it for the money."

"And the fire?" Ian stalked to the other side of the table, his mind trying to connect the pieces. "Was that just for money too?"

"Fire?" Maddok gave him a blank look. "The one at the sheriff's office? That was Bill."

Ian sent a side-eyed glance in Maddok's direction. "No, the fire that destroyed Widow Mars' home."

Maddok blanched, and for a second, Ian thought he was going to pass out.

"Is-Is everyone all right?"

"Bloody hell, Maddok!" Ian slammed his hand down on the table. "How can you ask that? I just told you there was a fire!"

"I know, but—"

"No! Everyone is *not* all right. In fact, they're all *dead.* Including two of your accomplices. Who was wearing my bloody coat, and how did they get it?"

"Last name is Franks," Maddok offered. "That's all I know."

The name meant nothing to Ian, but perhaps Henry would know.

"And the woman?"

Maddok shrugged. "George's daughter."

"Which is how you were able to get George to allow you to work the lighthouse," Ian surmised, the pieces beginning to fall into place.

"Yes." Maddok lifted his head and met Ian's eyes. "But I did not set that fire."

"No?" Ian flipped around a chair and straddled it before pushing Maddok a bit more. "Then who set the fire?"

"Isabelle." Maddok shrugged.

"Isabelle?" Ian repeated. "Explain."

Maddok studied him for several moments, and Ian half expected him to pretend ignorance.

"Isabelle paid me to take the heart, and Franks to my place," Maddok began. "The next day, I gave the gem to her and met with Geoffrey, just as she required."

"Then what happened?"

"You should ask Isabelle."

"I plan to," Ian barked. "For now, though, I want to hear your story."

"On April 5, George came to me with the news Henry knew about the lighthouse switch. I became nervous," Maddok told him. "That night, a man knocked on my door and suggested I leave town."

"In the merchant ship?"

"Yes," Maddok nodded. "I was not even aware Isabelle was in Boston until I saw her in the market."

Ian pushed away from the table, his mind working to connect all the information he'd been given.

"I need to speak with Isabelle," he told Jon. "Do you know where she lives?"

"I do," Jon confirmed. "Would you like me to go with you?"

Ian nodded and moved to follow his friend out the door.

"What shall we do with him?" Jon asked, thumbing over his shoulder toward Maddok.

"Shoot him for all I care," Ian retorted.

He heard Jon say something to the men who'd brought Maddok to the meeting. Except his focus was on the next confrontation. Would Isabelle have the stone?

"Are you sure you want to do this tonight?" Jon asked, setting the wagon into motion.

"I need this to be over, Jon." As the day had progressed, a sense of urgency had followed Ian. "Hope is waiting for me."

They traveled in silence, and it wasn't long before Jon slowed the wagon in front of a large home.

"This is where Isabelle is living?"

"Yes." Jon pointed to one side of the home, where a faint glow could be seen behind a window. "That is Isabelle's chambers. Her husband and children are on the opposite side."

"Wish me luck."

Ian hopped out of the wagon and made his way toward the house. He found a door, and with a few manipulations, was inside.

He easily made his way to Isabelle's chambers. They were lit with a single candle that sat on her dressing table. The heart rested under the candle's glow, and just as with his half of the stone; it seemed to breathe.

Isabelle was sitting close to it, seemingly mesmerized by the motion. But then he realized she was asleep. Before he'd completely thought through his plan, the stone was in his pocket, and his knife was at her throat.

"Now," Ian jabbed the tip of the knife hard enough, piercing her skin, "I have one thing I came for. If you wish to live, you'll give me the rest."

Isabelle opened her eyes, hatred instead of fear in their blue depths. "You," she spit. "What are you doing here?"

"Taking care of what's mine," Ian snarled.

"What's yours?" Isabelle frowned. "How is the stone yours?"

"The stone is a bonus," Ian replied. "But Hope is mine. And by extension, so is Geoffrey. Did you start the fire? Why did you take the stone? What were you thinking to gain?"

Isabelle's eyes glittered in the candlelight, and he kept expecting her to fight. Then she began speaking, almost conversationally.

"I'd hoped Geoffrey would come to his senses," she hissed. "His precious Hope was gone. But he still refused to come to me. So, I pushed a little more, thinking I'd find and return the stone."

"Just not before you also killed his oldest son," Ian added. "Or was that an accident?"

"Just part of the plan," Isabelle shrugged nonchalantly. "Except even after all of that, he refused me. He refused me!"

"Because he does not love you," Ian retorted. "How could he? Your love is dangerous. And what of the words you spewed to him and Christine?"

"I meant to cure my broken heart."

"Do you even have a heart?" Ian questioned. "Or is that what those words did? They took your heart and your hope, leaving you nothing but a bitter woman. I pity you."

"Geoffrey will change his mind."

However, there was a different tone in her voice. Not hopeful per se, but more hopeless, as if all fight had gone out of her.

"Here," Ian pushed a quill and paper closer to her. "Write the words you said that night. Perhaps they can be reversed."

"Why would I care about reversing them?"

Ian thought fast, as he felt he was dealing with limited time before her behavior switched.

"You said you wanted to cure your broken heart, yes?"

"That is what I said."

"Why is it Geoffrey cannot love you?"

"Because he still loves that twit, Christine." A little spark appeared in her eye. "You mean to heal Geoffrey's broken heart, do you not?"

"I mean to heal Geoffrey's heart," Ian acknowledged.

Once the words were written, Ian took the page and left Isabelle behind. With the two halves of the heart in his possession, he could complete his mission.

TWENTY-ONE

Henry's Home
30, November 1718
6:30 p.m.

Hope followed Faith into the coach, the ache in her back becoming sharper.

"How did we not know?" Faith exclaimed. "About your aunt, I mean. Why didn't Ellie tell us?"

"Well," Hope began.

"I mean, I know Ellie was sick," Faith barreled on. "So was Phillip. But still."

Hope winced. Since her return to Swan Harbor, she hadn't seen much of Ellie, Kitty or Phillip. Her energies had gone toward helping her father mend, and Ian. Then, when the sickness came to town …

"Maybe she wasn't sure she'd be able to carry the babes to delivery," Hope offered. "You know she's had difficulty before."

"I know," Faith hummed. "Is it not odd to think you have cousins just a wee bit older than your child will be?"

"And there are two of them." Hope rubbed her hands across her distended stomach, wondering how two could fit. "I just cannot fathom."

"Perhaps next time," Faith teased, just as the coach stopped.

Hope glanced out the window, surprised they'd arrived so quickly. "Henry's?" she questioned, as she'd thought they were returning to Faith's.

"I brought some supper for us," Faith grinned.

Hope followed Faith into Henry's, but she was torn. There was a part of her that wanted to be with her friends. The other part, though, wanted to go home and lie down, as the pain in her back had gotten worse.

"This is okay, is it not?" Faith asked once they were inside. "You had nothing else to do?"

"It is fine," Hope assured her friend. "I'm just a little tired. Plus, my back ..." She rubbed at the spot in her lower back that had been aching all day.

"Hope?" Faith was suddenly at her side. "Should I have Henry go get Doctor Williams?"

"No," Hope brushed away the thought. "I think I just bent over too much today."

Hope unwrapped the loaf of bread that had been packed and set about warming it. When Faith hovered worse than her father had been, she searched for a topic to distract.

"How is Henry's courtship of Felicity?"

Faith giggled, "I think it's going fine. It feels really strange though, to have him suddenly interested in her."

"It's not so sudden, sister mine," Henry replied as he entered the room. "I've had my eye on her for a few years, but she—"

"—Was but a child," Faith laughed. "I know."

"She was," Henry agreed. "Besides, it was not our time. I think it's our time now."

"Henry's right," Hope grinned. "Sometimes you have to be patient until it's your time."

"Unless you have your eye on someone," Faith muttered, "and your time never comes."

Hope winced. "Faith, I," she began, remembering they'd never talked about her friend's crush on Ian.

"I'm teasing, Hope, really," Faith hurried to explain. "Once I saw you and Ian in the same room, I knew you were meant to be together."

"Really?" Hope blinked, tears filling her eyes. "I was so scared to say anything."

"Women," Henry muttered.

"Yes, really." Faith hugged her. "Ian loves you, and now you're having a baby. It's so romantic."

A huge weight seemed to lift from Hope's shoulders. She felt like such a child for not talking to Faith earlier. After all, they were best friends.

"It is romantic. And now I'm …" she rubbed her hand over her belly and corrected, "we're starving."

Hope reached for a bowl of soup, and a cramp shot from the bottom of her stomach and traveled over the top. Then a warm gush of fluid flowed between her legs to splash on the stone floor.

"My baby!" Hope cried, her panicked eyes meeting Faith's, then Henry's. "It's too early."

Henry blanched. "Wha-What should I do? Get Doctor Williams?"

Another cramp jabbed her belly, this one traveling from side to side. Her stomach tightened, and the motion beneath her hands made her feel as if the babe was trying to jump through her skin.

"Not Doctor Williams," Hope grunted. "Anne." But then she remembered her brothers were home and still sick. "Wait, Alan and Luke …"

"I'll go," Faith suddenly took charge. "Henry can stay with you."

Another squeezing cramp had Hope bending over, her arms wrapped around her child, praying …

"Come on, Hope." Faith wrapped her arm around her waist and led the way toward Henry's bedchamber. "Here—"

"But I couldn't …" Hope tried to say.

"Hope," Faith told her patiently. "There's no other option. What if we get in the coach and …?"

Hope's heart sank as she knew her friend was right. She just hadn't thought this far ahead. In her mind, she was with Ian when their child was born.

She sat gingerly on the side of the bed. Before she could remove her shoes, another cramp arrived. This one ripped through her, taking her breath, and had her reaching for something to grab.

"Henry, give her your hand!" Faith screamed.

Hope took Henry's hand, her first thought of how she wished it were Ian's. When another cramp tore through her body, she didn't care, squeezing for all she was worth.

"Beggin your pardon, Hope," Henry whispered. "Try not to hold your breath with the pain."

"What?" Hope groaned.

"The pain," Henry repeated. "The professor said, when you hold your breath, it causes your muscles to tighten. If you breathe, they relax, lessening the pain."

"That's something the professor read, is it?"

"Oh, yes," Henry exclaimed. "He told me the same thing the last time I hit my thumb with a stone."

"And did it work?"

"It still hurt like a bugger," Henry admitted. "But I tried to do as the professor suggested."

Hope would try it. However, she was pretty sure there was no way *breathing* was going to remove the pain.

"I'm sorry, Henry," she murmured. His dark eyes, shaggy hair, and calm demeanor were so familiar, it helped. Except he wasn't the man she loved. "I'm sure you didn't sign up to take Ian's place."

Henry sent her a shy smile. "Ian's my friend. I would do anything for him."

"And we thank you." Hope hesitated and tried to breathe through another cramp. "Without your help, Ian and I wouldn't have been able to spend as much time together. We appreciate it."

"He's a good man. In fact," Henry released her hand and moved to the other side of the room, where a blanket had been thrown over something. He tossed aside the cover, revealing a beautiful cradle. "Ian made this for the baby. He was going to give it to you for Christmas."

Tears sprang to Hope's eyes, and she really wanted to explore the gift. She wanted to run her fingers over the wood Ian had lovingly carved for their child.

"It's beautiful," she pushed out before her breath was stolen from her.

"Breathe," Henry reminded.

"Breathe this," Hope muttered, instantly feeling contrition when Henry's face turned pink.

"Hope!" Anne came rushing into the room, her eyes immediately going to where Henry was holding her hand. "Is it?"

"Oh, no, no, no, no," Henry dropped Hope's hand and skittered across the floor. "It's the professor's."

"The professor's?" Anne's eyes met Hope's.

"The professor," Hope repeated, "is my husband."

"Your *husband?*" Anne shook her head as if she were trying to clear her thoughts. "You're married? When?"

Hope waited for the pain to subside and explained to Anne about meeting and falling in love with Ian. She also explained that they had been married by the minister in Timber Creek.

"You've been married since April?" Anne frowned. "Yet, you've waited this long to tell?"

"Papa was hurt," Hope murmured. "Ian and I had plans. We were going to tell my family and be remarried in February."

"Oh, you dear girl," Anne ran a cold cloth over Hope's forehead. "How you've suffered."

"I'm sorry, Anne."

"Sorry?" Anne's kind eyes met hers. "Why would you be sorry?"

"Because you told me a long time ago to tell you if I needed you ..." Hope's voice died when the worst cramp hit and her stomach tightened, feeling so hard she could have been holding a stone. It was a rolling pain, spreading from side to side and around her back.

"Breathe, Hope," Henry encouraged.

"Henry's right," Anne replied. "Breathing can decrease muscle tightness."

"See," Henry pointed out. "Your professor is smart."

Hope lay still for several moments, her body feeling as if it had been beaten against a riverbank. She could hear Anne bustling around her, but her heart and her thoughts were reaching out ...

Ian!

Boston Harbor

30, November 1718

11:15 p.m.

"Hope?"

Ian glanced at the letter in his hand, the sound of her voice so clear, it was as if she were next to him.

"Ian?" Jon asked anxiously. "Are you all right?"

"Fine, why?" Ian turned around, his eyes searching the docks.

"Well," Jon barked out a half-laugh. "Because we're alone and yet you act as if there is someone else with us. What is it?"

Ian knew he'd never be able to explain the connection he had with Hope. Knew he'd be locked up with the crazies if he even tried.

"I'm sorry, Jon." Ian handed over the letter he'd written to Hope that Jon's merchant ship would deliver. "It's been a long trip. I'm ready to go home."

"It won't be long," Jon assured him. "I'll make sure this gets to someone who will deliver it."

"Thanks, Jon. You've been a big help."

"Look me up again the next time you're back in Boston."

Ian grinned, "I'll bring Hope."

As soon as his friend had left, Ian imagined he'd heard Hope's cry again. She needed him ...

He stalked back to the El corazón, passing the Rosa along the way. Would D.D. understand what he'd decided, he wondered as he climbed onto the deck, on his way to his cabin.

His journal was open on his desk, and he knew he needed to complete an entry. Except he had no desire to write his thoughts. Instead, he took out his flask and crawled up onto his bunk. Perhaps if he were drunk enough, the night would pass, and he could ignore the feeling in his gut saying Hope needed him.

Ian had just begun to feel a buzz when the sound of footsteps had him watching the door.

"Friend or foe?" he called just before the door was pushed open.

"You knew who it was by my gait," D.D. scolded, stepping fully into the room.

"Maybe," Ian offered noncommittally.

He hadn't bothered to light the candle when he'd returned, but he could feel D.D. watching him.

"What?" he finally asked when he couldn't take the silence any longer.

The scrape of flint was the only warning he had before D.D. lit several candles in quick succession.

"Did you not find Maddok?" D.D. asked quietly.

"No, I found him," Ian retorted.

"He didn't give you the heart?"

"Maddok didn't have it," Ian shared. "He'd given it to Isabelle."

"Isabelle?" D.D. echoed. "Isabelle Williams?"

"Yes."

"That I hadn't expected." D.D. shook his head. "Had you?"

"No."

"And?"

Ian sighed and capped his flask before tossing it aside. He knew D.D., and there would be no rest until they'd spoken.

"I was going to talk to you in the morn."

"I'm here now." D.D. pulled a chair away from his desk and settled on it. "Go on."

In as few words as possible, Ian explained about the meeting with Maddok. He then told D.D. about speaking with Isabelle.

"The Broken Heart Cure?" D.D. repeated. "That's what she said?"

"Yes," Ian confirmed. "I have the words. Perhaps Anne, Isabelle's mother, can help me find the key to reverse it. After all, I would think she'd want to return hope to her daughter."

D.D. gave him a look that could only be described as skeptical, but Ian couldn't think of it like that. He had to hold on to his hope that all would work, and hope would survive.

"And you found the other half of your stone?"

"I did."

Ian took both halves of the stone from his pocket and laid them side by side in the candlelight. Just like every other time, the glass appeared to be alive, the light reflecting off the facets, so they appeared to be moving.

"Beautiful," D.D. hissed. "Are you going to search for the rest of the set?"

"I'm going to give the stone to Geoffrey Prince and claim Hope as mine. Having her by my side for all the days of my life is my most fervent dream."

"Like that?" D.D. asked. "And are you returning just their stone?"

Ian picked up the stones, two halves of a whole, he couldn't help but think. They were warm in his hand, which made no sense.

"The stones were never meant to be separated, D.D.," Ian tried to explain. "Whether you believe the myth that they are Vega's heart or part of Las Joyas del Mar, they belong together."

"It's interesting," D.D. Replied. "That Isabelle read the lines from a book meant to cure her broken heart, and yet they left her hopeless."

"They cursed my wife's family," Ian grumbled.

"But that's just it," D.D. remarked. "What are the chances that, out of all the places we've sailed over the last few years, we'd end up in Swan Harbor?"

"Come on, old man," Ian scoffed. "What are you saying? That a higher power is guiding my path?"

D.D. shrugged. "That you have the means to reunite the heart's other half has to symbolize something, do you think not?"

"Could the answer to reversing the curse be as simple as that?" Ian asked. "To reunite the halves of the heart."

"In more ways than one," D.D. pointed out. "That Hope's family has one half —"

"—And my family has the other—"

"—That binds you together," D.D. said, basically what Ian had been thinking.

"It's a good thing I asked Jon for the name of someone trustworthy who works with gemstones then, is it not?"

"To see if they can be reconnected?"

"Yes," Ian confirmed. "I'm to meet with him tomorrow at noon."

"You're a good man, Ian." D.D. sat there for several moments. "You did not have to help me rescue Richard. I thank you."

"Things worked out as they should," Ian proclaimed.

"And what of the Rosa?" D.D. brought up the subject Ian had been hoping to put off a bit longer. "What of those crew members who need to be returned to their homes?"

Here it goes, thought Ian. Would D.D. accept his decision or push for another outcome?

"I," Ian hesitated a beat before pressing forward. "I'm aware there are crew members on this ship still searching. I also realize there are men and boys on the Rosa who need to be returned home, including the ones taken from Serenity Cove."

"There are," D.D. confirmed. "We had several take their rewards and decide to stay in Boston. However, there is more work."

"There is more work," Ian agreed. "But I'm giving the Rosa to you. Take Freddy as your first mate and reunite the families. Then take Richard and go back home to your wife."

"What of you?"

"My place is beside Hope and our child," Ian murmured. "I wish to return to Swan Harbor, marry her again, and teach. Those are my passions. Our mission was to locate Richard, but we did so much more."

"And how will you get to Swan Harbor?" D.D.'s tone had Ian realizing his friend was going to push for another outcome.

"I'm going to sail El corazón, why?"

"Alone?"

Ian winced, as he knew it was going to be difficult, but figured, for a one-way trip, he could hire a couple of Jon's crew.

"I can handle it."

"You cannot." D.D. stood and prepared to leave. "I told you, Richard is my treasure. We'll give the Rosa to Freddy, and he can complete the mission. I'm sure Jon has some men you can hire to help us sail El corazón. My son and I will be by your side until you need us no longer. Now, goodnight."

Then, without allowing a rebuttal, he was gone.

Ian sat there staring at the closed door, wondering what had just happened. Realistically, he wouldn't have been able to do it on his own. Plus, it would be nice to spend time with D.D., Richard and Hope. So, he decided he'd let the older man win this round.

Alone in his cabin once again, Ian's thoughts traveled to Swan Harbor.

I'm here, Hope.

Henry's Home
30, November 1718
11:50 p.m.

HOPE LOST TRACK OF HOW LONG SHE'D BEEN LABORING TO PUSH her child free from her body. She'd also lost track of how many times she'd reached out to Ian with her heart. They were connected, and while she knew he couldn't really hear her, somehow, she knew, he knew. Somehow, he was reaching out to her as well.

"It's too soon," Hope moaned, not for the first time.

"Nothing we can do about it now," Anne repeated the same thing she'd said earlier.

"But ..."

"Hope," Anne tried again. "Your baby wants to be born ... tonight. Yes, it's early, but I'm going to do everything in my power for it. Just like I did when your mum birthed you."

"You were there?"

Another pain rolled over Hope, making her feel as if she needed to push, but Anne was shaking her head. She had to hold on, just a little longer.

"I was there," Anne confirmed. "You were a little early, and we were worried. But you were strong, and look at you—having a babe of your own."

"I can't hold back," Hope grunted, grabbing Henry's hand as another wave washed over her.

"Breathe," Henry reminded her.

"Quit telling me to bloody breathe!" Hope snapped.

He exchanged looks with Anne, and Hope had to wonder what that look meant.

"Won't be long now, Hope," Anne told her. "It's time to meet your baby. Are you ready?"

Didn't matter if she was ready or not, she thought, following Anne's directives and bearing down.

Ian!

"Once more," Anne instructed.

Her body was fatiguing. Hope dug into her reserves and imagined Ian was there. She wrapped his love around her and, with her last energy waning, brought her child into the world.

"Oh, Hope," Anne cried. "It's a boy. You have a son."

"A son," Hope whispered around the sounds of the newborn. "I have a son."

It was several more moments, and then Anne wrapped the baby in one of Henry's shirts and tucked him next to Hope.

He quieted, and with her heart in her throat, Hope glanced down into his little face. *So tiny*, she thought, wishing Ian were next to her.

"I'm your mama," she murmured. "You weren't supposed to arrive this early."

The baby snuffled, and Hope ran her finger down his petal-soft cheek. He turned his head, and she slid the tip of her finger between his lips.

"Do you have a name picked out?"

Hope hadn't discussed it with Ian yet, but she'd already chosen a name, "Meet Ian Geoffrey Jones."

"Oh, Hope," Anne exclaimed. "Your father will be pleased."

Hope brushed away her tears and picked up Baby Ian, cuddling him close to her chest. "Welcome to Swan Harbor, Little Man."

TWENTY-TWO

Hope's Home
18, December 1718
5:30 p.m.

IN THE DAYS AFTER GIVING BIRTH, HOPE'S LIFE TOOK ON A routine. She woke, ate, slept, and fed the baby. Her days and nights became intertwined. And just when she thought her strength was gone, the day would start anew.

It didn't seem to matter how much she loved the baby. Nor did it seem to matter how tightly she held on to him. She couldn't shake the feeling that, whatever Isabelle's words, they had sealed her fate. With her child's birth, her days were numbered.

Hope tried to pretend there was nothing the matter. Tried to ignore the worried looks of those who loved her. But how could she explain what she'd overheard between Geoffrey and Isabelle? How could she explain what Ian had learned in Boston? And with neither in Swan Harbor, she was alone.

It was then Christine returned to her dreams. Except where once her mother's visits had calmed her, they were no longer comforting. All they did was bring more fear until she woke, unable to breathe or think clearly.

Those were the times when she could close her eyes and hear Ian's voice, *Breathe, my love. I'll be there soon.*

She tried to listen. Tried to do as he requested. But with each passing day, it became harder and harder to get the very air she needed. Harder to hide what was happening.

It became even more difficult when Anne found her gasping for breath one morning. While she'd dutifully gone to see Doctor Williams, deep in her soul, she knew it would not help. The only thing that would save her was for Ian to find the key. Without it, all hope was lost.

Hope brushed her fingers across the baby's soft head as he lay in her arms nursing. He had wisps of dark hair, blue eyes, and his hold on her heart surprised her every day. For even if she'd known her life would end with his birth, she wouldn't have changed anything. Ian and the baby were her greatest joys.

When his eyes whispered shut, and his mouth grew lax with sleep, Hope wiped the tears from her face. She lifted him and gently placed him in his cradle. Then, just as she expected, when she stood, her head swam, and dark spots rushed in front of her eyes.

"Sleep, little babe of mine. Know that I'll love you till the end of time. I'll keep you safe and not be far. Just look up high, you'll see my star," was all Hope could manage before falling back into the chair.

It was several moments before she was sturdy enough to make her way across her room. As expected, the exertion brought on the cough that caused her chest to become tight, and the air to lodge in her throat.

"Hope," Anne knocked lightly on the door. "Are you all right?"

Hope swallowed the medicine Doctor Williams had given her. She leaned on her dressing table and took deep breaths, waiting for the medication to kick in.

"I'm fine," she tried to assure the older woman. "I was just dizzy for a bit."

Anne studied her for several minutes, her eyes all knowing, "It's not any better, is it?"

"No," Hope admitted, blinking the tears away. "But when Ian …"

"Are you sure I can't call Doctor Williams again?" Anne asked. "Perhaps there's—"

"No, Anne. Thank you." The medication kicked in, and as her head cleared, she stood up a little taller. "I'm better now. Besides, he told me he was giving me the strongest medication he had."

"If you're sure."

"I am." Hope hesitated as she knew the next few things she said were going to earn her an argument. "And now, I need a favor."

"Anything."

"Will you watch over the baby for me?" Hope took a deep breath and tried to hide her inner thoughts. "Ian's on his way. I need to see him."

"Why can he not come to your home?" Anne asked. "Your father is not here. Besides, you are married."

"I know," Hope admitted, unable to explain what she was feeling even to herself. "While I'm not sure exactly when he'll be here, I want to be waiting for him. And I want to wait at our place."

"Your place?"

"The cave overlooking the cove," Hope explained. "It's a place that has special meaning to both of us."

"A cave?!" Anne cried, but then immediately lowered her voice. "Hope, no! The weather."

Hope could acknowledge the weather was not the best, but there was an urgency inside of her.

"I have my cape, and I'll take a fur," Hope told her. "Plus, we'll build a fire. It's not like it's going to be forever, anyway. Just a few hours."

"What shall I do if Master Ian awakes?" Anne asked. "Have you forgotten him?"

Hope winced. "No, I haven't forgotten him. But he just ate and should sleep for a few hours."

"Hope ..."

"I'll be fine, Anne, really." She hugged the older woman and forced out a smile. "When I return, I'd like to introduce you to my husband."

"If you're sure," Anne sighed. "You were always stubborn. Take two furs."

"Thank you, Anne."

Once Anne was gone, Hope changed into breeches, surprised they were so much bigger than the last time she'd worn them. She gathered her things and, with a last kiss on the baby's soft cheek, stepped outside.

The day was gray, and there were snowflakes in the air. But it didn't deter Big Red as he galloped toward the cliff. And even when she arrived at the cave with a tight chest, it didn't change the feeling of excitement at seeing Ian.

Breathe, my love. I'm on my way.

Hope left Big Red under the overhang, ducked inside, and was instantly bombarded by memories. Fireside talks, picnics, and the first time they'd spoken of love. And just as she had the first time he'd joined her in the cave, she could feel him near.

Ian!

Her eyes filled with tears, and with nary a thought for her well-being, Hope ran to greet him.

"Ian!" she exclaimed, jumping into his arms.

"I've got you." His husky voice rippled along her skin as he slowly lowered her to the ground and cupped her face. "Come here."

When his lips touched hers, it was like coming home all over again. He smelled of the sea, and tasted like Ian, and all she wanted to do was to kiss him.

"Hope?"

The concerned expression on Ian's face told her he'd discovered there wasn't as much of her as there had been.

"Much has happened since you left."

"I can see that," he replied hesitantly. "Hope is, is the babe—"

"He's fine," she exclaimed.

"He?" Ian's eyes lit up. "We have a boy?"

Hope nodded, but with the snow swirling around, Ian scooted them inside. He wrapped her in a fur and set about building a fire. And the normalcy of the scene had her eyes once again filling with tears.

"Hope?"

Ian adjusted the blanket and pulled her against him, and the injustice of everything swept over her.

"Hope?" He kissed her lips and gently wiped her eyes. "Talk to me, love. You're scaring me."

"I'm sorry, Ian," Hope murmured, barely able to get her breath.

"Why are you sorry, love?"

"Because," she hiccuped and pressed her cheek against his shoulder, "I've brought you nothing but difficulty. And now ..."

"Hope, love." Ian kissed the side of her head and tucked her tighter against his chest. "Loving you has brought me more joy than I ever imagined.

Nothing, and I mean nothing, can ever make me regret falling in love with you. Tell me, Hope. Was our babe born on November 30?"

"Yes," she turned tear-stained eyes in his direction. "Our son, Ian Geoffrey Jones, was born on November 30. How did you know?"

"I heard you," he admitted.

"You heard me?"

"Yes, love." Ian kissed her head, and she could feel him trembling. "I'm so sorry I wasn't here for you. How?"

"Anne," she whispered, "and Henry."

"Henry?"

"Yes." Hope gasped several times, waiting for her breath to calm. Then she pushed the worries aside, needing to believe that all would be fine ... if only for a moment longer.

"Are you all right?" he asked quietly. "It wasn't too awful?"

Hope rolled her eyes. "It wasn't a bloody walk in the park, if that's what you're asking?"

He chuckled, and the sound vibrated underneath her ear. "I would have taken some of your pain if I could."

"No, you wouldn't have," she retorted. "I remember my father saying the same thing when my mother was having Alan. Do you know what happened?"

"He ran out of the house screaming?"

"No," Hope laughed. "The next time she cried out in pain, his face turned as white as the sheets. And I was given the task of taking my father to his den. Poor Henry's hands will never be the same."

"I'm sure he's fine," Ian assured her.

She could hear Big Red pawing the ground, and for a moment, she thought they should leave. But the feeling in her chest, she realized it wouldn't matter and selfishly decided against it.

"Ian, why don't you send Red home?" Hope suggested. "He'll go back to the barn where it's warm."

"Is that your way of saying we should go?"

"No," Hope denied. "It's my way of saying, I want to stay a little longer. When it's time to go, Henry's is closer. Then you can meet your son."

Ian studied her for a second, and Hope fought to act normally. When he nodded slightly and disappeared outside, somehow, she knew, he saw. And because he loved her, he said nothing.

"Hope," Ian returned to her side. "It's snowing pretty heavily out there. Are you sure?"

She placed her finger on his lips. "Just a little longer."

"I could never deny you anything," he murmured. "Even if it wasn't always in our best interest."

"I love you, Ian."

Their eyes locked in the firelight and, as if in slow motion, they came together. It was a clash of lips and tongues, and the longer it continued, the tighter her chest. She didn't want it to stop, though. Didn't want to believe that this was the end.

IAN SQUEEZED HIS EYES SHUT, UNWILLING TO ACKNOWLEDGE what he'd seen when he'd arrived. He was too late. Maybe if ...

"Hope, love." Ian dug into his pocket and pulled out the ruby heart, now whole. "Look."

"Swan Harbor's heart is whole again," Hope murmured. "How?"

"After I found the one on Isabelle's dressing table," Ian explained. "I realized the heart was never meant to be broken. I hoped that by reuniting one side with the other, it held the key ..."

Hope turned her tear-stained face up, her blue eyes meeting his. "I wish."

Ian's heart cracked a little, but he couldn't allow her to see that.

"Can you feel it?" he pleaded. "Your mother said two hearts connected would save Swan Harbor. Our love is all-powerful, is it not?"

"Oh, Ian."

She squeezed her eyes shut, tears ran down her face, and it was a struggle for her to get each breath. He wanted nothing more than to open his veins and give her his life. Yet, he was paralyzed to know what to do.

"Tell me," he cried. "Tell me what to do."

Hope swallowed and held herself up, and he had never loved her more. She was brave and strong, and he'd never felt luckier than to be the man she'd chosen to give her heart.

"Hold me," she requested. "I don't want to be alone."

Ian folded her in his arms and tucked her head under his chin and prayed for strength.

"How's that?"

"Perfect."

She was quiet for several minutes, and he couldn't stand it any longer. "How long have you known?"

"A few weeks," Hope admitted. "I wanted to believe you were right about the heart."

"I'm sorry, love," Ian choked. "I feel I failed you ... failed our son."

"Do not say that," Hope told him. "Fate is a cruel thing. This is mine, but yours lives on."

"How? How do I live without you?"

"You have to, Ian. For me, for our son." She hesitated, and as she struggled for air, he felt the sounds breaking his heart into little pieces. "You were led to me for a reason. While it's too late for us, I believe the answer is close. Find them. Just promise me you will not lose hope."

Ian was holding on to his emotions so tightly, he was trembling. How could he make a promise he was not sure he could keep?

"Promise me, Ian," she whispered.

"I promise I'll try," he settled on. "What do I tell our child?"

"I," she began breathlessly, "did as you asked, and journaled my pregnancy. There's also a letter for him. Tell him I wished not to leave him. Tell him I love him."

"Will you, will you come to him each summer as a swan?" he asked tearfully, "Just as you feel your mother has."

"I wish to live in the stars," Hope sighed. "There, I can keep watch over him, over you, and over Swan Harbor."

Ian turned them on their sides, so they were facing each other. He could see the struggle on her face to breathe, the hint of blue around her lips. But he wasn't ready to let her go. Wasn't ready to say goodbye to the best thing that had ever happened to him.

"Hope," Ian whispered. "I will always love you. Someday, I promise, I will see you in the stars."

"I'll be waiting. But watch the swans." she breathed. "Hope cannot die."

"Are you saying you'd rather I spend eternity as a swan?" he tried to tease, but it came across flat.

"You ... you'd make a handsome swan."

"Of course I would," he forced out. "My name would be Jonesy."

"Very original." Her voice had become so soft, though, he could barely hear her.

"If you can call your swan, Hope," he murmured. "Mine can be called Jonesy."

His heart stilled when she didn't immediately respond. Slowly, she lifted her hand and cupped his face. "Kiss me one last time, Ian."

Their lips met, and with their tears mingling, he prepared to set her free. Ian ran his thumb over her bottom lip and with a tremulous voice whispered, "Close your eyes, heart of mine. And feel my arms, one last time. Wait for me, I'll soon be near. Wait for me until I'm here. I promise you, Hope, I'll find the key. And on that day, we'll both be free."

"I love you," Hope sighed.

"I love you," Ian cried, tightening his arms around her, and burying his face in her hair. "I love you."

He lost track of how long he lay there, wrapped around her. Hoping, praying, there was some way to breathe life back into her. But just as their hearts were connected in life, so were they in death. While he held her, he could feel her heartbeat slowing until finally it stopped, and she slipped away.

"No!" he cried, the sound reverberating around the cave.

The ruby heart caught his attention where it lay on the ground. As the light of the fire hit the stone, just as always, it appeared to move.

Ian snapped up the stone and pressed it against Hope's chest. "Come back to me. Come back to me." He willed some of the power from the stone to be transferred.

It was useless, though. The stone's crack, where the two halves had been reconnected, was never more glaring.

He looked at Hope, and the thought that he would never again hear her voice, kiss her lips, or hold her hand overwhelmed him. His anger was at the stone, for if he'd not waited for it to be made whole, he would have returned sooner.

His wrath was so great, he grabbed the stone and raced outside. The snow fell heavily, blanketing the cliff in silence. Ian hurled it into the night, its destination unknown. At that moment, he cared not whether he lived or if he died.

Promise me, Ian. Do not give up hope.

But where was hope when the woman he loved more than life was taken from him?

What about your son?

His son would be better off without a father who'd allowed his mother to die.

Are you sure?

Ian refused to listen to his subconscious and crawled back into the cave. He curled around Hope's body and prayed to join her in the stars.

TWENTY-THREE
PRESENT DAY

Ava and Finn's Home
February 5
7:30 p.m.

KILLIAN FINISHED READING THE ENTRY AND GLANCED UP, HIS EYES meeting Emma's. Hers were red-rimmed, but he was pleased to see she'd been leaning on her uncle. They had disagreed fiercely over what was best for Jonesy, but reading the journals together seemed to allow them to find a common ground.

"What was the date, Killian?" asked Jack.

Killian flipped back a few pages until he'd located the information. "December 18, 1718, why?"

"Remember the mournful sounds of the wind in December?" Jack inquired.

"We were making cookies, right?" Ava replied. "Then the lights flickered, then the wind whined around the house. It gave me goosebumps."

"So, I was right," Jack responded. "Ian was lamenting Hope's death. I remember hearing it again in mid-January. When's the next entry?"

"The next entry is January 30," Killian shared. "Ian's journal doesn't fill us in on that six-week period.

"Perhaps, Henry's or Anne's," Aiden offered. "While I have them, I've not had time to look through them."

"Do we know why Hope died?" Emma asked quietly, while Aiden was pursuing the needed information.

"Of course, we know," Jack exclaimed. "She was cursed."

Killian exchanged looks with Emma and fought the grin that wanted to break free at her look of exasperation.

"I meant medically," Emma clarified. "Elsa, best guess?"

Elsa grabbed her phone and studied it for several seconds. "Difficulty breathing and a tight chest could have been symptoms of asthma. With the cold air and the fire, it would have dried out the air, making it harder to catch your breath."

"I thought asthma had been around forever," Emma replied. "Didn't they have a treatment?"

"The idea that people can be short of breath has been around forever," Elsa explained. "However, there was no proper treatment until long after Hope had died."

"But I wonder why it was never mentioned when she was young," Emma couldn't help but ask.

"Maybe she developed it after giving birth," offered Elsa. "There's research stating that hormones can cause adult onset."

"I don't need to hear that," Molly winced, rubbing her hands over her stomach, where her twin boys rested. "With all the issues these guys are causing, I guess I can understand. I haven't seen my ankles for weeks."

"I'm sorry, honey." Terri patted her on the shoulder. "Once those babies are out, you'll forget all the little aches and pains."

"Promise?" laughed Molly.

"Well, I survived one to have five more," Terri told her with a grin.

"Don't let her kid you," Elsa's mother, Patty, piped up. "It hurts like a bitch!"

"Mother!" Elsa exclaimed. "Come, let's get a snack."

Killian saw Liam wince, and his gaze followed his new wife out of the room. With Patty's Alzheimer's fluid, they were never sure what she was going to say. Or how much she understood. But since Elsa liked to give the caretaker a few evenings' reprieve, she'd joined the readings.

Which Killian had to admit had gone better than expected. He'd really wanted to jump ahead to what Ian had uncovered regarding the curse, but Jack had refused. He'd insisted that Hope and Ian's love story was one for the ages and as such deserved to be followed from the beginning to its end.

It was just bloody frustrating as, in a way, he felt as if he were living in Ian's shoes. And after the scene he'd just read, it was bloody uncomfortable.

"Killian?"

He glanced up to see his boss looking at him strangely and realized he was still holding the coffeepot.

"Did you need a refill?" Killian asked. "Freshly brewed."

Dylan glanced at the cup in his hand and shrugged. "Might as well."

After he'd replaced the coffeepot, Killian studied Dylan for a moment. They'd both been guilty of tiptoeing around Captain Jack's search for the key. Mainly, he thought, because they'd not had anything specific to latch onto. Except seeing everything play out through Hope and Ian's eyes somehow made it more real. Add to that, Dylan had lost more than one female family member at an early age, and while his situation wasn't quite the same, they both had much to lose.

"It was easier to think of it as the ramblings of the old before reading it," Killian sighed. "Wasn't it?"

"Agreed." Dylan hesitated a minute as if he were gathering his thoughts. "I remember comments about a key, but the reason the key needed to be found was never discussed."

"It makes no sense," Killian murmured. "But as I read Ian's last moments with his beloved Hope, I couldn't help but put myself in his shoes. I'm to marry the last Swan, and I have to admit, the thought of losing her ties my stomach into knots."

Plus, there was his nightmare, which he'd not even discussed with Emma.

"Tell me about it," Dylan agreed. "When Emma read that bit about Hope's fate being sealed after giving birth, it shook me. Not only is Molly pregnant, but so is Jessie."

"I thought Cameron was keeping an extra eye on her tonight," Killian laughed.

"He is," Dylan agreed, "and Jessie's already complaining."

"How are you holding up?"

Dylan drained the last of his coffee and set the cup in the sink. "I wish Jack had allowed us to skip ahead."

"Me too," Killian sighed. "If I know you, though, some of that was done when you found Geoffrey's journal ... without asking permission."

Dylan smirked. "Not only did I flip through Geoffrey's, but I also searched through Luke's."

"No luck though?"

"None." Dylan sent him a pointed look. "However, you can't tell me you didn't skip ahead."

"Well," Killian hummed. "I thought about it. But as odd as it sounds, I felt like I was taking something that wasn't mine yet."

"You know," Dylan blew out a breath and shook his head as if he couldn't believe what he was getting ready to say, "reading about my ancestors is kind of interesting. They've become real people instead of just a name in the Bible."

EMMA WANDERED TO THE WINDOW AND STARED INTO THE NIGHT beyond. It had taken her months before she'd entertained the possibility that Jack understood Jonesy. Now, there were Hope's thoughts of her mother watching over her as a swan. And Ian's comments about his swan's name, she was left to wonder about possibilities. Except the possibility that Ian and Jonesy were connected was almost more that her science-minded brain could handle.

"I found it." Aiden held up one of the books. "It's in Henry's journal."

Which was good, Emma decided, as it kept her from having to make sense of her wayward thoughts. She dropped onto the floor in front of Killian's chair for the next round of reading. Because, as independent as she believed herself to be, there were some burdens she enjoyed sharing.

"You can have the chair, Doc," Killian whispered. "I can sit on the floor."

"I'm okay." She dropped a kiss on his hand. "For now, anyway."

"Alright," Aiden was saying. "According to Ian's journal, Hope died on December 18. Henry Patterson wrote these next few excerpts."

18, December 1718

11:00 p.m.

El corazón docked earlier today, and I waited for Ian to come and see me. When he didn't, I assumed he'd immediately gone to see

Hope and his new son. I'm happy he's finally returned to Swan Harbor.

Faith and I went to see Hope and the baby last Tuesday, and she doesn't look well. After we left, my sister told me she's worried. That while Hope might not have the mysterious illness that has plagued so many, something is obviously wrong.

As I write this, I see the weather has taken a turn for the worse. I pray Ian and Hope have made their way to her home.

"The next entry," Aiden explained, "was two days later."

<u>20, December 1718</u>

11:00 p.m.

My hand is still shaking as I write this, as it has been a rather eventful forty-eight hours. It all started on December 18. I'd just blown the candle out when there was a fierce knocking at my door.

I assumed it was Ian, fresh from his visit with his new son. When I opened the door, my sister Faith rushed in. Her news sent a sense of dread through me. I know not why this was so, but when all came to pass, it made sense.

"Hope and Ian did not return as they were meant to," Faith cried the minute she rushed into my home.

Anne had sent a note explaining Hope had been gone for hours, and the baby was beside himself. When she'd checked and discovered Big Red had returned to the barn, her worry had increased. Since she was alone with Alan, Luke, and the baby, she'd been unable to mount a search.

I knew Hope and Ian had probably met on the mountain ... in the cave they claimed as theirs. But with the weather as it was, I hoped they'd made it to some type of shelter.

The only other place I could think of was Ian's ship. While I knew there was little chance they were there, I needed to exhaust all my options.

When I approached El corazón, the ship was dark, as if everyone were sleeping. I summoned the watchman to locate D.D. for me. Once the older man had been roused, it was just as I feared. Ian had not been seen since he'd left the ship.

"This is your town," D.D. replied. "Tell me what you suggest."

That the professor's friend will allow me to take the lead was comforting. But my fear was that I was the wrong man for the job. Who was I but a small-town lighthouse operator?

"You think they're at the cave?" D.D. tossed out before I could even formulate my thoughts.

"I do," I told him. However, with the snow coming down as it was, my worries were more for the searchers than for the ones we were searching for.

"We should go at first light, then," D.D. suggested, taking the words from my mouth.

"I believe so," I told him. A plan had been created, yet it still did not leave a good taste in my mouth. I feared no one could survive a night out in our weather.

When I returned home, Faith was pacing in my great room. The rest of the night was not for sleeping, but for praying.

When D.D. and his son arrived at first light, I led the way down to the small cove. And then up the path that landed close to the cave. The snow had blown toward the opening in such a manner we had to locate some large limbs to shovel the snow away.

As the snow was removed, I could smell the smoke and had hope that they had survived. But once inside, my heart broke at the scene.

Ian and Hope were under a fur, and he was holding on to her as if she were his lifeline. Once we uncovered them, it was obvious she was gone. And while Ian had some life left in him, at that moment, we were convinced he would be gone before the day's end.

"Now what?" I asked D.D., for the scene was nothing like I had experienced before.

D.D. brushed his hand through his hair, and I could swear he'd aged years in the time it had taken us to climb the mountain.

"We need a doctor," D.D. told me. "And someplace warm."

"The professor is welcome to stay at my home," I replied. "If I go get Doctor Williams, can you get Ian down the mountain?"

"What do you think, Richard?" D.D. asked his son. "Can we get the professor down to Henry's?"

Richard was a big man with a child-like expression, and I hated seeing the sad look on his face.

"We can do it," Richard proclaimed. And I had to trust they knew what they were doing.

"Go on," D.D. told me. "Richard and I will take care of the Cap'n."

"What about Hope?" I asked quietly. "I hate leaving her up here in the cold."

D.D.'s lower lip trembled, showing me he was just as affected by Hope's passing as I.

"There's nothing we can do for the lass now, Henry," he said. "We'll leave her be for now."

I knew he was right. Yet, that didn't make it any easier to leave Richard and D.D. to decide how to move Ian. Especially with the realization that the woman the professor loved was being left behind.

However, my job was to fetch Doctor Williams and trust him to save my friend.

The Doctor and I arrived at my house ahead of D.D., Richard, and the Professor. I was instructed to stoke the fire, warm some stones, and heat some water.

We heard the arrival of the other men before we saw them.

Ian was brought inside quickly, stripped of his clothing, and placed in a warm bed. With instructions to keep the room as warm as possible and rotate the hot stones, Doctor Williams took his leave.

For the rest of the night, it was up to me. There were moments when I felt a great need to go see what was being done with Hope. I had been tasked with saving the professor. And that was one job I took seriously.

D.D. must have seen the frustration on my face because he put a comforting hand on my shoulder. "Henry," he said. "This is your house. I love Ian as if he were my own son. I will take care of his wife."

"Are you sure?" I asked, especially since Anne would have no idea who he was.

"No," D.D. shook his head. "I'm not sure. Sometimes, though, when you're a man, you have to do things you don't want to do."

As I continue to rotate warming stones and massage my friend's limbs, I know exactly what he meant.

As soon as Aiden finished reading the passage, Emma glanced up at Killian. He sat stoically in the chair, a tic pulsing in his jaw. Not, she thought, because he was angry. It was because he was trying to hide his fear.

Share your burdens, he says … unless they're his burdens, she couldn't help but think.

"Five days go by before Henry gives an update on Ian," Aiden continued.

25, December 1718

5:00 p.m.

A week has passed since Hope's death and Ian's rescue. D.D. and Richard have moved in with me, and we are taking turns tending the professor. Doctor Williams comes daily, but I can tell by the look in his eye, he does not hold much hope.

Faith and my mother stop by regularly and bring soup. I have learned that since Kitty is nursing her twins; she has taken over the care of Baby Ian as well.

Geoffrey returned from Boston without Maddok and without Swan Harbor's heart. He has become reclusive since Hope's death, and my mother feels for Alan and Luke. They are so young and have lost so much.

"Over the next few days, Henry repeats the same story," Aiden told them, as he turned the pages looking for more information on Ian's well-being.

<u>10, January 1719</u>
10:00 p. m.
It has been almost a month since Ian was rescued, and he's said very little. He developed a raging fever, and during that time, he mumbled incoherently, but there were a few words I understood. 'Hope' and 'don't leave me' were repeated often. The despair in his voice tore me in two and had me second-guessing my pursuit of Felicity. Was I willing to allow someone to have that much control over my feelings? I did not know.

My thoughts were waylaid when there was a knock at the door. I was very surprised when I opened it to find Kitty Swan on the other side, holding Baby Ian. I'm ashamed to say, my first thought was she'd decided three infants were too much and was leaving Baby Ian at my home. However, I couldn't have been more wrong.

"Henry," Kitty greeted. "May I come in?"

A quick glance over my shoulder assured me the house was clean enough, and I let her in.

"How can I help you, Kitty?" I asked, for I was not sure what, if anything, she knew about my houseguest.

"It's not what you can do for me, Henry," Kitty told me. "But what I can do for you."

"All right." I stepped aside and allowed her in, feeling as if I did not, she'd barrel in anyway.

"Can I get you something to drink?" I asked as soon as I'd shut the door. It wasn't that I really wanted her to stay, but that I knew if I wasn't polite, my mother would have had a few words for me.

"No," she waved away the offer. "I need to see your patient."

"My patient?" I replied, as she'd taken me by surprise.

Kitty sighed, and tears filled her eyes. "Henry. I regret so many things, but my biggest regret is that when Hope talked to me about not wanting to marry a man of Geoffrey's choosing, I did not listen. Anne told me she was able to have some happiness with her professor."

During her speech, I relaxed my stance. "Hope and the professor had many happy times," I assured Kitty.

"I understand the professor is not responding to any treatment Doctor Williams tries."

I explained what Doctor Williams had told me. That sometimes a person's desire to live is not strong, and they fade away.

"I'm trying to bring back my friend," I admitted to her. "Except nothing I have tried has worked."

"He needs a reason to live," Kitty told me. "And I have the answer right here."

She held the baby up, and I could tell in the weeks since his birth, he'd grown.

"I, I know nothing about taking on a baby," I sputtered.

"Oh, no, Henry," she assured me. "You misunderstood. Come."

I followed her into my bedchamber, where Ian was lying in the center of my bed. D.D. and Richard were sitting on the other side of the room, playing a game of cards. As soon as we entered, they joined us at Ian's side.

"The child will become his reason to live," Kitty told me.

I had no idea what she was doing, but watched as she placed the baby on Ian's chest. I'm not sure how long we stood there, waiting for what we knew not, but then ... the baby mewed. For that was how it sounded. And slowly, Ian's right arm circled around the child's back.

"See," Kitty said with one of those smiles that all mothers have. The ones that say, 'I'm always right, and as soon as you realize that we'll both be happier.' "Your professor just needs a reason to live. He just needs hope."

"Will you look at that," D.D. murmured, slipping his arm around Richard. "But I have to agree with Mistress Kitty. Children give your life purpose."

"Here's what we'll do," Kitty decided. "Each day, the baby will come and lay with his father. And we'll see."

"All right, Kitty," I told her. "Shall I bring him back later?"

"This time, I'll come get him."

There was fear in my heart when I said goodbye to her. But it was being pushed out by ... dare I say, hope?

"Then one more," Aiden said.

<u>20. January 1719</u>

8:00 p.m.

The professor may be one of the brightest men I've ever met, but he's a bloody fool. The visits from his child were working. His color had improved, and while he'd done no talking, he had opened his eyes. Then, two days ago, I returned from my shift at the lighthouse to find him gone.

"Where's the professor?" I asked Richard as soon as I noticed Ian was missing.

"The professor?" Richard repeated, and then he smiled. "He's awake, and went to visit his wife."

I'd opened my mouth to give Richard a piece of my mind, but then D.D. walked in, and I realized Richard didn't understand.

Once more, the three of us were left to search for Ian. On our way up to the cave, we heard his cry. It was the sound of a wounded animal, and it sent chills running up my spine.

We brought him back and began the process again. However, it's as Doctor Williams says, we can give him food, shelter, and warmth. But we can't give him hope or Hope. He's going to have to dig for that himself.

TWENTY-FOUR

Henry's Home
30, January 1719
11:00 a.m.

"Sir, you can't go in there."

"And why not, Young Henry? Would you have something to hide?"

"No, sir. It's ..."

Henry's voice penetrated the silence surrounding Ian. He'd been hearing his friend's voice off and on for a while, but this tone, though, was different. And the other voice? Who was that?

"It's what?"

"Geoffrey," Henry pleaded again. "Tell me what I can help you with."

"I believe you know what I came for," Geoffrey told Henry. "Now get out of my way."

The door opened, and Ian heard what he assumed were Geoffrey's footsteps.

"Leave us, Henry," Geoffrey instructed. "We'll be fine."

"But Geoffrey," Henry's voice softened. "As you can see, Ian isn't ..."

"Tell me about Ian," Geoffrey replied just as quietly. "I know Hope loved him."

At the mention of Hope's name, Ian's heart clenched. He wanted to close his ears and ignore everything around him. Except he'd learned there were certain times when it was harder to do that. Sometimes, there was a warmth on his chest and a heart beating in time with his that brought him back from the edge.

"How, how did you—?"

"How did I know?" Geoffrey asked.

"Well, yes," Henry replied.

Geoffrey let out a light laugh. "My daughter took after her mother when it came to putting her feelings into words."

"Hope's journal?"

"Journals," Geoffrey clarified. "Hope documented her love story with Ian, just like her mother documented ours. She'd even started a new one for her son. I just wish..."

Ian felt a tear trickle down his cheek, and the warmth on his chest began to slide. Unconsciously, he reached for the heat to keep it steady, and there was a little squeak that pierced his heart.

"We all wish that, Geoffrey," Henry murmured. "My mother is concerned about my sister, Faith. She's blaming herself for not realizing Hope was so sick."

"It's the bloody curse," Geoffrey whispered, but his voice was so low, Ian wondered if he'd been heard.

"Excuse me, sir?"

"Nothing, Henry." Geoffrey sighed. "Has your friend said anything?"

"About ten days ago," Henry explained. "Kitty's cure worked, but then—"

"Kitty?" Geoffrey questioned. "This is Kitty's doing?"

Ian wanted to know what they were speaking about. What had Kitty suggested? And was Geoffrey angry or surprised?

"Kitty was trying to help," Henry defended Hope's aunt.

"How did Kitty know?"

"I cannot say, Geoffrey. She just appeared one day and said she hoped to give him the will to live."

"If it worked, then why ..." Geoffrey's voice trailed off.

The warmth around Ian's heart grew, and a mewing sound created ripples along his skin. Except the more he attended to those feelings, the greater the chance the pain would return. If he did that, he'd have to acknowledge ...

"Because Ian went back to the cave," Henry explained. "We had to start the process over again."

"He wishes to die," Geoffrey murmured.

"I'll not allow my friend to die, Geoffrey," Henry replied. "I just ..."

"Sometimes you must understand a man's mindset, Henry. Leave us now."

"But ..."

"Leave us."

Ian could hear the indecision in Henry's voice and had to wonder why. Hope's father did not sound angry.

"Shall I take the—?"

"Leave us."

There were quiet steps across the room, the door shut, and Ian knew Geoffrey Prince was in the room alone with him. With the scrape of a chair and he could hear the other man breathing. Then he waited to see what came next.

"Oh, Hope," Geoffrey's voice broke. "I'm so sorry. I failed you, and for that, I'll never forgive myself."

The weight on Ian's chest shifted, and Geoffrey's voice was closer. It was almost as if he were leaning over him—but how could that be?

"Ian," Geoffrey whispered. "It seems I have many things to thank you for. To begin with—for rescuing me from the fire. But none more so than for loving Hope."

Ian was surprised by what he was hearing, for he'd not expected to have Hope's father say such words.

"I understand your grief," Geoffrey went on. "And I know you can hear my words, as I've been where you are. You've locked yourself away in such a place that you feel no pain."

That is true, Ian thought. If he refused to allow the pain space, it stayed locked away. Except when the warmth on his chest was there. Then, it was as if his heart was being surrounded by a love so pure, it was thawing.

"When Christine was taken from me," Geoffrey whispered. "I wished not to go on. But then Anne would put Luke in my arms, or Hope would look at me with her big blue eyes, and my heart would tremble. It was then I realized I needed to live for my children. That if my love had created those precious beings, it was my job to care for them. For what kind of man willingly leaves his family to go it alone?"

But what child wants a father who killed his mother?

"Or are you blaming yourself for Hope's death?" Geoffrey mused. "Is that it?"

Ian could feel the despair climbing, the pain rolling over him in waves. He groaned, the sound loud to his ears. So loud, it triggered a piercing cry that went on and on, becoming louder with each breath.

"Hit a nerve, I see," Geoffrey chuckled. "However, you have nothing on me, Son. I've been there too."

The piercing cry continued. Each new gasp caused Ian's heart to flip. He could feel frustration—and a need—but for what?

"You have a pair of lungs on you," Geoffrey murmured. "Just like your mama had on her."

The warmth on Ian's chest was suddenly gone, and the piercing cry was farther away.

"There now," Geoffrey crooned. "You're all right."

It was quiet in the room, and without the warmth, Ian could have closed himself away. Except he found himself curious ... wondering what was next.

"I understand my daughter gave you my name," Geoffrey continued in a tender voice. "She made me proud. I just wish ..." His voice shook, and for several moments the room was filled with silence and someone sniffing. "I'm going to see that you—"

"Geoffrey," the door opened. "What are you doing here?"

"What does it appear I am doing?" Geoffrey tossed back. "I'm holding my grandson, Kitty."

"So, you know?"

"Of course, I know," Geoffrey grumbled. "It is my town after all."

Kitty snorted, "Your town? If it's your town, did you know about your daughter and this man? Did you know about the babe?"

"All right," Geoffrey agreed. "I knew not of Hope nor this man until it was too late."

"And if you had?"

Geoffrey was quiet, and Ian strained to hear what ... he could not say.

"I know not," Geoffrey admitted. "There are many things I want to say I would handle differently. But ..."

"Which is why I brought the baby here," Kitty explained. "To make up for not giving Hope's feelings the attention they deserved."

"I'm sorry."

"As am I, Geoffrey."

Kitty's voice was closer and, just as happened each time the warmth was removed, there was a soft touch on his shoulder.

"I hope you enjoyed your son's visit," Kitty whispered. "We'll see you in a couple of days."

The soft touch disappeared, feminine steps crossed the floor, and the door closed. Was he alone?

"Kitty is gone, Ian," Geoffrey sighed. "She's taken your son—my grandson—with her. It's just you and me. Open your eyes, and let's talk man to man."

Was he ready to face everything awaiting him if he opened his eyes?

"Don't think about what you've lost, Ian," Geoffrey pleaded. "Think about what's waiting for you. That baby needs his father, whether you believe that or not. He needs everyone who loved Hope surrounding him. It's the only way she can become real to him. We must all share the Hope we knew and loved. And that includes you."

Ian struggled to get his eyes to open, but they refused to listen to his command.

"What I told Henry was true," Geoffrey confided. "I did read some of Hope's journal. I hate to admit this, but I need your help. You need to help me find the key to break the curse once and for all. If we don't, my family, your family, and every family touched by ours will be tainted. Not just now, but for all time. Once hope is gone, so too will be Swan Harbor."

There was another scrape, and somehow, Ian knew Geoffrey was leaving.

"I brought these for you to read."

There was a sound as if something was set on the table, then Ian felt a hand on his shoulder.

"Come back to us," Geoffrey whispered. "Let's grieve for Hope together and find the key to set us all free."

Ian tracked his steps across the room and heard the door open.

"I'll be waiting for you, Ian," Geoffrey murmured, just before the door shut behind him.

Ian lay still and waited, but he wasn't sure what he was waiting for. Except with Geoffrey gone, the room was quiet, almost too quiet. The silence made it too easy for the screams in his head to be heard. And hearing the screams forced him to attend to the pain.

Don't think about what you've lost ...

Hope. How could he not think about what he'd lost? She was everything to him.

The door opened again. "Professor? Are you awake?"

It was Richard, and another Ian owed an apology to. He'd taken advantage of the gentle man and for that, he felt a different kind of sadness.

"I've been practicing my reading." Richard's soft steps came closer. "Shall I read to you?"

Then the scrape of a chair, and Ian could feel Richard was close to the bed.

"I've been practicing. But I still need help. When you wake up, will you teach me some more?"

There was a rustling of papers. Then Richard began reading in his slow, halting manner. "Ships are con—con—constructed using ..."

Another tear leaked from Ian's eyes and rolled down his cheek.

Think about what's waiting for you.

Ian's heart clenched so tightly he almost couldn't get his breath. It hurt, but he needed to talk to his love one more time ...

"Hope."

"I'm here, my love. You promised me."

"I said I would try," Ian clarified. "But it hurts too much."

"Ian," Hope pleaded. "You have to listen to what my father said. Think of what's waiting for you."

"Except then we'll no longer be able to talk like this," Ian cried. "I'll no longer be able to touch you, to kiss your lips."

"Don't think of it like that, Ian," Hope murmured. "I'll always be in your heart. Just look up. My star will be there, watching over you, our son, and Swan Harbor. When it's your time, I'll be waiting."

"Why, though? Why must it be like this?"

"Fate," she replied. "My fate was to love you and to become your guiding star. Your fate is to find the key. Then somehow make sure that our families are free."

"Do you really believe that?"

"I have to." Her voice grew softer, her blue eyes beseeching him to understand. "Your family and my family are meant to be connected. Our hearts tell us that. And just like we can feel each other's hearts' beating. Just like we can feel each

other's emotions, there are and will be more. Those connected hearts must come together to save Swan Harbor."

"It should have been our hearts saving Swan Harbor," Ian murmured, despair weighing him down.

"But it wasn't," Hope told him, saying nothing but the truth. "And until it's time, you must hold on to hope. Don't let the hope die."

"I promise, Hope," Ian whispered. "I'll find the key."

"And hope, Ian?"

"Somehow, someway, I vow to make sure Swan Harbor's hope stays strong."

"Thank you, Ian." Hope stepped into him and wrapped her arms around his waist. "Now, kiss me one more time. Others are waiting for you."

Ian tightened his hold on her and poured every ounce of what he was feeling into their kiss. He needed to make sure she was imprinted on his soul, so he would never forget her.

"It can take 100 trees to build a ship," Richard continued reading. "Ian, did you know that?"

Ian opened his ears to what was around him and once again fought to open his eyes.

"Richard!" Then there was a heavy tread across the floor. "Richard?"

"I'm here, papa."

"Richard," D.D. scolded his son. "You know not to disturb Ian."

"I'm reading to him," Richard corrected his father. "Not disturbing."

"But ..."

Ian opened his eyes to find D.D. staring at him.

"Ian?" D.D. rushed across the floor. "You're awake?"

Bloody hell, of course I'm awake.

When he opened his mouth to speak, he found his tongue didn't seem to obey his brain. And his thoughts were a jumbled mess.

"Thirsty," he managed to utter.

"Thirsty?" D.D. echoed.

"Ye-yes."

"Richard, he's awake," D.D. exclaimed, pouring cider into a cup. "Go tell Henry, please."

"Yes, papa."

"Oh, Ian," D.D. sat on the bed and helped him drink. "It's so good to see those dark eyes of yours. We've been mighty worried."

"So-Sorry." Ian's voice came out as weak as a babe's. And when he tried to hold the cup, his hand shook so much, the liquid sloshed onto the bed. "Ugh," he muttered disgustedly.

"Be gentle with yourself, my boy," D.D. consoled him. "It's going to take time."

"Ian!" Henry rushed into the room, with Richard close behind. "So, it's true! You're awake?"

"I'm awake."

"What can I get you?" Henry fluttered around, straightening the bedding, hovering closely. "Soup? Are you hungry?"

At the mention of food, Ian had expected his stomach to lurch. Instead, there was a gnawing hunger, and his mouth watered.

"Yes, soup," he agreed.

"Good, good," Henry murmured.

"That boy," D.D. chuckled as soon as Henry left the room, "has been a true friend."

"The best," Ian agreed.

"Here we are," Henry hurried back into the room, a tray in his hands. "My mother's vegetable soup and fresh bread."

Ian tried to push his body up in the bed, but when he was too weak, he sent a silent plea to D.D.

"Richard, grab the professor's other arm," D.D. instructed.

It took two of them before Ian was sitting up in the bed with the tray on his lap. For several moments, it was quiet while he ate. Not with much dexterity, as his hands were still shaking. However, by using the bread to dip in the broth, he was able to consume at least half the contents of the bowl.

"No more," he pushed the tray aside.

"But, Ian," D.D. grumbled. "You've barely eaten enough—"

"Doc Williams said that would happen," Henry broke in. "He said small meals until Ian is used to food again."

Ian's brows went up, for when had Henry spoken to the doctor?

"Doc Williams here?" he questioned.

"Yesterday," Henry confirmed. "I asked what I should do when you woke."

"I see."

"Anything else?"

"Nothing now." Ian relaxed back against the pillows. He longed for a bath, but knew he was still too weak.

"You scared us," D.D. told him. "We knew not if ... when you would awake."

"Sorry. I just ..." Except he wasn't ready to discuss what had transpired on the mountain.

"I heard Geoffrey Prince stopped by today," D.D. began in his direct way.

"I heard him," Ian admitted. "But I could not ..."

"Remember what I said," D.D. reiterated. "Be gentle with yourself."

How could he be gentle? There was a job that needed to be done.

"Plan," Ian sighed. "To find the key."

"So, you do not believe reconnecting the hearts was the key?" D.D. asked.

A bolt of rage raced through him, causing Ian to shake with anger. "Bloody hell, no!" Ian took a breath and plunged forward. "If it had, Hope wouldn't have ..." Then the words lodged in his throat.

"I'm sorry," D.D. murmured. "What can I do?"

"Plan," Ian repeated. "I must make a plan."

"That sounds like the Ian I know," D.D. agreed. "What shall I bring you from your cabin?"

It took Ian several minutes to remember what he needed, much less articulate it.

"My journal and my notes," he requested. "Please."

"I'll go now." D.D. returned the chair and asked again, "Anything else?"

Ian started to say no, but then he glanced down at his bare chest. "Clothes. Bring me clothes."

D.D. smiled. "It is good to have you back. While I'm gone, it looks as if you have some reading to do." He dropped Hope's journals on the bed next to him.

Geoffrey had read enough to know of his and Hope's love. But was he strong enough? Was he strong enough to read what she had written about them?

In the end, Ian couldn't make himself pick up the journal where Hope had written about their journey. Instead, he opened the one she'd started for their child.

1 August 1718.

Today marks the fourteenth day since your father once again sailed away from Swan Harbor. I understand he would much rather be with you and me, but he's searching for the key to undo the words spoken to my father and mother. Wouldn't it be wonderful if our love, Ian's and mine, as well as our love for you, broke the curse?

When he returns next month, I must work up the courage to tell him of you. I think he will be very happy.

15. August 1718.

For the very first time, I felt you move today. It was but a fluttering deep in my belly and reminded me of the bubbles in Timber Creek. If I place my hands on my stomach and sit quietly, will you reach for my hand? I'll be waiting …

TWENTY-FIVE

Phillip and Kitty's Home
30, March 1719
1:00 p.m.

It had been eight weeks since Ian had opened his eyes. During that time, he'd worked on getting stronger and making a plan. Once it was made, though, he no longer could just rely on himself, D.D., Richard, and Henry. For the next phase, he would have to trust others. That was going to be difficult.

Ian tugged on his boots and leaned against the wall. His strength was better, but not nearly where he wanted it to be.

"Do you need some help?"

He glanced up to see Henry standing just inside the door of his bedchamber, a look of understanding on his face.

"I need to do this alone, Henry," he tried to explain. "I've disrupted your life long enough."

"It's nothing you wouldn't have done for me," Henry began.

"True," Ian acknowledged. "But Felicity?"

Henry had been reticent about saying much regarding his courtship of Felicity Campbell. But Ian was determined to get the story out of him.

"We've no time to discuss Felicity," Henry retorted. "Now, get your coat. We must go."

Ian shook his head at the mulish look on Henry's face but slipped on his duster and followed him into the front room.

"You do not need to go with me," Ian repeated what he'd said before. "Just lend me your wagon or a horse."

"We've spoken of this many times," Henry sighed. "I'm going with you."

"Fine!" Ian threw up his hands.

He knew what was going on. Because he'd gone up into the mountains in January and relapsed, they were worried about him. Which meant he was rarely allowed time alone.

"Will you be holding my hand while I'm visiting with my son as well?"

"Quit being cheeky, Ian."

Henry set the horse into motion, and Ian couldn't help but notice the surrounding silence. The usual sounds of the busy harbor weren't present.

"Why is it so quiet?" Ian whispered. "It's almost eerie."

Henry glanced around. "The winter was grim. Maybe the town just hasn't woken yet."

Or maybe the town is losing hope.

Once they arrived at Kitty's, Ian climbed down from the wagon and steadied himself to get his balance. With slow, careful steps, he made his way to the door.

"Let me get that for you." Henry stepped in front of him to knock on the door.

"I can knock on the bloody door," Ian grumbled.

"Good day, Ellie," Henry greeted Hope's cousin. "May we speak with Mistress Kitty?"

"Who is it, Ellie?" Kitty came up behind her daughter, with an infant on her shoulder. "Oh!"

"May we come in?" Ian finally found his voice.

"Ellie, take the baby." Kitty handed the child to her daughter and led the men into the great room. "I'm pleased to see you on your feet."

"Thank you, Mistress Kitty," Ian inclined his head. "I should thank you for bringing my ..." the word hung in his throat, "... son to my sick bed."

"You got well," Kitty smiled. "That's what's important. Would you care to see your son?"

Ian cut a glance at Henry and then back again. "If it would not be too much trouble."

"Come with me."

Kitty led him into a smaller room with three cradles lining one wall. She indicated which crib his son was sleeping in, but he knew without being told. After all, he'd carved the cradle with his own hands.

"Baby Ian's been asleep for about an hour," she whispered. "Take as much time as you need."

"Thank you."

"Come on, Henry. Let them have some time."

"But ..."

"Henry," Kitty repeated. "Come have a cookie."

Ian glanced over his shoulder to see Kitty tugging Henry from the room. There was a part of him that would have welcomed his friend staying. But as he turned back toward the cradle, he understood. This was something he needed to do alone.

The baby was lying on his side, one fist curled under his cheek. Ian could tell, even without touching him, he had Hope's nose. And the longer he stood next to the cradle, the more he became aware that, just like with his wife, he could *feel* his son's heart beating. Could sense his contentment.

He didn't want to disturb his rest, but Ian couldn't help gently touching the infant's cheek. When the baby turned his head toward his father's hand, as if searching for food, tears immediately sprang to his eyes.

"Oh, Hope," he whispered. "I wish ..."

It was with a heavy heart that Ian said goodbye and turned to leave. Then he noticed there was a chair in the corner and, before he could change his mind, he lifted the baby and carried him across the room.

The baby continued to sleep peacefully in the crook of his father's arm. As their hearts were aligned, Ian would have known if something wasn't right. He would have felt it.

A need to assure himself all was well had him opening the blanket to examine his child. When the change in temperature brought forth a squeak, he found his heart aching, and a smile on his face at the same time.

Ten fingers, ten toes, and perfect.

"Your mama would be so proud of you," Ian crooned. "I'm going to make sure you know and love her as much as I did. That is my promise to you."

Ian once again settled the infant in the bend of his arm and relaxed in the chair. Time swirled around them, but his sole focus was on the child and the many expressions that crossed his face. Each new movement was filed away in his memory to be examined at a later time.

How his dark hair swirled around the cap of his head. The length of his eyelashes. And the way his eyes fluttered, as if he were having a good dream.

A quirk of his lips. Ears flat against his head. Cheeks that were baby-fine. Fingers that curled around his father's. Eyes that melted his heart.

The baby's eyes were blue, and when they locked with his, Ian was lost. He knew his life would never be the same, for from that moment on, everything he did would be for his child.

Hope's Home
30, March 1719
5:00 p.m.

"Ian," Henry slowly came down the back steps of Hope's home, "everything is taken care of."

"Thank you, Henry," Ian replied. "I know this makes no sense, but …"

"It does not," Henry agreed. "Especially since Geoffrey knows of you."

"I will explain everything soon." Ian took a deep breath and clapped Henry on the shoulder. "But just not yet. First, I must do this for Hope. She is waiting …"

Henry's confused gaze had him clamping down on saying anything further. If he told his friend where his thoughts were, he would sound unhinged and be accused of being overcome by grief. Except he was trying to follow his plan, which was the only way he made it through each day.

"All right," Henry nodded after several moments. "Follow me."

"Is she alone?"

"Yes, and in her room," Henry confirmed, leading them into Hope's family home. "My mother and sister are with Geoffrey and the boys."

Ian followed Henry up a narrow staircase and down a long hall. He stopped outside the last door on the left.

"You still wish to go in alone?"

"I have to," Ian replied.

Henry nodded and stepped back. "Shall I wait?"

"If you wish." Ian took a deep breath, knocked softly, and stepped into the dimly lit room. The older woman was lying in the bed, blankets piled on her, almost buried from sight.

There was a sense of urgency in the air that propelled him forward. "Anne, Anne Michaels. It's Captain ..."

"Hope's Ian." Her frail voice traveled the distance between them. "Come closer."

He took another step toward her bed and once again was bombarded by a strange sensation. It was as if someone or something was waiting. But for what?

"What did you call me?" He settled in a chair close to her bed.

"Ian," she repeated. "Hope told me about you."

Hearing his beloved's name said out loud still felt as if a knife was being driven into his heart. While he knew Anne had helped bring the babe into this world, he hadn't been aware Hope had spoken of them ... of their relationship.

"Hope told you about me?"

"She did." A smile came and went so fast he thought he was seeing things, then Anne admitted, "Hope told me about your marriage. You loved her?"

"More than life itself," he whispered.

"I'm the one who took the child to Kitty," Anne admitted. "When you ..." Her voice broke, taking a little piece of his heart, as Ian knew how she felt.

"You did what was right," Ian assured her. "And the child is doing well."

"Do you plan to claim him as yours?"

Ian ducked his head, ashamed to admit he had not thought that far ahead.

"I will do what needs to be done," he admitted. "But my child is not why I am here."

"What is it then?"

"The curse."

Anne blanched. "What did you say?"

"Come now," Ian scoffed. "Surely, you know of the curse. After all, it was your daughter whose words started this entire spiral."

She winced and seemed to shrink before his eyes. Which reminded him of the reason Hope had kept what she'd learned to herself. But if she hadn't then ...

"I'm sorry." Ian hesitated a beat. "I should not have blurted it out like that, as Hope did not wish for you to be hurt. But," his eyes bore into hers, "if she had, I cannot help but think ..."

"That Hope would be alive today?"

"Yes."

Anne nodded. "I understand. What do you know?"

Ian closed his eyes, and the memory of what he knew washed over him. "Everything."

"But how?"

"Hope overheard an argument between Geoffrey and Isabelle," he admitted. "Then finally, Geoffrey told her why he was trying to protect her."

"I was afraid Isabelle would do something," Anne sighed. "Except I never knew if she had actually followed through. I had hoped she was happy with Edmund and their children. Have you spoken to her?"

"Yes."

"Isabelle admitted what she had done?"

"She did," Ian confirmed. "Isabelle gave me this." He handed over the page where she had written the words uttered in anger all those years ago. "You can read them for yourself."

Anne pushed up in the bed, the exertion causing her forehead to glisten and her hands to shake.

"Isabelle willingly gave you this?"

With a little trickery.

"She did."

"How is she?" Anne asked softly. "The children?"

"I saw no children," he admitted. "Isabelle is bitter one moment ... then hopeless the next."

Anne closed her eyes, and Ian watched a transformation come over her face. It was only then he began to feel as if he'd made the right decision in speaking with her first.

"What do you need from me?"

"I want a way to bring back hope," Ian snapped, but when the woman on the bed winced, he regretted his tone. "Can it be reversed?"

"You want to bring Hope back?"

"Bloody hell, yes!" he hissed. "But I'm not daft and know that is not possible. So, I will settle for knowing that Hope is at peace, and that our son will live a long and fruitful life. My focus is on bringing back hope, with a lowercase h."

"The wish of every parent," she murmured.

"Can you help me?" He took a deep breath and plunged forward even more. "I fear that somehow the loss of my Hope and the hope of this town are intertwined."

"Why do you say that?" However, the tone of her voice and the look in her eyes told him she'd felt it too.

"There's too much silence in the air," Ian told her. "Plus, the swans have not returned."

"The swans?" she frowned. "It's early. Perhaps because the winter was so harsh, they are late."

"That's what Henry said," Ian sighed. "Except I feel it's more than that."

Anne glanced at the paper she was still holding, and he couldn't help but notice her hands were still shaking.

"When we left England, we had such high hopes," she told him. "But it wasn't until we saw the swans that our hope grew. Then, when I noticed they were being led by a black swan, I knew we needed to follow."

"What's special about a black swan?"

"They're a reminder to reclaim your personal freedom," she explained. "And that's what we were doing."

"Hope told me how the swans returned after her birth."

"They did." Anne smiled as if the memory were a happy one. "New eggs hatched, and whatever hung over the town seemed to disappear."

Ian's thoughts swirled, trying to figure out how everything was connected. And where the key fit into the picture.

"My Hope's birth brought new hope to Swan Harbor," Ian pointed out, "and yet Christine still died."

"Complications from childbirth," Anne offered.

"Maybe," Ian acknowledged. "According to Geoffrey, though, Christine felt hearts connected by love was the key. And yet," his heart broke, but he pushed on, "here we are."

"Geoffrey and Christine loved each other. The spiral began with Isabelle's words," Anne stated. "You and Hope loved each other, but it didn't save her. Is that what you're thinking?"

"Hope thought it was bigger than just us," Ian frowned. "But how? And what does that mean?"

"I've thought everything that was happening," Anne murmured, "harkened back to the heart being taken."

Ian winced, but immediately tried to mask his feelings.

"You know about the ruby heart?"

"I do." Ian searched for how much to say but could not bring himself to tell her of his thoughts regarding the ruby. After all, returning the heart to Swan Harbor whole had not saved his wife. And so, he settled on, "But the swans, they still came. And Henry believes the town can live without its heart but not without hope."

"Which brings us back to the town's hope," Anne sighed. "And whether with the passing of your Hope, the town's hope is doomed."

Some of Hope's last words to him had been to not allow hope to die. Had she been worried it was a possibility?

"Do you feel hope is dying?" Ian asked. "That you've been more hopeless this winter?"

"Do you?" she threw the question back at him.

He'd felt as if everything inside of him was dead until Geoffrey's visit. The words spoken by the older man—*think about what's waiting for you*—had stirred something, helping him grow stronger. Then, after he'd held his son, his heart had warmed, and his hope had returned.

"I cannot say it has died," Ian finally admitted. "However, you know Swan Harbor better than I. What are your thoughts?"

Her eyes locked with his, and he had to fight not to look away. This woman, who had loved Hope and helped her birth his child, seemed to be the only one who might have the answers he needed.

One moment stretched into two and then three until finally she nodded.

"I agree that somehow they are connected." Anne held up the paper with the words Isabelle had chanted. "Did it start with these words? It seems it is possible." She waved toward a corner of the room. "Can you bring me the book, *Magical Charms?*"

Ian raised a brow, unsure if he had heard her correctly. "*Magical Charms?*"

"Yes."

"Are you a witch?"

She reared back as if he had slapped her. "No! I am a healer."

He gave a subtle tip of his chin in acknowledgment and crossed the room to locate the book. When he handed it to her, and Anne began turning the pages, he had to fight the need to push her to move faster. She had almost reached the end of the book before she stopped.

"What did you find?" he asked when she remained silent.

"Did Isabelle tell you she was trying to cure her broken heart?"

"Yes," Ian admitted. "Isabelle called it The Broken Heart Cure."

"The Broken Heart Cure," Anne murmured, her voice so soft, he almost didn't hear her. "She must have not read all the words."

"It cured her heart by taking her hope, did it not?" Ian told her what he'd deduced after meeting with Isabelle.

"So, it seems," Anne agreed. "That is Isabelle, though. She has no patience."

"So, Geoffrey was right," Ian barked. "Isabelle's words started a spiral that has extended beyond just her and Hope's parents. Somehow, she took their hope as well."

"They perished from lack of hope?" Anne repeated several times, as if she were trying to make sense of what he'd said. "Except that makes no sense."

"Mistress Anne," Ian blew out a breath. "All I know is the woman I loved was taken from me and our child way too soon. Geoffrey believes that if we find this key, only then will our families be safe. But bloody hell, I've no idea what is meant by such a statement."

Anne met his eyes briefly before dropping hers to the pages of the book in her lap. "Will you give me time to research?"

"Do I have a choice?"

"I am sorry," Anne tried to console him. "However, I fear the solution will not be a simple one."

Ian grunted and had to bite his tongue to keep from saying something he would regret. But then he finally realized it would get him nowhere.

"How much?"

"As long as it takes. I promise, Ian. Once I find the answers you seek, I will get them to you."

"You give me your word?"

"I do."

He didn't want to walk out the door without answers, but realized he had no choice.

"Very well. I will wait to hear from you."

"Thank you."

Once he'd returned the chair, he knew he had no more reason to stay and made his way to the door. There was still something in the air he couldn't explain, but rather than making him anxious, it gave him peace.

He'd just touched the door handle when Anne's soft voice stopped him.

"I loved her too, Ian," she murmured. "Together, we'll find the key."

Her words should have soothed him, but with only a slight nod, he stepped into the hallway.

"Did you get what you needed?" Henry asked as soon as the door was shut.

"She is looking," Ian offered with a heavy heart. "Once she finds the answer, she will let me know."

They made their way back downstairs, and the closer he got to the door, the more the air closed around him. Ian wanted to ask Henry if he felt it too, but one look at his face showed nothing out of the ordinary.

Was it just him? Did it have anything to do with the fact he was in Hope's home? Walking on the floor she had walked on?

Henry pushed open the door and led the way down the stairs. "Are you alright? You look like you have seen a ghost."

"I'm fine," Ian assured his friend. "Thank you again."

"What now?"

Ian shrugged. "I wait."

"Will you be staying with me?"

Ian wasn't sure what he should do, but knew he needed to be alone with his thoughts.

"I will be there tonight, Henry," Ian promised. "As will D.D. and Richard. Our plan was for me to speak with Anne, which I did. Now, though, I need to decide what's next."

"What can I do?"

"Get your mother and sister home. I'll see you at your house later."

Ian stepped behind the line of trees that bordered the back of Hope's property. He was immediately bombarded with memories and wondered if this was a good idea.

"Ian?"

"Yes, Henry?"

The serious look on Henry's face reminded Ian of how concerned his friends were for him.

"You'll not do anything rash, will you?"

"No, Henry," Ian assured him. "I give you my word. But I just need to be alone with my thoughts, if that's all right."

Their dark eyes clashed across the short distance, and whatever Henry saw must have sufficed.

"I'll see you later."

Then, he disappeared back into the home, leaving Ian alone for the first time in months.

How do I go on?

You hold on to hope.

TWENTY-SIX
PRESENT DAY

Killian and Emma's Place
February 8
6:00 p.m.

When I stepped beyond the line of trees, the memories rolled over me one by one. So much so, I had to stop and regain my breath. That same feeling that had surrounded me in Hope's home was stronger in the woods. It almost felt as if she were standing next to me. Except I knew that couldn't be so and pushed on.

As I walked farther up into the mountains, I passed places that had been important to us. The spot next to the stream where we had enjoyed a picnic. A tree where we had carved our initials. The feelings were so strong that when I closed my eyes, I could sense her hand in mine and smell the food from our meal.

Yet none of the memories were stronger than when I happened upon the hot springs where she had spied on me bathing. Not only could I hear her laughter, but as plain as if she were in front of me, she spoke.

"It's bigger than just us, Ian."

Her words reminded me of my conversation with Anne. Of how Isabelle's words affected Christine and Geoffrey's happy ending. But even though Hope's and my heart were connected, it hadn't been enough. That seemed to reiterate the words, that it's bigger than us. What did that mean, though? And if it involved the swans, how?

The residents of Swan Harbor seem to believe the swans were the source of the town's hope. After living here for a short time, even I had fallen into the same thought. Except when I think of it logically, it makes no sense. And makes me even more curious about how everything is connected.

If the 'key' involves connected hearts, then why was the connection of Hope's and mine not enough? Our love was powerful, but yet ...

Hope believed my destiny was to find the key, and I will do that. But then, what is next for me? Do I stay and make my life in Swan Harbor? Or do I go back to England with D.D. and Richard? After holding my son for just a short time, this decision becomes even more important. For he is my reason for living.

I'd not expected to feel as much as I did when I held him. However, when our eyes had locked, I'd wanted to give him the world. Plus, something inside I'd thought dead had bloomed. Except what do I have to offer him? Is it fair to deprive him of the motherly love he's receiving from Hope's aunt?

As I climb onto the thinking stone high above Swan Harbor, I know I need to decide my next step. And just as I told Henry, I must consider D.D. and Richard. They promised to help me *complete my journey, which is more than I asked, but not more than I expected.*

I also have to trust that Anne will be able to give me the solution. The one to save Hope's family, my son, and the town, for without them, I have no doubt they will perish.

KILLIAN CLOSED THE BOOK AND TOSSED IT ONTO THE COFFEE table. There were bits and pieces of Ian's last few entries that kept swirling around in his head. Except were they what he needed to solve the puzzle regarding his town's teetering hope? Or closer to his heart, were they the pieces he needed to save Emma, unlike Ian had been able to save Hope?

Millicent, their mother cat, jumped on the table, her green eyes locked on him. The way she was looking at him made him feel as if she were trying to tell him something.

"What is it, girl?" he murmured, allowing her to crawl onto his lap. "Do you know why the pieces aren't fitting together?"

She butted her head against his hand until he began scratching her chin. Perhaps the hypnotic motion would allow him to pluck out the pieces he needed to examine.

"Killian?"

He glanced up just as his father and Liam came around the corner of the kitchen. Which meant they'd come up the stairs without him hearing them.

"Where were you just now?" Finn asked.

"1719," Killian grumbled.

"Visiting Ian again?" Finn surmised.

"Aye! Some bloody investigator I am." Killian kicked out, his boot catching the leg of the coffee table hard enough to knock it off. "Bloody hell." He reached for the journal, but it slid onto the floor.

Finn gave him a look but picked up the book, while Liam moved the broken table across the room.

"Killian 1, table 0," Liam quipped. "You're probably going to owe Emma a new one."

"Emma hates that table," Killian admitted. But knew that was his brother's way of giving him an opportunity to choose the direction of the conversation. "Were we to gather tonight?"

"No. However, after we read the other night, I could tell you had a lot on your mind," Finn explained. "So, we thought we'd have a brainstorming session, if you will."

"I see." Killian's jaw ached from where he'd been clenching his teeth. Except he couldn't get out of his mind, they were searching for something that hadn't been located in 300 years. "Is it just the two of you?"

"Elsa and Ava are with Emma," Finn told him. "Plus, Jack should be along shortly."

Killian had been surprised Emma's uncle had been so patient. He'd been looking for the key for over fifty years and seemed to think they finally had a chance of finding it. The question was, what was different?

The way his father was scrutinizing him said he was going to be expected to share his thoughts soon. Yet, how did he explain what he hadn't quite pieced together?

"We haven't finished reading Ian's journal," Finn pointed out. "So, I—"

"I'm aware of that," Killian cut him off. "But time—"

"Don't say it's running out," Finn scolded. "As long as there are pages to be read, there's time."

"I just keep thinking, what if ...?"

"What if something happens to Emma?" Liam guessed.

"Aye."

"Don't focus on what might happen," Liam reminded him. "Think about what we're trying to do to keep something from happening."

"In a way, that's how I've always kept my hope alive," Finn sighed. "There were many times I could have given in to the hopeless feelings. Except instead of thinking about the negative, I looked to the positive."

"I do the same when working on a case, but—"

"—It's bloody hard when it involves the woman you love." Finn's dark eyes met his and in them, Killian saw his father understood. After all, he was married to Emma's mother ... who was a Swan woman too.

"Right."

"Now, tell us ..." Finn began only to have Emma, Ava, and Elsa's arrival temporarily halt the conversation.

"Killian," Emma indicated the table. "Do I want to know?"

"The cats?" he offered.

She rolled her eyes. "Try again."

"Frustration," he admitted. "Liam said he could fix it."

"Bugger that, Killian," Liam laughed. "Emma, I told him to buy you a new one."

"Good, I hate that table."

"It does give us a little more room in here." Killian tried to look on the bright side.

Emma sent him a grin that said, 'I'll accept that response for now,' then excused herself to change out of her work clothes. While she did that, he took a few minutes to offer drinks to their guests.

"I'm sorry, but since we didn't expect you, we have no—"

"—Snacks," Ava snapped her fingers. "I left them in the car."

"Snacks?" Liam's eyes lit up.

"Pastries from Paula's," Finn told him on his way out to the car to get them.

While they were waiting for Emma, Finn, and Jack, Killian had Liam help him rearrange the furniture.

"Look who I found." Finn returned, bringing with him the yeasty smell of pastries and Jack.

"More journals, Jack?" Killian nodded toward the books the older man was carrying.

"Just Anne's and Henry's," Jack explained. "I thought we might need them."

"You feel it too, don't you?" Killian asked, somehow not surprised by Jack's comments.

"That there were some puzzle pieces in the last few entries," Jack replied. "Yes."

"But are they the pieces we need to find the key?"

"I hope so, son," Jack murmured, just as Emma returned. "I hope so."

"You hope what?" Emma asked, reaching into the box for a cinnamon bun.

"That you don't take the red velvet one," Jack grinned, helping himself.

"It's all yours." She handed her uncle a napkin and waited until he'd gone into the other room.

"Would you like coffee, Doc?" Killian jumped in before she could say anything.

"No." She closed her hand around his wrist, stopping him from what he was doing. "I'm going to make mom and me hot chocolate, and then you can tell them what you're thinking."

"Why me?" he responded, knowing he sounded petulant.

"Because they're here for you."

"But," his gaze locked with hers, "the key has been lost for 300 years. Surely, Jack …"

Emma kissed him, effectively shutting him up. "Killian, you know my thoughts on this. Jack believes you and I are part of the key. Plus, we," she reminded him, "decided our families should be involved. Besides, Swan Harbor doles out information in her own sweet time. Perhaps it's up to us to listen."

"Perhaps," he agreed, kissing her again.

"Of course, I'm right," she smirked. "You get the coffee, and I'll be in there in a minute."

Once everyone was seated, Killian flipped open Ian's journal and reread the last few entries. And just as before, there was a strong sense that there were pieces they needed to examine. As he read though, he realized why he was having such a hard time. He'd told his father that when working on a case, he focused on the positive. Therefore …

"Liam," he commanded as soon as he finished reading. "I need an extra pair of hands."

❧

Emma was surprised when Killian disappeared immediately after he'd finished reading … until he reappeared. She should have known.

"What?" He exchanged looks with her. "How many times have you said, 'you're the investigator, investigate?'"

"Not very many."

He arched that damn sexy brow of his, and she had to fight the giggle. "So, our search for the key is going up on an evidence board?"

"If it works," Killian murmured, already making a list. "My gut tells me the answers we need can be found by answering these questions."

The first item on his list was a question Emma had wondered about as well. He had written 'losing hope = death' on the board.

"How could losing one's hope cause death?" Jack asked.

"We see it in medicine all the time," Liam answered.

Emma understood that, as she saw the same thing working with animals.

"It's like this," Elsa explained, evidently noticing Jack's blank look. "There's been research on the power of positive thinking, especially with terminally ill patients. If two people have the same disease, their attitudes toward it can make a difference. Often, the person who keeps the most positive attitude will live a longer and happier life than someone who gives in to the disease."

"It's the same with animals," Emma stated. "A sick animal who has a loving family can have a stronger 'will' to live than an animal who doesn't."

"How does this fit with Christine and Hope?" Killian frowned. "Christine died of complications following childbirth."

"And Hope, we think, might have died from asthma," Emma added.

"It's the same as with terminal diseases," Elsa went on. "Hope developed asthma-like symptoms after having the baby. However, she had it in her head that death was her fate. Plus, since she assumed it didn't matter, she took chances. Being in the dry winter air, and the smoke from the fire didn't help."

"Yet when mom got sick." Emma clasped Ava's hand. "She looked on it as a positive sign and took the opportunity to create the life she wanted."

"Ava let me catch her." Finn kissed her mother's other hand.

"Or did you let me catch you?" Ava leaned into him for a kiss.

Emma met Killian's look across the room, as the fact their parents were married still felt weird to both.

"What I was trying to say," she laughed, "was that mom didn't give up on hope."

"Alright," Killian nodded, evidently satisfied with the answer. Then he went on to the next item on his list. "Thoughts on the solution not being simple?"

"It's like a business proposal gone wrong, I'd bet," Ava muttered. "You need to figure out where it went wrong and make sure there's a clause for each place things went off track."

"So that could tie into the comment about it being bigger than just Hope and Ian," Killian guessed. "It could also explain why, because of our connection to them, Jack felt that Emma and I were part of the key."

"If the spiral started with Geoffrey, Christine, and Isabelle, and Hope and

Ian's love wasn't enough," Finn murmured almost to himself. "Then it's not just you and Emma. You need someone connected to Isabelle."

"Catherine," Killian winced.

"Catherine?" Finn echoed.

"Aye, Catherine Gold," Killian replied. "Dylan dated her before he and Molly were married."

"And she's best friends with Killian's ex-floozies," Emma laughed.

"Oh," Liam nodded. "Perhaps I should talk with her."

"She doesn't care," Killian grumbled. "After that one time she met with us at Sally's, she said it didn't involve her."

"How could she say that?" Ava cried. "Doesn't she know this is important?"

"You'd have to know, Catherine," Emma sighed.

"Except in a way, she's right," Jack broke in.

"How?" Ava frowned.

"Catherine's mother was a Michaels," Jack pointed out. "Which means ..."

"She's a descendant of Anne's son or nephew," Ava realized.

"Right," Jack agreed.

"Which means," Killian murmured. "We need a Williams for them to be connected to Isabelle."

"I'll drop by the library tomorrow," Jack offered. "I'm sure Amanda would work on that for us."

"The timeline still doesn't add up," Killian complained.

"How so?" asked Jack.

"The date on the entry we just read is March 30, 1719. Ian wasn't seen in Boston until December 1719. If he lived in Swan Harbor all that time, how did no one know the story of Ian and Hope?"

"Good question," Jack acknowledged. "I remember hearing Rose, Teri, and Margaret Prince talking about digging through the archives at the library. That's how they found out about Hope. Was there anything in Rose's journals?" he asked Ava.

After Ava had found out she was Jack's niece, he'd given her a trunk that had been full of her Grandmother Rose's journals.

"No," Ava denied. "She didn't even know his name. Ian was always referred to as Hope's lover."

"There's also," Killian held up Ian's journal and pointed to the drawings on the back page, which he'd added to the board.

"But," Jack sputtered.

"I know you don't believe we should read ahead," Killian assured him. "However, these aren't new to us. And aren't you the one who said you felt these symbols were important to finding the key?"

"So, I did," Jack agreed. "Yet, we're still at a standstill, aren't we?"

"The chest where we found Hope's journal." Emma ticked off the first item, then moved to the second. "My bracelet has a key on it."

"Which Grandmother Rose said held the answer to finding the big 'key'," Ava added. "And the connected hearts," she went on to explain regarding the third item, "had to do with true love."

"Which leaves us with the last item - the heart with a lighthouse," Emma sighed. "What could that be?"

"Swan Harbor," Jack immediately replied. "At least the lighthouse is a symbol of our town. But the heart?"

"Another question that needs answering," Killian grumbled.

"But, Son," Finn reminded him. "The questions now are fewer than when we started."

"Aye, except are we missing something?" Killian murmured. "Or are we yet to learn it?"

"But it's not Ian we're waiting for, is it?" Emma noted. "Isn't it Anne?"

"Jack, you brought Anne's journal, right?" Killian asked.

"I did." Jack separated out Anne's journal and flipped it open. "Want me to read the last few entries?"

"Please," Emma confirmed.

While he was looking for the right page, she snagged Killian's hand and tugged him onto the sofa next to her.

"Are you alright?" he whispered.

"I'm fine," she assured him. "I ..."

He slipped his arm around her and pulled her back against him. "I've got you, Doc."

"Ian visited Anne on March 30, 1719," Jack reminded them. "Her first entry after that was on April 5."

5, April 1719

It has been several days since Hope's Ian came to see me. I want to say, I was shocked by what he had to say, but I cannot. On that day all those years ago when I discovered my missing book, I worried Isabelle would do something rash. Then the next day, I found it on the table and assumed I'd just left it out. It was easier to blame myself than it was to worry about my daughter.

And now, I must assume responsibility for the death of Christine, as well as my beautiful Hope. While I know it was not me who uttered the words, I should have expected it . How will I ever look Geoffrey in the face again?

However, as I try to come up with a way to undo the hate, my thoughts have not changed. I will do whatever is necessary to help Ian. It's the least I can do for the family I have come to love as my own.

<u>10, April 1719</u>

It's been ten days since I was given the cruel words said by my daughter. With the new happenings, I have an even greater regret for everything I have put this family through. But I am doing everything possible to help.

My thoughts continue along the same lines as they were in the beginning. That because everything started with Christine, Geoffrey, and Isabelle, the reversing of the spiral is more complex. If it only involved the connection of two hearts, Hope and Ian would have been able to have their happy ending. However, I am convinced connected hearts are the key. Except if it's not just two hearts, then who and how many are needed?

Which brings me to the other happenings. I was cleaning the kitchen after dinner and ...

"Is there something else you need?" Anne asked, when Geoffrey remained seated at the table long after what was normal.

"You know, do you not?" Geoffrey asked.

Her heart rate ticked up a notch at what could be on his mind. "I know what?" Anne inquired hesitantly.

"About Isabelle," he started the conversation she'd hoped to avoid. "About what she said to Christine and me the night we were betrothed."

Anne thought about denying everything, but she couldn't help but wonder, as Ian had, if they'd talked sooner ...

"I know," she finally admitted.

"And?"

"What do you want me to say, Geoffrey?" Anne cried, her voice thick with unshed tears. "You are like a son to me. Your children are like grandchildren. My heart breaks that my flesh and blood could have started this ..."

"Do you also know Isabelle is the one who shot me?" Geoffrey waved a hand in front of his injured eye and arm. "Who almost cost me my life?"

Her knees buckled, and she would have fallen if he hadn't caught her.

"I'm sorry," Geoffrey murmured. "That was uncalled for."

"But the truth?" Anne asked. "Isabelle shot you, and yet you told me not?"

"Hope decided there was no benefit."

A chill raced up Anne's spine at the amount of pain her daughter had caused Geoffrey. And to think that at one time, she'd hoped ...

"Do you wish me to leave?"

"Did I ask that of you?"

"No."

"Then we'll not mention it again." Geoffrey studied her closely, but rather than the anger she'd expected, she saw only pain. "Who told you?"

"You do not know?" Anne frowned. "Then how—"

"—Do I know?"

"Yes."

"I overheard you muttering," he admitted. "Now, who told you?"

Anne knew Geoffrey had met Hope's child, but he'd never asked about her part in the child's life.

"Are you sure you wish to know?"

"Was it Hope's Ian?"

"You know about Ian?" Anne gasped.

"Yes, I know," Geoffrey admitted. "I went to see him and asked for his help. Was it him?"

"Yes."

After my admission, I wanted to say more about Ian. To tell Geoffrey how much Hope had loved him. The chance was lost, though, when Luke ran into the kitchen for a cookie. I am now left to wonder what's next for the men Hope loved. As for me, I will continue my search.

TWENTY-SEVEN

Ian's Place
21, April 1719
9:00 p.m.

Ian adjusted the baby in the crook of his arm and pointed up into the night sky. "Your mum is shining down on you," he crooned to the infant. "She wants you to sleep through the night."

The child gave him a toothless smile and waved his pudgy arms.

"You think just because you're cute, I'm going to give in," Ian continued to lecture. "But a tired papa means a grumpy papa."

Baby Ian's eyes closed and opened several times before staying shut.

Finally, Ian thought, carefully carrying his son through the practically empty home. If he were lucky, he'd actually get the baby into the cradle before he woke up.

Somehow over the last few weeks his life had settled into a routine. He'd decided to move back onto the ship until Henry's mum had offered him an alternative.

A home had been started for Henry's sister and husband on a hill close to the tavern. When they had perished in the fire, the house had sat incomplete. Ian had offered to finish what needed to be done in exchange for a place to stay.

The small home allowed him to have his son with him most of the time. Once he'd configured his flask and a fine cloth for feedings, he'd not had to rely on Kitty as much. While it wasn't perfect, they were together.

"Sleep well," Ian whispered.

He placed the baby in the cradle and had just blown out the candle when there was a knock on the door.

"Bloody hell," Ian murmured. "Who's calling so late?"

Then he answered his own question and assumed it was Henry, D.D., or Richard. They still behaved as busybodies and kept a close eye on him.

"I told you," he began, opening the door. "Oh ..."

"Ian."

Geoffrey Prince was standing on the front stoop of Ian's home, his hat in his good hand.

"Sheriff." Ian tipped his chin. "What can I do for you?"

"We need to talk." Geoffrey stepped closer, making it impossible to shut the door. "Please."

Ian hadn't stopped hearing Geoffrey's voice asking him to *come back* to them. Or hearing him say, *Let's grieve for Hope together.* However, he'd wished to go to the older man with the 'key'.

"Come in."

He pushed the door open farther and stood back while Geoffrey entered the house.

"Henry told me where to find you," Geoffrey told him. "And Kitty explained your son is living with you."

"He is," Ian agreed. "We're managing."

Ian led the way to the great room, where a fire would keep them warm.

"Rum or cider?" he asked, stopping by a sideboard.

"Whatever you're having," Geoffrey murmured.

Ian had imagined this moment many times, but in his rendering, it was Geoffrey serving him.

"A bit of rum."

He handed Geoffrey the mug and sat on a bench across from his visitor. What the other man wanted, he wasn't sure.

"I suppose you're wondering why I'm here," Geoffrey began. Then, almost as if he were nervous, he tossed back the rum and stood to wander around the room.

"Why are you here?"

"What are your plans?"

"My plans?" Ian echoed. "To give my son the best life possible, why?"

"I," Geoffrey blew out a breath, "I'm mucking this up. Shall I start again?"

Ian saluted the other man with his mug. "By all means."

"Were you aware I visited you when you were ill?"

"I was." Ian debated how much to say, but finally admitted, "Your words reminded me of my purpose."

"The child?"

"Yes."

"When did you find out about the curse?"

Ian's lips curved into a semblance of a smile, the memory of climbing into Hope's room feeling just like yesterday.

"The night you were shot," Ian explained. "Hope told me what she'd overheard. We pieced it together after that."

"I'm sorry."

"For what?" Ian shot back. "You weren't the one who muttered words to heal your broken heart. This is all on Isabelle."

"I never imagined," Geoffrey sighed. "She's cost me so much."

"You're not the only one who's lost someone because of her," Ian reminded him.

"I'm aware of that," Geoffrey acknowledged. "After Christine was gone, maybe I should have ..."

"Geoffrey," Ian retorted. "Stop. Aren't you the one who said, '*Don't think about what you've lost*'? You were right when you said your children were what brought you back to the land of the living. It was the same for me."

He set his mug on the table and stoked the fire a few times, more for something to do than because it was needed.

"I blamed myself for Hope's death," Ian admitted. "Just as you suspected."

"But why?" Geoffrey studied him for several moments. "You weren't here when she became ill."

"I should have been," Ian barked. "Instead, I was in Boston retrieving the ..."

His words hung in the air, as he wasn't sure he wished to confess the reason.

"Retrieving the what, Ian?" Geoffrey pushed.

"The heart."

Geoffrey's jaw dropped, and Ian could tell his thoughts were whirling around in his head.

"But you did not take it."

"No," Ian agreed. "I did not take it." Then he went in a direction he hadn't anticipated. "Will you tell me about what happened with the heart in England?"

"In England?" Geoffrey frowned. "Why?"

"Curiosity," Ian offered. "Hope knew a little."

"The ruby was a gift to my grandfather and sat on a pedestal in my grandparents' home. I was young, six or seven, and there was a celebration. I remember loud music and dancing." Geoffrey's voice trailed off, and he was quiet for so long that Ian wondered if he was going to get the complete story.

"It was more than just miscreants who ran through the village, wasn't it?"

"Marauders," Geoffrey murmured. "There were many killed, including my grandfather. When it was over, only half of the heart remained."

"No idea who took it?"

"No," Geoffrey sighed. "However, it mattered not. The village continued to be fertile, and the water plentiful."

Ian was still unsure where his father had gotten it. The question was, what did he say to Geoffrey?

"My father ended up with the other half of the stone," Ian admitted.

"The stone led you here," Geoffrey guessed.

"So, it would seem," Ian whispered. "Then, when I found Isabelle, she had your half."

"Isabelle?" Geoffrey frowned. "But I thought—"

"Maddok?"

"Yes."

"Maddok took it during the fire," Ian confirmed. "But he gave it to Isabelle. It was her idea."

"What did you do with the heart?"

Ian winced but explained about having the stone reconnected.

"When yours and Christine's weren't *the* connected hearts, I'd hoped ..."

"That reconnecting the Swan Harbor heart was the key?" Geoffrey guessed.

Ian's eyes suddenly welled with tears, and he turned away. "I failed. When I realized Hope was gone, I threw it on the mountain."

"You threw it on the mountain?" Geoffrey repeated. "The Heart of Swan Harbor is—"

"—Somewhere on the mountain," Ian confirmed.

Geoffrey let loose a laugh, making Ian wonder if the other man had really understood what he'd said.

"You heard me, right?" Ian asked again. "Instead of bringing the stone to you, it's lost somewhere on the mountain."

"Oh, I heard," Geoffrey continued to laugh. "I should be angry, but how can I when I did something similar after Christine's death."

"You threw gemstones onto the mountain?" Ian shook his head. "Did you ever find them?"

Geoffrey shrugged. "Never looked. But why did Isabelle have it?"

"Part of her plan to get you back," Ian replied. "I made her think that if you cured your broken heart, you might love her."

"And that worked?"

"It did." Ian stopped at the window, and the moonlight hanging over the water had him longing for something different. "Now we wait and hope Anne finds the solution."

"And until she does?" Geoffrey wanted to know. "What had you planned had Hope lived?"

"I want to teach."

There had been a germ of an idea rolling around in Ian's head since he'd had time on his hands. He just didn't know what Geoffrey's thoughts would be.

"Teach?" Geoffrey came closer. "As in?"

"My crew isn't used to being so idle," Ian tossed out words as they popped into his head. "What would you think if we built a place where the children can go to learn for a few hours every day?"

"And you would like to do this?"

"I would." Ian decided he was all in and confessed, "Before leaving England, my plan was to go to the University."

"Well, that surprises me," Geoffrey smiled. "There was a dandy around town last fall. I heard he was teaching reading ...”

Ian ducked his head. “Yes, sir. That was me.”

“You?”

Geoffrey frowned, and Ian assumed he was trying to outfit him in dandy clothing.

“Hope felt,” Ian hesitated a beat, then two, “she said, ‘people see what they wish to see.’”

“And if she were seen with a dandy ...”

“Something like that.”

“When were you married?”

“Last April ... in Timber Creek,” Ian admitted. “I’d never wanted anything more.”

“Will you,” Geoffrey’s voice broke, and Ian’s stomach clenched on what he’d been about to say. But then he cleared his throat and continued, “Will you tell me of your love story with my daughter?”

“Did you not read of it in Hope’s journal?”

“Some,” Geoffrey acknowledged. “Except I wish to hear your side.”

Could he speak of her without sinking into the depths of despair? Or would speaking of her help keep her alive in his heart?

“I had heard her long before I saw her,” Ian began, his throat tight. “She had the voice of a Siren and lured me. Then, as I stepped from the tavern one night, she crossed my path. Her hair hung halfway down her back, and her dress was as yellow as the sun. It was what happened inside that caused me to take note. Warmth bloomed in the center of my chest, and I felt alive.”

Swan Harbor School

1, December 1719

Over the next six months, Ian became Professor Samuel Jones to most of Swan Harbor. He, D.D., Richard, and the crew went to work building a learning center. It was exactly the type of place he’d always imagined. And even before it was complete, he’d already organized his students.

“Do you think twenty-five is too many?” Ian frowned.

“Twenty-five seems like—” D.D. began.

“—The perfect number,” Ian answered his own question.

“I’m happy to help,” D.D. muttered tongue-in-cheek.

"Should we divide the space into several rooms?" Ian asked, stepping off the inside width.

"Well," D.D. followed suit, "I think—"

"Agreed," Ian once again answered his own question. "Two rooms are better than one. One for the reading ..."

"And the other for numbers?" D.D. surmised.

"I believe so," Ian agreed. "Faith said she would enjoy helping with that."

"Alone?"

Ian glanced up. "You doubt Faith can handle the numbers alone?"

"Children, they can be," D.D. shrugged. "Noisy."

"True. But the children who come to learn," Ian proclaimed, "will do just that ... learn."

"If you say so."

"I do." Ian stuck all his papers in a pouch out of the way. "Now, where's Richard? We need to go get the small tables I made for the children."

"Small tables?"

"Yes."

Ian led the way to the open wagon he'd borrowed from Geoffrey. He figured he'd need to make at least three trips. But since the school was close to his home ...

"What about chairs?" D.D. asked when they were on their way.

"Henry's father is making small chairs," Ian explained. "As soon as I've time, I'll make larger tables for each room."

"And learning materials?"

"Jon's merchant ship is bringing me some this week."

"You've really thought this out," D.D. mused. "Haven't you?"

Ian slanted a glance D.D.'s direction. "You sound surprised."

"It's not that I'm surprised you've done a thorough job," D.D. explained. "I'm surprised you seem happy, maybe even excited about this opportunity."

"I am," Ian began, but then he was quiet while he concentrated on lining up the wagon close to the door. "This should do it."

He'd built the tables in a shed he'd constructed behind the house. Then he'd moved them inside for smoothing, so he could hear the baby.

Between the three of them, they quickly loaded as many tables as possible and then climbed back onto the wagon for the return trip. As soon as they were on the way, he picked up the conversation.

"Did I ever imagine living in the Colonies and teaching young children? No, but I never thought about being a father either, and my son is my reason for everything." His voice faded, and when he continued, the sounds were huskier. "Do I wish things were different? Bloody hell, yes. But I want Baby Ian to grow up with family."

"He would have family in England," D.D. murmured.

"But not Hope's family."

D.D. said nothing until they'd arrived at the new building. "I want you to be happy, Ian."

"Thank you, D.D."

While they were moving the tables into the building, Henry arrived with another wagon.

"Thought you might need these." He hopped down and peeled back a tarp to reveal stacks of small chairs.

"Now we need the children," Ian grinned.

They carried in the tables and chairs, and he made a few notes. He'd need to decide how to separate the room but was fortunate they'd included fireplaces on each end. And then ...

"Now that it's all complete," Henry dug into his satchel, pulling out a metal plate, "Geoffrey and I decided you should put this somewhere on the building."

"What is it, Henry?" Ian took the plate that had his professor persona's name on it and the date.

"It's a way for others to know of your contribution to Swan Harbor."

There was a lump in Ian's throat at the sentiment, "I know not what to say."

"Say thank you," Henry laughed, "and come show me where you want it."

"What do you think, D.D.?" Ian showed off the sign. "Where shall I display it?"

"In a prominent place," D.D. proclaimed, leading the way outside. "I think it would look nice above the door. Everyone can see it."

Ian looked at the sign, but there was something that stopped him from displaying it in such a visible place.

"I think we need one that says, 'Swan Harbor Learning Center' there," he suggested. "Let's put this one on the corner."

Henry disappeared and returned with a pot of glue, and they stuck the sign on the building.

"Samuel Jones, December 1719," Ian read.

"I'm sorry," Henry murmured.

"Sorry?" Ian frowned. "About what?"

"I didn't even think," Henry blew out a breath. "It should say Ian Jones."

"No," Ian denied. "It's better this way. My friends and Hope's family know the truth. That's what matters."

"If you say so." Henry gave him a crooked grin. "I'll get to work on the Learning Center one."

"Thanks, Henry." Ian clapped his friend on the back. "Now, if you'll excuse us, we're due at Geoffrey's for a late dinner."

"Special occasion?"

"If I'm lucky, Anne will have figured out what needs to be done to set hope free."

"Good luck."

Henry climbed onto the wagon, and something had Ian asking, "Are you calling on Felicity tonight?"

"Not tonight." Then, saying no more, Henry set the horses in motion.

"He still will not say what happened with Felicity?" D.D. asked.

"No," Ian sighed. "But something tells me it has to do with me."

D.D. hummed but had no further words of wisdom. And while they closed the building down for the night, Ian decided he was going to have to speak to Henry. He'd tried, but apparently not hard enough.

"What about Baby Ian?" Richard asked when they turned toward Geoffrey's house and away from Kitty's.

"He stayed with Anne today," Ian admitted. "I left him when I borrowed the wagon."

"A might easier on Anne with one wee one," laughed D.D., "than Kitty and the three."

"I'm not sure how she does it," Ian admitted. "Now that Baby Ian is toddling everywhere, he keeps me busy."

"That they do," D.D. agreed.

Ian returned the wagon to Geoffrey's barn and followed D.D. and Richard into the home. He tracked his son's high-pitched voice into the great room to find him giggling at Luke and Alan.

The sight of his son interacting with family was the very reason he'd settled in Swan Harbor.

"Pa!" the child squealed. "Pa!" He toddled toward where Ian was standing, as fast as his legs would allow.

"Hey there, big guy," Ian said as he lifted his son high. "What are you doing?"

"We're playing, Professor," Luke informed him. "Baby, I behaved exceptionally well today."

Every time Luke spoke, Ian wanted to laugh, as he sounded more like he was sixteen instead of six.

"Did he now?" Ian set the baby back down. "That's very good to hear."

"Ian," Geoffrey came into the room from the direction of his study. "Everything go alright at the learning center today?"

Ian turned away from where the boys had gone back to playing, and the look on Geoffrey's face told him there was news.

"It went fine, Geoffrey," Ian assured him. "And Henry brought the chairs his father made. We're almost ready for the children."

"Good, good," Geoffrey murmured absently.

"Geoffrey?" Ian questioned. "Is there …?"

"Anne thinks she knows what needs to be done," Geoffrey told them quietly.

"That is good," Ian exclaimed. "Isn't it?"

"Good," Geoffrey sighed, "and bad."

"Bloody hell, Geoffrey," Ian retorted. "How can it be both?"

"Because," Geoffrey grumbled. "The words are not the problem. It's what she believes needs to occur before the words can be said."

Ian shrugged. "Tell me. Whatever it is, we'll figure out a way."

"I'm not sure it's possible without a miracle," Geoffrey told him. "We're going to need that higher power that brought the two stones back together. Otherwise, we're doomed."

TWENTY-EIGHT

Boston Harbor
10, January 1720
11:00 a.m.

Ian tugged open the door to Goodfellow's and stepped inside. It was surprisingly quiet for late morning, as compared to when he'd visited eight days previously. With only a cursory glance in the wooden cases, he made his way to the table where Elias was working.

"Were you able to complete my order?" he asked as soon as the other man glanced up.

Elias tilted his head for a second as if he were trying to place a new face. "I did. Are you ready for it?"

Several colorful thoughts flew through Ian's head, but rather than give in to them, he nodded. "Please."

"All right." Elias laid down what he'd been working on and disappeared behind a curtain, returning shortly holding a box. "I cannot say I've worked on a task such as this before."

I should hope not.

"You were able to complete the order to my specifications, though, right?"

"See for yourself."

Ian carefully looked over the ring with his family crest and slid it onto his finger. The bracelet with the charms held the answer to freeing hope. And the necklace would guard the words until it was time.

"Your work is exceptional, as Jon promised," Ian told the other man. "Did you use all the pieces of eight?"

Elias removed a small pouch from the box and dumped its contents into his hand. "These were left, sir. Did you require something else?"

"No, no," Ian assured him. "Keep those for yourself."

"Why thank you. Let me get these wrapped for you."

"The charms?" Ian asked. "They cannot be removed?"

"No, sir. They hang by a ring that was melted on."

"Good, good." Ian hadn't wanted to worry about one or more of them falling off before they were needed.

"Here you are." Elias gave him the package. "Good day."

"And to you."

When Ian exited the shop, there was a sense of anticipation that swirled around him. The first step in the plan to save Swan Harbor had been completed. The second step would not be as simple.

It had taken weeks of going over words and making plans after Geoffrey had explained Anne's findings. He'd been told the solution wouldn't be a simple one. That it would be such a drawn-out process, he hadn't expected, though.

A generation—a lifetime.

The town would only be freed when the connected hearts from the families involved worked together. Until then, they would have to rely on the small bursts of hope from engagements, weddings, and births. Would it be enough? Only time would tell.

Ian found D.D. in El corazón's galley listening to his son read.

"You're getting quite good, Richard," he complimented the younger man. "Before long, you'll be the teacher."

Richard preened. "Thank you, Professor. You're a wonderful teacher."

"And you're an excellent student."

"Did you get everything?" D.D. asked.

"I did." Ian held up the package. "Now we wait 'till sundown."

"Are you sure this will work?"

"No," Ian admitted. "But you heard Anne. It's the only solution she's able to find."

"Understood."

"I'll secure these items, and then I'm going to ask Jon if I can borrow a horse or a wagon."

"I took care of that," D.D. surprised him by saying. "Richard and I are going with you."

"No."

"Yes."

Ian's thoughts were muddled as he'd appreciated D.D. being by his side. However, he was reaching a point where the guilt was beginning to creep in.

"You need to think of your family," he tried to explain. "Your wife, your other children. Simon and Clarissa's child, whom you've never met, is three or four years now. My task is almost complete. Once done, I will return to Swan Harbor to live out my life."

"I am thinking of my family," D.D. assured him. "You have become just as much a son as Richard or Simon. We will go with you tonight."

"As you wish," Ian murmured. "We'll leave at sundown."

He left D.D. and Richard and made his way to his cabin. The paperwork was still spread out on his table, ready for the next step.

Ian set the bracelet and ring aside and took out the necklace. It was a heart-shaped locket with the Swan Harbor lighthouse on it. He planned to include the words Isabelle spoke that started the spiral all those years ago. He hoped that someday it would help save hope.

Once that was complete, Ian opened his safe place, stored the bracelet inside, and as he always did, took out the wedding rings. He'd known it wasn't normal to have a ring made for himself. Except he'd wished for others to understand, he belonged to Hope just as she had to him. Sadly, he'd been so eager to see her last night, he'd forgotten them. And then ...

The heart wants, Elias has carved inside the larger ring. And *what the heart wants*, inside the smaller. With the date *14/02/1719*.

His heart still ached when he thought of what could have been, even a year after her passing. So much pain, and all because of ...

Ian shut the hidden compartment in the wood and carefully opened the heart. It was going to take a steady hand to copy everything onto parchment that would last. Could he do it?

An image of Baby Ian came to his mind, pushing him to answer his own question. For his child, he would do what must be done.

The Williams' Home
10, January 1720
7:00 p.m.

D.D. slowed the wagon not far from Isabelle's home, and suddenly Ian grew nervous. However, if asked, he wouldn't have been able to give a reason that was so.

"You two should wait here," Ian instructed.

"We're coming." Richard jumped from the wagon and looked up with a mulish expression. "Papa said so."

Ian cut a glance toward D.D., "Papa said so?"

"I did," D.D. agreed, jumping down to tie the horses. "Ready?"

"I guess."

He led the way to the wing opposite where he'd entered the previous time. His hope was to catch the children, specifically the son alone.

"What are you doing?" D.D. asked when Ian went to work manipulating the lock, instead of knocking.

"What does it look like I'm doing?"

"But, but," D.D. exclaimed. "You cannot just barge in there!"

"And why not?" Ian shrugged and continued working. "It got me what I wanted the last time."

"But ..."

"I told you," Ian repeated. "You can stay out here."

"We're coming," D.D. grumbled. "Just hurry."

"All right." Ian twisted the handle and pushed the door in. "Shall we?"

They stepped into Isabelle's home and passed a few open doors before locating the son. He was a tall child, with blue eyes like his mum's, but there the similarities ended. His hair was pale blond to match his complexion. However, it was the look on his face that set him apart from his mother. There was curiosity, surprise, and finally recognition.

"You know who I am?" Ian asked as he, D.D., and Richard moved the rest of the way into the room.

The lad nodded but said nothing, his gaze constantly watching Ian.

"My name is Ian Jones," he introduced himself. "I'm here—"

"—From Swan Harbor."

"Yes."

"Do you know my grandmother, Anne?"

"I do," Ian assured him. "In fact, in a way, it was Anne who sent us here."

The boy tilted his head. "Why?"

And here it is, Ian thought, *the complex subject.*

"Well," Ian took the heart necklace from his pocket and allowed the chain to dangle from his hand. "A while ago, there were words said in anger. Somehow, those words have upset the hope surrounding Swan Harbor."

"The Broken Heart Cure?"

Ian swallowed and exchanged a quick look with D.D., "You know about that?"

"I'm not a kid," the lad retorted. "Plus, I heard my mother muttering."

Like mother, like daughter as that was how Geoffrey found out what Anne was working on.

"Then yes," Ian confirmed. "The Broken Heart Cure. But son, it cannot be reversed without all the families represented. This necklace holds the key to explain what happened to the hope of an entire town."

"What do I need to do?"

"Grow up, fall in love," Ian grinned. "Then set us, and Swan Harbor, free." He allowed the heart to pour into the boy's hand and closed the child's fingers around it. "Protect it."

"What are you doing here?" Isabelle's waspish question had him stepping back. "What did you just give him?"

Ian tipped his chin to the child and stepped back. "I gave him the key to set Swan Harbor free."

"You what?" she screeched.

"You heard me."

"I thought you were going to cure Geoffrey's heart, so he would love me."

"I said I wished to cure Geoffrey's heart," Ian confirmed.

Her eyes flashed blue fire. "You tricked me?"

Ian shrugged. "Not really tricked ..."

"Give me that, Griffin." Isabelle reached for the locket.

"No!" Griffin sidestepped her. "I liked Swan Harbor."

"You do not know what you've done!" Her eyes flashed again, and she pulled a pistol from her pocket. The same one she'd used on Geoffrey, Ian had no doubt. "Give it to me!" She held one hand toward her son, the other holding the pistol.

"I said no!"

The look on Isabelle's face turned to one of hatred, and she pulled back the hammer on the weapon. Richard pushed Ian, and Griffin pushed his mother, the loud bang from the gun ricocheting around the room.

Ian's gaze raced over Richard, D.D., Griffin, and Isabelle. What he saw caused his heart to break. Somehow he knew his life would never be the same.

Ian's Home
20, January 1720
5:00 p.m.

"When I lifted my head," Ian explained. "Isabelle was lying on the floor, a pool of blood already forming around her head. I could tell by the vacant look in her eyes that she was gone."

"Her son?" Geoffrey whispered.

"Yes, when he pushed her, she hit her head." Ian brushed his hand over his face, fatigue wearing him down. "The ball grazed Richard's side, but he's going to be fine."

"Then what happened?"

"The shot brought the caretaker and Isabelle's young daughter," Ian sighed.

Geoffrey winced. "Where was her husband?"

"I'm not sure," Ian admitted. "He showed up when I was trying to calm down the caretaker."

"And what is Edmund going to do?"

Ian's stomach clenched. "I cannot say, but I worry he could be trouble."

Geoffrey sent him a look that said he knew exactly what was on his mind. "What will you do?"

"Whatever needs to be done to protect my son."

"Damn, Ian, I'm sorry," Geoffrey sighed. "I wish ..."

"We cannot change the past," Ian reminded the older man. "It's as you said. We must not think of what we lost, but of what is waiting for us."

"No matter how hard it is," Geoffrey agreed. "And the reason you were in Boston? Were you successful?"

Ian reached for the package he'd brought to show Geoffrey.

"I gave Griffin, Isabelle's son, a locket which has the original words inside. This," he laid the charm bracelet on the table, "will go to Kitty and Phillip's sons. One of them will keep it."

"And I've recorded the location, just as Anne said."

"The solution will be kept safe," Ian assured Geoffrey. "Someday, just as a higher power used my half of the heart to guide me here. So too, will everything align to save hope."

"Are you sure of that?"

"Am I sure?" Ian questioned. "Honestly, no. We have no choice, though, do we?"

"No, son, we do not." Geoffrey stood and put on his hat. "And now, I shall go break the news to Anne about her daughter and grandson."

"I will—"

"No," Geoffrey interrupted him. "I'll take care of it."

He saw the older man off and had just shut the door when he heard a call from the other room.

"Pa!" Then it was quiet for a few moments. "Pa!"

"Is someone looking for me?" Ian peered around the door to see Baby I, as Luke called him, standing in his cradle.

"Pa!" the child shrieked and hitched his leg over the side.

"No!" Ian lunged for the baby, catching him just as he tumbled out. "I've got you," he crooned, trying to quiet the tears.

"Up."

"You wanted up?"

Baby I nodded, "Ye."

"Yes," Ian gently modeled. "I think it's time you slept in your big bed."

"Be?"

"Bed. Yes." Ian carried him across the room and showed him the child-size bed he'd built. "A new bed for you."

Baby I studied it for several minutes and patted the blanket. "Be."

"Would you like to try your bed?"

The baby looked up, and a pucker developed between his brows. "No!" he exclaimed and took off running.

For the next few hours, Ian enjoyed the best part of his life. He fed his son and talked about Hope. When it was time for bed, he took the baby out onto the front step and looked into the heavens.

"Tar," Baby I murmured.

"Yes, love," Ian agreed. "Your mum's star is shining down on us."

When his son wrapped his arms around his neck and snuggled in, Ian couldn't keep the tears away. He couldn't understand how holding his son brought him both the greatest joy and a deep sadness.

"We'll get there," he sighed. Just when, he had no idea.

"Ian!"

"Henry?" Ian wiped his face and stepped down onto the ground. "What brings you in this direction?"

"I heard you were back and ..."

"We've not been back long," Ian admitted. "I was just going to put Baby I to bed. Would you like to come in?"

Henry's grin flashed white in the dark. "All right."

Good, thought Ian, taking the baby to bed. *Perhaps I can find out what happened with Felicity.*

"I'll be right back."

"Take your time."

It took longer than he'd expected to get his son to stay in his small bed, and by the time Ian returned, Henry had stoked the fire.

"Whiskey or ale?"

"Whiskey." Henry hesitated a beat. "I heard what happened in Boston."

Ian handed Henry a mug and sat across from him. "How?"

"Overheard Geoffrey telling my father."

"Was anything said about Anne?"

"Geoffrey said she had left to tell her son." Henry tossed back his whiskey and set the mug on a side table. "He said it was as if she'd expected it."

"I was lucky," Ian admitted. "If Griffin hadn't shoved her, or Richard pushed me ..."

"So, now what?"

"I teach," Ian shrugged. "Is that what you mean?"

"Will Edmund keep quiet to protect Griffin?"

"I know not," Ian admitted. "However, I did speak with my friend Jon, who is on the Governor's Council."

"And the men from El corazón?" Henry asked. "Will they be happy?"

"Freddy Taylor is the captain of the Rosa," Ian told Henry. "He's going to take on most of the men."

"Will D.D. and Richard be going back to England?"

"As soon as it warms," Ian replied. "He's been gone for many years."

It was quiet except for the popping from the fire for the next few moments, and Ian decided it was as good a time as any.

"What happened between you and Felicity?"

Henry loosened his cravat, and a look of unease crossed his face. "I'm not sure what you expect me to say."

"Henry," Ian chided. "You were ready to request her hand in the fall, and then ..."

A look crossed the other man's face as he was speaking of the fall. It took Ian back to his initial thoughts.

"Does this have something to do with me?"

"What do you mean?" Henry frowned.

"When you were taking care of me," Ian continued, working to ferret out the truth. "Was Felicity unhappy that you weren't attending her?"

"I ..." But Henry's voice died, and he wandered to the window. "I know not what you wish me to say."

"How about the truth?"

"Truth," Henry sighed. "What is that?"

"I thought you loved her."

"Love," Henry murmured. "I'm beginning to think it's underrated."

"Henry!" Ian exclaimed. "You know how much I loved Hope. How happy she made me."

"I know that when she died, you no longer desired to live," Henry shot back. "I'm beginning to believe an arrangement like my parents had might be more suitable."

How did he argue with Henry's comment, as he was right? Living without Hope hadn't been something he had wished for.

"Henry," Ian waited until his friend was looking at him before continuing, "You're right, I loved Hope with my whole being. When she died, something inside of me died with her. But when Geoffrey came to see me, he said, *don't focus on what you've lost. Focus on what's waiting.* I'm living for my son."

"But the pain ..."

"Is the greatest pain I have ever known," Ian admitted. "Except it's better to have loved and lost, than to never have loved at all."

Henry studied him. "Are you saying that if you had known what was going to happen, you would have fallen for Hope anyway?"

"In a heartbeat," Ian admitted. "Listen to your heart, my friend. It always knows."

"I'll think about what you've said," Henry murmured noncommittally.

"That's about all I can ask."

Henry smiled, except it didn't quite reach his eyes. Long after his friend was gone, he couldn't shake the feeling that there was more to the story. However, that was a tale for another day.

Ian shut down for the night, leaving a low flame in case he had to check on the baby. He crawled into his lonely bed and settled in, hoping to dream of his love.

His thoughts drifted, and she was there waiting, just on the fringes of his mind.

"Pa."

Something brushed across his cheek, and Ian buried his head deeper into his pillow.

"Pa."

Again, something brushed across his cheek. Slowly, Ian opened his eyes to find his son beside the bed.

"Pa,"

"Why are you out of your bed?"

"Up."

"For just a moment."

Baby I snuggled against his chest, and as their hearts aligned, Ian once again felt whole.

TWENTY-NINE
PRESENT DAY

Liam and Elsa's Cottage
February 10
9:00 p.m.

Killian turned the page in Ian's journal and scanned the group seated around Liam and Elsa's kitchen table.

"There's one more entry."

"Well, what are you waiting for, son?" Captain Jack replied. "Read it. We still don't know how to break the curse."

"Alright. It looks like it was written on the same date we've always thought the ship was left in Swan Harbor.

> *14 February 1720*
>
> *I was readying for the day when there was a knock at the door. It was Geoffrey, and the look on his face caused my heart to feel as if it had been crushed. For before he began talking, I knew what he was going to say.*
>
> *A wanted poster had just arrived on the Swan Harbor's sheriff's desk for Ian Jones. While Geoffrey tried to convince me*

to stay, I couldn't. There was no way I could subjugate my family to all the what-ifs.

As soon as Geoffrey left, I began to make my plans to leave Swan Harbor and return to England. The thought breaks my heart, but not nearly as much as the thought of leaving my son behind. However, the journey over the sea is no place for a small child. I will wait to hear from Geoffrey and return as soon as possible.

El corazón has been cleaned of all my belongings. My plan is to write a letter to my son and instructions for Henry regarding the ship.

As I sit to write the letter, I'm wavering between what my head and my heart are saying. My head says I need to leave to protect my family. Except my heart is saying, if I leave, I might as well be dead, for my will to live would not be with me.

I will, of course, do what is best for my son. Better to have a father who left to protect him, than to have a father killed as a murderer.

Henry will see to it that everything identifying El corazón is removed. And I will leave silver for the care of the ship and my son. While I am hopeful that I will be reunited with my family soon, I fear the future.

I've already created a place for this journal on El corazón. Someday, a descendant of mine will uncover it. I am hopeful that means they can then set us all free.

The solution, as Anne has said all along, is not simple. Because of Isabelle's words, the circle of those involved will most certainly grow. But I've attempted to account for everything by leaving the pieces with those originally involved. However, while I have left the pieces, they will only come together at a time when hope is at its most optimum. <u>This is part of the key.</u>

Isabelle's family holds the locket, guarding the words that took the hope.

Geoffrey's family has the location the hope was taken, and where it must be restored.

Christine's family has the bracelet holding the charms with the solution.

And the words for returning hope are in a safe haven. When the time is right, they can be located by solving these riddles.

When it's time,
To save the line.
The questions are here,
The answers are near.
They are hidden, safe and secure.
Waiting for hearts whose loves are pure.
You need not go far,
To find where they are.
Just look in that place,
And find the space.
For there, hope's waiting with the key.
And forever then, we'll all be free.

Once the location has been discovered, it takes solving one more riddle.

You hear me when in love.

Geoffrey was right. We do need a miracle for all the pieces to come together at once. But I have faith that the higher power which guided me to Swan Harbor and Hope has a plan. Until then, the town will have to rely on the bursts of hope from the *special occasions. And I will bide my time by lending my hope to the tiny town that holds my heart.*

As for Hope's journals, I am torn. I want to take them with me, but I have read them so many times, the words are imprinted on my heart. I will lock them away with what should have been our wedding rings, in the place that meant so much to us. My hope is our love story will show others what I said to Henry. That it is better to have loved and lost, than never to have loved. While in life, we did not get our happy ending; it does not mean we will not in death. We were brought together to save Swan Harbor, just not in the manner we wished.

After I complete the writing on this last entry, I will lock my journal away in its resting place. My last goodbyes will be made, and D.D., Richard, and I will leave by horseback. We will travel to Timber Creek, where we will board one of Jon's merchant ships. Once in Boston, I will leave the Colonies as Professor Samuel Jones. My heart, though, will always be in Swan Harbor.

Killian's voice faded as he finished reading. His thoughts were already trying to break apart the pieces Ian had given them.

"That poor man," Ava murmured. "He lost his wife, and to save his child, he left him behind. I can't imagine how much that must have hurt."

"Just like I've always said," Jack looked around the room. "Ian went back to England and died of a broken heart.

"Do we know when he died?" asked Terri.

"My sister found the date in a family Bible." Aiden opened his notebook. "Ian died in July 1722."

"He lasted two years," Jack sighed. "A long time without the family he loved."

Killian exchanged looks with Finn, wondering how far he'd gotten in searching for Jack's lost love. Edythe had left him at the altar because she'd learned about the curse. They were yet another couple who'd lost their happy beginning.

"Did you bring your evidence board?" Liam teased.

"What do you think?" Emma deadpanned. "Wouldn't leave home without it."

"Don't besmirch my board," Killian exclaimed. "Who's the investigator? I'll just get it."

He brought the board into the kitchen and propped it up. Then wrote out a couple of lines from the book that stood out.

"This line is new information," Killian explained.

Geoffrey's family has the location the hope was taken, and where it must be restored.

"Any ideas, Dylan?" he asked the Sheriff.

"Unless it's in Geoffrey's journal, I'm not sure where to look," Dylan replied.

"We know when the words were said, right?" asked Emma.

"Yes," Aiden confirmed. "Anne wrote about it in her journal. It was December 1695."

Dylan was quiet while he searched for the dates in his ancestor's journal.

"There are only two entries in Geoffrey's journal in December 1695," he told them. "The first one is just him preparing to ask for Christine's hand. But the second one ..."

20, December 1695

It was late, and I probably shouldn't have snuck Christine from her home. Except I was afraid that Isabelle's hate was going to make her regret, she'd promised to be my wife.

We rode up the mountain, to one of our favorite places. The 'thinking' stone, which is protected by ivy year-round, had become our hideaway. Somewhere we could shut out the world for a few hours and make plans for our life together.

We'd just gotten comfortable on the stone when we heard the unmistakable sounds of another approaching. I worried it was her father, but then Isabelle crashed through the ivy. The words she muttered were inconsequential. It was the hatred in her eyes that frightened me.

"Does anyone know where The Bride's Veil is?" Dylan frowned. "There are multiple hot springs surrounded by ivy on our mountain."

"I know," Terri replied, a melancholy smile on her face. "Dean proposed to me once up there."

"Once?" Harper questioned. "Grandpa had to propose more than once?"

Terri chuckled, "Oh honey, our road to the altar was not a straight line. But that's for another time."

"I'm going to hold you to that," Harper murmured.

"Do you think you can tell us how to get there?" Killian asked, already making notes on his board.

"I keep telling you," Terri retorted. "While I may be ninety, I'm not senile. But yes, Killian. I have no trouble getting us there."

He bit his lip to keep the smirk off his face and moved on to the next line.

"Here's another part that stands out," Killian pointed to the board. "It parallels why Emma and I felt all of you should have been involved."

"Because our ancestors were involved in Hope and Ian's relationship, right?" Gray Hunter questioned. "Cameron and Jessie always made sense because she's a Prince. But Sadie and I ..."

"That was what we originally thought," Killian agreed. "However, now I think it's closer. Look at this line."

Because of Isabelle's words, the circle of those involved will most certainly grow.

"I think in the beginning, we were just focused on the Swan and Prince families. But could it be extended families as well? Which means the Hunters could be involved because of some other connection besides Jessie."

"Killian," Jack jumped in. "If we tried to trace the connections of the residents of Swan Harbor to the beginning, we'd be here for years."

"But ..."

"Why not just involve all the connected hearts in the town?" Terri offered.

"After all, Jack's always said when there's a love match, it gives the town a burst of hope."

"I do, don't I?" Jack preened.

"Alright, Jack," Killian placated the older man. "We'll figure out how to involve the whole bloody town."

❧

EMMA EXCHANGED LOOKS WITH KILLIAN AND THOUGHT ABOUT wading into the conversation he was having with her uncle. Except he'd stayed out of her argument with Jack over Jonesy, so ...

"Is Killian okay?" Elsa whispered.

Emma glanced at Elsa and scooted farther away from the table. "He's been edgy lately."

"Because of the wedding?" Elsa questioned. "Or because he's stuck dealing with this?"

"I think he's worried," Emma offered. "And no matter how much I hint for him to share his burdens, he's been pretty tight-lipped."

"I'm sorry," Elsa sighed. "My family wasn't even involved, and yet, I feel responsible somehow."

"You're here," Emma squeezed her friend's hand. "That's what's important."

"Any more wedding details that need to be taken care of?"

"Ask my mother," Emma laughed. "I swear if she wasn't involved in her mentoring program, she would have made a good wedding planner."

"She is very organized," Elsa agreed. "I know I couldn't have done without her help."

"Next," Killian was continuing, "we have the riddle."

Emma wrinkled her nose. "Another riddle. Who solved the last one?"

"Terri Patterson," Elsa nodded toward the older woman. "Said she figured it out because she reads romance novels."

"Oh, that's right," laughed Emma. "Mom did tell me that."

"These words lead us somewhere," Killian tapped the board. "Suggestions?"

When it's time.

To save the line.
The questions are here,
The answers are near.
They are hidden, safe and secure,
Waiting for hearts whose loves are pure.
You need not go far,
To find where they are.
Just look in that place,
And find the space.
For there, hope's waiting with the key.
And forever then, we'll all be free.

"Is the house Ian lived in still standing?" Ava asked. "Maybe he hid something inside it."

"Do we even know where the house was located?" asked Killian.

"Behind the Patterson tavern somewhere," Jack offered.

"Which was where?" Killian pushed.

"The Beachside Inn and The Beach Shack have been owned by the Pattersons for centuries," Terri told him.

"And there are no homes in the cliffs behind it," Dylan added.

"What about the school Ian built?" Terri suggested.

"I can ask Molly to check tomorrow," Dylan offered. "She still teaches first grade at Swan Harbor Elementary."

"How's Molly feeling?" Emma asked.

"Pregnant," Dylan shrugged. "Tired. Happy."

"When is she due again?" Terri inquired.

"May."

"I can see if Amanda at the library can give some guidance about the layout of the town in the 1700s," Jack volunteered.

"What about the pictures in the Underground Museum?" Aiden replied. "Harper and I were in there in December, and there are a few artist's renderings from the 1700s."

"I'll look tomorrow," Jack promised.

"One more," Killian pulled everyone back to the board. "Look at these lines."

However, while I have left the pieces, they will only come together at a time when hope is at its most optimum. This is part of the key.

"We believe the pieces come together means the descendants of the families involved, right?" Killian tossed out.

"Or, in this case," Jack reminded everyone, "most of the town."

"And when hope is at its most optimum?" Killian followed up.

"Remember in Hope's journal," Emma stated. "When she was speaking to Jenny?"

"She was talking about the times when hope was most alive," Ava picked up, "even when the swans weren't around."

"When there was an engagement, a wedding, or a new baby," Terri grinned. "Times of optimum hope."

"So, I was right," Jack had his *You should have always trusted me* grin going. "Geoffrey's family has Molly, who's expecting twins. Christine's family has Ava and Finn's wedding and Emma and Killian's engagement and wedding on February 14."

"We're still missing Isabelle's family," Killian sighed.

"We'll get there," Jack assured him. "It's all coming together."

Emma hoped so, but she'd reached the point where, if their wedding went off without a problem, she was going to be surprised.

"Stop it," Elsa scolded.

"I'm sorry," Emma murmured. "It's just ..."

"I get that. Have you checked on Jonesy?"

"That's another huge weight," Emma tried to explain. "We released Jonesy into the wild. He's in warm water, and the cave protects him from the elements."

"But he still hasn't perked up?"

"No. If it really is his hope ... or will to live, like we talked about the other day, his really is waning."

"And you—"

"No," Emma interrupted Elsa before she'd gotten far. "I keep telling Jack, avian medicine isn't my specialty."

"Except he doesn't believe you?" Elsa guessed.

"It's not that he doesn't believe me," Emma remarked. "More like he wants me to perform a miracle. But even the specialists are stumped."

"I told you it was Jonesy's hope, long ago," Elsa grinned.

"Haha," Emma intoned.

"I'm going to get some coffee. Want some?"

"No thanks, I'm fine."

"Alright," Killian was pulling everyone back to the board. "We have the pictures that were on the last page of Ian's journal. On the left, the date is 18, December 1718, and an open chest."

"The date Hope died, and the chest where her journal was kept," Jack guessed.

"It does look like that chest," Killian agreed. "But why? Hope's journals didn't have clues in them."

"And the picture on the other page, the ship is named Hope's Haven," Jack frowned. "Why?"

"The chest is closed, though." Killian turned the journal around. "However, the dates match—14, February 1720."

"Is that the same chest as on the back page?" Jack asked.

"The pictures are small ..." Killian began.

"Wait," Aiden pulled a file folder from his briefcase and took out a sheaf of papers. "I blew up those pictures. Chest, the heart locket with the lighthouse, the—"

"Elsa!" Patty grabbed the piece of paper Aiden had just laid down. "Look!"

"What is it, mom?" Elsa frowned.

"The hope locket! See!" Patty shoved the page toward Elsa.

Emma saw Elsa glance down at the paper and look back up at her mother.

"What did you say?"

"The hope locket."

All color drained from Elsa's face. She dropped the paper and rushed from the kitchen.

Emma went after her at the same time as Liam, both arriving to find Elsa searching for something.

"Elsa, love," Liam took her hand and tried to get her attention.

"The locket." Elsa's gaze bounced off Emma. "Remember last fall when you went with me to the jewelry store?"

"We went to Joanne's several times, El," Emma reminded her.

"I know," Elsa went back to searching, "but here it is." She held up a small bag with the Joanne Gems' logo on it. "Come on."

Emma exchanged looks with Liam, who shrugged, and they followed Elsa back into the kitchen.

"Elsa, what's going on?" Jack frowned. "You looked like you'd seen a ghost."

"I might have," Elsa muttered and poured the contents of the bag in her hand. "Isabelle's." She was holding a silver heart-shaped locket, the long chain dangling over her hand. And on the locket, a lighthouse.

"Bloody hell," murmured Killian.

"Bugger that." Liam tugged Elsa into his arms and kissed the side of her head. "When you said you had walked the streets, stood on the cliffs, and looked out at the sea, you weren't joking."

"No wonder it felt like home," Elsa sighed.

"I'm assuming by Patty's reaction," Jack guessed. "The locket came from her family."

"It did," Elsa confirmed. "Right after mom was diagnosed with Alzheimer's, she wrote me a letter and gave me this locket." She fished the letter from her pocket and read.

And before I forget (no pun intended), I'm including a locket that's been in our family for many generations. My father told me it held hope. And my hope for you is health, happiness, and love.

"Then mom saw me holding it," Elsa smiled. "She said, 'You found the hope locket.' I asked what she meant. Then she said, 'The hope locket. My grandfather used to tell me it held enough hope to fill an entire town'."

"Ian's first step was to give it to your ancestor, Elsa," Killian murmured. "Can you open it?"

Elsa played with the lock for a minute and handed it to Liam, who did the same.

"It needs a key." Liam glanced up.

"What about this one?" Emma held up her arm with the charms. "It opened the chest Hope's journal was in."

"Worth a shot," Liam agreed. He handed the necklace back to Elsa and unfastened the bracelet. "Here goes nothing."

Emma wanted to scoff at the possibility of the key from her bracelet being small enough to open a locket, but something told her it was going to work.

"It opened," Liam whispered, handing Emma her bracelet. "And there's a piece of parchment in it."

"Read it," Jack instructed.

"Hey, Jack," Liam retorted. "It's Elsa's family who cursed us all, I'll let her read it."

Elsa elbowed Liam but took the parchment and carefully unfolded it.

"Are you sure I should read this out loud?"

"Just read the bloody words," Killian groused.

"It's okay, El," Emma assured her friend. "Read it."

Elsa took a deep breath and read.

> "On the day you say I do.
> The countdown for hope will begin for you.
> And for every line,
> Throughout time.
> Every seed you sow,
> Will fail to grow.
> As my heart shatters, and the pieces fly,
> They will mix with the stars in the sky.
> And on the day when hope dies,
> I'll rejoice when I hear your cries.
> Because of you, all hope will be lost.
> Are you willing to pay the cost?"

"Now we have the words," Killian retorted. "How the bloody hell can we undo them?"

"Solve the riddle," Ava reminded them. "And study Emma's bracelet. According to Grandmother Rose and Ian, the answer lies within the charms."

"I remember Rose wearing that bracelet," Jack smiled. "Except the charms were just charms."

"List the charms for me, Doc," Killian asked. "I'll add them to my board."

Emma held up the bracelet, allowing the charms to dangle freely. "There's the key, the number 2, a heart, an eye, a swan, a ruby, a timepiece, and a cluster of stars."

"Bloody hell," Killian grumbled. "This is cocked up."

"No, it's not," Terri assured him. "It's a piece of cake."

"Then what's the answer?" Killian shot back.

"That I don't know," Terri admitted. "Let me think about it for a little while."

THIRTY
PRESENT DAY

Captain Jack's Fine Dining
February 12
8:00 a.m.

There was a part of Killian that wished he were at the cove with Emma, checking on Jonesy. As she'd said, though, he was the investigator, and his job was to investigate. Except after studying the charms on the bracelet and coming up empty, he'd turned back to the riddle. He had solved hundreds of cases in his career. Just none more important than finding the key to save Swan Harbor's hope. Was he correct in thinking the answer lay somewhere on Ian's ship?

He could only hope, he thought, as he drove into the restaurant's parking lot to find his brother shifting his weight from one foot to the other, a large cup of coffee in his hand.

"You look awful."

"Wanker," Liam shot back. "Multiple Vehicle Accident on the Cove Highway," he yawned.

"Aren't you the chief paramedic?" Killian retorted. "Doesn't that mean you get to choose the best shifts?"

"Paramedic Chief," Liam corrected. "And I'm still training the guys."

Killian knew Liam had taken on a big job at the fire department, but he also knew his brother loved it. Plus, having family around was ...

"There's dad and Aiden," Liam nodded as two other cars drove into the lot.

Then before they'd parked, Dylan arrived behind them.

"Alright, Killian," Finn began. "What do you need us to do?"

"We found Ian's journal hidden on his ship, right?"

"Yes," Liam grunted. "But that's not new."

"Ian wrote, *'And the words for returning hope are in a safe haven. When the time is right, they can be located by solving these riddles.'*" Killian indicated the ship that had been turned into a restaurant. "What if the ship is the safe haven?"

"A safe haven," Aiden repeated several times. And then his face suddenly lit up, and he took off toward his car.

"Cousin Aiden had an epiphany," Liam grinned.

"Be nice, Liam," Finn scolded.

"What is it, Aiden?" Killian asked when his cousin returned holding a folder.

Aiden removed a piece of paper and held it so all could see.

It was a copy of the page from Ian Jones' journal Aiden's sister had found in England. The drawing had led them to locate the hiding place of the book inside the ship. But until reading the journals, they had assumed the ship's name was Hope's Haven, as was written on the paper.

"What if it's not Hope's Haven," Aiden posed, "as in a name? Perhaps hope is with a lower-case h, so it's hope's haven?"

Killian turned it over in his head a few times. Haven equaled a safe place, which the ship had been to Ian for many years.

"It fits," he agreed. "Now, to the next step, which is to interpret the riddle and find the exact location inside the ship."

"Jack's been searching the ship for years," Finn reminded them. "And the journal wasn't found until Aiden brought the riddle."

"Don't remind me," Killian grumbled. "Emma doesn't believe Jonesy has long. And if that bloody swan dies ..."

"Don't go there, Killian," Finn encouraged.

"Right." Killian tipped his chin and opened the journal to the riddle.

"When it's time,
To save the line.
The questions are here,
The answers are near.
They are hidden, safe and secure,
Waiting for a heart whose loves are pure.
You need not go far,
To find where they are.
Just look in that place,
And find the space.
For there, hope's waiting with the key,
And forever then, we'll all be free."

"Any suggestions where to start?" he asked. "I would assume it's in a place out of the way."

"And someplace that wasn't affected when the ship was converted to a restaurant," Dylan added. "I would start in the captain's cabin."

"Why?" Killian tossed back.

"Because in his journals, Ian speaks of a safe place," Dylan explained. "It was where he kept the silver, the heart, etc."

"Bloody hell," Killian grumbled. "How did I miss that?"

"It's why I'm the boss," Dylan quipped.

"That must be it," Killian muttered tongue-in-cheek.

"Shall we?" Liam took off without waiting for the others. "If I stop, I might fall asleep."

They were halfway to the ship when Killian remembered they had no way to get inside.

"I forgot—"

"I didn't." Finn tossed him the keys. "I stopped and got them from Jack."

"I'm surprised he didn't come with you."

"He's going to the cave," Finn explained. "Jonesy and Emma were on his mind."

"Good," Killian murmured, hoping Emma would be alright with that.

As soon as he'd unlocked the door, his father turned off the alarm system and flipped on the lights.

"This way," Finn led the way.

There was a hush inside the old Spanish galleon that wasn't usually present. Did the ship somehow know they were on a mission? That the secrets protected for three hundred years were getting ready to be exposed?

"Here it is," Finn pushed open the door.

The cabin had been turned into Jack's office, but he hadn't changed the look of the space. Much of it remained as it was the last time Ian sailed from Boston to Swan Harbor.

"What are we looking for again?" Aiden asked.

"A safe place," Killian told him.

He thought back on Ian's words, and while he'd spoken of opening something, there'd been no sign of where.

"Read the bloody riddle again," Aiden sighed after they'd looked for half an hour with no success.

Killian opened the book to the shorter riddle. "*You hear me when in love.*"

"What the ...?" Liam began.

The answer rolled around in Killian's head, and then his eyes met Dylan's.

"We're looking for a heart, mates," he grinned.

"How do you know that?" Liam asked.

"When your heart speaks ..."

"It's best to listen," Liam completed. "I must be more tired than I thought."

"I could say something," Killian smirked.

They began searching the walls, looking for the outline of a heart. The wood was old, and there were multiple blemishes, but nothing that stood out.

"Is this it?" Aiden indicated a faint mark next to the bookshelf.

"Leave it to the current Professor Jones to find what the past Professor Jones left," Dylan remarked.

"Does it open?" Killian asked.

Aiden pushed on the heart, and a part of the shelf popped open.

"Will you look at that?" Finn whispered.

"It looks like the chest Hope's journal was in," Killian murmured, when Aiden pulled a small wooden box from the safe place.

"It's locked," Aiden complained.

"Of course, it is," Killian groaned.

"Where's Emma's bracelet?" Liam asked the obvious.

"I have it." Killian reached into his pocket but, when it wasn't there, realized he hadn't picked it up when he'd left the apartment. "Bloody hell, it's still on the kitchen table."

"Go, go," Liam shooed him out the door.

"I'll lock up, and we'll meet you at the cave," Finn shouted.

Killian thought about sending a quick text to Emma but decided to wait. He wanted to make sure they'd found the right chest.

Lover's Cove
February 12
7:00 a.m.

Emma lost track of how long she knelt next to Jonesy with her stethoscope pressed against his chest. Even when Jack and her mother had climbed into the cave, she hadn't stopped listening. She was focused on the swan that had appeared after her mother's birth.

For fifty years, he'd been coming to Swan Harbor. And unless there was a miracle, the town was going to have to figure out a way to go on without him.

"Is he?" Jack whispered.

She glanced up to see he'd moved closer. "I can still hear ..."

The swan's heartbeat had gradually grown slower and slower. But every other time she'd thought it was the last—she'd heard another. Until now ...

Emma closed her eyes and silently asked for a miracle before checking the time. The knowledge that it had been too long between beats broke her heart.

"I'm sorry, Jack," she cried.

Her breath caught, and the ache inside grew, threatening to climb over her. She looked up, her eyes meeting Jack's dark ones; his pooling, the tears spilling to roll down his face.

"I'm sorry," she murmured. "I'm so sorry."

"Hey now." Jack pulled her up into his arms. "This is not your fault."

"How can you say that?" Emma mumbled against his shoulder. "He was fine until last year. Maybe if I ..."

"Emma," Jack hushed her. "Just like Ian had a destiny, so did Jonesy." He hesitated and tilted her chin, forcing her to look at him. "Just like you do."

"But ...," she sniffed. "You've been saying Killian and I are bringing things full circle. That we're part of finding a way to give Swan Harbor its happy beginning. That—"

"Take a breath," Jack cut her off. "You and Killian have given Swan Harbor its possibility again, Emma."

"What do you mean?"

"After your mother was born, Jonesy appeared in Swan Harbor," Jack reminded her. "Just like Hope's birth gave the town hope all those years ago, so did Ava's. For fifty years, Jonesy kept coming and waiting. Then Killian moved here."

"And six months later, I moved here," Emma murmured, beginning to understand where he was going.

"Then Elsa followed you," he completed the circle. "Without you, we never would have known how to find Isabelle's descendants."

"Except," she glanced down at the swan, and again her heart twisted. "We failed."

"There's always hope." Jack hesitated and tilted his head, the sound of slamming car doors reaching them. "Perhaps that's it."

"Emma," Killian called. "We found it."

Instead of running to tell them it was too late, Emma reached for her stethoscope and slipped it into her bag. She followed Jack toward the mouth of the cave, but her legs were heavy, her steps feeling like they were mired in mud.

"Emma?"

"Jonesy's gone."

Killian's wild eyes traveled from her to Jack to where Jonesy lay, then back to her. "Gone?"

"Yes," she barely got out before he pulled her into his arms. "He's gone."

"But we have the words, Doc," Killian repeated. "We can set him free."

"Don't you think he's free?" She shrugged. "He's dead and no longer responsible for all the hope in Swan Harbor."

"What about Ian and Hope?" Killian whispered. "If he's been loaning his hope to our town, the least we can do is cut him free."

"Does it matter?"

"Don't you think Ian and Hope deserve a happy ending, Emma?" asked Jack.

"Of course."

"Then the least we can do is reward Ian for his hard work."

"How, though?"

"Liam, are you still tapped into Swan Harbor's gossip line?" asked Jack.

"Yes," Liam confirmed. "Why?"

"Come," Jack waved him along. "We have quite a few connected-heart couples to notify. We'll see you on the mountain."

"But Jack," Emma stopped him. "What about?" She thumbed back toward the swan.

Jack glanced toward the back of the cave. "I'll take care of my old friend later. Let's set him free first."

"Harper and I will take this to the University and make copies," Aiden snatched the chest Killian was holding. "How many copies should I make?"

"A lot," Dylan muttered. "I'll go get Terri to show me where The Bride's Veil is and set up some emergency lights."

"Finn and I will contact Sunset Cliff Retirement Village," Ava told them. "If Lois, Rupert, and the gang are home from Florida, they'll want to be involved."

Suddenly, it was almost too quiet, leaving Emma unsettled.

"Are you ready to go, Doc?"

The concern on his face when she looked at him was almost more than she could handle.

"I can't explain what I'm feeling." Emma frowned and, without thinking, cleaned her hands and repacked her bag. "It makes no sense."

A little pucker appeared between Killian's brows. "Doc," he took her hand and led her out of the cave, "remember the first time I brought you here?"

"How could I forget?" she murmured. "It was very romantic."

"It was," he agreed. "As is the legend behind the cave."

"That if you make love here, you'll be engaged by year's end?"

"Aye, that one." He grinned. "Did I ever tell you that when I arrived at the cave, a vision of a pirate ship sailing into the cove floated through my head?"

"No."

"It did." He ran his fingers over the cave walls. "Was this the cave Hope died in? Perhaps, as I'm sure, the land has shifted in 300 years. Except even if not, this was Ian's cove."

"True."

"Then perhaps that's what you're feeling," Killian mused. "The past and present coming together."

"Maybe." She took one last look at Jonesy before following Killian toward their cars. "But I don't like leaving him there."

"Which makes sense," he assured her. "However, after fifty years, perhaps Jack has earned the right to say goodbye to his friend alone."

That she could understand. But it didn't stop her from wishing things had been different.

The Bride's Veil
February 12
6:00 p.m.

THE BRIDE'S VEIL WAS LOCATED NOT FAR FROM AN ABANDONED building Finn had purchased as an investment. Except Killian found the area nothing like it had been depicted in Hope's journal. Moss still hung from the trees surrounding the flat stone. However, the hot springs had long dried up, and there were markings on the rock. He assumed they were evidence of lovers left behind through the years.

With the help of the Hunters, Dylan had arranged for multiple construction lamps to light their way. Not only the area where they would all stand but the path leading up.

"Are you cold, Doc?"

"Aren't you?"

Killian tugged her against his chest. "I've got my love to keep me warm."

"You're still corny."

"And you still love me."

"I do," she whispered. "I'm still cold, though."

"Hopefully, it won't be much longer," he murmured.

He'd lost track of the number of couples that had joined them on the mountain. The descendants of the original families were closest to the stone, and everyone fanned out from there. There was still a large part of him that felt what they were doing was ridiculous. However, he loved Emma and was doing it for her. And she loved Jack. Which had him wondering if that held true for many of the residents of Swan Harbor as well. That after so many years, they had come to support him.

"Killian," Emma frowned. "Did you ever figure out how my bracelet holds the answer to breaking the curse?"

"No." He fingered the charms, but just as before, the only one that stood out was the key. "I've no idea, Doc. Maybe your grandmother was mistaken."

"Rose wasn't mistaken," Terri corrected, stopping next to them.

"How can you say that?" Killian grumbled. "Have you been *thinking* about it?"

"I have." Terri handed the papers she'd been passing out to one of her granddaughters and fingered Emma's bracelet. "The answer is two hearts."

"Bloody hell, Terri," Killian groused. "We know the answer is connected hearts. How do you get that from these charms?"

She sent him an indulgent grin. "The number two, then H from heart, E from eye, A from swan, R from ruby, T from timepiece and S from stars—2 hearts."

"Alright," he conceded. "I'll give you most of that, but don't you think A from swan is a stretch?"

"Probably," she shrugged. "How about A is for animal?"

He groaned, earning a girlish giggle from Terri.

"You're just not reading the right books." She patted his shoulder. "Read more romance books. They might help you in your line of work. Let me know the next time you get stuck on a case."

"Shall I buy you some romance books to read on our honeymoon?" Emma teased once Terri had moved on.

Killian tugged Emma back into his arms. "I'm pretty sure I'll be able to find other things to do on our honeymoon. You did see the pages I'd turned down in the newest Rebecca's Fantasy, didn't you?"

"Maybe," she murmured.

Before he could respond further, Jack climbed up on the stone, and a microphone sprang to life.

"Where did that come from?" Liam grumbled, moving to the other side of Emma, away from the speaker.

"Tyler," Killian named the owner of Siren's Song, a club on the pier.

"Figures," Liam retorted.

"Be nice, Liam," Elsa played the peacemaker. "You got the girl."

"Thank you for coming out tonight," Jack began, cutting off any more conversation. "I'm sure you're all wondering why you're here, and when you can go home."

"Why are we here?" someone called.

At the same time, someone from the other side of the group yelled, "Whatever you need, Jack."

"Thank you all—"

"Hold it. Hold it," Jack was interrupted again. "We just got back."

"Lois, Rupert, and gang," Liam replied in response to Killian's raised brow. "They just got back from Florida."

"Now that everyone is here," Jack continued. "Does everyone have a piece of paper with the poem?"

There was some shuffling, and before Jack continued speaking, it started snowing.

"Bloody hell," Killian murmured, looking up into the cloudy sky, snow swirling around them.

"Most of you know," Jack went on, "how much Jonesy has always meant to my family. I'm sad to say that he passed earlier today, but I have hope that these words will set him ... and all of us free. Please, each of you read them out loud with the person your heart is connected to."

Here goes nothing, Killian thought.

All around them, he could hear people reciting.

"ON THIS DAY,
We'll have our say.
And with the key,
We'll set hope free.
Gather your line from far and wide,
You need them all by your side.
Our hearts are full of a love that's true,
That began with the words I love you.
Then listen and watch far above,

As you seal the deal with words of love."

"I love you, Doc," he murmured, staring up into the snowy sky.

"I love you too."

"Is something supposed to happen?" Liam asked.

"I wondered the same thing," murmured Emma.

The microphone came to life again. "Read the poem once more," Terri instructed. "Everyone should know that in a romance novel when they seal a deal, that means you kiss."

"Apparently not everyone knows that," Killian pointed out. Then, once again, everyone read.

"On this day,
We'll have our say.
And with the key,
We'll set hope free.
Gather your line from far and wide,
You need them all by your side.
Our hearts are full of a love that's true,
That began with the words I love you.
Then listen and watch far above,
As you seal the deal with words of love."

"I love you, Doc." He kissed her. As the kiss went on, there was a whoosh, and the light was bright behind his closed eyes.

Slowly, he opened them and looked up at the sky—and had to blink rapidly several times.

"Are you seeing what I'm seeing?" Emma whispered.

"It depends," he whispered back. "Are you seeing two swan necks entwined, forming a heart over the cove?"

"I am." She tangled her hands in his coat. "Is that Ian and Hope reuniting in the stars?"

"Surely not," Killian muttered, just as the image faded.

The chatter around him, though, assured him others had seen the same thing as he had.

"What do you expect, son?" Finn laughed. "This is Swan Harbor."

"That it is, dad." Killian shook his head. "That it is."

"Now that Jonesy has been taken care of," Elsa linked her arm with Emma's, "tell your bride-to-be you'll see her at the altar."

"Wait," Killian began before Liam and his father directed him in the opposite direction. "Where are we going?"

"You're getting married in two days," Liam reminded him. "There's a bachelor party and ..."

THIRTY-ONE
PRESENT DAY

Lighthouse Inn
February 14
1:00 p.m.

The past two days had rushed past, and Emma had spent the morning being pampered at the Foxy Lady. With lunch over, she opened her suitcase to get dressed, and her ever-present checklist was lying on top.

"Emma." Ava knocked on the door and pushed it open. "Do you …?" Her voice faded as she came farther into the room. "Is that your list?"

"It is," Emma grinned. "Except how did you know?"

Ava let out a light laugh. "I've always had a penchant for writing everything down. When you were young, you used to ask questions. After Grandpa Leo died, and Peter moved out, I saw the list hanging in your room. I wasn't aware you still added to it."

"I was fifteen," Emma sighed. "With everything else in my life chaotic, somehow setting goals and checking them off helped me stay in control."

"Look how far you've come," Ava smiled.

"And much of that since moving to Swan Harbor," Emma added.

"We've all gone through changes since you moved to Swan Harbor," Ava told her. "However, you made me promise—no sentimental talk before the wedding. Therefore, I'll just say you'd better get dressed. The carriage will be here to get you and Elsa before long."

"Okay, mom."

Except she couldn't get dressed until she read through and added to her list. It had started short and continued to grow.

Goals equal success, she had written at the top of the page. Below that, she'd listed her goals.

Graduate from High School. ✓

Graduate with Bachelor's. ✓

Get into Veterinary School. ✓

Graduate from Veterinary School and pass licensure exams. ✓

Get a job. ✓ Heck, she owned her own Veterinarian practice.

Make Business a success. ✓ - at least according to Sadie, her business manager.

Hire a staff. ✓ She had Sadie, Leroy, and even Maggie, who offered to help when needed.

Make new friends. ✓ She had more friends than at any other time in her life.

Partner? Not yet, but Doctor Thatcher was there to cover when she needed him.

Find a man. ✓ When her heart had spoken, she had finally listened.

Fall in love. ✓ She couldn't pinpoint the exact moment she'd known she loved Killian. Some days it felt as if she'd always loved him. On other days, though, it felt brand new.

Get Engaged. ✓ He'd proposed in June, with the help of the entire town.

Marriage. ✓ *In just a few hours, she'd be escorted down the aisle by her mother and Finn on one side, and her father and Amber on the other. Possibly a little odd for a twenty-eight-year-old professional woman, but after everything she'd gone through, it was only fitting.*

Her next goal was family, but something had her amending it.

Family.

Relatives. ✓ *In addition to both of her parents' remarrying, she'd gained an uncle. And while Jack was eccentric, he was hers.*

Children. Not yet, but someday …

"Emma," Elsa stuck her head in the door, "you need to hurry."

"I know, but I had to make sure my list was up to date."

"And is it?"

"It is." Emma grinned. "Come on in and talk to me while I get ready."

Elsa laughed. "It's just like when we were in college, and you had a date. You needed me to talk to you so you would stay focused."

"Actually," Emma clarified, stepping into the bathroom, "I needed you to talk to me so I wouldn't cancel."

"Oh, now the story comes out."

"What can I say?" Emma asked. "I never had much confidence in my choices."

She stepped into her long, off-the-shoulder white dress with simple lines, a fitted waist, and three-quarter sleeves.

"Zip me, please."

Elsa zipped the dress, and their eyes met in the mirror. "Ever imagine when we were freshmen at Brown, we'd someday stand up for each other?"

"Never," Emma blinked. "But you promised no sentimental talk."

"I know," Elsa's blue eyes glistened. "Except what are matrons of honor for but a little sentimental talk?"

"Is that your excuse?"

"It is," Elsa dimpled. "How did I do?"

"Seriously though," Emma squeezed Elsa's fingers, "I'm really happy you're here."

"I'm glad too." Elsa's eyes flared. "You've no idea how uncomfortable I've been feeling since we found out my family cursed yours. It's just ..."

"Freaky?" Emma offered.

"Very."

"Yeah," Emma sighed. "When Jack first said the destinies of the Swan and Jones families were decided long ago, I freaked."

"Why?"

"I don't really know," Emma admitted. "In fact, I'd already made a comment about how fate had played a role in bringing our parents together to Killian. I wanted to feel we'd chosen each other."

"And now?"

"Now?" Emma shrugged. "There are so many things that happen in Swan Harbor no one understands."

"Hello, swans forming hearts in the sky on a snowy night," Elsa tossed out.

"Yes, exactly." Emma agreed. "I decided that while a higher power might have led us here. We chose to fall in love. We chose to get married."

"Emma," Ava rushed into the room, "it's ... oh honey, you look beautiful."

"Thanks, mom." She studied herself in the mirror. "I feel beautiful."

"The car's here for me." Ava hugged her. "You'll be ready for the carriage in five?"

"Yes, mom," Emma assured her.

"Alright." Ava hugged her again. "I'll see you at the church."

Emma smoothed her skirt down and took a deep breath. "I just got nervous."

"Just as long as you don't trip walking down the aisle, you'll be fine." Elsa crammed a couple of tissues in the center of her bouquet and handed it over. "Shall we?"

"We shall," Emma agreed, hitching up her skirt. "Think Killian's nervous?"

"Killian?" Elsa laughed. "Something tells me Liam is keeping him calm."

"As long as he's not getting him drunk," Emma mumbled.

Swan Harbor Church

February 14

3:00 p.m.

KILLIAN STARED OUT THE WINDOW OF THE SMALL ROOM IN FRONT of the church. He could hear the music and knew in a short time Emma would arrive. If he focused on those thoughts, his throat tightened, and his heart raced. The dream of losing Emma was still too vivid for his peace of mind.

"Are there any questions you need to ask before you say I do?" Liam suddenly materialized by his side.

"Excuse me?"

"You know, questions," Liam repeated, "about marriage."

"Bloody hell, Liam," Killian retorted. "You've been married two months."

"That's two months longer than you have," Liam pointed out.

"Alright," Killian acknowledged.

"I can punch you if you're nervous," Liam offered.

Killian side-eyed his brother. "Why would you offer to punch me?"

"It's what you did—"

"Right," Killian cut him off. "From where I'm standing, though, you're the one who's nervous. What's going on?"

"It's not important," Liam brushed it off.

Which was typical of Liam, Killian knew. He kept his problems to himself while helping everyone else. But that had changed since he'd moved to Swan Harbor, or at least he'd thought it had.

"What's going on, Liam?"

"I don't want to dump my issues on you," Liam sighed. "After all, this is your big day. Are you looking forward to a week in Aruba?"

"No work, no sun, and Emma in a bikini," Killian grinned. "I can't wait."

"It's a nice escape in the middle of winter ..."

"Bloody hell, Liam," Killian interrupted. "You want to keep me from being nervous? Dump your problems on me."

"It's not something you can solve," Liam muttered. "This is something I need to figure out on my own."

There was a tone in his brother's voice that had Killian turning from the view outside. Liam's expression was atypical for his always affable brother. He was somber, as if he were carrying around some extra weight.

"What's going on, Liam?"

Liam glanced up, but then his gaze dropped back to a spot on the floor.

"Is it Patty?" Killian tossed out.

He knew Elsa's mother's Alzheimer's was a stress that no one could understand unless they were in the middle of it.

"In a way," Liam admitted.

"Alright," Killian pondered several directions that could go. "Something to do with her diagnosis?"

"In a way."

"Liam," Killian groused. "I'm an investigator, not a mind reader. Just tell me."

"Elsa wants to have a baby."

Killian's first instinct had been to smile, but then he'd gotten a look at Liam's expression.

"I thought you wanted children."

"Someday." Liam blew out a breath and took his earlier stance at the window. "I love Elsa and want to have a family with her."

"Then what's the problem?"

"It just feels ..."

"What?"

"Rushed," Liam finally offered. "I moved here in October and within a couple of months, I'd started a new job, and we were married."

"But you got married so quickly because—"

"—Of Patty's disease," Liam confirmed. "Which is why Elsa wants to have a baby."

"Because she wants to have one before Patty doesn't know who she is?"

"Yes," Liam sighed. "There's a part of me that wants to grant her wish ..."

"The other part, though, is worried you're not ready for that responsibility?"

"Something like that."

Killian had to admit that if he were faced with that decision, he wasn't sure how he would feel.

"Have you talked to Elsa and explained what you're thinking?"

"Not yet," Liam winced. "Every time she mentions it, I've ducked out."

"That's what caused your problems with her before," Killian reminded him. "Talk to her."

"I'll try," Liam promised. "I hear the music. Are you ready?"

A quick flash of the Killian Reade who'd moved to Swan Harbor rolled around in his head. He was definitely not the same person who'd run from New York City. Emma had made him a better man.

"I'm ready."

As he stood in front of the church and looked out at all their friends with successful marriages, his confidence faltered. Could he give Emma what she deserved?

Suddenly, the music changed, and there she stood, in the back of the room.

She was a vision in white, surrounded by parents who hadn't really been there for her when she was a child. But who'd finally grown up as well and found their own happy beginnings.

His eyes met Emma's, and as clear as if she were next to him, he heard, *I chose you.*

We chose each other, he sent back.

With those words, his nerves evaporated. It was as he'd told Liam before he'd married Elsa. There were going to be times when they disappointed each other. When those times happened, they'd talk and move on together. That was what marriage was all about. That was what he wanted with Emma.

The sight of her so mesmerized him, he barely registered when it was time to step forward.

"You look beautiful," he murmured.

Her eyes sparkled. "I know."

He took her hand, and as they turned to listen to the singers, the rest of his fears floated away.

Lighthouse Inn
February 14
6:00 p.m.

THE NEXT FEW HOURS FLEW BY QUICKLY, AND JUST WHEN EMMA thought she had her emotions under control, something new would set them off. She truly felt like a princess who had somehow won the lottery.

Ava gave her a knowing look. "You're having a hard time believing it's real, aren't you?"

"Is it that obvious?" Emma glanced around to make sure people weren't staring. "But how did you know?"

"Because I feel the same way every time Finn looks at me."

"Are you talking about me?" Finn appeared and handed Ava a glass of wine. "Was it good?"

"I'm not going to tell you," she laughed. "You don't need a bigger ego."

"I bet I know how to get it out of you."

He whispered a kiss across Ava's cheek, and there was a part of Emma that wanted to look away. But when a pink tint dotted her mother's cheekbones, she couldn't help but smile.

"I'll talk to you later," Ava retorted primly. "I believe I promised this dance to Jack."

Emma laughed when her mother glanced back over shoulder and winked. "She's happy."

"So am I," Finn grinned. "May I have this dance?"

It was quiet for the first few minutes, while she enjoyed his smooth dance moves. Then, she realized, he'd danced them into a position where he could watch her mother.

"You did that on purpose, didn't you?"

"Who, me?" His dark eyes twinkled. "I'm just dancing with my new daughter-in-law."

Emma giggled. "Caught your son's attention too."

Finn swung her around a few times. "He and Liam are giving Aiden advice."

"Advice about?"

"Harper."

"Is Aiden listening?"

"I'm not sure," Finn twirled her around again so he could see his sons. "Aiden looks like he's listening, though."

"Does this mean I'm to throw my bouquet into Harper's arms?"

"That might push the matter," Finn agreed.

"I'll see what I can do."

Finn grinned, but rather than saying anything, moved them across the floor in a few intricate moves. Then, once he'd settled, he moved on to another subject.

"Did your mother tell you what Rocky did?"

In November, Ava and Finn had found a mother dog and her newborn puppies in a cave. They had adopted the mother and one of the puppies.

"She didn't," Emma laughed. "However, since he's about fourteen weeks old, I can guess. What did he chew on?"

"It's more of what he didn't chew on," Finn grumbled. "One of Ava's red shoes, one of my brown ones, my briefcase."

"And what does mom say?" Emma asked, knowing her mother had never had pets before.

Finn shook his head. "She just says, 'Rocky's a baby, he'll learn.'"

"Do you want me to talk to her?"

"Not yet," he grinned. "It's worth a new pair of shoes or two to see the smile on her face."

"If you say so."

"I do."

But as the song came to an end, Emma made a mental note to look into obedience classes.

"Thank you for the dance," he bowed, showing off his old-world charm. "Looks like we finished just in time."

"That's right." Killian tucked her against his side. "I believe this is our song."

"Our song?" she frowned.

"How soon they forget," he sighed dramatically. "Listen."

They swayed to the music for several minutes, and the memory of their first dance floated through her mind.

"Do you remember now?"

"Dancing with Zorro?" she giggled, referring to the masked dance they'd attended in New York City on New Year's Eve. "Of course, I remember."

"So, what you were saying," he dropped a quick kiss on her lips, "is you were so enamored with me that night, you paid no attention to the song?"

"That's exactly what I was saying," she quipped.

"I thought so."

"Your self-assuredness is definitely one of the traits I love about you."

"Are you keeping a list?"

"It's pinned right next to my list of goals," she teased.

Killian chuckled, and his hot breath blowing across her ear sent a shiver up her spine.

"Now tell me," he whispered. "Did you pack any of your Rebecca's Secret purchases for our honeymoon?"

"Maybe," Emma murmured. "I guess you'll just have to wait and see."

"How much longer do we have to stay?"

"Not much longer," she promised.

"Good." He tucked her a little tighter against his chest. "I'm looking forward to the honeymoon."

The music continued to swirl around them, and her eyes lightly touched on each person in the room. Sometimes she couldn't believe she'd only lived in Swan Harbor for eighteen months. But since her ancestors had followed the swans, it all made sense. From the first moment, the town had felt like home.

"Do I need to ask what you're thinking about?" he murmured.

"Jonesy," she admitted.

"Have you spoken to Jack?"

"Spoken to him, yes," Emma murmured. "About Jonesy, no."

"Jack had a few drinks with us last night," Killian confided.

"Did he say anything?"

"While we were inside, no," Killian explained. "When we were leaving, Jack pointed to a group of stars that were bright enough to be seen through the cloud cover. He said, 'see those stars? That's Hope, Ian, and their son. After three-hundred years, they finally have their happy ending.'"

"Now, Jack needs a happy ending." Emma peeked over Killian's shoulder to see Jack dancing with Terri. "I worry without Jonesy to think about, he's going to be lonely."

"You know," Killian hummed. "Ian threw Swan Harbor's heart onto the mountain. And there was never any mention of its being found."

"You think that should be Jack's next mission?"

Killian shrugged, "You're the one who said you didn't want him to be bored."

"I don't ..." Then she realized he was teasing her. "You know something, don't you?"

"Oh, I know a lot of things." His voice was husky, and the way his blue eyes were diving into hers threatened to steal the words from her head.

"I'm sure you do. But you know what I mean."

"I do?" He tilted his head teasingly. "Well, let me see ..."

"Killian!"

"I love you, Doc." He turned on the charm. "When you thought of a happy beginning, was this what you had in mind?"

Emma glanced across the room where her mother and Finn were laughing at something her father was saying. And in another corner of the room, Jack was talking to Elsa and Liam.

"It's more than I could have ever imagined," she admitted. "What about you, Killian? Is this what you had in mind?"

"Oh, Emma," he cupped her face, his lips hovering just above hers, "you've been my happy everything since the moment your untuned car stole my peace."

"Should I apologize?"

"No." His lips dropped even lower. "Except I should have pulled you over that day for disturbing me. We might have been doing this much sooner."

"In Swan Harbor Killian, things happen when they're meant to happen. You know that."

"I do ..." was all she allowed before grabbing his lapels and meshing her mouth with his. Sometimes, he needed to understand that actions spoke louder than words.

EPILOGUE

Mountain View Lodge
December 7
1:00 p.m.

Gray drove up in front of the burned-out lodge and
stopped next to his father's truck. "So, what do you think?"

"I think it's going to take work," Cam responded. "But if we can keep the
main entrance, then perhaps ..."

His brother took off toward the front of the building without finishing his
thought, but Gray stayed back to take in the entire property. He had to admit
there was something aesthetically pleasing about the Lodge. The wood and
glass blended naturally with the environment—but was anything salvageable?
If not, could they recreate what was once grand without changing what had
made it special?

Gray stuck his hard hat on, tossed his tool belt over his shoulder and
grabbed a ladder. His job was to see whether the old building was structurally
sound. Until they knew that, everything else was just tentative.

The Mountain View Lodge was in the foothills that surrounded Swan
Harbor. It was built in the mid-1950s and, except for the back side, shaded by

large trees. When you followed the patio around, the trees framed a view of the harbor that took one's breath.

It was best known for its live performances in the nightclub, but there were also rumors that circulated about the owners. However, in December 1995, a fire had closed its doors. After that, the building had been empty for many years. But Finley Reade, a newcomer to Swan Harbor, had taken an interest in the property. What his plans were, Clint had yet to share.

"Gray found his father standing in the middle of what had once been the nightclub. "Dad, are you alright?"

"I'm fine," Clint assured him.

"But?"

"I just hadn't anticipated the memories," he murmured.

"You and mom?"

"Yeah." Clint crossed the room to a spot off-center from the stage. "There used to be tables here, here, and here," he indicated. "The night I proposed to Mary, we were sitting exactly where I'm standing."

"You proposed to mom at a nightclub?" Gray exclaimed. "Why haven't I heard that story?"

Clint shrugged. "You never asked. It was a shame when the place burned. I'd hoped they would restore it, but ..."

"Who owned it?"

"The Desmond brothers," Clint frowned. "Fred and Rick."

"Wasn't there talk Rick was in the mob?"

"Rick was in trouble with the law more than once," Clint confirmed. "And Fred's son had no interest in the business. I guess it just got to be too much, as one by one, the family members all disappeared.

"So, the Lodge set empty for close to twenty-five years?"

"About that," Clint murmured. "Until I got the call from Finn Reade, I hadn't given the old building much thought."

"Does Finn want to reopen the Lodge?"

"He wants to turn it into a retreat," Clint explained.

"A retreat?" Gray repeated. "What type of retreat?"

"A couple's retreat," Clint went on. "Finn says that since Swan Harbor has been so good to the Reade family, it seems a shame not to share the good fortune."

"Which would give Swan Harbor bursts of hope." Gray laughed. "At least, that's what Captain Jack would say."

"That he would," Clint agreed. "But now, I should go wait for Finn. He'll be here in a few minutes."

With his father gone, Gray took out his notepad and began making notes. Standing in the center of what was once the nightclub, he had to admit there was a certain feeling to the old building. And he couldn't stop thinking about the stories she could tell. Were they lost, or would they eventually come to light?

He worked his way through several rooms, and in each new one, various fanciful thoughts floated through his head. It was easy to imagine stories with mystery, adventure, love, lust, and even death occurring between the walls. Secrets that may or may never be discovered.

Gray worked his way into a long hallway, with multiple doors and a set of stairs going down to the basement. However, before he could get started, the view outside caught his attention.

After a few minutes of convincing, the door opened, and Gray stepped onto the patio. He was immediately bombarded with a sense of anticipation he would be hard-pressed to describe. It felt as if there was a secret hanging in the air that Swan Harbor was getting ready to share.

He shook off the feeling and hurried toward the railing to look out over his little town. Swan Harbor was spread out below, so breathtaking, Gray snapped a photo and sent it to his wife.

Sadie: Beautiful. Are you looking to move?

Gray: No, Legs. I like our house.

Sadie: Me too. Where are you?

Gray: The old Mountain View Lodge.

Sadie: The view should sell the property.

Gray: My thoughts as well.

Sadie: When will you be home?

Gray: A couple of hours, why? What did I forget?

Sadie: Furniture shopping, remember?

Gray: Do we have to?

Sadie: I'll make it worth your time.

Gray: Did you get something new from the
Rebecca's Fantasy Catalog?

Sadie: Maybe …

Gray: I'll see you in a couple of hours. But I'm not
getting rid of my recliner.

Sadie: We'll see. Love you.

Gray tucked his phone back into his pocket and took a last look around. With Swan Harbor spread below him, she reminded him of a jeweled brooch he'd seen his grandmother wear.

Except it was winter, and the colors weren't as vibrant as in the summer.

"Gray," Cam called from inside the open door. "Where are you?"

He took one more look at the view, then returned inside to find Cam sketching one office.

"What have you found so far?" Cam asked. "Can this building be saved?"

"Hold on," Gray laughed. "I just started."

"What have you been doing?"

"Checking out the view." Gray thumbed over his shoulder. "There's something ..."

"What?" Cam murmured, but there was a tone in his voice that had Gray curious.

"Come here."

"What?" Cam asked again.

"Just come here." Gray pushed open the doors once more. And just as before, there was a sense of anticipation that caused his pulse to tick up a notch. "What do you feel?"

Cam's green eyes met his blue. "I thought I was imagining things."

"No," Gray sighed. "I feel it, too. Anticipation?"

"Yes," Cam murmured. "What piece of information is Swan Harbor getting ready to spill?"

"I just hope we're ready when we find out," Gray replied.

"It's Swan Harbor," Cam grumbled. "She doles out when she's ready."

"That she does," Gray agreed. "Want to check out the basement with me? I want to talk to you about a project."

Cam sent him a look. "What are you thinking?"

"Sadie's Christmas gift," Gray grinned. "I want to build her a ..."

In Book 7, Gray & Sadie's marriage will be tested. Dylan will meet an enemy, and Captain Jack is struggling. Download a copy of Book 7 and get caught up with Swan Harbor.

The Memory of Love

https://sophiebartow.com/book/the-memory-of-love/

Sign up for my newsletter and receive a link to download a bonus Hope & Ian scene. The extra chapter fits smoothly between chapters 19 and 20.

A Day at Sea.

https://www.subscribepage.com/swan-harbor_bonus_scenes

THE MEMORY OF LOVE BLURB
THE MOUNTAIN VIEW LODGE TRILOGY BOOK 1

Can Love Forgotten Be Found Again?

Sadie and Gray Hunter had their happily ever after—then lost it in a tragic accident. Now, Gray's left with no memory of the past few years ... or of his loving wife.

Meanwhile, Captain Jack has problems of his own. He knows *something* is wrong with him. But is the problem with his body, or his mind?

Sheriff Dylan Prince, on the other hand, knows *exactly* what his problem is. He's got a serial killer on the loose in his small town, and he won't rest until the culprit is behind bars.

Can Sadie and Gray find their way back to each other? What does the future hold for Captain Jack? Will Sheriff Prince find the killer, or become the next victim?

Only Swan Harbor knows the answers to those questions ... and she's not telling *anyone* until she's ready.

Watch the trailer, read an excerpt or download the book.
The Memory of Love
https://sophiebartow.com/book/the-memory-of-love/

Mystical Waters Canyon
Where hearts can be heard.

WHISPERS OF LUCK

WHISPERS OF THE PAST

WHISPERS OF A MIRACLE

December 2025

WHISPERS OF LOVE

February 2026

Hope & Hearts Series
Without hope, there would be no happy endings.

FROM DARKNESS INTO LOVE

KITTENS, PUPPIES & LOVE

BROTHERS, HOPE & HEARTS

KISSES, FAMILY & HOPE

A TREE, MISTLETOE & A SUNSET

HOPE, HEARTS & FOREVER

THE MEMORY OF LOVE

THE INNOCENCE OF LOVE

THE FORGIVENESS OF LOVE

THE POWER OF LOVE

THE CHRISTMAS LOVE SONG

THE KISS OF LOVE

THE LESSONS OF LOVE

THE HEART OF LOVE

THE JOURNEY TO LOVE

Bonus Hope & Hearts

CYGNETS & DREAMS

Hope & Hearts Historical Novellas

GUIDED BY LIGHT - 1952

GUIDED BY HEART - 1964

GUIDED BY LOVE - 1969

WELCOME TO SWAN HARBOR- 1979

FINDING HER LOST HEART- 1983/1990

GUIDED BY A KISS - 1995

ABOUT THE AUTHOR

Sophie crafts small-town mystery romances that weave intricate plots with richly developed characters. Her female leads are intelligent, resourceful, and resilient, while her male characters, often stubborn, exude sexiness, wit, and a protective nature. She delights in building slow-burn romances, savoring the tension and delaying that first kiss for as long as possible. No matter the trope, every story she writes has a happy ending.

After a fulfilling 30-plus-year career as a speech-language pathologist, working with adult post-stroke and Parkinson's patients, she is enjoying her new journey. With their four children spread out, Sophie and her husband live in South Florida. They share their home with a pampered cat named Irma.

You can find her on her website: **https://sophiebartow.com/** *Sophiexo*

facebook.com/SophieBartowAuthor

x.com/SophieBartow

instagram.com/sophiebartow

goodreads.com/sophiebartow

bookbub.com/profile/sophie-bartow

pinterest.com/SophieBartow

9 781965 510155